The Banyan Tree

Marion Lindsey-Noble

With love to Tanya

Marion

Cashmere Publishing

First published in Great Britain in 2015 by
Cashmere Publishing
Brompton Regis
TA22 9NW
Somerset

marion.lindseynoble@btinternet.com

A CIP catalogue record for this book is available
from the British Library

ISBN 978 0 9557932 4 0

Printed and bound in Great Britain by Booksprint

This book is dedicated to Joshua Lindsey-Noble, my delightful, kind and gentle grandson, an American who loves his English heritage.

The Banyan tree is a type of fig tree *Ficus Benghalensis*.
It grows mainly in South Asian and Far Eastern countries and is the national tree of India. It has elliptical, large, leathery, dark green, glossy leaves, never flowers and is famous for its aerial prop roots.
Early travellers observed that traders and merchants were often gathering in the shade of a Banyan tree to do their deals. In Gujarati language the word banyan stands for grocer or merchant rather than the tree.
Portuguese travellers brought this meaning for banyan to Europe in the 1500s. To this day, Banyan trees have remained the shady places under which villagers gather, chat and trade.

Song

The lotus flower smiles when the bee is talking.
Why don't you smile at me when I am talking to you?
When spring comes, kissing the earth,
Why don't you come to me in the same way?

Like the clouds in the far away sky,
Drifting by in the air,
Why are you not like them
Drifting through my dreams?

Like the night is sprinkled with the light of the noon,
Why don't you sprinkle me with your blessings?

Like the bird is welcoming her partner
Into the nest,
And is loving him,
Why don't you love me in the same way?

Original: *Oliro kotha shune bokul haashe.*

Translation by Marion Lindsey-Noble
performed in Bengali by Hemanta Mukherjee
available on You Tube

Chapter One

ᘓ‍ᘔ

Ali Khan stretched his tanned arms, forming an arc above his mop of dark brown hair. He linked his fingers and turned his palms into the blue Bangladesh morning sky. He smiled imagining his wife Martha shuddering at the sound. It was not the only thing she had to get used to.

He loved this time of day before the chatter of the waking children would seep from their dormitories; when the sun had not yet driven away the freshness of the night and had not silenced the bird song of *doels, mynahs, tuntuns** and kites. Ali listened to them before it was drowned out by the screeching of the tiya, the riotous parrots, and the croaking of the ever present crows. His favourite bird was the *babui** which had taken to dangling its delicate nests from the orphanage's tallest palm tree. How different the mornings had been in New York!

Martha, his wife of almost six months, was still asleep in their bungalow on the crisp cool sheets of their marital bed with the American covers, a small concession to her origins.

Soon everybody – Martha, the staff and the six hundred children and young mothers – would wriggle one last time in their beds beginning to feel uncomfortable as the sheets and blankets would slowly begin to stick to their bodies with the creeping heat of the morning.

This was the life Ali had dreamt about: educating Bengali children who otherwise would have no chance to ever getting near a school, but best of all, he had the woman he loved by his side, a soul mate who was equally committed to making a difference.

* See Glossary at the end of the book.

He also had the blessing of his mother Karin and a less enthusiastic nod from his sister Jasmine who both lived in England. He shook his head in admiration, remembering the stories of how his mother had met and married his father Raj in the late 1960s, had made every effort to live in the Bangladesh of over forty years ago and had finally failed and rescued herself and her children, Ali and Jasmine, to begin a new life back in the West.

There were still a great number of his father's relatives in various parts of Bangladesh but he rarely saw them since his Abbu's death. His mother had come over during her ex-husband's last days and had attended the funeral for as long as she was allowed as a western woman, but then she had flown home, moved from London to Manchester to be close to her daughter and grandchild.

Ali shook his head thinking about his unpredictable sister. Jasmine was a successful lawyer who had always been pragmatic about relationships, but had surprised everybody by announcing that she was pregnant and that she had no intention of marrying the father of the baby, a colleague of Indian heritage. Ali wondered whether the poor man even knew.

Karin's move to Manchester had been a blessing not only for Jasmine but also for a young woman called Serena whom she had met on the flight and who had been at a loss how she could attend teacher training college with her three year old son in tow. Now the problem was solved.

Jasmine and Karin had joined forces to buy a three-bedroomed house where grandmother would look after the baby granddaughter, and where Serena could drop off Omar in the mornings. It was an ideal arrangement and a wonderfully satisfying occupation for Karin, which she considered to be her tiny contribution to the emancipation of Bengali women. Luckily, Serena's husband Mohsin was supportive, too, which was not usual amongst Muslim men.

Ali yawned and stretched again, arms high up in the air, hands clasped making his knuckles crack. It was good to know that the women in his family were safe and happy.

Ali stretched one last time, looking at the drooping roots and branches of the old banyan tree which swayed in the gentle morning breeze. It stood in the middle of the square surrounded by the low buildings of the Children's Village.

What was it his mother had said? 'Lucky boy!' He hoped it wouldn't turn out too good to be true! He smiled and turned to go back inside the bungalow where he heard Martha making coffee.

ഇ⊂ൠ

The excited chatter of several hundred children drifted across from the assembly green and was the sign that it was nearly eight o'clock, time for Ali, the new deputy headmaster, housemaster for the boys and English teacher, to join them.

He grabbed one last piece of toast, took a hearty bite out of it and washed it down with thick sweet espresso which gave every fibre in his body a jolt. Martha came out of the kitchen dressed in shorts and a T-shirt. Their bungalow was the only place where she could wear them. She would have to change later into a *shalwar kameeze*, a kind of trouser suit, for her lessons.

At first the headmaster had insisted that she learn to wear a sari but she had argued that the complicated process of winding five metres of silk artfully around herself would most certainly delay her morning routine, and that she was much more likely to be punctual for lessons putting on the trouser suit.

Today she was timetabled to teach from nine o'clock, so she could take things easy and have a leisurely start. Her duties so far didn't amount to much but she was confident that as time went on and she had opportunities to prove herself, she would be given more responsibilities. She had great plans!

Ali hadn't expected to wear tie and suit for his job either; Bangladesh was far too hot. He had taught inner city children in the United States where jeans and T-shirts had been his and Martha's quasi uniform, a relaxed attire to blend in. However, in order to avoid antagonising Dr Abdullah, the headmaster of the Children's Village, Ali had given in, accepting that he, in his position and as the new member of staff, had to set an example for impeccable dress. His new boss was of the old school; the generation who had taken their cues from the British whose influences were still felt so many years later and had morphed into instinctive second nature.

9

Martha straightened Ali's tie, kissed him heartily on the lips and pushed him out of the door, opening it only by the width of her husband's shoulders and shutting it quickly behind him so that no one would spot her in her state of relative undress.

Ali crossed the cobbled yard, passed the Banyan tree and turned the corner to the left to go round the back of the reception building. There he found everyone assembled and the staff trying to quieten the children for the headmaster's appearance. Ali took his place at the front of the boys' queues.

There was a sudden hush as Dr Abdullah − a tall, light-skinned man, sporting a salt-and-pepper moustache, and dressed in a black gown and mortar board − approached with a book under his arm. The children fell silent and stood motionless. Not even the staff moved. Only the birds continued to chirp.

'Good morning, children!' the headmaster's deep voice boomed across the assembly green.

Good morning, Dr Abdullah,' shouted the children in unison at the top of their voices.

'And now let's greet your teachers,' Dr Abdullah continued and the children fell in happily with his request: 'Good morning, teachers!' who in turn replied: 'Good morning, children.'

Formalities over Mr Abdullah opened his book and read out his favourite poem by his favourite poet Rabindrannath Tagore *Where The Mind Is Without Fear*. He declaimed with great pathos almost entirely by heart, hardly ever looking at the written text. When he had finished, he closed his eyes moved by the fine words and shut the book. There followed a moment of grave, respectful silence. His young, adoring audience realised how important it was to him that those words should seep into their hearts and minds. Then he broke the spell standing aside and asking the PE teacher, Mr Uddin, to lead the morning exercise. This consisted of stretching arms into the air, touching toes, gyrating heads and waists, breathing exercises and sitting on the grass in cross-legged posture to meditate for a few minutes, elbows resting on thighs, middle fingers and thumbs forming 'o-s'.

'Do we have any messages?' asked the Headmaster.

A short list of announcements was read out ending with a round of Happy Birthday singing for a little girl called Arima.

She blushed and pulled her headscarf over her face overcome by shyness.

'Mr Khan, do you have anything to add?' The Headmaster looked encouragingly at his most recent recruit.

Ali stepped forward, turned to face the children and smiled: 'As you know I have been thinking about a motto for our school since the day I arrived. Some of you came forward with good ideas. I also remembered the motto of my previous school in America. I didn't think any of them were quite suitable. I was really agonising over this, when I received a letter from my mother who reminded me of my own school's motto: Quo quis est doctior, eo est modestior. I still like it! It is Latin and means that the more learned a person is, the more modest he or she becomes. What do you think that means for us, Tarique?' he asked a tall, skinny boy at the front of his queue. The boy looked baffled and then stared at the ground.

Ali shortened the boy's agony and answered the question himself: 'It means that the more we learn, read and study the more we realise how little we know. Knowledge should make us humble and grateful that we have an opportunity to learn and better ourselves. And what should we not do?'

A gangly arm shot up a little behind Tarique: 'We should not be immodest, Sir.'

'Well done, Safir! We should remain modest and resist being boastful and looking down on people who have not had the same opportunities that we have been given. I shall ask the boys in the carpentry workshop to carve our new motto on a board. This will be hung up in the dining room hall where everyone can see it every day. So let's hear our new motto: Quo quis est doctior…' Ali paused and listened to the enthusiastic chorus. 'Eo est modestior.'

'That was fantastic! Give yourselves a big round of applause.'

In his last school in New York this would have been an invitation to wildly riotous screaming and whistling, but the children in the orphanage responded with restraint, polite clapping. They liked their new teacher. He often made them smile.

'Thank you, Mr Khan,' the headmaster took over again. 'Now, in an orderly fashion, everyone to the classrooms, please!'

The children filed away in various directions each led by their class teachers.

၈ာလ

'Ali, can I have a word with you sometime this morning?'

'Yes, of course, Dr Abdullah.'

'Oh, spare me the formality, Ali. To you I am Shamsur.'

The two smiled at each other. There had been an inexplicable bond between them from the moment they had met. Maybe Dr Abdullah saw his younger self in his new Deputy?

Ali admired the way his boss ruled the orphanage with kind discipline and was pleasantly surprised how well organised the administrative side was; nothing was left to chance, efficient transparency ruled which made life easy and predictable; a rarity in a third world country.

Ali was pleased to think that their relationship was like the meeting of two minds and almost on equal terms.

He thought fleetingly that for Martha her reduced role had been a bit of a shock, but he was convinced that things would settle down and that she was more than capable of carving out a niche for herself before long.

Chapter Two

Cೞ৲ಐ

It was mid-morning in England. Karin Khan, Ali's mother, checked her watch: Nine fifteen. She drained her cup of coffee, rinsed it under the tap, left the Shaker style kitchen and walked upstairs to the pink boxroom where little Esme held her morning nap. Karin looked down into the cot of her ten months old grand-child. Esme was fast asleep, sucking on an imaginary nipple.

Ali used to do that, Karin thought and smiled at the memory of her little brown son lying in the crook of her arm, moving his lips in exactly the same way. It was a long time ago when she had lain in that sparkling white room in a private Dhaka clinic which — like a protective womb — had provided her with a sense of blissful isolation from the blistering heat and alien world outside.

Karin checked her grand-daughter's forehead as if feeling for a temperature, converting it immediately into a gentle caress. The little girl was healthy and robust although softer and with a sunnier disposition than her mother had ever been. Considering that Esme's father was Indian and Jasmine, Karin's daughter, had inherited her father's Bengali complexion, the little girl was astonishingly fair-skinned, more like her grandmother, a distinct nod to their genetic link.

Karin pulled the feather-light duvet up to the baby's shoulders, planted a gentle, noiseless kiss on her forehead and left the room.

Karin had hardly begun to busy herself with household chores when the telephone rang in the landing. Luckily she had turned down the volume of the ringtone so that it wouldn't wake the baby.

'Hi Mum,' Jasmine sounded harassed and gulped after the first two words; then she coughed. 'Sorry, I am just having a sandwich on the hoof… I have to go to court in half an hour.'

There was no need for Karin to say anything; she simply shook her head at the boundless energy her daughter displayed. It had been only ten months since Jasmine had become a mother; pregnancy and birth had not managed to stop her pursuing her aim: to become the best and most successful lawyer ever.

'Good luck then!' Karin managed to say before hearing the click that ended their conversation.

She smoothed a grey wisp of hair from her eyes. Some weeks ago, her daughter had pressed her into abandoning the bun, the severe and easy-to-manage hair-do of her solitary years in London. She had finally given in and was dragged to a stylish salon where Jasmine seemed to be well known.

'My treat,' she had said and Karin had shuddered to think of the cost. She had, however, drawn a line at having her hair dyed. Now she had to grudgingly admit that the new bob suited her as it had done when, as a young wife, she had followed her husband to Bangladesh.

Karin was still slim, maybe a little less upright than she used to be when she had practised yoga every day, but somehow her cheeks were more rounded and glowing with health, a sign of living well and enjoying life. Her daughter had termed it 'blossoming'. Karin certainly led a more interesting and fulfilled life since they had joint forces, bought this lovely 1930s house in a village outside Manchester and had moved in together.

The doorbell rang.

'Hi there!' It was Serena with her six year old son Omar.

'Hello, poppet,' Karin bent down and stroked Omar's thick, unruly black hair; no sooner did she remove her hand than the straw-like strains sprang back up to stand away from his head like hedgehog spikes.

'Where is Esme?' he asked with the inquisitive persistence of an almost five year old.

'Don't you say "good morning, Auntie Karin"?' his mother admonished him with a disapproving frown while she shook rain drops from her umbrella.

Omar dutifully mumbled the requested greeting, ready to get on with more important things.

Karin laughed: 'Esme is still asleep but she will wake up soon and then once we have given her a fresh nappy and changed her clothes we can all go to the park.'

Omar's school had closed for half-term. Serena who was in the middle of her teacher training, a most stressful affair by the sounds of it, had no holiday.

'Can we go to the swings?' Omar persisted.

'Of course, we can and remember, we shall also feed the ducks on the lake.'

Omar cocked his head to one side, smiled triumphantly and began to rummage around in his mother's tote bag before holding up triumphantly a plastic container full to bursting with bread cubes, the lid almost falling off.

'You remembered – brilliant! The ducks will be pleased.'

'I can see that I'm not needed,' Serena quipped in mock-disappointment, and added: 'I let you get on then…. I better be going myself; for once I want to be on time for my lecture,' but instead of turning to go, she lingered and sighed: 'We shall find out today which schools we shall be allocated to for our practical.'

'Good luck then! And see you tonight.'

'Around six?'

'Whenever you can – you know that!'

Another sigh, this time with relief: 'I am so lucky. One woman on my course has her baby in a nursery. She pays five Pounds extra for every ten minutes she is late to pick him up.'

'How much do they charge nowadays?'

'The fees are sky-high! Over a thousand Pounds a month and you have to pay even when you keep your child at home, when it's sick or during holidays.'

'How can people justify that? It sounds like exploitation!' Karin was incensed how people could take advantage of others' predicaments.

Serena nodded, gave a warm hug to her friend and finally turned to leave, her long, thick plait of black hair swinging across her back like a pendulum as she walked away.

Karin shut the heavy oak door which gave out a tiny squeak while its Victorian picture window threw colourful patterns of stylised lilies onto the thick-pile, cream carpet. Karin was tempted to take Omar's small hand in hers, but knew from experience that he wouldn't thank her.

'Go on then,' she encouraged him and he stormed up the stairs with Karin trailing behind him.

Chapter Three

C(380)

'Come in!' Dr Shamsur Abdullah called from behind his office door which was only ajar. It was far too hot to keep doors shut.

Ali wiped his sweaty hands on a handkerchief which he carried constantly with him. It had been Martha's idea when, one day during their first week at the Children's Village, he had complained that he felt like a trussed-up chicken ready for the oven in his formal suit. Waves of heat were constantly flooding his body, setting his face alight and sprinkling his forehead with beads of perspiration as if it had been splashed with water. It felt as if he was standing in a furnace all day long. It was a matter of getting used to Bangladesh's hot, humid air, so different from the dry heat of the Eastern Seaboard of the United States. A handkerchief at the ready would be a great help.

'Sit down, Ali'.

His boss was considerably taller than the average Bengali man; he was probably in his fifties, slim and upright and had a full head of dark, well- trimmed hair greying at the temples. He pointed to a brown leather club chair in front of his desk. Ali had come to admire him as a disciplined man, the personification of fairness, a deep sense of responsibility and a genuine love for his charges.

No wonder he was adored and respected by children and staff alike. What made life even easier was his British wry sense of humour which Ali, having grown up in England, had missed amongst his American colleagues. Looking at the Headmaster's face with the kind brown eyes under bushy brows, the classical wide nose and an almost permanent smile around his lips, Ali was sure that the children in this orphanage would be safe for as long as Dr Abdullah remained in charge.

'Ali, I wanted us to put our heads together on an issue which is bothering me.'

He looked at his newest member of staff and, when a smile was the only reply, he continued: 'Our oldest pupils will soon be ready to leave the school. There are four boys and three girls who, in my opinion, should carry on with higher education.'

'Do you mean my tutor group?'

'Yes, the children I am thinking of are Vijay, Iqbal, Ismail and Sajjad, and the girls are Rani, Salma and Sultana.'

Dr Abdullah paused. Ali kept looking at him expectantly until the headmaster got up from his high-backed wing chair, upholstered in solemn black. He folded his hands behind his back and began to pace the room: 'I have spoken to them but with little result: None of them want to leave here. They are afraid of the outside world and would rather stay amongst the people they know. It would be such a pity if they wasted their opportunity.'

His voice had risen with passion. 'They are able young people but I have failed them. I must have failed to nurture their self-confidence. I thought youth equalled natural curiosity and a sense of adventure. But not with them; they don't want to go. To be honest, we can't really keep everyone here after a certain age, but more importantly, they could do so well for themselves if they only tried.'

The Headmaster blinked and looked both baffled and pleading: 'Would you speak to them? You might present them with a new perspective; you are a young man yourself and have experience with adolescents. Our group of seven might listen to your advice more than to that of an old man.'

Ali laughed: 'So you think I can do better than you? I doubt it but of course, I shall try, Shamsur.'

'I knew you would!' The Headmaster clapped his hands with relief. 'I am counting on your powers of persuasion!' and then added without the slightest embarrassment: 'I told them you would expect to see them at seven o'clock this evening in the dining hall.'

Ali was taken aback by the speed with which his boss had organised this important meeting, leaving him not much time to prepare his arguments. Nevertheless he could see that it was a worry for Shamsur, and he as his right-hand man was happy to oblige. He would just have to think on his feet.

'Will you be there as well?' Ali enquired.

'No, I took the initial soundings which were disappointing; now it's up to you. I hope your powers of persuasion and scope for diplomacy will exceed mine − at least with the boys...' He fell silent and seemed to puzzle over something before finally repeating: 'I really don't understand why they don't jump at the chance! I hope you can change their minds.'

Ali couldn't think of anything more to say; they would just have to wait and see.

'Do you want a written report?' he asked after-thought.

Shamsur laughed out loud:

'You are not in America anymore, Ali. We don't leave paper trails of how we tackle problems. As long as we solve them, that's all we need!'

Ali couldn't help feeling a little uneasy about that last statement, but at the same time he was relieved; it certainly would safe time.

Ali had an hour to spare before afternoon classes and decided to spend it with Martha. It would give him the opportunity to talk to her about tonight's mission. Martha was intuitively compassionate and intelligently practical and would help to organise his strategy. He absolutely adored her!

There were two more lessons in the afternoon once the worst of the noon heat had dissipated. However, to the new teachers from America it didn't feel any better. The heavy heat of the day sat on the ground like a cloud of bad smells over a bowl of rotting fruit. The skin felt forever damp and sticky; there was only the hope that taking another cold shower would provide prolonged freshness.

'Shall I come along,' Martha offered eagerly twirling a wet curl clinging to her forehead.

'Let me have a go first, but you will probably have to speak to the girls separately. I can't imagine them making any decision; they will be too busy feeling awkward sitting next to the boys.'

Martha nodded, her mind already working on a way to persuade the girls that this was their once-in-a-lifetime chance, more than any other Bengali girls might have, and that they mustn't let slip away. They were as good as the boys!

She also knew that it would be difficult to break through the barriers of their traditional thinking, their belief that their place in society was different from that of the boys, however clever they were. They did not see it as their natural right to fulfil their potentials. Society had instilled in them that their first duty was to be obedient and not to bring shame on those around them. Martha did not want to be the brash American who would change their world within months but she was determined to set these girls on a path of greater independence, self-reliance and confidence, and prove to them that people would still be proud of them.

She would have to tread very carefully, though.

'I'll be alright with the boys,' she heard Ali cheer himself on.

'I'll come with you for support,' she said whilst gathering her curls into a pony tail.

'I am not sure that's wise,'

'Why?'

'I am not sure, Shamsur wants you involved at this stage. Let me try first.'

'Suit yourself then.' She shrugged her shoulders and turned away.

Ali could hear the disappointment in her voice. She just would have to learn that in this country women took a backseat rather than be the driving force.

He didn't see the big tear rolling down her cheek as he left.

'Good luck!' she whispered as she watched him crossing the square and looking up at the umbrella-like roof of the Banyan tree as if to implore it for inspiration.

ৎেওঙ

Ali almost laughed at the predictability of the situation which met him as he entered the dining hall. The boys were sitting at one table and the girls with their backs to them at another, almost at opposite ends.

Habits die hard, Ali thought; no such thing as emancipation or equality. In a way, he found the girls' attempts at preserving their dignity endearing.

'Good evening everybody,' he began but got immediately tired of moving his head from one side to another to make sure they all felt spoken to.

'Girls, would you mind terribly to turn round and move your chairs a little closer? My head will come off if I have to swivel it between you and the boys.'

They giggled and obliged bringing the chairs just a little closer to the middle of the room.

'Thank you!' Ali said with a grateful smile. 'You know why we are here. Dr Abdullah and I and all the other teachers feel that you should be given the opportunity to study further after you finish with us. You have excelled and deserve to carry on with your education. Unfortunately, we cannot provide this here and you will have to go to college in Dhaka.'

He paused to gauge the effect of his words. The boys, Vijay and Iqbal, were congratulating each other with high-fives while Ismail and Sajjad looked at him with a sullen expression. The girls pulled their scarves tighter round their heads in embarrassment, staring at the table tops as if this did not concern them. No one said a word.

Ali decided to continue. He tried a different tack: 'What are your plans for the future? What would you like to do once you finish school? What would you like to be?' No one was volunteering. It was like extracting treacle from a tin. 'Come on, you must have thought about it. You must have dreams!' Ali was sure that they had; however, something held them back to dare believing that there might be the remotest possibility for their dreams to come true.

'It is not up to fate or a Higher Power. The opportunity is there and it is entirely up to you what you make of it. Your career, your happiness lie in your own hands.'

Ali looked at each and every one; all had lowered their eyes and stared at their knees, lap or the table top.

'Sajjad, what would you like to be?' Ali prodded and, after waiting till the sheepish smile around the boy's mouth had vanished, he heard a faint: 'A doctor, like Dr Chowdhury.'

'Good!' said Ali, noticing the astounded expression in Sajjad's face that this idea was not rejected out of hand as complete nonsense.

'Next, Vijay.'

Vijay first looked at his friend Sajjad and took courage when he nodded: 'Also a doctor.'

'That's more like it; I am all for high aspirations!' Ali tried to preserve the momentum.

'Ismail?'

'An engineer,' was the sullen answer, and before Ali could ask the last boy Iqbal blurted out: 'A carpenter.'

'Excellent. You all have plans. Now to the girls…' They shrank into the chairs they were sitting on: 'Sultana!' She was the most studious amongst them. 'Come on, be brave!'

'I would like to be a teacher,' she said with surprising confidence.

'A teacher for…?' Ali dug deeper.

'I don't mind; little ones or for English or Bengali. I like books and I like to write stories.'

This was more than Ali had hoped for, but he was less lucky with the other two girls. Rani wanted to get married and Salma only shook her head. She either did not want to think about her future or she didn't want anyone to know.

'We shall prepare you for the entrance examinations and also help you move to college halls. Of course, once you will have moved to Dhaka, we shall keep in constant contact with you and shall visit you regularly. We wouldn't dream of just abandoning you in the capital. We shall be like any other parents whose children go to college.

'We don't know anyone there,' Sajjad almost whimpered.

'As I said, we wouldn't just abandon you. If need be, one of us would go with you and stay until you have settled in. In the end you will love it. It's such a great opportunity, opening up fantastic career prospects and a prosperous future. And just imagine how proud we all shall be, knowing that you represent us at college in Dhaka! And…' Ali grinned, 'if you miss us so terribly you can always come back with your degree and make yourself useful here.' He let his words sink in.

'Would we come back during holidays?' Vijay asked.

'Of course! Just imagine, all these little ones hanging on your every word about your studies and college life. You will be trail-blazers! Everybody will be so proud of you, just like we are of Dr Chowdhury.'

Dr Chowdhury was been an old boy. He had, after university and a gap year in England where he had stayed with the founder of the orphanage, Mrs Bellamy, returned to the Children's Village to establish a small clinic and to look after everybody with the help of the three Ss, three young nurses called Shazia, Safda and Sufi.

'Would we go together with the boys?' Sultana whispered greatly concerned. No one laughed because 'mixing with boys' was a serious matter, probably the biggest stumbling block for the girls.

'There are separate colleges for boys and girls, but once you get to university you would mingle.' There was no point to pretend otherwise. Ali took a deep breath trying to regain the lost enthusiasm.

'We still have six months to decide. Meanwhile it is your task to study for your final examinations as hard as you can.'

The boys looked more positive, their eyes shining and cheeks reddening with the fire of excitement. Vijay with his longish face and hair that stood on end over his forehead like an awning; the short and stout Iqbal with dimples in his cheeks and a permanent grin fixed on his face; even the skinny Sajjad with the spindly arms and legs, and the computer geek Ismail with over-sized glasses and a faraway expression.

Ali turned to the girls. There they sat, fiddling with their hands, bangles or the ends of their achols, trying to avoid their teacher's eyes. The cute Rani with that heart-shaped face, beautiful dark eyes and full lips who would make such a good nurse with her caring demeanour; the tall, slim, studious Sultana, who moved slowly and graciously at all times and whose green eyes now fixed him with seriousness and quiet expectation; and the already womanly looking Salma who loved to help, was wonderful with the little ones in the village and had a lovely singing voice; she would make a fantastic nursery nurse.

There must be something I can do to change their minds, Ali thought

'You may go,' he said, a little defeated, and watched as they filed out silently and with bowed heads.

Chapter Four

⚜

'Hi Mum, hi Esme!'

Karin loved the exuberant tone of her daughter's voice; not a tinge of tiredness after an exhausting working day.

Esme, her little grand-daughter, was sitting at her feet, cushions scattered around her in case she toppled over. The podgy little hands tried to place wooden animal shapes into a puzzle board, and Esme shrieked with delight when she succeeded.

'You clever little girl! Now let's show Mummy.'

Karin got up from her chintzy armchair, which, with its kaleidoscopic colours, stood out rather flamboyantly from the rest of the almost bare room. I think it's called post-modernism, Karin mused shaking her head. It wasn't her cup of tea and she couldn't help herself, occasionally scattering little flashes of colour in the shape of Indian cushions around. She picked up her grand-daughter and carrying her past a low coffee table of sustainable wood, a permanently reclining creation of a chair made of steel and with only an armrest on one side, and an expensive Italian designer settee in grey whose sweeping curves of a frame were an artwork in itself. The only concessions Jasmine had made to her mother, when they had decided to share the house, were that chintzy arm chair and a wall of bookshelves which Karin had filled in no time.

'You are getting heavy, young lady,' grandmother teased grand-daughter who duly began to giggle.

With Esme in her arms, Karin walked out into the corridor to greet her daughter.

'How is my little honey-bun girl?' Jasmine cooed.

It never ceased to amaze Karin how her career-driven, almost cold-hearted daughter had changed into this doting, almost soppy mother persona. She wondered whether her colleagues at court had noticed a difference or whether Jasmine shrugged off her professional image like a cape when leaving the office.

Esme stretched out her short, plump arms and squealed with pleasure when her Mummy dropped the stylish leather satchel to the floor, grabbed her daughter by the waist and swung her round like a carousel.

'You show Mummy what a clever girl you are. I'll make us a cup of tea.'

When she came back to the sitting room with a tray of tea and chocolate brownies, mother and daughter were crouched over the puzzle, laughing triumphantly whenever they managed to fit all the pieces into the hollow animal shapes.

'Hmmm – I needed that,' said Jasmine grabbing a brownie and biting heartily into it, and then looking at her mother, she suggested: 'Shall we go for a walk? It's such lovely weather and so mild; almost like spring!'

It had been a mild winter indeed but there was always a chance that the most eager of plants showing already the tips of their leaves in their small and jungle-y garden, might get an icy shock later on.

'I shall prepare dinner meanwhile. You go and have some fun! But wrap up warm; the sun is treacherous.'

Jasmine went quickly upstairs to change into jeans, t-shirt, wind-cheater and trainers and put up her shoulder-length black hair into a ponytail, while her mother wrapped and strapped Esme into the buggy.

'Off we go then; bye-bye, Granny!'

Karin waved after them. Suddenly, she became aware of a white envelope with the unfamiliar handwriting on the hall table. It had arrived this morning. She must remember to give it to her daughter.

ೞℭ℞

After the walk it was time for dinner. They made a point of including Esme at every mealtime, sitting in her high chair, waving her plastic spoon about or hammering the mashed food in the plastic plate with it. This was less an exercise in feeding the child than in getting her used to communal eating. She would have her bottle of formula milk before going to bed.

Jasmine insisted on a healthy diet for herself; it suited her mother fine to have mainly salads, fish or lean meat cooked with olive oil, garlic and herbs. Today it was chicken drumsticks.

'What did you dip them in?'

'Egg, breadcrumbs and parmesan cheese.'

'They are lovely! Did it take long?'

'No, about ten minutes preparations and 20 minutes in the oven.'

'Gosh, it sounds so easy. Before you came, I lived on microwave ready meals, bought sandwiches or the odd lunch in a restaurant.'

'No need for that. It just takes a little bit of planning, patience and a good, simple recipe. That's all.'

'You must teach me sometime!' She knew her mother would love that, but the chance of finding the time would be a challenge.

She handed a sliver of an olive to Esme who duly put it in her mouth, pulled a face and spat it out. A piece of chicken was more palatable and after chewing it for a while, her little fingers fished it out again and put it neatly on her plate.

While Karin cleared the table, Jasmine disappeared with Esme to give her a bath. Judging by the loud screams and laughter, which could be heard even downstairs, they were having a lot of fun. Then it was story time and after that, Granny was called to sing the obligatory 'Guten Abend, Gute Nacht'.

'I remember you singing that to us in Bangladesh,' Jasmine had pleaded, and so it had become part of Esme's routine as well.

To the young Karin it had been a matter of clinging on to a tiny piece of her own culture whilst living abroad, an attempt at preserving something of her own identity. The memory made her smile wistfully.

Mother and Granny kissed the little girl 'good-night' and pressed the button to set off the musical mobile Karin had bought; it played the same song. Esme was fascinated by the colours, the movement and the sound and was soon lulled into sleep, whilst the two women tiptoed to the door and closed it gently behind them.

ುುಲಿ

'Let's have a glass of wine,' suggested Jasmine. 'I have something to tell you.' A conspiratorial smile played around her lips.

'I have something to tell you as well,' thought Karin but had forgotten what it was.

'You are not pregnant again,' she blurted out instead.

'Oh Mum! You are priceless!' Jasmine laughed hysterically.

Yes, it was probably ridiculous. Jasmine had broken up with Esme's father before she even knew that she was expecting. Karin wasn't even sure whether the poor chap knew; his name was never mentioned.

I wonder what he was like,' Karin mused and quickly shook her head in self-disapproval; it was undignified to be nosey, and it was entirely up to her daughter to tell her when she was ready. There was probably nothing to be done anyway. Jasmine could be headstrong and determined once she had made up her mind.

'I have been offered a pupillage,' she beamed. 'Chambers think that I should apply.'

'My daughter, a barrister!' Karin said proudly and wasn't at all astonished knowing the girl's determination. This deserved a hug and a squeeze, however awkward her daughter might find it.

She didn't and returned the hug.

'It will mean even more work, but with your help, I think I can risk it. It's rather complicated and takes a year; two six months periods called 'the sixes'. During the first six months, I shall just observe and assist, albeit under strict supervision, and after that I shall work as a trainee barrister and have to prove myself.' She sipped the last drop of wine and checked her watch. 'Who knows, in a few years' time I might even go for Silk.'

'What's that?' Karin asked.

'Oh, the really successful barristers can apply to become QCs, Queen's Councils.' Jasmine yawned. 'I better turn in now. I have a court case tomorrow.'

Karin suddenly remembered: 'You have a letter on the hall table.'

'It will keep till tomorrow. Good night, Mum.'

After clearing away the glasses, Karin climbed up the stairs to her own bedroom which, compared to the minimalist décor of the rest of the house, was cluttered and mildly untidy. She had relaxed and become less pedantic, and it showed. They had formed a happy family unit and their life was near perfect. What a blessing!

ಸಿಂಛ

The next morning, Jasmine was unusually lost in thoughts, eating her light breakfast of Muesli and strawberries without a word.

'Have you slept well?' Karin enquired cautiously.

'Hmm.'

'Esme slept through?' Karin tried again.

'Yes, I fed her at six. I just put her down again.'

'Oh, I can hear her,' Karin laughed, 'I'll go.'

And so another day began. As Karin tidied away the breakfast dishes and changed the bedclothes, she couldn't see the letter or the envelope anywhere. Why had Jasmine been so monosyllabic? She might have just been preoccupied with her court appearance this morning; after all, she was now working towards a significant professional goal.

The letter was probably not important at all.

Chapter Five

CЗВЭ

'We have good news, children!' Dr Abdullah beamed and waved a piece of paper above his head.

'As you all know, it will be Independence Day next month and we are going to have very important visitors to our celebrations.' Dr Abdullah paused for effect, to emphasize the importance and to create tension as to who the visitors might be. Finally he tossed the names into the excited expectancy like hand grenades: 'The founder of the Children's Village, Mrs Victoria Bellamy and her husband Jeremy from England will grace us with their presence.'

There was stunned silence pervaded by a feeling of awe. They knew that their benefactors came from England which was far away, worlds away, and that it was a great honour that they would take the trouble to travel all this way. None of the children had any idea how long it would take them – days, weeks? Even the teachers were impressed, although they had known for some time that a visit would be imminent.

'So I expect you all to put your minds to how we can welcome and entertain our honoured guests. Discuss your suggestions with your teachers, please!'

Before the astonishment could wear off, the children were asked to sing the national anthem and were dismissed to go to their classrooms or workshops.

'Can I have a five minute meeting with the staff, please, Dr Abdullah sounded harassed. And indeed, it turned out that he was. He clearly wished that he had been given a little more notice of this visit and he hinted that he would have to cancel some private plans. As nobody knew what he referred to, everyone put it down to nerves and promised to stage a worthy show for the guests.

Formal lessons were cancelled for the day, so that teachers and pupils could put their heads together to come up with ideas. Soon they made long lists: a dance, a play, a cricket tournament, an art exhibition. The children proposed to make some gifts: a hand-embroidered shawl and a straw-painting were mentioned and threw up more questions: which fabric, which colours, what sort of embroidery and for the picture, which topic, how big – the problems were endless, but everybody was enthusiastic. They liked their formal lessons but this was even better!

ℰᏬᏨ

'It is amazing how quickly the children entered into the spirit,' Martha commented at the end of the day, appearing from the shower, wrapped in a white bath towel and rubbing her curls dry with another.

'It would have been a much bigger battle in New York!' Ali grinned. Martha laughed out loud at the memory. He loved her throaty laughter, like a seal's greeting.

'Most of them would have shrugged their shoulders, walked out and left the problem to the teachers. Nothing to do with me, Sir!' he imitated teenage grunts.

'I have heard worse!' giggled Martha.

ℰᏬᏨ

The Children's Village became a beehive of activity: The carpentry workshop set about to carve welcoming boards and sign for the new school motto. The embroidery classes and tailoring sheds began by discussing the designs and colour schemes and settled on white, green and pink shawls as gifts. The blacksmiths had already produced some stunning clothes hooks which would grace any hall in an English house; and the cooks decided on a variety of menus adapted for English taste buds.

The girls of under ten formed a little dance group under the guidance of Sara, the receptionist, who was so popular with them that in their hearts, she held the same status as a teacher. They would perform a folk dance whilst the older girls wrote a one act play in English so that the guests would be humoured and entertained.

A guided tour through the fields and vegetable gardens was planned to show off this year's crops; it was left to Dr Abdullah to organise prayer sessions with the local Imam.

Ali would be dispatched to pick up the guests from the airport and to bring them to the Village while Martha was in charge of the reception committee consisting of all 600 children either singing in the choir, greeting the guests with flower garlands or waving little paper Union Jacks and small replicas of Bangladeshi flags, a red ball like the sinking sun on a dark green background. The rest of the staff would have to help with crowd control.

Dr Abdullah strutted around with confidence and gravitas, while everyone else was getting nervous and overawed. They had exactly six weeks for their preparations which included the thirty days of Ramadan, observed by some of the older children and most of the Muslim staff. Eid would follow on the first night of the New Moon.

Ali had heard of Mrs Bellamy. The children had chatted about her, their hands clasped over their mouths, but their eyes shining with glee. He pictured their description: A tall, willowy woman with grey hair woven into a thick plait down her back and eyes deep blue like the sky overhead; her skin was pale, the children whispered, and speckled with little brown spots on her nose and cheeks as if they were dancing there; her voice had disconcerted them at first as it was astonishingly deep, like a man's but they had got used to it quickly. Nobody had seen her husband before as he had stayed behind in England to look after his business and, it was rumoured, to look after their two cats. Nobody knew what sort of business he was in; it had become a matter of pure speculation amongst the gossips, but someone had seen a photograph of the cats which were dark brown with yellow eyes. Mrs Bellamy had spoken about them as if they were her children which no one could understand; in Bangladesh cats and dogs were considered rather dirty animals, roaming free, scavenging any rubbish heap, full of fleas, quick to bite or scratch; all in all, disgusting creatures.

It was rumoured that the wealthy from Dhaka would bring pedigree cats back from their trips abroad, and set them free, when their children had lost interest in them. It was considered an odd thing to do.

Ali liked what he had heard about Mrs Bellamy and was convinced that having founded the orphanage, she must be naturally kind`. There was no reason to panic.

Chapter Six

Jasmine was not her usual self even the next morning at breakfast. She hadn't brushed her hair and had tucked unruly strains absentmindedly behind her ears while nibbling listlessly on a piece of plain toast. Her blank stare suggested that she was unaware that or what she was eating. Her coffee had gone cold and apart from 'Good Morning,' she had not said a word.

Karin recognised the signs: Her daughter had a problem and was working on a solution. It wasn't her style to discuss details, to blurt out the various options, to unburden herself and get all worked up about whatever it was. She preferred to work things out in her head and announce her decision. It was best to let her be.

Karin ate her egg and toasted soldiers in silence and gave occasionally a strip of bread to her grand-daughter who was sitting in her high-chair, happily burbling indeterminable sounds, scraping off the butter with one finger, licking it off, kneading the bread into a little ball and finally stuffing it into her mouth with both hands. Karin couldn't help smiling. A couple of times the toasted soldier broke in two and ended up on the floor, Esme leaning over her chair observing its fall. Under normal circumstances, Jasmine would have issued a stern 'Esme', but today she was absent-minded and didn't even register that her mother bent down to pick up the bits of breakfast from the cream-coloured carpet.

Jasmine got up wordlessly and went upstairs, Karin assumed to get ready for work. She was, however, back within minutes and almost slammed an unfolded letter next to Karin's plate.

'Here – you need to know sooner or later anyway.' The pout of her lips and the steeliness of her eyes indicated bitterness and exasperation.

Karin picked up the sheet of paper, looked at typed text which filled three quarters of the page and ended with a signature: Hamid. Karin had an uncomfortable inkling that she knew who Hamid was without ever having met him. She began to read:

My dear Jasmine,

It has been far too long that we have not spoken. I have always regretted the way we parted and often thought that we should have fought more for our relationship. Now this might be our chance!

I know that our main problem was that I was looking for a wife and you wanted to concentrate on your career. I admit that I might have frightened you off, but now things have changed. Through friends I heard that you had a baby several months ago. Unless I totally misjudged you, I am quite certain that the child is mine. Why did you keep something so life-changing and important from me? It isn't fair.

So here is my suggestion: As the father I would like to take an active part in our child's life and to help and support you whichever way you want me to.

I am delighted at the thought of being a father, so please, let's meet up and discuss the future.

Hamid

The signature was followed by a mobile phone number and an e-mail address.

Karin handed the letter back to Jasmine, whose face had crumpled into angry wrinkles.

'I wonder who that gossip was!' she snorted then shook her head as if this thought wasn't worthy to waste time on and declared: 'I really can't be doing with this now. I shall ignore it and see what happens.' By now, her face had set in her professional mask of fierce determination.

She stormed upstairs again to collect her bag and coat and was gone within minutes. Her sudden transformation was almost miraculous.

'O dear!' Karin laughed looking at Esme's startled little face covered in butter right up to her nose. Sometimes it was a relief when her daughter left.

℘৩৫

However, Jasmine had underestimated Hamid. He had probably foreseen that she might stall him and decided not to wait for an answer. A couple of afternoons later, the door-bell rang and Karin was taken aback by the appearance of a doppelgänger, albeit a younger version, of her late husband, Raj.

She stiffened and looked at him with a polite but uninviting smile. This was a tricky situation, and she wished Jasmine were present to handle it.

'I am Hamid.' He said simply. Karin observed that he was rubbing the tips of his fingers nervously against each other.

Karin recognised the name: 'Are you a friend of my daughter?'

'Yes...at least I was some time ago.'

'She is not here, but would you like to leave a message?' Karin felt uncomfortable, unsure of what to say; she wanted him gone.

However, rather than retreating, Hamid seemed to gain in confidence and announced: 'I think I am her baby's father! I came to see my child.'

Karin stepped back in shock, feeling vulnerable and at a loss how to react.

Hamid had meanwhile taken to staring at his fidgeting hands as if suspecting that his request was hopeless.

He was proved right.

'Hamid – it was Hamid, wasn't it?' he heard Karin say. He nodded.

'Hamid, you know I can't do that, not without Jasmine's permission, but I feel for you and I'll tell her that you called.'

'Who are you?' Hamid suddenly changed tack.

'I am Esme's grandmother.'

'Esme...' he let the syllables roll over his tongue, tentatively as if to savour them.

'Can't I see her now, just for a moment?'

It was heart-breaking, but it was not her decision; Karin shook her head: 'I'll do my best,' was all she could promise.

She heard him say: 'Thank you!' before slowly closing the door on him.

₼₽₾

'Mum, why did you not slam the door in his face? The gall, just turning up on my doorstep unannounced! It is harassment! What were you thinking of, promising him to talk to me!'

There was no point reasoning with Jasmine when she was in a temper like that. In a way, Karin could not find fault with the man and thought it rather endearing that, as soon as he had heard that he might be the father of Jasmine's child, he had made contact and offered to share the burden. He could have just shrugged his shoulders, turned away and escaped responsibility. But he hadn't!

However, Karin knew better than to interfere in her daughter's personal affairs and waited for Jasmine's fury to blow itself out.

Just like her father, when something didn't go his way, Karin couldn't help thinking.

'Sorry, Mum!' The sensible Jasmine eventually re-surfaced: 'You were not to know. I hadn't told you much anyway. It's between him and me,' and after a pause she added defiantly, hitting the dining table with her flat hand: 'I am not going to let him see Esme and share parental rights! I went through the pregnancy and the birth all by myself. I don't need him now; Esme is mine! So no more visits, phone calls or letters!'

It would have been unwise to point out to Jasmine, that she had actually kept the pregnancy from the poor man; that she hadn't even wanted her mother at the birth, and that Hamid had not even managed to cross their threshold yet.

Chapter Seven

ೞ⊱ಬ

'Come in!'

Ali saw Vijay skulking outside his office door which he had left ajar to let in some of the fresher evening air.

'Is it about college?' Ali asked with interest. He put down the list of events for the Independence Day celebrations he had been scrutinising and looked encouragingly at his pupil. The boy looks a bit pale, he thought fleetingly.

'Not really, Sir.' Vijay was subdued and reluctant to speak.

'Well, you must have come to see me for a reason. Shall I shut the door to give us privacy?'

Vijay nodded. When Ali had returned to his desk, Vijay suddenly unbuttoned his shirt and pointed to his chest, his eyes brimming with tears.

'You want me to have a closer look?' he asked.

Vijay nodded.

Ali leant forward to inspect the patch more closely. There were various lesions on Vijay's skin.

'Do you know how you came by them?'

Vijay shook his head: 'They just appeared. At first I thought I had hurt myself playing cricket, but then more appeared, and I don't know why. They hurt.'

'I can well imagine.'

Vijay was buttoning up his shirt.

'You better see Dr Chowdhury.' Ali took his jacket from the back of his chair, walked around the desk and put a sympathetic hand on Vijay's shoulder.

'Let's go!'

He marched the boy swiftly across the Banyan tree square to the Village's very own mini-hospital.

Dr Chowdhury was an ex-pupil, the pride and joy of his former teachers. He had returned a qualified doctor after years of studying, some of them in England. They were proud, too, that instead of going into the lucrative business of private consultancy, he had returned to the place where he had been given shelter, food and an education as a little orphaned boy. He was a cheerful man, in his thirties, happy to repay his debt with a smile and never-ending patience. He was well liked by his staff, the three Ss – Shafia, Safda and Sufi – girls who had, with his help, qualified as nurses and were running the tiny, sparklingly clean hospital ward with efficiency and diligence. It was rumoured that all three of them were in constant competition for the handsome doctor's approval and affection.

He was just wiping his black-rimmed glasses, when Ali entered the surgery with hurried steps, his arm still reassuringly around Vijay's shoulders. Ali gave a brief explanation.

'Have you got any other symptoms, Vijay, like headaches, nausea, and diarrhoea?' Dr Chowdhury asked after peering at the sores with concentration. Vijay nodded to headaches and confirmed to have had 'loose bowels' for quite some time.

'We'll do some tests. First a blood test, and let me have a sample of your urine, too. We'll get to the bottom of this and nip it in the bud,' he promised with a reassuring smile. 'We don't want anything nasty spreading in the village, do we, particularly during the summer months and Ramadan when everybody is a little weaker than usual anyway.'

'What do you think it could be?' asked Ali after the boy had provided his samples and gone back to his dormitory. 'He has never been ill, and it is quite unlike him to complain. But this looks different, not like a sport's injury.'

'I am not sure; let's wait for the results.' Dr Chowdhury was non-committal. He didn't want to spread worry just yet. However, if his suspicion was confirmed, the whole Children's Village would be in danger.

ॐ

Ali thought it necessary to inform the headmaster whose face grew dark and his brows knitted together with worry. If he had his suspicion he didn't say, but he seemed to know more than he let on.

The samples would now have to be taken to a Dhaka hospital and the results would not be back before two weeks.

Meanwhile, Vijay didn't remain the only child with inexplicable sores.

After the symptoms had been mentioned in assembly, children of all ages came forward, often accompanied by their tutors. Most admitted also to headaches, feeling sick and sometimes vomiting. Everybody thought it was a type of bug which would be cured in no time by giving their tummies a rest for a couple of days, drinking lots of water and in the worst cases, taking antibiotics. The approaching summer's heat was always draining and harbouring germs and viruses.

When the test results were finally delivered by the local postman on bicycle, Dr Chowdhury rushed immediately to the headmaster, and both men called the staff to a lunch time emergency meeting.

The speakers, for all to see, looked perturbed and their pressure of speech revealed that fast action was needed:

'As you all know strange lesions and sores have been discovered on the skin of some of our children. Urine samples tested for an unacceptably high level of arsenic. The most likely source of this is our drinking water.'

There was stunned silence. It was almost summertime when everybody was encouraged to drink lots of water. What would they do if their drinking water was poisoning them? Murmuring grew from whispering voices, like far away rolling thunder.

'But we have relatively new wells!' shouted Malik, the mechanics teacher.

'Yes,' said the doctor but was interrupted by the headmaster: 'We might not have dug deep enough.' Everyone looked puzzled.

'What do you mean? How can that happen?' asked Sara, the receptionist, with amazing calm.

'Well,' Dr Chowdhury had thought about how to explain this phenomenon in a simple way: 'Arsenic occurs naturally in rocks which are washed along by the rivers from the Himalayas. At that stage, arsenic is harmless. However, once it reaches lower river basins, bacteria present in the soil, release the arsenic from the rocks in a soluble and more toxic form. That seeps into the shallow aquifer. This has happened for millennia but with an increase in population and water demand the arsenic sinks even into the layers of the water which we pump up for drinking.'

'So what's going to happen?' someone shouted.

Dr Abdullah took over again:

'I have rung the Ministry for the Environment and Water Ways and they will send someone as soon as possible to assess the situation.'

'And in the meantime? Are we all going to be poisoned?' The panic stricken, shrill voice of one of the cooks cut through the din of outrage.

'Of course, not! Dr Chowdhury and I have decided to switch over – at least for the time being – to bottled water until we find out which water source in the Village contains the arsenic. Dr Chowdhury will begin with the tests immediately and I have dispatched Harun, our caretaker, and his two assistants, to buy as much bottled water locally as possible. I hope to place a large order today for a whole lorry-load from Dhaka. For the time being, do not drink well-water and make sure the children don't either. The kitchen staffs have begun to boil huge vats of water for household use.'

'And what's the long term solution?'

'We don't know. We hope the Ministry will tell us.'

හඟ

'Did you know that 60 million Bangladeshis are poisoned every year by arsenic in drinking water?' Martha had looked up research papers on the internet later that evening.

'That's astonishing; I had no idea!' Ali commented. 'Does that mean that so far we were just lucky?'

'It says here that poisoning often occurs when lots of new wells have been dug. That's exactly what has happened in the Village in the last couple of years. They dug lots of wells to irrigate the new paddy fields and the vegetable plots, and to fill the fishing pond. How deep do you think they have dug?'

40

'No idea; maybe a hundred feet?' Ali guessed.

'Here is our answer without waiting for the Minister: Wells should be dug at least 450 feet deep to avoid the aquifer most likely to carry arsenic."

'I wonder whether the Head knows about this, if it is so common in Bangladesh.'

'You know,' Martha twirled a lock nervously, 'I worry much more about what happens to the children who have been affected. It says here that the symptoms of arsenic poisoning are lesions which can result in cancer of the skin, lungs, bladder and pancreas. Over a period of time, it inhibits mental development in children and can cause cardiovascular disease. - how appalling!'

'So are our vegetable plots and paddy fields and their crops poisoned, too?' Ali was horrified at the prospect. 'I am not sure but it says here that arsenic will not be present in rice grains, even if grown in poisoned fields.' Martha closed her laptop

'One thing is clear,' she concluded, sniffing like an irate bull, 'as usual, the poor are suffering the most.'

Ali agreed but it wasn't helpful to criticise.

'Keep on looking,' he said instead.

Martha nodded. 'I shall take whatever we can find to Dr Abdullah and Dr Chowdhury. They need all the support they can get. I bet they don't sleep well tonight!'

ৰাজ্ঞ

Indeed, the doctor had not gone to bed at all but equipped himself with as much knowledge from books and the search engines of the internet as he could find. It wasn't helpful to find out that Chinese medicine had used arsenic for over 2,000 years for conditions like syphilis long before penicillin was discovered; nor was it relevant to learn that artists had used pigments of arsenic compounds for emerald green paint, often poisoning themselves unintentionally: Cezanne had suffered from severe diabetes, Monet was totally night-blind and Van Gogh had clearly had a neurological disorder.

Dr Chowdhury waded through more historical information, terrified that he might overlook some vital information. He read on:

The famous murder cases in the Middle Ages and the Renaissance popped up on the screen, when arsenic was used by the ruling classes to get rid of opponents. The Borgias in Italy were particularly adept at administering it, helped by the fact that the symptoms were similar to those of cholera.

The use of arsenic was so wide-spread in the 19th century that it acquired the pseudonym of 'inheritance powder', a frequent solution to inheritance disputes. It was rumoured that arsenic's most famous victims had been Francesco I di Medici, Grand Duke of Tuscany; George III of England; and Napoleon Bonaparte who, it was suspected, had inhaled arsenic-laden fumes lurking behind wallpaper in his exile residence.

And finally, in Victorian times, a combination of vinegar, chalk and arsenic had been used to whiten people's skin to be fashionable.

All very interesting but I got totally side-tracked, Dr Chowdhury scolded himself. He needed to concentrate on how to combat the existence of arsenic in the drinking water, how to treat the symptoms and how to avoid a worsening of the children's health.

He found some suggestions like ointments for the sores, vitamins and garlic for prevention, but he decided to contact colleagues for further advice. The situation was far too serious to rely on the opinions and conclusions of one person.

Come to think of it, it was a nightmare scenario: Six hundred children, some with their destitute mothers and the entire staff poisoned and further weakened by the steaming heat outside, desperately trying to prepare a cherished festival and a visit of their founder and most important sponsor.

No time to lose! He wouldn't be able to sleep anyway. Dr Chowdhury grabbed his largest torch and went out to take samples from the wells.

Chapter Eight

~~~~~

'Hi, Mom!' Karin often experienced a moment of surprise when her son's faintly American voice came over the phone.

'Hello, Ali. How lovely to hear from you. It's a rather dull morning here.'

'It's boiling over here, and it's not even full summer yet.'

'I well remember!' Karin smiled to herself.

'Are you are both keeping well?'

'We do, but some of our children have developed symptoms.'

'Symptoms of what? Cholera?'

'No, symptoms of arsenic poisoning.'

'Oh my goodness!' Karin exclaimed. 'Is that still going on?'

'Do you know anything about it?'

'A little; it used to be really bad in the villages. No one knew at first why people developed sores and started to vomit. Later on it was discovered that the rate of cancers increased in the same villages. It took a long time until scientists made the connection between those pockets of grave illness and the drinking water. I remember that after months of research it was finally blamed on new wells which had been dug to irrigate the paddy fields; but how the arsenic got into the water, nobody could tell.'

'We are waiting for the Minister of Environment and Waterways to tell us why this has happened to us and what to do about it. Our wells are relatively new.'

'Couldn't the arsenic be filtered out?'

'No idea.

The line crackled ominously.

'We are not breaking up already?' Karin shook her head in exasperation.

'I hope not.' Ali laughed drily.

During most of their weekly telephone conversations, the line was suddenly taken over by noises of ocean waves between them, their voices fading by the second as if the speakers at either end were drowning.

'How are the children coping?'

'Some of them really don't feel well and their sores hurt. They were prescribed ointment and bed rest which in this heat is not pleasant.'

'Is anyone fasting?' His mother still seemed to remember vaguely the Islamic festivals.

'No, thankfully not! Eid is in August this year, so Ramadan begins in July.'

'That's a blessing!' Karin breathed a silent sigh of relief. Fasting, she remembered, was difficult, even for adults, at the best of times; it would only further weaken the little patients.

'So, have you taken any precautions yet?'

'The sick children don't feel like eating anyway, and all the others have been forbidden to drink anything except bottled water. The caretaker went to buy up locally as much as he could get his hands on.'

'I am so sorry to hear this. Would you like me to make enquiries about what can be done? Maybe I can find a specialist firm here who can advise us.'

'No, Mom, but there is something you could do for me: Would you mind ringing the founder, Victoria Bellamy in London and explain to her what has happened, and that we might have to postpone her visit until this is sorted out?' Ali took a deep, sorrowful breath. 'None of us is in a fit state for visitors. The children can't practice or rehearse anything, and of course, we don't want to run the risk that our founder is poisoned, too. We just begin every day by praying that no more new cases are coming forward.

'Of course! I shall ring her straight away. Mrs Bellamy will understand.'

What's her telephone number?'

She took quickly paper and pen which lay next to the telephone on the thin, long hall tale, and wrote the number down.

'It's just a shame because she was meant to come for the Independence Day celebrations. At this rate, there won't be any at all.'

'Well, let's hope you caught the outbreak early. And once you know the source you can get on with finding a solution which will protect the children.'

'I have a feeling that whatever the outcome and advice, the solution will be horrendously expensive.' And the Ministry might be some time to turn up. Karin kept those thoughts to herself.

Just then the line began to crackle once more and, after hasty 'good byes', it cut them off altogether.

ℰ❀ℭℛ

'Some of the orphans have developed symptoms of arsenic poisoning,' Karin reported to Jasmine at dinner.

'Bloody hell! What a backward country!'

Karin hadn't expected such an unfeeling outburst.

'It's not a kind thing to say' she admonished her. Jasmine sensed disapproval and averted her eyes from mother's stern look.

'Don't forget, you were born there. They are trying!' She suddenly found herself defending the country she had left over forty years ago.

'It's something to do with digging wells for drinking water and to keep their paddy fields submerged. I am not sure whether they use the same wells for both. Come to think of it, the villages had this problem already when I was there. Dhaka drinking water was always safe, but we still boiled it.'

'So in all these years, they didn't manage to get to grips with arsenic in the water? It doesn't sound as if they have made much effort!'

Jasmine's analytical brain could not understand that a problem of such huge proportions could be allowed to remain unsolved.

'What do they have a government for? Don't they want to make progress, improve their country? It's the same with the floods: Every year we read that thousands of people have drowned or

45

lost everything they had, and nobody seems to care. We in the West seem to care more than their ruling classes do. This time it's arsenic in their drinking water. Will it ever end? When will they ever learn?'

'Stop ranting, darling,' Karin rebuked her. 'Only people my age are allowed to do that,' she added jokingly to break off the spike of sarcasm. However, in her heart she silently agreed. The people of Bangladesh deserved better! Where had all the money from the United States, the UN and Europe gone which had been destined to solve some of Bangladesh's biggest problems? Probably on pet projects of the various Governments or worse, corruption. The eternal excuse was that whatever hardship befell people it was to be borne as God's Will.

'Do you want me to make enquiries?' Karin heard her daughter's conciliatory question.

'That would be nice. Maybe we can find something out, Ali can't.'

'They should sue the Government or at least the builder of the wells!'

Jasmine was still fuming.

Karin burst out laughing: 'Fat chance! They won't dare and Ali would probably be thrown out of the country.'

'Well, at least we would have him back and he could do something useful in a civilised country; like concentrate on his career instead of do-gooding in such a hopeless place!.'

Karin was shocked to hear her daughter dismiss the country of her father so lightly; she sounded arrogant and heartless. After all, it was a country full of people who like everybody else in the world, fought to scrape together a living and who deserved a little happiness and support.

Karin was also pained to hear how dismissive Jasmine was of Ali's attempts at making a difference to other people's lives. Yes, it would never bring him great riches or lead to an illustrious career, but this was not what he and Martha were after. They wanted to fill their lives with good deeds and to bring love, hope and education to people less fortunate than themselves. Karin understood that desire so well; this was what she had always wanted to do but, as part of an eminent Dhaka family, had never been allowed to do. Karin was very proud of her idealistic son and daughter-in-law.

'I'll make enquiries,' Jasmine said a little chastened. Her outburst had dissipated, and she looked sheepishly at her mother's horrified face.

'I'll ask around,' she repeated with what Karin hoped sounded like contrition.

Chapter Nine

All preparations for the Independence Day celebrations and the visit of the founder, Mrs Bellamy, were cancelled.

The Headmaster had looked really relieved when Ali had told him that Mrs Bellamy had been happy to postpone her visit, and that she sent her very best wishes for the children's quick recovery. Soon afterwards, she rang him personally to enquire whether there was anything she could do to help, reassuring him that, of course, she understood that her visit could not take place. There would be plenty of time later, once the children were well again and the adults had figured out how to provide safe drinking water.

'Damn, I had almost forgotten about her visit.' Dr Abdullah muttered.

Ali looked at his boss with astonishment at his choice of words and lowered his face to hide a grin. The stress had taken hold of everybody in the Village.

When she wasn't teaching, Martha was furiously scouring the internet for information, sifting through various theses, essays, speeches and articles, and to her big surprise, her sister-in-law Jasmine in Manchester had sent various website addresses on the subject of arsenic poisoning and the most recent research results. It looked as if the World Health Organisation had known about it for years and had tried to keep an eye on developments but of course, it hadn't been enough. The latest findings had come from scientists sent by American Universities as prestigious as Stanford, Columbia and Delaware, independent research funded by outside institutions.

Ali laid the print-outs on his boss's desk: 'We shall know more about it than the Minister,' the Headmaster said, smiling kindly at Ali and thought gratefully what a blessing this young man had turned out to be. The wife was a bit of a nuisance because she wouldn't stay in her place but he had hopes that soon she would be overtaken by events and be busy with a baby. After all, they were a young married couple, surely longing for a child of their own. Until then, she would have to learn to play second fiddle to her husband which shouldn't be too difficult. She did have a few lessons to teach and could help keeping an eye on the girls. Dr Abdullah sighed: A pregnancy couldn't come too soon.

'Any news from the Ministry yet?'

The Headmaster could only shake his head: 'I shall follow it up today,' but his furrowed brow and hunched shoulders gave away that he wasn't hopeful that he could speed up proceedings.

❧❦

'Why don't you ask Shamsur to send a delegation to Dhaka?' Martha suggested when Ali told her about the Headmaster's defeatist attitude. 'I wouldn't mind doing it. An American voice might chivvy them on!'

Ali doubted that – in fact he feared that an American voice might make things worse – but it was kind of her to offer. He found it hard, too, to just sit and wait while the sick children were suffering and the rest were on tender-hooks whether to eat and drink at all. Normal lessons were almost completely abandoned and only the housemasters tried to keep those children occupied who were still well. Even some of the staff began to feel queasy. It was an unbearably tricky situation: The hottest time of the year approaching, the fasting month only a few weeks away, both requiring more drinking water than at any other time in the year and their own wells unusable. How would, how could they cope?

They were still desperately waiting for the results for the water samples the doctor had taken and sent to an official laboratory.

'At least, it would give me something worthwhile to do,' muttered Martha.

Ali hadn't listened, busily thinking about how to speed up the visit of the officials without annoying or prejudicing anybody.

'What did you say?' he turned to his wife.

'Never mind!' She gave him a friendly slap on the back and pressed the latest stack of printed research papers into his hands.

Chapter Ten

⊂ঙ৪০

The next morning, Karin noticed how tired and stressed Serena looked when she delivered Omar for child-minding. Dark rings under her eyes, as if sprinkled with kohl dust, and a heavy smile gave away nights spent hunched over books or the computer.

'You haven't slept much, have you?'

'No, I was belly-aching over another bloody assignment.'

'Mummy!' exclaimed her five-year old in horror before giggling. Serena clasped her hand in front of her mouth that such words could have escaped her mouth.

'You are tired!' Karin laughed.

'Sorry,' Serena whispered with lowered eyes, ruffling absent-mindedly her son's already unruly hair.

'I won't keep you now, but would you like to have a chat sometime after work this week?'

Serena's eyes lit up for a moment and then dimmed.

'No time,' she said sadly.

'I could make an early dinner for us all so you won't need to bother when you get home?' Karin tried to tempt her.

Serena's smile grew more relaxed, and she accepted gratefully, squeezing Karin's hand. Somehow this older woman had become her surrogate mother, her confidante and her trusted friend.

'Tomorrow will be good because Mohsin is on late shift, so he won't be waiting for me.'

'Excellent. Tomorrow it is! Jasmine won't be back until late either, so we shall be undisturbed.'

৪০ঙ৪

In the event, Serena was over an hour late and flustered.

'This school, the college sent me to, is horrendous. If all inner-city comprehensives are like that I pity the children and the staff. I don't know how teachers can spend their entire career there!'

'Why?'

'Where shall I begin? For a start, none of our tutors have prepared us for the reality of an inner city class room. Our heads are stuffed full of well-meaning theories, but most of them don't work, not in a sink school. You know what I feel like?' she looked at Karin who nibbled at her lower lip with pent up anger against this ridiculous system of putting prospective teachers through the wringer.

'What?'

'I thought bringing up my own child would have prepared me and given me an advantage but I feel like a totally inexperienced, untrained social worker who is thrown in at the deep end. This has nothing to do with teaching. It's about ironing out the mistakes other parents have made; it's about compensating for their neglect and setting of wrong examples. It's heart-breaking!

'I feel for the kids – it's not their fault – but if I try to introduce discipline, so that I can actually teach, even the little ones ignore me or threaten to sue me or to send their parents 'to duff me up'. If that is what I shall have to face every day of my working life, I don't think I am born to be a teacher!'

Karin had listened quietly to the stream of anxious words pouring out of Serena's distraught mind. When she finally stopped, Karin put her hand across the table on her young friend's arm and said:

'Hold on, your college wouldn't have sent you there if they thought that you couldn't cope with it...' She hoped that her face didn't show that she wasn't entirely convinced herself.

It does sound like a baptism of fire; she thought and got angrier by the minute. Why did teacher training colleges have to make it so hard for their young, idealistic recruits?' They seemed to defeat their own object: instead of winning them over, they seemed to do their best to put them off the profession.

'And then there is the way to school every morning,' Serena sighed. 'It is half-way across the city. It takes me almost an hour and a half to get there. It's a struggle to be on time and in the evenings, I take the bus back weighed down with books and exercise books, like a mule.'

Karin pressed her lips together and shook her head in disbelief.

'It seems crazy. But listen, it's not going to be forever, is it?'

'No, we are meant to change schools next term.'

'There you are. The next one might be pure heaven and just round the corner from where you live.'

Serena shrugged her shoulders as if to say that that was very unlikely.

'Even Mohsin thinks that I have bitten off more than I can chew. He is worried that I might neglect Omar. I am seriously considering giving it all up.'

'Have you spoken to your tutor?'

'Not yet.'

'Why don't you think it over during half-term when you had a few good nights' sleeps?'

'Chance would be a fine thing! We are back at college at half-term, plus I have to hand in a five thousand word essay on discipline afterwards.'

This really seemed unnecessarily harsh: When all the other teachers could have a breather and get organised for the new term, the trainees were expected to carry on with their studies without a break.

'Don't you think it's worth battling on for another few months? Just imagine, you will kick yourself when, in summer, the others on your course celebrate, and you haven't given it your best shot.'

Serena looked up at her confidently smiling friend and recalled fleetingly the moment she had met this reassuring woman on a plane to Bangladesh.

'Thank you for the kick up the proverbial. I needed that,' and she laughed with relief, free like soap bubbles blown into the air.

'And how is Jasmine?

'Oh don't ask! We don't want to depress ourselves again. I'll tell you some other time.

There was a lot to tell indeed!

৪৩৫৩

53

The following morning the postman brought a letter from Martha which added to Karin's worries.

Chapter Eleven

Martha and Ali sat in wicker chairs outside their bungalow, enjoying a gentle evening breeze. The ground was uneven and the tough grass showed already signs of burning; soon the summer's heat would leave only brown, dusty patches. The thought had crossed Martha's mind that she might try her hand at gardening, if only to grow a few flowers or maybe some vegetables; she may even plant a fruit tree. She loved the banana palms which would have never grown in the USA, never mind England. She was fascinated by how tiny green sticks grew upwards in bunches into thick, soft, yellow fruits.

'Look at the branches of the Banyan tree,' remarked Martha, 'as if they are sweeping away the heat and troubles of the day.' Her laughter tinkled like little bells on a dancer's ankle bracelet.

'My very own poetess!' Ali grinned, stretched out his legs and began cracking his knuckles in contentment.

'Huh, don't do that,' she admonished him. 'It sounds horrible and it's not good for your joints; it leads to arthritis in old age.'

'Not long to go then,' he quipped but looking at her he was confused at the serious frown above the bridge of her nose and the sudden sharpness of her tone.

They were quickly distracted by an approaching figure waving a sheet of white paper in the air.

It was Dr Abdullah, who almost ran the last few steps towards them.

'At last! It's from the Ministry,' he shouted breathlessly before he had reached them. 'The Minister himself will be coming tomorrow with his team of experts.'

'They don't give us much notice, do they?' Ali shook his head.

'Well, I am glad they come at all,' beamed the headmaster, obviously relieved and grateful for the imminent support and possible swift solution of his problems.

'Would you like a cup of coffee, Shamsur?' Martha offered, already getting up, but he declined by gesturing that she should sit down again.

'I must prepare for tomorrow.'

The poor man sounded happy and harassed at the same time, twitching a little around the eyes, obviously not sure what to expect but very hopeful that the Minister would bring the answer to his prayers.

౭つ◌౩

Everybody was up early in anticipation of the visit of Government officials. Harun, the caretaker, made sure that the road from the entrance gate to the Village was free of debris and litter, and ordered some of the older boys to sweep the grounds of the square. This was where the honoured guests would leave their cars shaded by the Banyan tree. Everything and everybody was ready by 7 o'clock. The usual timetable would be suspended for the day, and the children who had not succumbed to the sickness, were kept busy with arts, crafts and music under the supervision of their teachers. They might as well rehearse for the Independence Day celebrations which would now be very low key.

The minutes of the morning ticked away and the sun rose towards its midday zenith bringing the landscape beneath it to a slow boil. The Village and its people began to wilt with the heat, frustration and disappointment.

Finally, close to midday, someone spotted the caretaker, who had kept guard at the gate, racing his rickety bicycle along the drive, shouting and waving with one hand, the other holding on to the handle-bar. He was closely followed by a cavalcade of cars whose roofs were glinting in the blistering sun. The reception committee consisting of the headmaster, Ali, Martha, Dr Chowdhury and his three assistants hastily reassembled and welcomed the visitors with words of delight and gratitude. The Minister looked disapprovingly at the women in the group who – exept Martha – quickly lowered their eyes in deference; he seemed annoyed as if everybody was wasting his time.

He looked out of place in his well-tailored, navy, pin-striped suit, a paisley-patterned tie, very much like the ones Liberty's in London were famous for, and black, highly polished leather shoes. His dark, shiny hair was neatly parted on one side and brushed carefully to lay flat above his high forehead. His eyes were shaded by large sunglasses which he didn't take off.

He was obviously not the person to do the examining of the wells.

He interrupted the headmaster's words of welcome with irritation in mid-sentence and barked orders to his minions, a group of men in shabby suits and narrow ties like strings around their necks. They shrugged off their jackets, rolled up their sleeves and asked to be taken to the existing wells. Dr Chowdhury and his nurses obliged.

'My scientists,' was the short introduction of the disappearing backs. Then the distinguished visitor indicated, dabbing his forehead with a pearl-white handkerchief that he would prefer to retreat indoors.

Ali felt like taking his own handkerchief out and wiping his face but didn't dare; he didn't want to be accused of making fun of the Minister.

This is surreal, Ali thought. The scene reminded him of a day in the USA, when he had stepped on a nail and had to go to the doctor's; every other patient before him had limped, so when Ali was called into the consulting room, Martha had whispered, giggling that he was only copying the others. It was funny then; it wouldn't be funny now.

Ali decided to let the beads of sweat run over his face rather than having the use of a handkerchief misconstrued.

The Headmaster, one eye lid twitching violently and anxiety etched in his face, led the Minister to his office. He hoped that this man would listen and understand what the last weeks had been like for him, his staff and their charges. He hoped fervently that his guest wouldn't mind if the pent-up worries and emotions would gush out of him; The Headmaster needed a sympathetic ear, a fair exchange of opinions and some reassurance that he was not to blame.

For the moment, all he could do, while the scientists were at work, was to keep his illustrious visitor fed, watered and humoured. The two men were sitting opposite each other on soft cushions in rattan arm chairs, a little coffee table between them. Sara, the receptionist and secretary, served tea and nimki, assorted snacks. She took the opportunity to scrutinise the Minister from under her respectfully lowered eyelids while placing cups and saucers on the low table. The men remained silent and when she was lingering a little longer than necessary, The Headmaster gave her a sharp look and indicated with a nod to the door that she should leave them alone.

At first the men indulged in small talk about the weather and the condition of some of the sick children. Then the Minister imparted his knowledge how arsenic came to be in drinking water, the sequence of Himalayan rocks floating down-river harbouring the non-toxic version of arsenic which with time turned into the lethal stuff that seeped into the shallow levels of underground water.

It wasn't news to the Headmaster – after all, he had read Martha's print-outs carefully – but he nodded courteously. However, he wasn't prepared for the rebuke in the next sentence: 'You should have dug deeper to find safe drinking water for the Children's Village. Now we have a huge problem and children might die. Even the people in the surrounding villages might suffer.'

Dr Shamsur Abdullah, the highly respected headmaster, crumpled. He felt miserable enough, without someone blaming him.

He really couldn't imagine what else he could have done: When the wells were under construction, he himself had kept a keen eye on things to make sure that rules, regulations and deadlines had been adhered to. He owed it to the children, his staff and their benefactors. He had particularly queried the depth of the wells, but the engineers had assured him that he was worrying unnecessarily and that they were highly skilled and experienced in that field. In the end, he had to trust them, admit that he was not an expert and had stopped interfering. It was reassuring that they had called in their own qualified surveyors and Government inspectors to check and sign off the various stages of completion.

The Minister fidgeted in his chair still ranting about the inefficiency and carelessness of today's workers. He seemed more concerned with finding a scapegoat rather than expressing sympathy for the orphanage's misfortune or offering a solution.

'And the rumour-mongers make it even worse.' He looked sternly at the Headmaster as if he personally had spread gossip.

'There has already been a small report in the Dhaka News. Goodness knows how quickly word will spread and the whole country will be in panic. We have to keep this secret as much as possible. No journalists, no television, no newspapers.'

Now we know, what is really important to the Government, the Headmaster thought clenching his teeth.

The Minister totally ignored the crestfallen expression of his host. When his rant had run out of steam he declared imperiously: 'I shouldn't be discussing any of this with you prior to the test results. I have to remain unbiased and impartial.'

That would be a first, thought the Headmaster not even looking at his guest. Instead he decided to ask the questions which had haunted him more than any other:

'What can be done about the poisoned water wells? Can we dig new bore-holes, deeper than the existing ones? And will the Government help us to pay for them?' He looked up, straight into the Minister's eyes.

The Minister stared at him as if he had gone mad and remained silent. When he saw the despair in his hosts face he began to twist uncomfortably in the chair and finally spoke to his knees:

'Well, this is a charity. We would hope that your organisation will stump up some money. I shall see what I can do, but I am mainly here to make sure that the situation is kept under control and that rumours don't spread. You have made arrangements for other sources of drinking water, I presume?' He looked again at his host, eyebrows raised, as if speaking to man known for his forgetfulness.

The light of hope had gone out in Dr Abdullah's eyes. He nodded like an automaton.

'I shall dictate a report to the Prime Minister as soon as I get back to my office.' It wasn't reassuring.

Suddenly, the Headmaster was gripped by fury. He had nothing to lose any more but a right to defend his position:

'The money we get is for looking after the children, to feed, accommodate and educate them. We live on donations from England.'

This remark was met with stony silence. The Minister had obviously nothing more to say.

'Would you like to have a look at the Village now?' Dr Abdullah suggested escaping the oppressive atmosphere. 'The children would be most honoured.' He had to save some of the goodwill he hoped his guest had on offer.

It was declined on the grounds of the heat outside. The children who had hoped to show off some of their paintings, silk printing and musical skills would be waiting in vain.

The next half an hour dragged on like eternity. The headmaster, unable to get on with work, was at a loss what to do with his prominent guest who was sitting there admiring his polished finger nails and sighing every so often. More tea had been declined. By now, both of the Head's eyes were twitching with the anguish of it all. Occasionally the men smiled faintly at each other or picked over another morsel of small talk until the Minister suddenly lost patience, got up, stormed outside and instructed his chauffeur to recall the team they had brought along.

To the Headmaster's surprise, the Minister became agile and animated as the square turned into a hub of activity. The samples of water, plants and soil were collated and stashed away in the ministerial car while the scientists gathered their tools, rolled down their sleeves, straightened their ties, put on their jackets and scuttled back into theirs.

'When will we have the test results,' the Headmaster almost shouted before the chauffeur could shut the car door.

'We shall be in touch,' was the hardly audible answer and with a click the Minister was protected from any further enquiries

Everyone in the Village had gathered to wave the visitors off, bewildered by the group's hasty retreat. Now they dispersed totally confused and unsure of the outcome of the day's exercise.

'Won't the samples be contaminated?' whispered Martha. 'They haven't even bothered to put them in sealed boxes.'

Ali looked on open-mouthed, the wave of his hand coming to a standstill, before he finally stuffed his fists angrily into his trouser pockets: 'Maybe that was the whole idea.'

Martha stared after the disappearing cars, eyes blazing with fury.

'Shamsur looks devastated,' she remarked.

Ali put his forefinger over his mouth: 'Psst, let's leave him alone!'

Before she stomped back to their bungalow, Martha looked once more at the helpless, disheartened and miserable face of Dr Abdullah.

Chapter Twelve

೦೪೮

Karin leafed through a tourist guide of Manchester while Esme had her afternoon nap in her pretty cot, festooned with soft toy animals tied to the bars and a bird mobile turning slowly above to gentle classical music.

After months of settling in and helping with child care, Karin realised that she hadn't seen any of the sights in her new home town. She simply hadn't had any time to herself.

Come to think of it, her life now was almost as monotonous as the one she had left behind in London, only less peaceful. Of course, she loved her grandaughter dearly and found her endlessly amusing; of course, she was of great help to her daughter who was aiming high in her profession and hoped to go even higher within the next couple of years, but Karin wondered what Jasmine would have done if her mother hadn't been able or willing to move away from London? Some young people didn't even have parents at all to fall back on.

Karin felt a buzz of excitement at the thought of going out on her own.

She was sure that Jasmine would understand her need for occasionally breaking out of her daily routine to feed her soul with the arts and interests of her own.

Where would she go first? There seemed to be an awful lot of Shopping Centres in Manchester; the Arndale, praised as the biggest of its kind in Britain, and its smaller version, the Triangle. Then there was The Royal Exchange Shopping Centre and the Barton Arcade which sounded rather pricey; Afflecks' Indoor Market and the Lowry Outlet Mall seemed to be more to her taste. However, shopping would not be her priority. The small shops in the village, where they lived, catered for all their daily needs.

Sport was next on the list, something of which the Mancunians were proud: The two football clubs, Manchester United and Manchester City and the Salford Quay water sports centre. Karin shuddered at the thought of the bungee jump on offer.

One thing, however, she was pleased about: Many of the attractions were free of charge.

It was important to her to maintain her financial independence. That's why she had insisted on sharing the mortgage with her daughter rather than living rent free against child-minding services rendered. It was her grandchild she was looking after; she would have felt ashamed to accept payment. Her pragmatic daughter had frowned and would have preferred to tie her mother down with a contract, but Karin refused to be regarded as an employee. She wanted to preserve the freedom to make decisions and to change her mind. She had assured Jasmine that she had no intention to let her down or to leave her in the lurch, but she certainly didn't want to be beholden to her either.

They had finally agreed that should their arrangement become tiresome or unworkable, or unnecessary, for example when Esme would be old enough to go to school, they would talk about it rationally and make the necessary changes without rancour on one side or the other.

Hence, she had to make do with her modest pension and free entry to places was certainly a bonus.

Karin took a note pad and a pen from the telephone table in the hall and began to make a list in her neat handwriting and in order of interest:

Manchester Art Gallery
The Lowry
The Royal Exchange
The Town Hall on Albert Square
The Cathedral
The Museum of Science and Industry
Salford Quays, out of town

For transport in the inner city, it said, she could use a system of orange, green and purple buses known as the Metroshuttle;

for anything to take her further out of the centre, the guide suggested the Metrolink trams. That seemed easy enough.

The Curry Mile near the University, Chinatown and the nearby Gay Village sounded intriguing and inviting.

I think I'll start with The Bridgewater Concert Hall and the Manchester Art Gallery. She rubbed her hands in anticipation. After that, she could explore The Whitworth Art Gallery which promised works of Picasso, Turner, van Gogh, Hockney and Hepworth, and if there was time she might see a movie at the ultra-modern Cornerhouse.

Goodness, she would take years to see it all!

Karin looked up and listened intently. She thought she had heard a whimper upstairs. All remained quiet, and she went into the kitchen to brew herself a cup of tea.

As she sat down again and had found the first sip too hot, she picked up on her previous thoughts and wondered whether it had been wise to slip so willingly into the routine of her role as a doting grandmother. The way her new life had turned out seemed to be based mainly on convenience for her daughter rather than an independent fresh start with the odd bit of grandmotherly duty thrown in.

Her duty to Omar would come to an end with Serena's that of studies. They had discussed this already: Serena was determined to find a part-time teaching job, so that she would not be dependent on a child-minder again.

If she began to feel trapped, Karin had only herself to blame. It had happened before in her life. Now she was over forty years older and should know how to preserve her independence. She would steel herself against Jasmine's persuasive arguments and appeal to her sense of fairness. She had to get it off her chest and talk to her with honesty how she truly felt.

Karin picked up the little guide book with renewed determination: The Cathedral of Manchester, described as 'an architectural salad' and boasting beautiful stained glass windows and lots of wrought iron, looked certainly worth a visit.

Picadilly Gardens sounded lovely for a relaxing stroll and a cup of coffee; and the Victorian Royal Corn Exchange, previously England's largest trading room, now housed the most breath-taking modern theatre.

Her thoughts strayed again: What exactly was the role of a grandmother, she asked herself?

She had heard of grandparents whose entire retirement seemed to be taken up with calls to babysit or help out the distressed, exhausted and busy young parents; some even moved closer to their grown-up children to be close at hand.

Once she had left Bangladesh, where nannies were almost forced upon her, she had tailored her career to the needs of her children. Admittedly, she had struggled financially because, once she had been divorced, she had forfeited any chance of contributions from her husband but she and the children never went hungry and had always a roof over their heads. Yes, she might have bartered with traders at the end of a market day to let her have vegetables at reduced prices, and her furniture might have originated from house clearances, but she and her children had been happy and had fun. She did not resent the interruption of her career as a linguist but re-trained as a teacher instead to have as much time with her children as possible. Not for a moment had she resented anything; she had thought that it was self-understood to make sacrifices the moment one had children. As long as she had enough money for basic necessities and a good education for her children, she had been content. She smiled at the memory of scouring the free local papers for weekend entertainments and events which didn't charge entrance fees. In a big city like London there was always something on offer. Nowadays she would probably be classified as poor, but it hadn't felt like that. She simply hadn't dwelled on it, had made the best of the situation and had been determined to enjoy her new life, free from the restrictions of her previous life.

Karin decided that it might even be a blessing if Jasmine had to spend a little more time with her baby daughter.

She listened again and could now hear the happy babbling of her grand-daughter. Esme was such a good child, rarely crying without good reason; a sunny child who smiled at almost everyone.

Karin put the booklet back onto the shelf and went to check on the little girl.

છા૭

Jasmine was even later back from work that evening than usual. She had rung to say that she had to see a client a little after office hours, and after that she had to prepare papers for the following day's trial.

'I have to make myself pleasant if I want to keep the pupillage,' she stated.

Karin had dinner with Esme and then put the little girl to bed, promising that Mummy would give her a kiss as soon as she got in.

Unsettled, Karin leafed through the booklet again and found an interesting section on Manchester's history.

It started off as a fort and market settlement under the Romans; after their departure this seemed to disappear, only to reappear under the Saxons, earning a mention in the Doomsday Book as Mamecester; however, it remained obscure until the 14th century when the town became well known for its wool and linen trade. In the 17th century, cotton took over from wool as the main product, waterways were built and soon Manchester became a centre of textile production. Driven by the Industrial Revolution, Manchester developed not only into a national but a global market place and an industrial powerhouse.

When the new wealth didn't trickle down to the working classes, Manchester became the hub of protests resulting in the birth of the Labour Party and the Suffragette Movement.

In the 1930s, everyone was hit hard by the Depression and during the Second World War the mobilisation of the city's industries to support the British war effort resulted in heavy bombardment by the Luftwaffe. The industries and, with them, the wealth of the city declined. Half-hearted attempts at revitalisation were made in the 1980s; however, the IRA bomb attack in 1996 was a catalyst for renewed efforts and investments. Today, the booklet proclaimed, Manchester is pronounced by many the UK's second city.

Karin heard a key turning in the lock of the entrance door.

'Hi, Mum,' Jasmine shouted breezily as if she had come from a party. 'Is Esme already in bed?'

'Her bedtime is seven o'clock, remember?' Karin allowed herself a surprised and slightly sarcastic look.

'I know, I know. I am a bad mother,' Jasmine said laughingly without any conviction. 'I am starving!'

'We'll talk about that later. Now, go up and give your daughter the kiss I promised her.'

ℰↃ𝒞ℛ

'So what was it you wanted to talk to me about?' Jasmine was confrontational and straight to the point as usual. Karin could imagine that her daughter would probably intimidate a great number of adversaries in her job, and that she might be considered fearless and brilliant in getting results for her clients.

However, in private life, an attitude such as this was unbecoming.

'I was looking through a brochure of Manchester today, and thought that I haven't really seen anything yet. I would like to take the occasional day off and do my own thing.'

Karin was proud to have found a way to express her wish in a reasonable manner.

'There is a lovely exhibition at the moment at the Whitworth and I thought I might have a look on Sunday.'

'That's a bit sudden,' Jasmine frowned and then fixed her mother with a stare as if suspecting a hidden agenda. Karin imagined that that was how she would look at a particularly awkward witness of the prosecution.

'I haven't really had a day off since I moved up here.' Why was she defending herself? She was not the young girl who had to explain everything in great detail and justify any ideas of her own to a domineering husband. That was ages ago. She should have moved on from there.

Karin sat up straight in her arm chair and looked straight at her daughter: 'Jasmine, I do need to have a life of my own. I need time to myself away from you and your child, and I need to fill my life with interesting things and maybe make some friends of my own age.' She gazed steadily into Jasmine's face which twitched ever so slightly – either with irritation or impatience. Karin could almost see Jasmine's brain working out the new situation and the adjustments that would have to be made.

'I cannot remember that that was mentioned when we discussed your role,' Jasmine said finally, half shutting her eyes

67

in a menacing sort of way, as if trying to make sense of words from a slightly dim opponent.

'Jasmine,' Karin's patience snapped, 'I am your mother, not your au pair or nanny. I am doing for you and Esme what I can, but in no way am I beholden to you. I promised you that I won't ever let you down, but don't take me for granted! I am emotionally and intellectually not dead yet; I wanted to start a different life from the one I lead in London, so I want to be more sociable, enterprising – all the things you are. The difference is that you have a responsibility to your child, I don't. I can only promise to help out. I thought that that was the deal.'

'I have a huge case beginning next week, and I had hoped to go into the office and get a lot of the work done on Sunday. Now you want me to look after Esme because you plan to see an exhibition. It's not fair to spring this on me!' Jasmine's voice sounded like ice-cold steel.

Intuitively, Karin felt a sudden change in her daughter's demeanour as if she had realised that she had forgone her good manners that she had inkling that her mother might have a point and that she, the cool, collected lawyer was in the wrong. Karin could see that something irked her, and that she was about to lose her composure. Karin bit her lower lip, as Jasmine got up, about to leave the room.

'Sit down,!' Karin said sharply, 'you can't have been that partisan and self-absorbed that you didn't expect me to take occasionally time off to do my own thing. Most people have weekends to themselves.'

Jasmine sat down again in shock.

They sat stiffly opposite each other in silence until Karin relented: 'I tell you what. You can do your work this Sunday, and I shall stay at home, but in future I expect you to devote one full day of the weekend to your daughter; let's say two Sundays and two Saturdays a month. I wouldn't even mind a weekday sometimes, if that would be more practical for you. We make a timetable at the beginning of each month, so that I can plan my outings a little in advance.'

Karin looked at her daughter and almost laughed: Jasmine pouted as she had done as a little girl when things didn't go her way.

Karin got up, went across to Jasmine, bent over her and gave her a hug: 'Alright?'

Jasmine nodded. She didn't really have much choice which probably bugged her more than having to devote more time to being a mother. She hated not being in charge.

'I'm going to bed now. See you in the morning.'

Karin left her daughter sitting there, so that she could get used to the new regime. She almost chuckled as she went up the stairs.

Nice to know I still have it in me; she thought and was really proud of herself.

Chapter Thirteen

ℭℨ℘

'Sir, Sir!' Sajjad ran as fast as his spindly legs would take him.

He could hardly get the words out he was so out of breath.

'Doctor Sir, Vijay is not very well. He vomiting; he close eyes, he look …' his eyes widened before he almost screamed the word: 'dead!'

Dr Chowdhury took his emergency bag without a word and followed Sajjad, who had already turned back, at a trot. One behind the other, they ran towards the boys' dormitory and disappeared through the door.

Everyone nearby had heard the commotion and soon word spread throughout the village. The crowd around the doorway to the dormitory grew steadily until the Headmaster and the teachers came rushing out of offices and classrooms. They had seen Dr Chowdhury running across the square and had put two and two together.

'Go away!' The Head shouted with less composure than usual. 'You are not helping by standing here. Make space, in case we need to call an ambulance.'

A gasp of shock rose into the air, followed by whispered murmurs, before they fell silent, undisguised horror in their eyes.

The Headmaster looked as if he would collapse with the strain of it all. His face had gone bright red, unruly strains of hair had fallen into his forehead and he gulped for air. He waved weakly for Ali to take over before he sat himself down awkwardly on a hurriedly procured chair.

'Right, children! Now listen carefully,' Ali began. 'We all know that some of you are ill from something that was in the drinking water. We still have to be vigilant, but switching over to bottled water, should make a big difference. Those who haven't shown any symptoms so far are unlikely to fall ill at all. Those, who have already shown symptoms, will be ill for quite some time, but we all hope and pray that they will recover fully. Youth should be on their side. So do not worry over-much. We shall keep you informed and tell you more as soon as we know ourselves. Now, be good and go back to your classrooms or workshops or wherever you have been before coming here! That would be most helpful! Thank you.'

Reluctantly they did as they were told, sloping away in stunned silence.

ॐ

'We better call the ambulance,' said Dr Chowdhury to Sara, the receptionist. He had left Shazia, his assistant nurse, with the lethargic, almost unconscious Vijay.

'What is it, Aresh?' The Headmaster had quietly approached the doctor and his patient, quivering with fear.

'Vijay had convulsions, blood in his urine and his breathing is laboured. He needs to go to hospital urgently. We haven't got the equipment here to treat him properly.'

'Do what is necessary,' the Headmaster nodded. 'What is the prognosis?'

The doctor shook his head sadly before looking straight into his face, desperation in his eyes: 'He might die. I think his liver, kidneys and lungs are already affected. But we mustn't give up hope!'

There was not much more to be said. Sara had already called the ambulance who in their turn had alerted Dhaka Hospital.

'Who is going with him?' Dr Chowdhury asked. I can't really spare the nurses considering how many other children are ill.'

'Oh, not another problem!' The Headmaster wrung his hands then rubbed his left arm as if in pain.

He is certainly not in a fit state to do anything, thought Ali, looking with concern at his boss, never mind accompanying a sick child to Dhaka.

'What's the news, Ali?' Martha had come into the dormitory.

'I'll tell you later. I'll be back in a couple of minutes. I want to make sure everybody is okay. Wait till I am back. It shouldn't take more than a few minutes.'

He left for the classrooms to reassure pupils and staff that everything was being done to make Vijay better. Everyone was upset, because they knew him as a kind, caring boy with a great sense of humour and they didn't want him to… it was too ghastly to think about.

The Headmaster answered Martha's question:

'Vijay is very poorly.' There was no point beating around the bush. 'He needs to go into hospital and someone must go with him. I can't.'

She nodded in agreement: 'I shall go!'

She looked at Dr Chowdhury for approval but he refused to meet her eyes. She turned back to the Headmaster who sat there on his chair head hung low. Ali wouldn't mind; he would understand and even be proud of her.

A grunt came from the chair; Dr Adullah swung back and forth as if wrestling with a decision, then stopped and slumped back into it as if past caring. Dr Chowdhury kept his own council whether it was wise to send the newcomer, an American and a woman; he had to trust Martha's common sense. What her husband would make of it was another question.

When the ambulance came with two medics, they transferred the feverish Vijay gently onto a stretcher and carried him to the vehicle. Ali still hadn't returned.

'Is anybody coming with him?' one of them asked. They had to decide quickly, right now.

'Yes, I am,' said Martha, without a moment's hesitation. It earned her a curious look from the ambulance crew. But she was sure that this was the right thing to do. She didn't have time to notice the uneasy glances which followed her to the back doors of the ambulance.

Ali had just come out of a classroom and ran over to the small gathering just in time to overhear Martha.

'Martha, I really think you shouldn't go!' he shouted, waving his arms, aghast at the development.

She turned round and said in a low voice just audible enough

72

for him to hear 'Ali, as I have hardly any lessons to teach, I won't be missed. I like doing something of importance, remember?'

'Here take this,' he pressed his mobile into her hand. 'Call Sara as often as you can, with news about Vijay and - that you are alright.'

He is really afraid for me, she thought, her heart softening.

'I shall, darling. I presume a hug is out of the question?' she grinned knowing the answer. 'Don't worry! We'll probably be back in no time.'

She turned away and climbed into the back of the ambulance to join Vijay. She knew it wouldn't do either to squeeze in the front seat next to the ambulance driver.

৪০০৪

What have I done? Martha thought.

It was difficult to get comfortable in the ambulance. She had sat on a bench opposite Vijay's stretcher but the car was shaking so much on the uneven roads that she had to hold on to the edge of her seat. Goodness knew how painful it must be for the patient. She decided to crouch on the car floor next to Vijay; that way, she was nearer to wipe the sweat from his forehead.

Her secret fury at the inertia, indecision and lack of initiative at the Village had evaporated, and she conceded to herself that they had probably done the best they could under the circumstances. This wasn't America and she had to stop making comparisons.

She knew Ali would worry about her, and she herself became a little unsure of how she would cope without him in a Dhaka hospital. She knew neither the admissions nor the medical procedures nor did she know anybody who could guide her. She would just have to learn quickly.

Martha scolded herself. As usual, she had been headstrong and impulsive, not good qualities in an emergency, well-meant perhaps but potentially unwise, particularly in a country with such a different attitude to women. She hoped she hadn't embarrassed her husband in front of his colleagues. She prayed that they would see the goodness of her intentions; that she was on their side; that she wanted to play an active part and help to make things better.

73

She would hate to be considered as 'the brash American' who waded in without sensitivity, knew everything better and imposed her ideas.

A few silent tears rolled down her cheeks as she looked at the softly moaning boy.

It was hard being part of Ali's dream.

Chapter Fourteen

Cらる♡

Karin put the key in the lock. She was exhausted. She hadn't been on a day-long outing for months but today had been a great success.

She had gone into Manchester without a fixed plan, only her little list of 'poossibles'. She had feared it would be just like another city with huge, jostling crowds of grey looking people, the air blowing dust in her face and ear-splitting noises. London had been like that, overwhelming at times; whenever she had gone out, she had felt sucked into frenetic haste which left her more lonely than if she had stayed at home in her little flat. She remembered bewildering streams of people for whom this seemed to be a daily routine, and what had thrown a ring of isolation around her was the fact that everyone seemed familiar with it except her. She had felt bullied, waved on, ignored, hunted when crossing a road and eventually, she had been too anxious to enjoy any treat the city offered. After a few mishaps – when she had boarded the wrong Underground train; or when her handbag had been snatched by pickpockets; or when she had got lost walking in the wrong direction, swept along by a gushing stream of people – she had given up. Whatever glorious exhibition, concert or play, with which she had meant to cheer herself up, hadn't been worth the effort of wading through the treacle of fears.

To her surprise, Manchester had felt different, more welcoming, more personal.

It had taken her little more than a quarter of an hour to walk from her house to Poynton Station for the 9.30 train. She had been excited like a young girl on her first trip alone.

Not that she minded her usual routine, looking after her grand-daughter, Esme and on certain days, young Omar, but Karin was ready for a break, to do something adult, something for herself, if only for a day.

The sun shone through the window as the train set off and sped through the landscape, only stopping three times at Head Green, Cheadle and Burnage before arriving at Manchester's Piccadilly Station.

There she stood on the platform, smiling to herself, feeling adventurous, even a smidgeon reckless.

I have to gather my thoughts and calm down, she told herself, and decided to walk down to Piccadilly Gardens to have a coffee and decide on a programme.

She chose the nearest pavement café opposite the vast green expanse of the Gardens teaming with people: children playing hide-and-seek, mums or dads watching them, teenagers kicking a football or chasing each other, and couples strolling along arms slung around each other. The cafe was still empty and the waiter hovered and then rushed over to her like a spider to prey in the centre of its web.

She ordered an espresso and a glass of water while he fussed over her table, moving a little vase with a lonely gerbera from the table centre to the edge. It was unnecessary, she thought fleetingly; her espresso wouldn't take much space but still it was nice that someone fussed over her. He stopped, looking at her as if for approval and she smiled at him before he turned to get what she had ordered.

Karin took out a Manchester Guide from her handbag which she had put on the chair next to her. She wanted to check the opening times for the museums and galleries − as she realised − éé for the umpteenth time.

It must be old age, this constant checking and reassuring myself, an unsettling thought which she discarded immediately. She was here to have a good time!

She paid the waiter and, in her cheerful mood, left an unusually large tip. He had, after all, been quite helpful pointing her in the right direction to the Royal Exchange, her first port of call: Straight on, along Market Street.

As she stood outside the Grade II listed building which had been once the largest trading room in England, she realised that it was now part theatre and part craft centre, mixing the classical Victorian style with a bold modern art scene. She had a quick look over the craft stalls but without much interest; she hadn't come here to shop.

Karin stepped out into the sunshine again and crossed Exchange Square towards the Cathedral. She noticed the big Ferris wheel in the distance which would give her a fantastic view over the city but she had never been one for heights and had avoided torture of that sort all her life.

The large television screen in the Square made Karin smile; she had put it to the back of her mind that Manchester was famous for its sporting events and home to two football clubs whose games were regularly transmitted here for those fans who could not get tickets.

Karin quickened her step towards the entrance of the Cathedral.

The volunteers at the reception gave her a leaflet which she now studied: Manchester and its parish church had been mentioned for the first time in William the Conqueror's Doomesday Book. Around 1215, the Lord of the Manor and Baron of Manchester, Robert Grelley, decided to build a church next to his manor house. By 1311, due to the lack of a Grelley heir, it fell into the hands of the de la Warre's. Thomas de la Warre became not only the Baron of Manchester but also the rector of the parish church. During the subsequent centuries, the Cathedral had undergone several refurbishments, not all an improvement; the Victorians had imposed their sombre ideas of worship and later, damage had occurred from bombings during the Second World War. What had been preserved to this day was the Perpendicular Gothic style and the only surviving item of the Middle Ages was the small carving of a little angel with a scroll, now exhibited in the nave.

The leaflet bombarded Karin with names of benefactors, architects, craftsmen and incumbents – even a link to Margaret Beaufort, the mother of King Henry VII was mentioned.

She decided to just savour the tranquillity and beauty of the building; she could always read up the details later.

Sitting in the middle row of the pews, she looked around and was captivated by the wonderful woodwork of the root screen and the misericords, the hinged seats in the choir stalls, said to be the finest in Europe.

Karin's eyes wondered to the dazzling West windows of modern stained glass. She took out the leaflet again, looked for that particular section and learnt that the magnificent Victorian stained glass windows had been blown-out in the bombings of 1940 and that ever since, Mancunians were making efforts to replace them. So far, the artists Margarete Traherne and Linda Walton had created the Fire Window and the Healing Window, and Antony Holloway had been in charge of the restoration of the five Western Windows of St. George, St. Denys, St. Mary, The Creation and The Apocalypse.

Karin put the leaflet in her blazer pocket and waited whether there would be any bells ringing to indicate the full hour but the bells and the magnificent looking organ remained silent.

She got up, walked past the now crowded Visitors Centre and out through the impressive main portals.

As her eyes adjusted to the light outside, Karin noticed that it had begun to rain. She dug to the bottom of her handbag and brought out a pocket umbrella. As she opened it, she spotted the Triangle Shopping Centre, rushed over and took refuge. On the outside, it looked a fusion of the traditional and the ultra-modern, and the plaque at the entrance informed her that the building had been damaged in the 1996 IRA bombing and had been restored in this typical Mancunian style, preserving the old façade and adding a fashionable new shopping experience on the inside.

The stalls offered lovely home-made crafts and jewellery. She hadn't intended to buy anything but she was tempted by a silver bracelet with aquamarine stone insets, perfect for her grand-daughter.

If I can't spoil Esme what's the point of being a grandmother, she thought and paid.

Her stomach rumbled; it was definitely time for lunch. She found a café on the lowest level with the pretty name of Tiffany's and decided that she fancied a seafood panini and a salad which were rounded off by a large café latte. She had brought a thin paperback with her to read in case she felt conspicuous sitting on her own, but it wasn't needed. People passing by were far more interesting to watch, and amazingly, most looked relaxed and some even smiled in her direction. Manchester grew on her.

She looked at her guide book again: She would give the football museum a miss, the Lowry Gallery was near the South Quays, too far to walk; it would have to wait for another visit. She had only about 3 hours left to entertain herself.

Why not try the Manchester Art Gallery, she thought. She could pick and choose what to see and then take a leisurely walk back to Piccadilly Station.

Just as she was stowing away the guide book, a large woman with a bulging shopping bag approached the table.

'Is this seat free?' She dropped the bag on the floor and let herself flop into the chair with a sigh of relief.

'Yes, of course. I am just going.'

'Oh, don't go on my account,' the lady said hastily. Karin hesitated.

'Are you a tourist?' the lady asked.

'Not really…. Well, in a sense I am,' Karin stuttered. 'I have recently moved from London to Manchester and live now with my daughter, but I haven't had a chance yet to see the sights.'

'So what have you seen today?'

Karin told her.

'Any plans for this afternoon?'

'Well, I thought the Manchester Art Gallery might be nice but it looks a little far out.'

'It isn't really, and you can take a bus anyway. Have you got a Daysaver ticket?'

Karin shook her head.

'Well you can get one from the driver, or buy a single ticket from the machine at the stop.'

'Excellent! You obviously know your way around here.'

'Yes, I live up by the University, 'she chattered on happily. 'You know what? I fancy coming with you to the Art Gallery. I am just having a coffee and, if you don't mind waiting, I shall join you. I haven't been to the Gallery for years. It's always like that, isn't it, whatever is on your doorstep you take for granted…'

Karin agreed silently. How lovely that she wouldn't have to find the way by herself. She leant back and felt her spine touch the back of the chair.

What a nice woman…

'I am Tilly,' her new companion introduced herself.

'I am Karin.'

'Karen?'

'No, Karin; my parents were German.'

'My family is not half as interesting. We are Mancunians for generations,' she laughed heartily.

Tilly ordered and when the Latte was served, she drank it greedily, wiped her mouth with a paper napkin and declared: 'Let's go!

૭ჿ૭

With Tilly leading, they were soon in Moseley Street outside the imposing Art Gallery.

'What are you interested in? Pre-Raphaelites? Gainsborough? Impressionists? Dutch School?'

Karin was impressed with the choice. She had always loved the impressionists, Renoir, Pissarro, Degas, Gaugin, Corot, and opted for them, while Tilly branched off to the English collection with the Gainsboroughs, Hogarths, Turners and Constables.

After an hour, the women met up again.

'I never expected to see such wonderful paintings,' Karin admitted.

'…and you have only scratched the surface. You must come again!'

'Would you like to meet up sometime?' Karin felt unusually bold but was prepared to accept a refusal.

'I would!' Tilly replied eagerly. 'Since my daughter has moved to Australia with her husband, I live on my own. It will be nice to have company. Do you like music? '

'Classical?'

'Oh yes. My education of pop music stopped with the Beatles and the Bee Gees.'

They exchanged telephone numbers, promised to investigate about forthcoming events and to come up with suggestions for their next meeting.

Tilly waited with Karin until her bus came and waved her off like an old friend. The bus took her straight back to Piccadilly Station and she didn't have to wait long for her train either.

Karin was elated and couldn't help smiling to the trees flying past outside.

෨⠀ා⠀ଔ

Karin turned the key and pushed the door open. It was quiet in the house. She hung up her blazer in the hall, put her handbag on the table underneath and entered the sitting room full of enthusiasm.

She was greeted by Jasmine's sullen stare. She had a women's magazine on her knees which she now closed with an air of exasperation.

'Hi, Jasmine.'

Silence.

She tried again: 'Is Esme in bed?' Jasmine still fixed her with that unnerving stare.

Surely she couldn't be angry about her mother taking a day off and going out? It had all been discussed beforehand and agreed as fair.

'Esme's father was here,' Jasmine said in that ice-cold tone of hers when she disapproved. Karin noticed that Jasmine could not even get herself to mention her ex-boyfriend by name.

'Oh dear,' was all she could say, feeling sorry for the poor man. It was funny really how her daughter, so brilliant at and unflappable in her job, was quite easily upset by the twists and turns of her private life; more worryingly, she was not very good with personal relationships. Somehow she got terribly irritated when they couldn't be pressed into her set of rules and views of how things should turn out.

'What did he want?' Karin tried hard to be sympathetic.

'Access to Esme!' Jasmine, outraged, threw the magazine on the couch table with a thump.

81

Karin was tempted to ask 'why not?', but knew better than to stoke the fire.

'He had the audacity to suggest a holiday with the three of us.' Jasmine shuddered visibly at the thought.

Karin sat down in her chintzy arm chair and looked kindly at her daughter: 'It's up to you, Jasmine, but don't you think it would be nice for Esme to spend some time with her father? At least he shows interest.'

'I could do without it! I had never planned to involve him.'

'He obviously didn't know that.' Karin couldn't believe that she had raised such a calculating and selfish young woman. Where had she gone wrong? Maybe genetics played a bigger part in people's developments than she had anticipated? Jasmine's father hadn't been exactly the self-sacrificing type.

Karin put her thoughts aside, got up and declared: 'I shall go to bed now. I had a lovely but tiring day. I suggest, you sleep on it, too. Good night, darling.'

'How did it go?' Jasmine suddenly remembered that she had not taken any interest in her mother's outing; she wasn't ready to quit yet; she needed company and a sounding board, and someone to agree with her.

Her question sounded predictably rhetorical and polite.

'I made a new friend,' Karin was about to blurt out with happiness, but Jasmine was not in the right frame of mind; She wasn't really interested; she might even become suspicious. So Karin kept it to herself: 'I shall tell you all about it tomorrow,' she promised and walked up the stairs to her room, looking straight ahead in spite of Jasmine's exasperated sighs following her. She would not allow anyone to dampen her elation.

Chapter Fifteen

❦

Martha sat on a low-backed, wooden chair which kept her stiffly upright like a climbing plant tethered to a trellis, and whose top plank dug into her ribs. Vijay lying in a large bed next to her, looked pale, almost translucent, sleeping the heavy sleep of the drugged; occasionally restless for a few moments and then lost to the world again. Poor boy!

When they had arrived masses of people seemed to want to help to get him out of the ambulance and before she could climb down herself, he and his stretcher had disappeared in a cloud of white coats and a tangle of loud voices. As she rushed after them, she was stopped and reminded by a gesticulating male receptionist that someone had to help with the boy's admission. Martha gave the pathetically few details she knew about Vijay – where he lived now, his approximate age, the history of his illness; she was shocked how little she knew about his past and background.

At last they seemed to have finished formalities. The receptionist was still scribbled away without lifting his head. Martha breathed a sigh of relief and knocked impatiently on the separating glass pane to get his attention: 'Where is he now?'

'Wait here,' he pointed to a few wooden benches along the walls. 'Doctor will come find you.'

'How long will it take?' She realised that it was a silly question and wasn't surprised when the young man replied with a dismissive shrug.

I can't possibly sit here and do nothing, she mumbled more to herself than to him who had lost interest in her.

I shall ring Ali, she thought glad to have found something to occupy her mind.

It was Sara, the self-declared dogsbody of the Children's Village who received her call.

'How is he?' Sara asked with a voice trembling with concern.

Martha didn't want to be more dramatic than necessary. So she said simply: 'No change. He is with the emergency doctors at the moment, and I am waiting for their report.'

'Keep us informed, Martha.'

'Of course, I will. And,' Martha added hesitantly, 'tell Ali I am fine.'

ॐ

Later that day, sitting at Vijay's bedside she had plenty of time to reflect. She felt like holding the boy's hand for reassurance but she didn't dare; it lay there on top of the white sheet; needles and tubes protruded from almost every inch of his emaciated body, and she feared she might dislodge something. At least he was breathing regularly rather than in those short, uneven burst in the ambulance which had frightened the life out of her.

Martha looked round the room. It was light and airy, cooled by air conditioning. The windows were closed to keep the heat outside, but it also kept birdsong and the scent of flowers out. Not that the patients would have noticed…

She looked over to the other two young patients, all wired up. They were a sorry sight, a little boy with meningitis whose family had visited and cried profusely around his bed, obviously fearing the worst. The mother had stayed behind by his bedside. She never looked up but, from time to time, Martha could hear her sobbing.

The teenage boy next to Vijay had been visited by a young woman, maybe his sister, who had entered on tiptoes as if not to disturb him in his recuperative sleep. Martha had overheard that he had been involved in a motorcycle accident and had sustained severe injuries to the head.

When her glance returned to Vijay, she couldn't help feeling that he wasn't so much fighting for his life than life, ever so slowly, ebbing away from him. Dread and worry had formed a ball of nausea in the pit of her stomach and for the first time in her life, Martha felt helpless.

84

Please, God, no, she prayed silently. Please, save him!

Vijay had so much potential to fulfil, so much to give to his society, a whole life to experience. He was only at the beginning of it all. He was such a nice boy. He had such a big heart and so many dreams…

Martha nodded to the intensive care nurse who had entered on noiseless soles; only a soft, cool draft through the opening and shutting door had announced her arrival.

'No change?'

Martha shook her head.

When the nurse had left, Martha leant back on her hard chair and thought of Ali. Warmth wrapped itself around her heart. She smiled. He was such an idealist, so warm hearted, but also surprisingly ambitious. He really was determined to make a difference to these children, to this orphanage. She knew that secretly he had his own big plans for it but of course, he was wise enough to keep them to himself for the time being. He would bide his time, get established, gain experience until he would be given a bigger say in the running of the organisation. Ali realised that the Headmaster, was not a man to be pushed aside; he had become a father figure to the children and an authority to be reckoned with, a much loved and respected benefactor. He had made the Village into what is was: A well-run home and educational centre for children who would otherwise have neither; who would have been reduced to begging or miserly paid labour, fodder for exploitation by the more fortunate and cunning.

I am glad, Martha thought, that we have come to Bangladesh to do this work. The only thing which bothered her was the vagueness and fluidity of her position. It felt honorary, unimportant, as if they had desperately tried to find something for her to do. Any important decisions and tasks were allocated to her male colleagues. It was not what she had been used to nor had expected when both she and Ali had been offered the jobs by Dr Abdullah.

In America, she had been the leading light, the efficient organiser, the unflappable solver of enormous problems. Not even Ali had had such a load of responsibilities, the heavy burden of dealing with the maimed souls of American teenagers, children who behaved like rogue adults, who thought that this was the way of the world, that this was the life they were supposed to lead, that this was the only way to survive in a country of plenty and high living standards.

Now she dealt with maiming of a different kind, true poverty and neglect in a country which was poor itself, chaotic and run by people who had never experienced deprivation of any kind; who lived in gilded mansions and led almost westernised lives; who had inherited wealth, status and had enjoyed an education, ninety-five per cent of the population could only dream of.

Martha had come here full of zest, ideas and energy. What she hadn't expected was to be side-lined, hindered at every attempt to do something useful, that any shoots of initiative would be quickly buried and smothered, that most of her efforts were hampered – not because she was inept, inexperienced or ill equipped but simply because she was a woman. Ali, to his credit, kept her in the loop of all goings-on and informed her about problems in the Village when they chatted in the evenings but she wished she wasn't just treated like a delicate Victorian wife who shouldn't worry her little head about things. In her stifled efforts she felt much like a volcano whose vent was clogged up by magma.

It was not in her nature, she decided, to be just an appendage to her husband. What was the point of her working for a charity at all if she wasn't allowed to do anything? She and Ali would have to have a serious talk soon.

Martha was fairly certain that Ali understood her completely and her feelings of frustrations. She was sure that he was on her side. He would fight her corner discreetly and bring about changes on her behalf with the diplomacy and patience that escaped her. He had just been so busy since their arrival to establish his own position and to adjust to their new surroundings. She was sure of his love and support; all would be well!

I wonder how Sara copes with being second best, Martha mused. She is always so cheerful and she never seems to question anything. She had grown fond of the young woman.

Martha resolved to speak to Sara when she and a much improved Vijay would return to the village.

Martha smiled at the sleeping Vijay, brushing gently a strain of hair from his forehead. She decided to give herself a break, to get a coffee and to try again ringing her husband. She needed to hear his voice.

Chapter Sixteen

Karin hated it when her daughter was cross with her. The following morning, the atmosphere was thick with resentment and they tried to avoid each other, waiting until the other had gone downstairs or left the room before entering the same space. Jasmine's voice was clipped and business like. She only let a little cheeriness filter through when she addressed Esme, her little girl.

Not that they had had a blazing row, but the few comments Karin had made about the possibility of Esme's father being involved in their lives, had made it clear to her highly intelligent daughter that her own mother disagreed with her to keep him at bay. In a way, Karin was flattered that her daughter should mind what she thought. She usually went ahead regardless.

I wonder, Karin thought, whether she has doubts herself, and that's why she is so prickly.

On the third morning of their spat, Jasmine's ice-cold demeanour seemed to melt a tiny bit. An uncertain smile played around her lips and she looked frequently at the carpet.

I wonder what she wants… Karin mused, but wasn't going to make it easy for her. She hated emotional roller-coasters!

Karin had wandered into the kitchen to make herself a cup of tea and found Jasmine standing with the back to her. Then Jasmine turned round slowly.

'Shall I make you a cup of tea?' When had her daughter last wanted to be helpful?

Karin mumbled: 'I can make it myself,' but then nodded.

As they stood there sipping their morning tea, Jasmine

drummed nervously with her fingers onto the working surface as if working herself up to a crescendo in a circus tent.

Karin waited for the announcement:

'Mum, I won't be here at the weekend. I have been sent to Edinburgh to meet an important client. He is only free over the weekend to discuss his case, so I'll be back on Monday evening.'

Halfway through this speech, Karin looked up from her cup of tea and stared at her daughter in disbelief.

Jasmine cleared her throat in embarrassment: 'I know we had agreed that you could have Sundays off but I really need you to do this.'

Karin was aghast. After a pause she said in her own ice cold-voice, which she had obviously handed on genetically, but had rarely used in the past:

'Jasmine, I am not your employee, I am your mother!' Outrage sparkled in her eyes.

'I know, Mum. I didn't mean it like that…'

'What did you mean then? Will you please, kindly adjust your tone of voice when you speak to me?'

'I'm sorry, Mum.' Jasmine's voice faltered and she dropped her chin onto her chest. 'I can hardly refuse during my pupillage…' Her haughty composure had crumpled.

Karin felt a tiny bit sorry for her but not much.

'They know you have a child.'

'I think it's a test whether I am up to the job. They expect me to make arrangements.'

'And I am the arrangement, am I?' Karin was seething.

Jasmine swallowed visibly and whispered: 'Please, Mum,' stretching the syllables in an urgent plea.

'Jasmine, I don't really feel like giving up my Sunday after you have ignored me for days and bitten my head off on the rare occasion when you did speak!'

Jasmine stood there, eyes lowered as if in the dock awaiting her sentence.

Karin turned away to hide her considerable effort to control her fury and disappointment that she should have to shelve her plans for the weekend. She would not be able to go out and meet Tilly. It hurt. She hadn't realised how much she craved

89

the company of someone she could talk to, an adult with whom to exchange views and opinions, a sounding board away from family responsibilities.

She turned back to face her daughter:

'I shall do it as long as you promise not to make a habit of it and realise that I need a life of my own. Esme is your child not mine, however much I love her.'

She could see relief sweeping over Jasmine's face. And was there a spark of contrition?

'Of course, Mum. Thank you.' She had rarely sounded so solicitous.

'And as we are at it being honest to each other: It would be nice if occasionally you could enquire whether there was something you could do for me!' Karin knew that she sounded like a teacher admonishing a pupil, peering sternly over her reading glasses.

It worked. Jasmine's posture softened, she leant forward to embrace her mother. Karin sighed and hugged her back.

'Need to dash,' Jasmine whispered, and five minutes later, she was out of the door.

☙❧

An hour later, the doorbell rang.

That will be Omar with his mother, Karin thought and sure enough it was. She was due to mind him today.

'You look harassed, Serena,' Karin remarked

'Oh everything went wrong this morning,' the young woman moaned. I am late for college, I have still to write a five thousand word essay before Monday and now Mohsin just announced that he will attend a conference in London all over the weekend. I have no idea how I am going to do it all. And poor Omar is piggy-in-the-middle.'

'Well, I didn't have a particularly good morning either,' Karin conceded, 'I had to cancel my plans for Sunday. Jasmine has been sent to Edinburg to   a client who can only meet her at the weekend.'

'Oh, you poor thing! You were so much looking forward to it.'

Why did Serena understand her so much better than her own daughter?

'I tell you what: Why don't you bring Omar on Saturday morning. Esme will love having him around. You can pick him up when you have finished your essay on Sunday.'

'I can't ask you to do that,' Serena shook her head. 'It's really kind but you do enough as it is.'

'I'll be very happy to do that, honestly!' Karin smiled encouraging for her to accept.

'Are you sure? I don't want to exploit your generosity.'

'You don't! I am determined that we shall have fun! We might as well.' The laughter was liberating. She was cheering herself on, pretending that the new plan was not quite so bad, and that she could rescue some shreds of enjoyment.

'That's absolutely wonderful.' Karin received the second hug of the day.

ℰᏅ

'Tilly, it's Karin.'

'How lovely to hear from you! I am looking forward to Sunday. We are still meeting, aren't we?'

'I am afraid I can't come up to Manchester. My daughter will have to be away, and I have to look after Esme, my grand-daughter.'

'What a pity!' Tilly's sunny voice darkened.

No, she would not allow Jasmine to ruin everybody's weekend: 'I tell you what: Could you come out and spend Sunday with us? We can pick you up from the station and then we'll have a nice day together. There will be a little boy, Omar, as well, but he is no trouble.'

'Goodness, you are busy! As far as I am concerned, the more the merrier! Are you sure you don't mind me coming as well? It's ever so tempting.'

'I will be delighted to have a bit of grown-up company!'

'Me, too!'

Interesting… thought Karin. It contradicted the picture of the bubbly Tilly she knew.

'That's settled then. Come as soon as you can, and I shall make a plan of action. Hopefully, the weather holds so that we can spend some time outdoors.'

'I'll give you a call as soon as I have the train times; and I shall bring some goodies for tea.' Tilly sounded excited as if she had been invited to a big adventure. 'I haven't been outside Manchester for years,' she admitted, 'It just never happened.'

Karin was equally thrilled and suddenly didn't mind at all having to babysit.

℘)℘

They were lucky. The weather was glorious, so Karin took her little troupe of children along Chester Road to pick up her new friend from Poynton station.

The little ones were in good spirits, Esme in the buggy and Omar skipped along the pavement.

'And when we have picked her up, we go for a hike and a picnic,' he reminded himself and Karin of her promise.

'Yes, if the weather stays like this, definitely.' Reassured, he continued to skip along the pavement until they had reached the platform.

℘)℘

'I am not sure whether I can manage a hike,' groaned Tilly in fake desperation when Omar told her. 'As you can see,' she padded her belly, 'that's something I haven't done for a while.'

'We could just go for a little walk?' relented Karin, but when Tilly saw the disappointed faces of the children, and when Omar promised that he would pull her along if she got tired she relented to give it a go.

'But I can't give you a piggy-back,' he pointed out looking up at her.

They all laughed, imagining the picture: 'That's alright,' Tilly spluttered with mirth, 'I'll be fine!'

Luckily, Poynton Park was easy to reach, only a short distance along London Road. They turned off to the lane which skimmed the edge of the Park. The adults were glad when they found a gate so they didn't have to worry about passing cars anymore.

'Now let me look at my little map,' Karin made everybody stop.

'Goodness, you are well prepared,' Tilly remarked.

'We got this yesterday from the Information Office, didn't we, children'

They both nodded and their new friend said that she was very impressed.

'I think we have to do this hike back to front because it's meant to start at the other end of the Park.' The children looked uninterested and just wanted to get going, while Tilly mumbled: 'You are not getting us lost, are you?'

'Of course not,' Karin padded her reassuringly on the arm. 'Let's go!'

They went past the so-called Pool, along a couple of lanes which became narrower as they ended on the edge of a meadow. They climbed the stile with great hilarity as Tilly pretended to be clumsier than she really was, heaving her stout body over it.

'What a stupid thing to build,' she grumbled.

'Well, I don't think you would have preferred a kissing gate!' Karin laughed, and then she had to explain to the children what a kissing gate was which made them giggle even more. Walking across the meadow they could see Tower Farm on their left. Looking at Tilly, who kept up valiantly, but obviously struggled, Karin decided to choose the shorter route. They retraced their steps to the Park and followed the signs to The Pool, a lake of considerable size.

The children threw themselves into the grass when Karin declared that this was the right spot for their picnic.

'Now you have to eat up everything,' said Tilly, 'I am not going to carry the food back home!' Her eyes twinkled and they knew that she was joking. Karin spread a table cloth onto the grass, unpacked her cucumber and egg mayonnaise sandwiches while Tilly distributed four parcels of tin foil, one for each. They contained crumbed chicken nuggets, a little plastic container with potato salad, cherry tomatoes and a small bar of chocolate.

'What a feast! And look at me with my sandwiches!'

'Have we got something to drink?' the children asked.

'Oh, I almost forgot.' Karin pulled a bottle of lemonade from her rucksack whilst Tilly suddenly looked sheepish and produced a bottle wrapped in a kitchen towel. She held it in one hand while proffering four plastic champagne flutes with the other: 'I know it's naughty and a bit early in the day.' It was a bottle of bubbly which they opened with loud encouragement from the children and an even louder bang.

The sun was still beating down on them and, after everybody had eaten and drunk well, the two women stretched out in the grass whilst the children explored their surroundings.

'Do stay near, so that we can see you.' They promised they would. Tilly had a nap whilst Karin enjoyed listening to the birds, the soft waves lapping on the shore and breathing in the wonderfully fresh air, always keeping an eye on Omar and Esme who seemed to play 'catch me'.

'Come on, you two,' she shouted across when Tilly had woken up and they began to pack up. They made their way back through the Park and the children were treated to an ice cream from a seller who smiled out from his van as if he had been waiting for them especially.

'Now home for a nice cup of tea,' said Karin. 'Not far to go.'

ഇറ

'Poynton looks very community minded,' Tilly had come into the kitchen where Karin was making tea and hot chocolate.

'Could you put the doughnuts from that bag onto the plates?'

Tilly set to the task immediately.

'Sorry Tilly, what did you say? I thought I had heard the children quarrelling.'

'No, they are absolutely fine. They are playing with the doll's house. Well, I was just remarking that Poynton seems a nice place to live. So many events and clubs! I had a quick look at your *Poynton Post*.'

'Yes there is a public swimming pool, an entire sports centre, a club for most interests and a Fair in August.'

'There were two which really caught my attention: The Gilbert & Sullivan club and one for Egyptologists. They sound interesting. Do you belong to any?'

They carried the drinks and doughnuts into the sitting room and called the children. Omar and Esme gobbled down the cakes

94

and hot chocolates and disappeared back in the children's room eager to get on with their play.

'No, I haven't joined anything yet because I have been so busy looking after Esme and the house. But all this will change now,' she sat up straight, brushed a few crumbs from her skirt and took a hearty sip from her cup of tea.

'In future, I shall insist on my free time, and as Esme is growing up, those times will be extended and more frequent. I really felt that my brain was getting numb. Talking to a child all day is not great stimulation – it's tiring, and keeps you on your toes, but it doesn't stretch one intellectually. At the end of a day, I am ready to talk to an adult, and my daughter is not always a willing and attentive conversationalist after her day at work.'

'Mine rings me once a month, if I am lucky,' said Tilly wistfully, but then was back to her normal cheerful self:

'Why don't we both join one of the clubs, maybe one in the afternoon so that I can get here and go back in the evening.'

'You wouldn't mind coming out every week?'

'I need more fun in my life, too, Karin. I haven't even got a grand-child to talk to. Cities can be lonely places. So why don't we both join something together. It's less embarrassing,' she grinned.

'Well, I am sure, Jasmine wouldn't mind if you stayed overnight, so we could even consider something that takes place in the evening. Let me buy the new Poynton Post tomorrow and we can have a look what we fancy.'

They agreed that Karin would make enquiries during the week about the Egyptology class, the Gilbert & Sullivan Club and the Volunteers Office. Neither Tilly nor Karin was keen on sports; they were just not fit or competitive enough.

As the afternoon drew to a close, they made arrangements to meet up in Manchester the following Sunday, before Karin, Omar and Esme took Tilly back to the train station.

'When will you come back, Auntie Tilly?' Omar asked, and Tilly nodded as if she had thought the same thing.

'Soon, I hope. It's lovely here, and you are such good children. I had a whale of a time.'

A couple of minutes later, the train arrived and Tilly got in.

'Come back soon!' they shouted, waving wildly with both arms in the air as the train pulled away. Tilly blew kisses at the little group who, once the train had disappeared, set off to walk back home talking excitedly about the wonderful day they had had.

Jasmine didn't need to know that.

Chapter Seventeen

Cঙৎ9

'Hullo, is that Sara?'

'Yes. It's good of you to ring. Martha. How is Vijay?'

'No change, I'm afraid. He is still sleeping. I have just come out to have a coffee and speak to Ali. Is he there?'

'Yes, I gave him your last message and he said to fetch him if you'd ring again.'

'Oh thank you, Sara. That's good and very kind of you. I'll wait.'

'Why don't you ring in five or ten minutes again? Saves you holding on.'

'That's true. I shall do that, Sara. Give my love to everyone!'

Martha had never known herself to be so impatient. The five minutes' wait seemed to pass by in slow motion; in the end, she waited an additional three minutes to make sure Ali would be able to reach reception. She dialled again with jittery hands like a young girl ringing her boyfriend for the first time. She had no idea how he would have taken to her impulsive escapade. With a thumping heart she dialled:

'Hi, Martha, he is here. I hand you over.'

Martha heard that Sara was leaving the room. Ali didn't speak until she had shut the door.

He cleared his throat; finally he spoke. It sounded sad and concerned rather than angry: 'Hi, Martha! How are you doing? And how is Vijay?'

'Honey, I am fine,' she blurted out feeling so relieved to hear his voice. 'Vijay is still asleep in the intensive care unit. I just sit with him. I wish I had brought a book.'

This last thought had not struck her before. Why was she saying unimportant things?

'You didn't give anybody time, Martha, least of all yourself.' He rarely called her Martha; Darling, Honeybun, Sweetie, yes, but not her name; it sounded like a reproach.

'I'll come back as soon as Vijay is better. I can't leave him with all these people he doesn't know. What if he wakes up? Someone needs to explain to him what has happened and where he is. And who better than someone from the Village.'

'I see. So you are determined to stay?'

'Yes, don't you agree that that's the best for Vijay?'

'I am worried about you!'

'But I am in the hospital. I am totally safe.'

'And what do you do for food? You will have to go out. You don't know Dhaka at all. You as a woman are not supposed to go round without a chaperon.'

'I am not hungry, and I might be able to get something later from the staff canteen.'

'You are not wearing jeans, are you?'

'No,' she said guardedly, not understanding why it was important what she wore. 'I am still in my teaching shalwar kameeze.'

'Good, but please remember, Martha, this is not America. Where are you going to sleep? You can't spend more than a night sleeping in a chair. Be sensible. I shall send the caretaker to pick you up tonight and I expect you to return with him. The nurses and doctors can look after Vijay.'

'Excuse me, Ali? Since when do you make my decisions for me?' she said hotly, her voice almost choking with tears of frustration. Why didn't he understand? She wanted him so much to be on her side. She couldn't just leave Vijay in hospital on his own.

'Martha, you are not his mother! I'll send somebody else to stay with him.'

'He hasn't got a mother; he hasn't got anybody except us. So I am going to stay! I am not going to die of hunger; and what if I am a little uncomfortable at night. It's nothing compared to what Vijay is going through!' Big sobs stuck in her throat like meatballs.

All the endearments she had wanted to say to her darling

husband and hear from the one person in the world who loved her, floated away. He didn't understand, he didn't agree; he had turned near enough into a Bengali husband, worried what her actions would look like to others rather than upholding their shared principles. He had changed into someone she didn't recognise. Amongst all her emotions, defiance won out.

'I'll send Harun!' she heard him say again, 'I want you home and safe!'

'Don't bother!' She pressed the off-button on her mobile and burst into tears. People around her sitting in the 'relatives' room' didn't take any notice. This was a sad place and everybody was engrossed in their own, personal tragedy.

ℰℐℂℛ

I need to speak to somebody, Martha thought, somebody who understands, and she suddenly remembered her mother-in-law. I shall put a quick call through to her. If nobody understands, she will. She was a wonderful emotional safety net.

Unfortunately, she was thousands of miles away; so the telephone had to do.

It turned out to be a good idea and a good call.

She walked slowly back through the corridors to the intensive care station, still chatting to her mother-in-law.

'Don't worry too much!' she heard her say. 'I know what you are going through. Have patience and all will be well!'

'I am back at the room now, Karin. I better go…'

When Martha opened the door, she saw an unfamiliar man bobbing around Vijay's bed, taking photographs of the sleeping boy with a professional's camera. As a bright flash lit up the room, Martha hissed: 'What are you doing? Who are you?'

'Martha, are you alright?' came the worried voice through the mobile phone she had forgotten to switch off.

'Sorry Karin! I have to ring you back later,' She quickly pressed the off-button.

The young man hardly interrupted positioning himself and clicking away, then he announced without looking at her:

'I am from the *Daily Star*. That boy will be famous!'

'You have no right. Get out!'

99

He took one last photo of the patient, turned round, took a picture of the furious Martha and rushed out of the door.

'Get out!' she screamed after him until she was hoarse.

Martha stared after the disappearing figure when a nurse came past:

'We had someone from the press here taking photographs of my patient. Could you please, make sure it doesn't happen again.' Martha sounded harsher than she had intended, but the nurse understood the gravity of the situation and checked on Vijay before calling for assistance. There would now be a guard sitting outside the sick room.

Chapter Eighteen

CREW

'Hi Mum,'

'Oh, Ali. What a lovely surprise.'

'I hope, I don't ring too early. I keep forgetting the time-difference. It's already lunchtime here.'

'No, no, I have been awake. I am enjoying the luxury of reading in bed, and a little later I shall meet Tilly for lunch.'

Ali was surprised at the new name: 'Who is Tilly?'

'Someone I met on my excursion into Manchester. She is about my age and lives on her own near the University. Her daughter has emmigrated to Australia. So as it is Sunday today, and Jasmine is devoting herself to being a mother, I shall be meeting my new friend.'

'Good for you! Don't let Jasmine take advantage of you; she is good at that.'

Karin chuckled: 'That's all sorted out.'

'Good. Mum, can I run something past you? I need your advice.'

'Of course, Darling, fire away.'

He told her about Vijay, the Minister's visit to the orphanage and Martha's hasty decision to accompany the sick boy to hospital.

'We had an awful row over the telephone.' He swallowed hard to supress his torment and to be able to continue.

'Mum, you of all people know what Martha is going through; how she is thinking and feeling. I hate having to tell her off. On the other hand, I am the husband who – to the thinking here – has lost face and control over his wife. You know what it is like…'

Karin nodded into the telephone without noticing.

'Everyone here,' he carried on, 'is holding their breath what I am going to do about her. I wouldn't worry if we were in America; Martha can look after herself but it's different in a Muslim country. I wish she would see that she has to adjust. My colleagues treat me with kid gloves, but I can feel the disapproval through their good manners.'

Poor Martha, poor Ali! Karin's forehead wrinkled with strenuous thinking what best to advise.

'What can I do, Mum?' Her boy sounded desperate.

'Why don't you ask the Headmaster for a few days off and join Martha?'

'We have to cover already her lessons. Dr Abdullah would not be pleased to lose his Deputy as well.'

'I am sure, he can find a solution to this; a little reorganisation for a few days should not be beyond him. He could give the children a few more study periods, or a bit more sport or games. Do I need to go on? If you all put your mind to it, you will see that it can be done. And your relationship with Martha must be worth the effort!'

She could almost hear a stone fall from his heart:

'Mum, you are an angel; actually, you are brilliant; that's exactly what I shall do! The Headmaster can deal with the problem; he is getting the big salary. I need to save my marriage!'

'The sooner the better,' she admonished him.

'Yes, got your message loud and clear. Thank you! So if you don't hear from me for a few days, I shall be in Dhaka to sort things out with Martha.

'Yes and your main object will be to support her! You do love her for who she is, don't you?'

'Yes, I do.'

'Now, if you will excuse me, we are both in a hurry to go places. Good luck, and give Martha a big hug from me.'

'Shall do, and you give my love to Jasmine and Esme and… to Tilly. I shall keep you posted, and have a nice lunch.'

'I shall intend to,' she laughed.

Her afternoon would certainly be more pleasurable than his.

❦

She had hardly found the place in the book, where she had left off, when the phone rang again. Ali probably forgot to tell her something. To her surprise, it was Martha.

'Hello, Martha. I just had a call from Ali.'

'Did you?' Martha didn't sound her bubbly self.

'He is worrying about you.'

Instead of launching into a complaint, Martha said:

'That's very sweet of him, but he doesn't need to. I wish I could return home, too, but I can't leave Vijay alone in hospital with people he doesn't know.'

I love that girl, Karin thought. She is so caring and trying hard to please everybody, but ultimately, her moral principles win out every time.

'Life for a woman seems to be so hard in a society ruled by men,' Martha continued. 'I just don't know what I am supposed to be doing here. I came to make a difference, and all I do is upset people, even my husband.'

'Martha, be patient. You have only been there for a few months. You will find your niche, and Ali will work on your behalf. He just has to be diplomatic.'

'Sure,' Martha didn't sound convinced and rather near tears.

'He will, you mark my words! He needs you. He loves you just the way you are, your enthusiasm, your initiative, your compassion. He couldn't do what he is doing without you!'

'I guess so... When did you stop minding?'

Karin knew what she meant:

'You mean, minding to play second fiddle, waiting to be summoned and ordered to do things rather than doing them under your own steam?

Well... my situation was different: At the beginning I didn't mind at all; I loved to play the part of a good Bengali wife. I was totally naive, didn't know who I was and was perfectly happy to act out the role expected of me, even to be submissive. Your case is different: You have experienced freedom and equality all your life; plus you and Ali have a mission; and are used to supporting each other.'

'Do you really think I still have his support? Don't you think Ali might find it easier to change....'

'...into a Bengali husband?' Karin laughed: 'Of course not!

He would get a thick ear from his mother. Don't worry. Just be patient, Martha, and all will be well. And if you need another pep-talk, give me a ring – any time!'

There was a hard little laugh from the other end, but a laugh nevertheless: 'Thank you, Karin. I needed that.'

Martha seemed to be walking along a corridor; Karin heard footsteps.

'You do understand that I can't leave Vijay on hisown?'

It was safe to say: 'Of course, you stay put and don't worry!'

Martha suddenly seemed distracted, and Karin could hear the sounds of a commotion through the line.

'I have to ring you back later,' Martha said hastily and hung up.

₨␍

Oh dear, the joys and troubles of marriage! Karin had lost interest in her book.

Time to get dressed and ready, she decided.

She left a note for Jasmine and Esme, who seemed to have gone on an early morning stroll or to the playground, and made her way to the station.

Chapter Nineteen

☙❧

The following morning, Martha had a text from Ali: DID YOU INFORM THE PRESS? VERY UNWISE. SHALL TRY TO BE WITH YOU TONIGHT, it shouted at her.

No 'Ali', no: 'Honey' or 'Sweetie', not even a disapproving 'Martha'. Ali was furious with her, and she hadn't done anything to deserve it!

She sat on her hard chair for the rest of the afternoon, staring into space, confused and disconsolate. She didn't even want to go down to the kiosk and buy the wretched newspaper. She had no idea how they had got hold of Vijay's story about the arsenic poisoning. She could well imagine what the reporter had written, a sob story about the tragedy of an orphaned boy topped by a picture of the comatose patient and possibly her railing against government officials, when, in fact, she had been railing against the intrusion of the photographer. The orphanage would be dragged into it one way or another, and that was the last kind of publicity it needed.

What it needed more than anything else was a grant from the Government to build new wells and provide safe drinking water. The article would not endear the cause to the people in charge of distributing aid.

She listened.

There were loud voices outside the intensive care-unit obviously an argument was going on. Suddenly the door was flung wide open. It was the Minister, who had visited the Village. Without introduction or explanation he started on Martha, who looked at the guard for help but he stood in the door frame, shrugging his shoulders apologetically. He had obviously been pushed aside and was over-wrought by such an exalted visitor.

'So you are here, like it said in the article,' the Minister began his imperious tirade, 'what are you doing here, if I may ask?'

Martha stood up as if protecting Vijay from the Minister. She raised herself up to her full height and replied with defiance:

'I came in the ambulance with the sick boy.' Martha could just stop herself from adding: and it's none of your business!

The Minister shook his head at the inappropriateness of her action.

'No idea, have you, you silly woman!'

She was about to defend herself when he interrupted her rudely:

'Why did you call the newspapers?' His eyes narrowed threateningly. 'Are you planning on a smear campaign against our Government, and, in particular, me?'

He almost shouted taking no notice of the seriously ill patients in the room and the wide-eyed relatives sitting at the bedsides.

'Of course not!' Martha retorted with spirit, hands on hips 'The photographer was in the room when I returned from making a phone call; that's why there is a guard on the door now.' She pointed at the puny young man in the door frame who seemed to shrink with embarrassment.

'Who tipped him off then?'

'I have no idea. Could we please, discuss this outside? There are sick people in here!'

The Minister ignored her plea though he realised that his line of enquiry was leading into a cul-de-sac.

'Did you read the article?'

'No.'

'To give you the short version: The newspaper accuses us of either negligently or deliberately poisoning the poor and vulnerable. There will be riots in the streets if you and your colleagues are not careful…'

'That's hardly our fault! This article has nothing to do with me or the orphanage,' she retorted hotly. 'All I came here for was to accompany my sick student and stay with him until he recovers and I can take him home.'

The Minister was not about to give up trying to intimidate

her: 'You do realise that your involvement gives the whole affair a certain perspective: Americans again interfering in other people's affairs?'

'That is totally unfair,' Martha refused to be cowed, 'and you know it!'

The Minister looked triumphant. He was not used to being opposed and he was not about to get used to the insolence of an American woman now. If her husband tolerated such nonsense, fine, but she was not going to win over him, a representative of the Government!

'You should have stayed with your husband...' He stopped in mid-flow, looking a little confused as he was interrupted by the unit's matron who began to bustle around to indicate that even a Minister's visiting time was limited.

'Can I have a word with you outside?' he said in a more conciliatory tone, flashing a broad smile at the nurse who duly ignored him.

Martha nodded and followed him.

'We are in discussion amongst Government departments how to help the orphanage; how to solve your problem. We thought of giving you a grant to dig fresh wells. However,' he paused meaningfully, 'this article has put a different complexion on the whole matter and my colleagues might feel that you prefer to fight dirty.' He looked smug.

'That's not true. You know that we are desperate for the grant. We need to safeguard the children's health and improve our water supply.'

'Well, I am not sure I can change their minds.' Martha knew that he was being deliberately disingenuous.

'We can ask the newspaper to print a disclaimer in one of their next issues,' she bargained.

'That won't help. The minds of the so-called needy and vulnerable have already been poisoned by the idea that the Government, and in particular my Department, don't care, ignore their plight and can't be trusted. What a preposterous suggestion, after all we have done for them!'

I am not surprised, Martha thought, but kept it to herself. Suddenly, the Minister grabbed her hand and pulled her so close that she could smell his breath, a mixture of garlic and cigarettes:

'There is, of course, another solution,' he hissed in her face, 'if you could find a way to be nice to me, I might reconsider…'

Martha flung his hand away as if she had been stung, turned round and fled back to the room, when she heard a familiar voice:

'Martha, wait! What's the matter?'

The Minister turned on his heels and disappeared down along the corridor, only briefly nodding when he passed Ali.

'Was that the Minister? What is he doing here?' Ali asked breathlessly.

'He tried to threaten…' she couldn't finish the sentence and buried her face in his shoulder. He heard her muffled sobs.

'You can tell me later. Let's go and see Vijay first,' he said.

Nothing that had happened in the past 48 hours seemed to matter anymore. His fury had evaporated, and all he wanted to do was to console his wife. He stroked her unruly hair.

'I shall stay with you until we know what's happening with Vijay.'

For a moment, he remembered his mother's advice with gratitude.

Chapter Twenty

The two women had a great afternoon.

Tilly had come to the station to pick up her friend.

'Have you chosen a restaurant?' Karin took Tilly's arm, looking straight into her face, eyes sparkling with curiosity.

'There is a nice carvery near where I live.'

Karin's pursed her lips in disappointment. She had hoped for something more adventurous.

'You don't sound enthusiastic,' Tilly remarked trying to think quickly of something else. But she didn't really know much else.

'Well,' began Karin, 'have you ever been to an Indian restaurant?'

'You mean, have I eaten curry before? Yes, I have, but it usually comes from the supermarket – not often though. I tend to cook quick and simple meals for myself.'

'Takeaways are not the real thing. I wonder whether we find an authentic restaurant on the Curry Mile? Would you be up for it?'

'The food is not going to be too hot, is it?'

'No, trust me!' said Karin squeezing Tilly's arm. 'Bengali cooking is not meant to be hot; it's full of spices and fresh herbs and quite delicious if it is well cooked.' Tilly grinned as Karin got carried away and, licking her lips unconsciously, salivated in anticipation.

Tilly raised her eyebrows like question marks: 'I was wondering about something when I came away from our meeting last Sunday…'

Karin looked baffled: 'Fire away!'

'I hope …ahm… you don't mind me asking,' Tilly stuttered with embarrassment, 'and I don't want to be intrusive …ahm … is Esme's father… hm… Indian?'

Karin laughed: 'Oh dear, I thought it was something really serious. Of course, I should have explained before, Tilly – I was married to a Bangladeshi and lived in Bangladesh for a few years.'

Tilly looked at her open-mouthed and muffled a nervous laugh with her hand: 'We have lots of Indians, Pakistanis and Bangladeshis around here, but I have never met an English woman who was married to one. What was it like?'

'Colourful, dramatic, exotic – ultimately, in my case, disastrous, but I wouldn't change it for the world…'

'Go on,' Tilly stared at Karin in fascination.

'Today I shall introduce you to the food – a very important part of Bangladeshi society.' She could see in Tilly's expectant face that she would have liked to hear some more intimate titbits – it could wait.

'One last question: Is your daughter half Bangladeshi?'

'Yes. Jasmine gets very annoyed in summer when her skin tans more than that of others. I think, she is a very pretty woman. A bit too ambitious for my taste but she is a good girl. And I have a son as well; he is called Ali is married to Martha, an American, and they both live at an orphanage in Bangladesh.'

Karin looked at her friend quizzically as if expecting another question.

Thankfully, Tilly recognised that her friend was not offended at her curiosity. Some people she knew would have been cagey, suspicious or even annoyed. She had never understood why. To her, people were fascinating and interesting with their various backgrounds, pasts and opinions, different to hers.

Tilly sighed with relief and let herself be pulled along to the nearest bus stop.

When they got off the bus and walked along the Curry Mile, they peered at menus hung up outside until Karin chose the Shapla which advertised Bengali home-cooking. As they had a peek through the door, wonderful exotic cooking smells and Indian music wafted towards them. They looked at each other and nodded in unison.

'We shall give that one a try, shall we?' asked Karin already inside the door. 'I'll teach you to eat with hands,' Karin was in her element. It never leaves you, she thought.

Tilly looked doubtful and said: 'Oh dear!' Her new friend provided her with more adventures than she had had in the last ten years.

୪୦ଔ

The Bengali meal proved a great success. Tilly hadn't taken to eating with hands. Karin was highly amused by her friend's attempts and gave her plenty of encouragement and praise, but soon Tilly resorted to fork and knife. Then she tucked in.

'I won't eat for a week!' Tilly announced when the plates were empty, sat back in her chair and took a deep, satisfied breath. 'It was delicious, apart from the lentils. Mine are better.' They both laughed.

When coffee had given them a caffeine boost, and the restaurant began to fill with other customers, they paid and said their good-byes to the staff who, standing in the background by the bar, had taken delight in watching one English lady clearly introducing another to their cuisine.

'I don't think I can walk you back to the station,' Tilly mumbled mournfully, 'full as I am.'

Karin still smiled and said absent-mindedly: 'Your home is somewhere near here, isn't it?'

Tilly nodded and nibbled at her lower lip: 'I would like to invite you to my flat but it's really… it's really not fit to receive visitors. It's tiny.' She looked embarrassed now.

Karin put an arm around her shoulder and said with passion: 'Tilly, you don't need to worry. If I come to your place it's because I want to see y o u not your flat. But not today! I must get back myself. I'll take the bus from here to the station, and next week, we meet again in Poynton? We must sort out which club to join.'

'That would be lovely!'

Tilly waited with Karin until her transport came. She would have liked to hear more about Karin's colourful past, but decided to leave it for another time. Heavy with food, they had gone quiet and only smiled occasionally at each other. Finally the bus came into sight.

111

Before boarding, Karin turned round, gave her friend another hug and said: 'Thank you for being such a good sport! Have a good week and see you at the weekend.'

They waved until they lost sight of each other.

ଛଠଠ୫

Sitting on the train, suddenly Ali's and Martha's calls popped into Karin's head.

How happy they had been, when they had arrived in England! They had left their lives and careers behind in the States and had chosen a future in the orphanage north of the Bangladeshi capital where they would put their knowledge, experience and compassion to good use. However, before starting their new life, they had wanted to get married in England.

What a pity that circumstances put them at odds with each other. It was true that most marital quarrels were about other people. They were such a wonderfully matched couple. They had in common a mission in life – to do 'good', to make a difference to the lives of others – but they also had a strong desire for adventure and fun. Karin would have loved to lead their life when she had been young but she hadn't chosen a suitable partner.

Everybody had been so excited when Karin, soon to be a mother-in-law, Jasmine and Esme had picked them up from the airport. Martha had been overcome by emotion and had wept a little into Karin's shoulder which was understandable; after all she had just left everything behind she had ever known, just like Karin had done over forty years ago. The older woman gave the younger one a warm, reassuring embrace. Martha was a great girl, full of zest for life and idealism. She would make Ali a wonderful wife and partner.

As Karin had gleaned from sporadic letters and telephone conversations from the USA, Martha had grown up in a family of academics and career-minded people, and everybody had expected her to toe the line. Now Karin couldn't help the feeling that Martha – in spite of professing the greatest respect for her parents – was a disappointment to them, an outsider, not committed to making as much money as possible. It sounded as if she was not quite the black sheep of the family but certainly an odd-ball amongst them. In their eyes, she would never amount to anything; she would never be rich, famous or fêted.

Karin had to admit that, in a small way, she had been like this as a young woman but she hadn't been brave enough to upset everyone and to follow her instincts. She had trusted that she would be able to put her idealistic ideas into practice within the frame work of her exotic marriage. As it had turned out, it wasn't to be.

Never mind, Karin thought, that's all long in the past. The important thing was that Ali had found a wife who not only supported his charitable ambitions, but was a driving force herself.

Neither of them would allow anybody to hold them back. They would be unstoppable! Karin felt a warm wave of pride fill her heart.

Once the young couple had unpacked their suitcases, had had their first English dinner with the family and had chatted well into the night, another task had beckoned: Organising the wedding; nothing elaborate, only the closest family as witnesses but of course, they had all wanted to make it the best day in the couple's life.

Karin had volunteered to pay the Tourist Information Office another visit to collect ideas of what was on offer.

Jasmine had had no experience with weddings either, but had made some enquiries amongst colleagues. She had come up with some whacky ideas like a reception in the Lowry art gallery or in Manchester United's football grounds or something to do with Media City, the new home of the BBC. Jasmine was definitely not the romantic type. Karin, however, was and suspected that Martha was, too. She had to enlist more help.

'What do you think, Serena,' she had asked her young friend when she came to pick up her son. 'The art gallery is not too bad, but football grounds? Television studios? I thought of a river boat trip but we are not really enough people to hire one.'

'I shall make enquiries when I go shopping on Saturday.' Serena had offered. 'The library might come up with something.'

And it had done so! What could be more romantic than getting married in the same setting as Jane Austen's Elizabeth and Mr

Darcy; Lyme Park, a short drive north of Manchester, would be perfect!

Karin, now sitting on the train, remembered the wedding day with pride. The sun had been shining in support. There had been several more people than they had anticipated: Not only the bride and groom, herself, Jasmine and Esme, Ali's closest family, but to their surprise, Serena, her husband Mohsin and young Omar had almost insisted on attending and contributing.

'Why not ask Esme's father along?' Ali had suggested but had instantly regretted his frivolous remark, when he was hit by his sister's un-amused dagger- looks.

Karin had felt sorry for Martha who would not have any support from her side of the family, and she had told her so.

'Oh, you wouldn't want them here,' the young woman explained in her thick American accent. 'Nothing but a huge event would do; I am not prepared to put on a show for them; that's not us, it's not our style. I broached the subject with them some time ago, but they didn't understand. So I didn't tell them before we left. They will find out in time and sulk for a while, but I want this day to be our wedding day, the way we want it, small, fun and romantic.'

They had set the time for the wedding ceremony at St Peter's in Disley at two in the afternoon.

The little group had all been decked out in their finery. Karin had looked very elegant in her lilac, short sleeved, knee-length dress and a little purple pill box hat; Serena had predictably worn a sari, silver with purple embroideries, which gave her an air of sophistication; Hamid had put on his best dark suit and had just been glad that, for once, he hadn't been on duty in the hospital.

The little ones had felt very important and had looked ravishing in their outfits: Esme had been terribly proud of her yellow summer dress with little butterflies flying all over the fabric and had kept twirling – with the faltering steps of a one and a half year old – to make the skirt fly. Her pride and joy had been the tiara in her dark hair.

Omar had been reluctant to be pressed into any outfit other than his usual jeans and T-shirt, but had conceded that he had to make a better effort in honour of Martha's and Ali's special day; so he had agreed to wearing old-fashioned fawn breeches, cream coloured knee-length socks, black buckle shoes and a white shirt which would have made Mr Darcy jealous.

'All he needs now is a horse,' his father had joked.

The two children had been assigned to strew rose petals from little baskets they had carried while guiding Martha into the church; there Ali and the small group of wedding guests had been waiting. Esme had been so eager in her duty that she had toddled up to the altar, standing with the bride and groom in front of the altar, still spreading rose-petals, until her mother had sneaked up on her and had pulled her gently back to the pews. Her little scream of indignation had made everybody giggle.

Ali had looked at his bride and had been astonished: She had always said that she would sew her own bridal outfit; she must have done it in secret while still in America. She had looked simply ravishing in a grey satin Madame Pompadour style costume hugging her curves, and a small grey hat with a delicate veil falling over her forehead. Nobody had been let into the secret beforehand, and now everybody was gasping with admiration.

They had sung their hearts out to fill the big church and had nodded in agreement when the vicar had held his brief, encouraging sermon and had pronounced Martha and Ali husband and wife. The organ had played them out and once outside, the children had thrown the rest of their flower petals into the air. To their amusement, Ali had had to brush off the flakes which had got stuck on his eye lashes and one on his lips. Martha had just left them clinging to her costume.

It had been a wonderful day, Karin mused now, still sitting on the train. She remembered that, after the ceremony, a surprise had waited for the new Mr and Mrs Khan: A horse-drawn carriage had taken them from the church to Lyme Park, the grand country house, which had offered them a small room to have a meal should the weather be inclement. As it happened, the entire park had glowed in blazing sunshine, and their favoured plan had been put into action: The carriage had stopped by the famous 'Pemberley' lake, where restaurant staff had put a festively decorated table, chairs and a large hostess trolley keeping an entire wedding meal warm. A waiter had been assigned to stay behind to help and serve them.

They had started with a lobster bisque, continued with beef medallions, jersey potatoes and a selection of the finest baby vegetables; the meal had ended with a knickerbocker glory, Martha's most favourite desserts, followed by coffee and a piece of wedding cake. Esme and Omar had fought over who could keep the wedding couple figures perched on the cake.

'Why don't you have one each?' the bride had suggested, but by the end of the day, Omar had lost interest, and Esme had hidden them quickly in her fabric pouch which matched her dress.

Tipsy from champagne and all the excitement of the day, they had tried to coax Ali into throwing himself into the lake to emerge - like Mr Darcy in the television adaptation of Pride and Prejudice - with a wet shirt clinging to his broad chest, but Ali had laughed off the suggestion, pointing out that he had no need to impress his wife any longer, as they were already married.

They had heard the clopped-di-clop of horse hooves along a path. Probably other tourists were now taken on a ride. However, to the wedding-party's surprise, the horse and carriage had approached their spot again. They had looked at the debris on the table but the waiter had assured them with a shake of his head that it would all be cleared away in no time.

'A little treat awaits you,' he had said mysteriously and had waved them good-bye as they had piled into the carriage. The children had had to sit on the laps of the adults which had given them an even better view. They had pointed out deer grazing in the distance while the horses had trotted through the park. Lyme Hall had come into view with its sweeping background of the moors, and the children had discovered a tower in the distance. Getting closer to Lyme Hall, they had skirted along the edge of the formal gardens and had stopped outside the grand colonnade of the main entrance.

Another smiling gentleman in morning suit had welcomed them.

'Our sincere congratulations on your marriage,' he had said with a bow. 'If you will allow me, I shall take you on a private tour through the Hall, with the compliments of the house,' he added quickly when he saw Karin reaching for her purse.

Martha had been visibly moved, her eyes brimming with tears of joy. 'This is what I always dreamt, England would be: So much history, so much beauty, so romantic!' She had turned to her husband, had kissed him and had ambushed him with a passionate embrace.

'Help,' he had yelped in mock-horror, and the high-spirited children had run to his aid freeing him by pulling at the bride's arms and legs, until she had let go of him and had chased them up the grand stairs.

Karin had felt a tiny bit proud; proud of having succeeded in fulfilling Martha's dream; proud of Serena to have come up with the idea in the first place and proud that they as a family had managed to organise the day so well; but also proud of England, its history and heritage. Although having been brought up in Germany, there was nowhere else she would rather be!

Lyme Park and the Hall, they had learnt, dated back to the 14th century.

'The United States weren't even founded then!' Martha had whispered to Ali.

'It was given to Sir Thomas Danyer by Edward III for services rendered,' the guide informed them. 'After Thomas's death, the estate went to his eldest daughter, who had married Piers Legh, known as the Black Prince in the battle of Crecy. From then on, itt stayed in the Legh family until it was handed over to the National Trust in 1946.'

'And,' the guide had said conspiratorially, 'for the children, an especially lovely story: The Legh family always had dogs, and they particularly liked mastiffs. Now, at the battle of Agincourt in 1415, Sir Piers Legh II was badly wounded and his mastiff stood over him for many hours to protect him while the battle still raged around them. They both survived and this dog became the father of many generations of Lyme Hall Mastiffs, the ancestors of today's breed.'

'Good dog; so brave!,' the children had chorused and had looked in admiration at a dog portrait hanging on the wall amongst the 17th century Mortlake Tapestries.

The wedding group had seen the Library and its famous Lyme Caxton Missal, a 500 year old prayer and chant book; they had walked through the Dining Room with its magnificent stucco ceilings; then they had followed the guide through the Elizabethan Drawing Room to the Stag Parlour. Martha couldn't get over the stone fire place and as they had walked on, she had kept looking back at it in admiration.. The Grand Staircase had taken them up to the Saloon on the first floor with Rococo ceilings and precious wood carvings.

The children had become restless and were told to find the garden. An un-equal race down the Grand Staircase had ensued. Serena had had to help Esme to get down safely and to catch up Omar. Soon the wedding party had strolled in the formal flower gardens where the tour had ended.

'Children, did you see the Tower in the Park?' They both had nodded.

'It's called The Cage, and it served through times as a hunting lodge, a keeper's cottage and a lock-up.'

'You mean a prison – for bad people?' They could see that Omar was very keen to know more about the gory details.

'That's enough, Omar,' his father had said, 'you don't want to spoil the day.' Omar had given in reluctantly and had scampered off after Esme.

'I feel like a real life princess,' Martha had said looking around her new family.

Karin had given her a big hug: 'You are our princess and you truly look like one.'

'There is more to come,' Ali had said, 'after all, we are going on honeymoon tomorrow!' And turning to his mother and her friends, he had said, almost croaking with emotion:

'Thank you so much for organising all this. What a wonderful wedding day we had – quite unforgettable!'

Karin welled up with emotion at the memory of it all.

Just before leaving Lyme Park, they had grouped together for photographs and had taken it in turns to take pictures. Then they had asked guide to call a taxi. Mohsin had brought his own car, so they had said good-bye with promises to keep in touch.

'I'll see you next week anyway, Karin auntie,' Omar had shouted, waving as he followed his parents.

The newly-weds had spent the evening packing and had an understandably early night, while Jasmine and Karin had tried to get an over-excited Esme to go to sleep. The following morning,

Ali and Martha had been off straight after breakfast in their hired camper van, heading to another wonderful place, Castle Howard.

∞∞∞

Karin shook her head as if to wake herself from a dream. Her heart ached comparing their wonderful wedding day and the problems they were facing now. Maybe they had taken on too much too soon – a new marriage, moving to a different continent and trying to save the world?

Karin hoped fervently that Ali's and Martha's love would not waver, that their dreams of a future together and a joint mission to do their bit for the world, would survive.

She would write them a letter as soon as she got home.

Chapter Twenty-One

'Martha, you look exhausted. Did you sleep at all since you arrived?' Ali was shocked at the dark shadows under her eyes and her tired voice.

'In the chair,' Martha said quietly and stroked wearily a curl out of her forehead.

'I'm here now, so you can have a rest. I want you to sleep in a bed. I am sure they have spares for relatives. It's my turn to guard Vijay.'

Martha was grateful. Now that she could relax, she felt so tired and had trouble putting one foot in front of the other.

When the nurse returned Ali presented his request and a solution was found immediately, a box room with a bed, on the same floor.

'Sleep well, Honey.' He put his arms around her, pulled her close and kissed her gently on the forehead. She would sleep well: A big, heavy stone of mixed emotions and fear had fallen off her shoulders, and her heart had stopped feeling squeezed with anxiety. Ali was here.

'Honey, I have worked out a plan to make use of our time in Dhaka.' He greeted her the next morning.

Ever the organiser, Martha grinned to herself. She had slept all night without waking once and had just appeared in the door, freshly showered for the first time since she had arrived; her hair was still hanging around her face in dripping curls and she was wearing fresh clothes – white baggy trousers and a blue kaftan type top with white embroideries. It had been the first thing she had picked out from the over-night bag Ali had brought with him

– not her favourite outfit, but it was fresh, and she was grateful.

'I shall make an appointment with the Minister. I want to secure that grant for the orphanage,' he continued, 'and now, that his Excellency has behaved so badly, I might be able to shame him into writing out a cheque.'

'He is truly horrible! I never want to see him again!' Martha said with a visible shudder.

'You won't have to. I shall go there as soon as he will see me. You stay with Vijay and maybe read the letters from England.'

'Oh, have they written? How lovely!' Martha always looked forward to Karin's, Jasmine's and Esme's letters; the little girl usually drew a picture for her new auntie and signed her name with the help of her mummy. Martha settled comfortably in the chair next to the still unconscious Vijay and began to read.

'I'll make the phone call then. Wish me luck!'

Martha blew him a kiss.

ℰℭℜ

She read about Karin's plan to take her new friend for Sunday lunch; as the letter had winged its way to Bangladesh for a week, Karin and Tilly had probably been on their outing already, Martha calculated. Good for them!

Suddenly she heard Vijay moan. She looked up, saw his eye lids flutter and his body wriggle ever so slightly.

'Vijay... Vijay, it's Martha; you are in hospital; Ali is here as well.'

She wiped his clammy forehead with a cool, damp sponge: 'All will be well now,' she murmured tiptoeing to the door to call the nurse who had just passed: 'Nurse, I think Vijay is waking up.'

The rest became a blur to Martha. The nurse called for assistance, then rushed in to see for herself and kept speaking to the patient in soothing, reassuring tones while checking his pulse and blood pressure. All of a sudden the room was a-buzz and Ali was by her side again.

'Thank God,' he said with relief. 'Let's hope that it's the sign we were waiting for, and that his recovery can begin.'

Martha leant against her husband.

'We shall keep him in intensive care for another couple of

days until he can be transferred to another ward for observation,' said the doctor to Ali, obviously relieved himself that things were looking up for his patient. Without waiting for a comment, the consultant turned swiftly to leave the room.

'Well done,' Ali beamed at Vijay and a shadow of a cheeky smile appeared around the boy's lips. 'Now you must concentrate on getting better every day, and we shall stay with you until we can take you home.'

'Did you get hold of the Minister?' Martha suddenly remembered.

'Yes, he fitted me in this afternoon at four, pending my confirmation. Now that our young man here has woken up, I think I can risk leaving you both for a couple of hours.'

'Of course, you can,' Martha said full of confidence. 'I'll guard him and will make sure he behaves himself,' she joked.

'No slacking now, Vijay; your days of idleness are over; we want you home as soon as possible!' Ali continued the banter, and turning to Martha he said:

'Okay, I shall go and make my phone call and get some instructions how to find the Minister's office. I might as well leave a little earlier.'

A happy Martha waved him off, and even Vijay tried to lift one hand from the bed sheet, dropping it back immediately with weakness.

ℰᘛᘘℭ

The Minister had offered to send an official car to pick up Ali from the Shishu Childrens' Hospital but Ali didn't feel that he wanted to accept favours from the man who had propositioned his wife. All he wanted to achieve with this visit was to have confirmation of the grant to dig fresh water wells for the Children's Village or even better, take a cheque away with him. If necessary he would shame the Minister into it. However brave Ali intended to be, he had no idea what sort of welcome he could expect and whether the Minister would even listen to him.

Ali made his way through the crowded hospital corridors and took a deep breath of warm, humid air as he reached the outside. He walked away from the building, along the path framed by lawns to the main entrance gates. Looking rather startled at the sudden wall of street noise, he turned back to the gate guardsman and asked him to hail a taxi for him.

'Too much traffic,' the guard shook his head in disapproval, stepped out bravely into the busy road. For a moment, Ali lost sight of him in the chaos, only to see him re-emerge with a baby taxi, a kind of motorised rickshaw, trailing behind him. Then, from a respectful distance, Ali could see that negotiations were developing into a full-blown shouting match.

'Where you want go, Sahib?' The guard shouted back to Ali.

'Jatiyo Sangsad Bhaban – the Parliament House.' A shadow of surprise crossed the gate man's eyes, and when he related this news to the rickshaw wallah, it had a similarly effect on him, leaving him wide-eyed and mumbling with contrition. Obviously and strangely, Ali's destination had elevated his status.

He smiled inwardly – let them think whatever they want as long as I get there on time!

Ali reached for his purse for baksheesh but the guardsman shook his head: 'My pleasure, Sir!'

'Tell me, how did you manage not to get run over?' Ali was full of admiration. 'You are a courageous man!' which produced a short, proud laugh and a salute.

'At your service, Sir!' The gateman even clicked his heels

Ali returned the salute with much less accuracy, which produced another wry smile. It was so easy to make these people happy.

With much apologetic bowing from the rickshaw driver, Ali was ushered into his seat. Non-existent specks of dust or dirt were brushed off the faux leather seats and Ali was asked repeatedly whether he was comfortable. Finally they were ready to set off.

As the rickshaw pulled away, Ali felt as if he had jumped into a cauldron, the bubbling cauldron of Dhaka's vastly over-crowded streets; it felt as if he was drowning in the cacophony of hooting of car horns, millions of people shouting, engines roaring, bullocks bellowing in protest of having to pull heavy carts, constant ringing of shrill cycle bells, revving motorcycle engines – a congealed mass dragging itself along inch by inch under the blazing sun.

Luckily they didn't have to go far. The National Parliament

House was in the same district of Dhaka, Sher-e-Bangla Nagar, as the Children's Hospital. As they approached, traffic calmed down and a wide plane of lawns, paths and lakes came into view. Ali would have liked to ask the driver about the building but his Bengali wasn't good enough and the driver didn't seem to speak any English; anyway, the noise of the traffic would have drowned out their conversation.

Ali was stunned how modern the building was, utopian cylinders rising into the sky. When was that built? By whom? This was a third world country! It was an odd feeling to arrive here, like being spat out onto a different planet. The Hospital had already been a pleasant surprise with its modern building, smooth organisation and the latest medical techniques but this seat of the Government, Jatiyo Sangsad Bhaban, was something else, another Brasilia, surrounded by a different kind of jungle. Four major roads surrounded the expanse like a picture frame.

He paid off the rickshaw wallah who seemed to have expected a larger than usual tip from his eminent passenger. The man drove off without a word, looking sullen.

'Obviously not happy,' Ali grinned.

As he strolled along a wide, smooth path between lawns he was met by joggers and skate boarders. Many people who looked like tourists strolled around taking photographs of the silo-like buildings.

Ali was twenty minutes early for his appointment but it would probably take him a while to find the Minister's office.

As it happened, he met the Minister outside, leaning against a wall smoking a cigarette.

'You are early,' the Minister said obviously annoyed that his cigarette break would be shortened.

'Don't hurry because of me. I don't mind waiting. Maybe I shall have a look around. This is a magnificent building. Where can I get some information?'

'There are brochures and guide books in the foyer but I don't mind telling you what I know.'

'Okay.' Ali didn't want to appear over-friendly but didn't want to antagonise the Minister either. After all, he had come to ask a favour.

'Well, the complex is divided into the Main Plaza, the South Plaza and the Presidential Plaza.'

The Minister indicated with an outstretched arm the directions in which each of them lay.

'The main building is surrounded by a lake on three sides but you have probably seen that already.'

Ali nodded.

'We shall be going in through the South Plaza which is the main entrance for MPs; it houses the administration; they prettified the concrete on the outside to look more welcoming.'

Ali stayed silent, looking vaguely into the distance, until the Minister continued:

'The Prime Minister's residence is in the North-West corner and is only a five minute walk. However, I wouldn't recommend that you head that way because, as you can imagine, it is highly guarded by the security services.'

The Minister looked at Ali to check whether his visitor was bored yet, but Ali enjoyed learning more than he had expected:

'Who built it?'

'Construction started in 1961 instigated by the then President of Pakistan, Ayub Khan. The first architect was Muzharul Islam, a Bengali architect who soon tried to recruit help from Alvaar Alto and Le Corbusier, world-renowned architects at the time, but they were both unavailable. So he enlisted his former teacher at Yale, Louis Kahn.' The Minister flipped the ash from the cigarette and took a deep drag on the remaining stub before continuing: 'However, the project was interrupted for years. As you will know, we had an Independence War and reconstruction of the country took priority, but eventually the complex was finished and opened in 1982.'

'It's quite stunningly modern,' Ali interjected and just stopped himself from adding: … and looks outrageously expensive.

'Yes, and in spite of all the reinforced concrete on the outside, it is rather beautiful on the inside. Louis Kahn's aim was to bring as much natural light into the assembly halls. For example, each space reaches directly up to the roof, without the light being blocked by another floor.'

The Minister checked again that his listener was still with him and decided to was worth to continue: 'The Parliament Chamber can seat up to 354 members during sessions. A huge composite chandelier is hanging from its parabolic shell roof; this chandelier is a metallic web which spans the entire chamber and supports the individual light fittings. Quite amazing…' and, after a pause, he added proudly: 'After all, it received the Aga Khan Prize for Architecture in 1989.'

'Impressive!' said Ali politely. The Minister looked at him with a grin whether he was being sarcastic, but Ali was genuinely impressed.

The Minister gave a short bark of laughter: 'They should employ me as a tourist guide here!' He then stepped on his cigarette butt, left the butt on the pristine concrete pavement and indicated to Ali to follow him:

'But you didn't come here as a tourist, did you? We better get back to business.'

Ali wasn't looking forward to it.

ৡ৩ড়

The Minister had described the interior of the Parliament building well: If the exterior was simple with the silo shapes in re-enforced concrete, the interior looked surprisingly stylish. Huge spaces were flooded with light but the heat was somehow kept at bay; Ali suddenly discovered something ingenious: each white wall was inlaid with bands of white marble from which light bounced off into the rooms.

The two men went up to the second floor.

'We are now in the 'Bhaban,' the Minister explained, 'the main building. It consists of nine individual blocks and eight peripheral ones. The central ones rise to 155 feet and the outer ones to 110 feet. And all our offices are there.'

One of the doors to what looked like an assembly hall was open, and as they passed Ali could see that it was built like a sumptuous amphitheatre.

The Minister looked back to check that this hadn't escaped Ali's notice and was pleased to see that his guest was impressed.

'Here is my office. Come in.'

Ali took a deep breath and crossed the threshold.

The office couldn't have been more modern, minimalistic to

126

the point where one doubted that work was ever done in here at all. The beautiful mahogany table was devoid of any paperwork or other office paraphernalia. Only a miniature telephone of a most recent design reflected itself in the polished surface.

The Minister pressed a button on it and spoke into an invisible microphone:

'Satija, could you please bring us,' and whispering to Ali 'tea or coffee?'

Ali shrugged his shoulders. He didn't really want either. He wanted to get on with the business and leave, but as the Minister seemed to wait for his all-important answer, he said: 'Cooffee, please.'

'Coffee, Satija. And after that I will be unavailable for 15 minutes. So no phone calls, please.'

Ali could hear but not understand a girlish voice replying, followed by a click ending the call.

They sat there in silence until a connecting door slid aside with a gentle whooshing sound and revealed a middle-aged woman carrying a tray with coffee, white square-shaped plates and cups in the form of the building's architectural silos. She went back and appeared a second time with a plate of fine chocolates, a sugar bowl and cream jug.

Ali didn't want any of it but the Minister's personal assistant was well trained and took her task seriously.

'You know, amongst the 345 MPs here, 64 of them are women, Mr Khan,' the Minister declared haughtily but got no reaction from his guest.

It's not the numbers, it's how you treat them, thought Ali with rising anger.

'That's all, Satija. Thank you. So no calls for fifteen minutes,' she was reminded. She nodded and stepped through the connecting door which, seconds later, closed with the same gentle sliding sound.

He is giving me fifteen minutes, Ali thought, that's my limit. Right, my performance begins!

'As you have seen for yourself, Minister,' but he was interrupted.

'Do call me Ashraful.'

Ali became irritated with his opponent's attempts at diverting

127

his attention. He ignored him and continued with determination: 'The water supply of our Children's Village is laced with arsenic and as we have seen, it was almost fatal. We need to dig new and deeper wells to provide safe drinking water for the children, for us all.'

'What about your charity? Wouldn't it be their duty to raise money?' Ali registered that the Minister smirked. He pressed on regardless:

'They can't give us any more. They have a certain number of members and their donations have to go towards the running of the orphanage. And to be frank, Minister,' Ali was aware that he was rejecting the offer of calling him by his first name, 'the poisoned boreholes had been built on the recommendation of the Government's engineers and officials. We stuck to every rule and regulation they came up with although at times, we disagreed. So we really think that we have kept our part of the bargain, but your people have let us down badly. We don't want this to carry on and have deaths of children on our hands, do we?!'

The Minister considered this rather long and passionate speech, staring at his desk, finally saying in a clipped voice:

'I can't see how I can help.'

'You have come to inspect the Children's Village; you have seen with your own eyes what needs to be done and how much it is going to cost. I believe it is your duty to safeguard the health of our children. In short, we need money!'

'Otherwise your wife will go to the press again?' The Minister's words were laced with sarcasm.

'As you bring up this point, Minister,' Ali steeled himself taking a deep breath and half expecting to be thrown out after this, 'she didn't invite the press. It wasn't her fault. The journalist slipped through the hospital's security system. But you are right: I do think you owe us!' Ali looked the Minister straight into the eyes; he was astounded by his own courage, riled and fired on by a very unflattering picture in his head of the man sitting opposite him.

The Minister leant back staring towards the other end of his office, avoiding Ali's gaze. For the first time he looked uncomfortable.

After a prolonged silence, during which the Minister seemed to be deeply in thought, he pressed the telephone button and called his PA back.

Before she came in, he took a golden pen from the inside pocket of his tailored jacket and scribbled something on a piece of brilliant white paper he had magic-ed out of a silently sliding drawer.

'Satija, please do this immediately. Mr Khan will wait for it. I have to go to my next meeting.'

Ali wasn't quite sure what that meant. Was he dismissed?

Satija took the paper, nodded again with gravitas and disappeared into what Ali presumed was her office.

'I am sorry, Mr Khan,' the Minister got up from behind his desk without looking at Ali. 'I have another appointment. I think this should help towards solving your problems… and I hope it will appease Mrs Khan.' He bowed slightly. 'Give her my compliments!' he grinned arrogantly and left the room.

Ali felt like hitting him and clenched his fists in his trouser pockets, but thought better of it. No point jeopardising what he had achieved.

Minutes later, Satija came back with an envelope addressed to The Headmaster of the Children's' Village.

'This will give you permission to begin the work and a guarantee that the Ministry for Environment and Waterways will pay the bills against receipts. There is also an initial cheque so that work can commence.'

Ali was astonished by the self-assurance of this lady who minutes before had been reduced to the status of a waitress. For the first time, she smiled as she handed him the envelope: 'Good luck, Mr Khan. And if there is anything else we can do for you, let me know. I enclosed my direct number.'

'You are very kind!' Ali stuttered. 'You are so very kind!'

'We are here to help, Sir,' and with those words she opened the office door for him and let him slip out.

'Shamsur,' Ali was hardly outside when he dialled the number and shouted into his mobile, 'Shamsur, I have a cheque.'

The Headmaster croaked with emotion: 'Come back soon, and thank you, Ali.'

'Oh, and Vijay has woken up, He'll be out of intensive care soon.'

'What wonderful news! Thank you, Ali. Thank you!' Ali could hear through the telephone that the old man was moved to tears of relief.

Next Ali rang his wife. Luckily, she was in the canteen to receive his call.

'Martha, the Minister caved in. I can't believe it − he caved in. I have a cheque and a letter of guarantee!'

Martha laughed: 'Well done you, husband. I am so proud of you!'

They didn't know that the following day, the Minister would be in the newspaper again − but for an entirely different reason.

Chapter Twenty-Two

൙൙

'I can't believe he is doing this to me!' Jasmine had just come home from work, was struggling to take her coat off, had thrown her fine leather satchel on the floor and had opened her mail.

Her face was creased in frowns of outrage. Hamid, the father of her child, had applied at court to have regular access to his daughter. Jasmine stomped around the house until Karin pointed out that this sort of behaviour was upsetting the little girl, who had been waiting for Mummy to come home.

'And it's not very nice for me either!' said Karin shaking her head in disapproval.

What she kept to herself was the question, why Jasmine was so surprised. In fact, she felt that Hamid acted honourably. He wanted to be part of his daughter's life. He didn't shrink from the responsibility of having fathered a child out of wedlock. In Karin's opinion, he was perfectly entitled to have access. Of course, Karin realised that another thing was at stake for Jasmine, professional pride. They were both competitive lawyers and hated to lose. Karin was convinced that it wouldn't have come to a confrontation in court, had Jasmine behaved in a more conciliatory way. After all, they had had an affair. Yes, they had split up, but Jasmine had kept from him that she was pregnant at the time. She had only thought of herself when deciding whether to have an abortion or to become a single mother. She had not wasted one thought on the father of her child. It never occurred to her that she was doing her former boyfriend an injustice, that he was involved in the matter whether she liked it or not. Karin shivered thinking about the ruthlessness and clinical logic her daughter had applied to such a complex, emotional dilemma.

When the wind of Jasmine's fury had blown itself out later that evening, when neither mother nor daughter felt that there was any point in trying to get to sleep, Karin suggested to have a conference between them. They sat at opposite ends of the dining table. Karin was the first to speak: 'Darling, you can't go round ranting. It's not good for you and goodness knows what it might do to Esme. With all your other professional responsibilities, do you really want to burden yourself with a legal dispute about access?'

Jasmine looked flushed. Her eyes were dry, but red as if she had been crying. She bowed her head towards the table top and put both her hands over her face. Karin had never seen her daughter so distressed and vulnerable.

'You don't need to cope on your own. I love you and do what I can. Maybe you should see it as a blessing in disguise that Hamid wants to get involved; especially now while you are so busy?'

Jasmine's hands had slumped on the table and Karin put her palms soothingly over them.

'Look at me, Jasmine!' Jasmine slowly lifted her head, and Karin could see that her eyes were brimming with tears and her mouth was quivering with the unsuccessful effort of keeping emotion at bay.

'I'm trying so hard to cope, Mum, and I do not need the additional burden of being in a relationship. It just complicates matters. I do not want to begin to rely on someone, and then that someone would let me down or would disagree with everything I did. Look what happened to you and Abbu.'

'You can hardly compare the two, Jasmine. I would have loved if your father had focused more on us.'

'I don't want to ever get into the same situation, to be bullied, discarded, dominated, all the horrible things men do to their wives.'

Karin was shocked: 'I am so sorry, Jasmine, if this is the impression you grew up with. I thought I had hidden my troubles fairly well.'

'You did, but I came to my own conclusions. I see it daily in my job, and I remembered quite a lot from when I was small. I hated him shouting at you, and, I think, he hit you as well.'

There was nothing Karin could say; it was the truth. She was only sad that this seemed to have coloured her daughter's attitude to relationships and family life.

'Well, I don't think, Hamid means to propose to you. He just wants to see his little girl regularly. In my opinion, that is laudable, and it might help you cope better, someone taking up the slack when you are madly busy.

He is probably quite sensible if you try him.'

'I am afraid, Mum. I don't want anybody else having a say in my life. I want to be free to follow my career, to bring up my daughter the way I see fit and to have the odd adventure and fun with her. Marriage has never featured in my dreams.

'Maybe allowing him access doesn't look so frightening when you have weighed up the advantages and disadvantages. It's your decision whether you prefer to go to court and having to accept the outcome, or whether we could find a way to come to a private arrangement which suits you both.'

I know what I would choose, Karin thought. Going to court would end in bitterness and – knowing Jasmine – years of cat and mouse games, trying to outwit her opponent, It would turn her daughter into a vengeful shrew, an unpleasant person to be with. And what would that do to Esme? She would probably grow up into a man-hater, emotionally constipated like her mother, preferring success in a career and lots of money in the bank to personal fulfilment and happiness.

There has to be a balance somewhere, Karin thought. I must put a stop to this nonsense! Now was the time, while Jasmine showed a chink of weakness.

'Hamid is not a bad man, and if you explain to him, why you don't want to share your life with him nor anyone else, why you are worried for Esme…. Just open up to him, explain and negotiate. We are all human beings, we all have feelings. He will understand. And he is intelligent enough not to take advantage if you give in a little.'

Jasmine had taken to staring at her folded hands in her lap. She was obviously struggling as much with her own stubbornness as with the idea of accommodating Hamid in a niche of her life, frightened as she was of relationships; frightened of closeness and having to reveal her true self, and also frightened of losing control, to trust someone else except herself.

'Why don't you invite Hamid for a discussion? It can be here or anywhere you choose. Talk to him, find out what he expects without making promises.'

There was a stern look from Jasmine across the table. She seemed to have recovered her composure.

'That sounds like a good plan,' she said business-like.

Karin sighed, realising that she had missed the moment to make an impact, to soften her daughter's heart. She had to give it one last shot: 'I think it is your best chance of getting more peace in your life.'

Jasmine got up from the table without another word. This time, she didn't hug her mother.

ॐ

Karin was most surprised when Jasmine announced the following evening.

'Hamid will be coming for Sunday lunch.' It sounded as if she had booked someone to read the gas meter.

'Shall I go out? I could take Esme with me; maybe meet Tilly. Or do you want me to cook lunch for the two of you?'

'Oh, it's your day off – I had forgotten.'

'This is more important.' Karin could have kicked herself for saying it. In truth she was disappointed, but she would make sure that she would have time off in lieu.

'I really don't trust myself with Hamid on my own. Could you stay, at least for some of the time?'

Now there was a surprise!

'I tell you what: I shall cook us all lunch, but afterwards we leave you two to talk. Just keep your cool like you do with your clients and you might even be surprised how easy it will be to find a solution. Hamid does not strike me as unreasonable.'

'Yes, you mentioned that before,' Jasmine said, pulling a face to underline the sarcasm in her comment.

ॐ

134

'Tilly, would you mind coming out next weekend? I need moral support!'

Tilly was wise enough not to ask why their plans to go to the movies in Manchester had to be changed.

'Everything alright?' she asked sympathetically.

'Can you come on Friday? I thought of checking out the groups we might join. I could make appointments for us.'

'Sounds like a great idea. Will your daughter be there?'

'Yes, but she will have to deal with affairs of her own. Esme will have to come with us though.'

'That will be lovely. She is such a sweetie! So, to be clear, shall I buy a day return ticket for Friday?'

'No, Tilly, would you be so kind to stay with us over the weekend? I need a bit of sanity around me.'

Tilly laughed: 'I am not sure I can provide that, but I will give it my best shot. So do I stay over two nights?'

'Three if you want to.'

I shall get an open return ticket so I can go back any time.'

'We shall be delighted to have you with us, Tilly. It will break up the tense atmosphere we have here at the moment.' And then she decided to tell her friend anyway, painting the situation in broad brush strokes.

'Oh Tilly, they always say young and old shouldn't live together. I think I have made a mistake. I can't bear these ups and downs anymore. I want peace and harmony in my life and a bit of fun, but at the moment I have none of it, just worry.'

'I'll be there,' her friend reassured her.

∞∞

Karin and Tilly were very busy on the Friday. Esme was in Kindergarten for a couple of hours, so they could go and meet people in Poynton and even attended a rehearsal of the Gilbert & Sullivan Society. It lifted their spirits and they decided to join. The rehearsals would be on Friday evenings which suited them both. Jasmine simply would have to be at home to look after her daughter.

On Saturday, they fled because Jasmine was running round the house, cleaning, hoovering and dusting as if she were possessed.

It struck Karin as strange: Why would she bother about cleaning? Why would she want to impress Hamid?

Karin and Tilly offered to help but were shushed away by an exasperated Jasmine.

She had been cross when she had heard that Tilly would be joining them for the weekend. It wasn't so much that the spare bedroom would be taken up, but that there would be another witness to her possible defeat.

'Can't you ring her and cancel?' she had suggested to her mother. 'Any other weekend would be fine, but not this one. I am on edge as it is.'

Karin had understood but had remained firm:

'Tilly is coming for my sake, Jasmine. You are quite irrational at the moment; it's very wearing. A bit of distraction and sanity won't do us any harm. It might lighten the gloom that has descended in this house.'

Jasmine had stayed silent and bitten her lip.

On Saturday afternoon, the two friends wrapped up Esme in her red coat and sneaked out of the house. Once outside they laughed hysterically. It was all a little surreal.

'Let's go and have a coffee and you, young lady, will have a hot chocolate. Then we shall write our shopping list for tomorrow's lunch… and then we shall go and buy it all.' And that's what they did.

By the time they had finished, the house was sparkling, and Jasmine decided to have an early night. She wouldn't even stay to eat the take-away fish and chips. Everybody else tucked in. Once Esme was in bed, Karin and Tilly had a nightcap and watched a bit of television before retiring to their rooms.

None of them slept well that night.

☙❧

Tilly helped with the preparations for Sunday lunch. It would be roast leg of lamb, roast potatoes, beans, carrots and cauliflower.

'That should be safe, whatever his religion,' she remarked. 'Not that I know much about it…'

They smothered the meat in butter and covered it with sprigs of rosemary before putting it into the oven. They went easy on the garlic, though. Usually Karin made slits into the meat and inserted slivers of it.

'We don't want anybody to get self-conscious.' Karin chuckled at the thought that nobody would open their mouths for fear of having garlicky breath. She might have just hit on a solution!

She simply bashed a couple of unpeeled garlic cloves, which was quite therapeutic against the creeping nervousness, and put them underneath the leg with some onions, carrots, celery sticks and olive oil. As Jasmine had asked her mother not to make a fuss, Karin decided against a dessert but kept a tub of good ice cream in the freezer, just in case.

'Ready!' she announced, taking her apron off, about 10 minutes before Hamid was due. The dining table looked lovely with a bunch of old-fashioned pink and purple roses in the middle which Tilly had gathered from the garden.

Hamid was punctual and when she saw him again, Karin couldn't help thinking that he seemed to be a nice man.

Esme toddled straight up to him and wasn't bothered by her mother's little yelp.

'Who are you?' she asked innocently.

Everybody held their breath thinking the unthinkable, that he might tell her the truth, but he said simply: 'I am Hamid.'

'We have big lunch and ice cream!' she announced. 'I like ice cream!'

He bent down and whispered in her ear: 'me too!'

When Jasmine suggested that they should adjourn to the dining room, Esme took his hand and led him in. Not a muscle twitched in Jasmine's frozen face.

Hamid was well groomed in an unfashionable sort of way. He wore frameless glasses which enhanced rather than hid his brown eyes. His black hair was cut short and was already greying at the temples – Jasmine had once indicated that their age difference was no more than four or five years – his long face with a slim and slightly hooked nose and full lips gave him a serious but boyish look. The calm restraint, with which he proffered a box of chocolates, was endearing rather than charming. He was certainly not one for flattery.

However, he gave the impression that he had come to listen and to negotiate but that he would not be a pushover. Jasmine had met her match.

Having lunch together had not been a good idea. Everybody was tense and not really interested in eating. The wine bottle had remained uncorked because everyone wanted to keep a clear head, so they emptied the jug of water between them.

Sporadically, they made polite conversation mainly revolving around Esme who was alone in enjoying the meal, chattering between mouthfuls. For some, to her, unaccountable reason she was the centre of attention and made the most of it.

I am sick of this, thought Karin. Tilly noticed her friend stuffing food mechanically into her mouth without enjoying it, looking fed-up, unsmiling, fidgeting and fussing with the cloth napkin, ready to jump up like a coiled spring, ready to bring an end to this farce. Tilly tried to catch her eye to send a reassuring smile, but Karin hadn't looked up since the beginning of the meal.

'I think we should leave them to it,' Karin muttered when they met in the corridor carrying plates.

By the time they had cleared the table and had fled to take the protesting Esme to the swings in the nearby playground, Karin was furious and once Esme was out of earshot, she burst out:

'If my daughter chooses to be unreasonable and to complicate matters; if she insists on walking all over people's feelings, I won't be part of it! That poor man has every right to see his child! What must he think of us?' Then she saw Tilly's horrified face and added quickly: 'I am so sorry, Tilly. It's not your problem and I shouldn't have bothered you with it. It's not fair on you either!'

'Don't be silly,' Tilly said. 'What are friends for?' Calming people down was one of her specialities, and she was pleased that it came in handy now:

'Let's go over to the swings and push Esme. She is the important little person here. Your daughter and her boyfriend will have to sort themselves out for her sake.'

⚡⚡

Jasmine kept her tightly folded hands on the table top. She

could feel Hamid's cool gaze upon her, and it irritated her. She couldn't bear to look at him, but eventually she had to.

'You start!' she said sounding officious.

'My point is quite simple: I want access to Esme.'

'Why all of a sudden?'

'I didn't know that I had a daughter. Now that I know, I want to be part of her life.'

'We are quite happy as we are,' she said.

Hamid shook his head: 'For once, this is not about you, Jasmine. It is about giving our daughter a family.'

'She has got one,' Jasmine retorted.

'She has got half. She hasn't got a father or a grandfather.'

'It would be terribly confusing for her, if you suddenly ….'

He interrupted her: 'Not more than other children, who have a father …'

They were sparring now, both taking great pains that their voices should not betray their emotions.

'And how do you propose, we arrange it?' Jasmine spoke as if she was challenging a particularly awkward child.

'If you wish, we can arrange it privately, honouring each other's promise like civilised people; If that isn't enough for you, we can take it to the Family Courts,' Hamid countered coolly.

'You have it all thought out, haven't you,' she was stung by the allusion, that she might not be civilised.

'Of course, what did you expect? I am a professional. So are you.' Hamid slumped back in his chair and swallowed hard. The conversation was clearly not going in the direction he had hoped for.

'And if I refuse?' Jasmine sat up as straight as she could, staring at him like a prize fighter going in for the kill. 'You are not mentioned on Esme's birth certificate!'

'How dare you, Jasmine!' Anger and frustration were rising within him. 'You have not given me a chance to stand by you, to support you, and let's face it, you robbed me of the unique opportunity to look forward to the birth of my first child!' and after a deep sigh he spat out: 'I had no idea that you could be so cruel!'

'And what you are doing now is not cruel, suddenly turning up,, interfering in our lives?'

139

'What are you talking about? We seem to be going in circles. I thought I knew you quite well, but I don't recognise the woman I once loved!'

It sounded more like a bomb exploding between them than a compliment.

'You never loved me. You wanted a wife, a housekeeper and a broodmare. You never bothered to ask what I wanted, and I want to be a barrister!'

They were shouting at each other now.

'I wouldn't have hindered you! Being a couple, even getting married doesn't mean that we have to be each other's prisoners.'

'It would have been with you and your precious family!'

'Jasmine!' Hamid's voice rose to a crescendo. 'Leave my family out of this. They are an entirely innocent party. It hurts me to think that they don't even know that they are grandparents.'

'Do you mean, you want access for them as well? No chance!' Jasmine stood up and pushed her chair underneath the table, as if this was the end of the discussion.'

'Hold on, Jasmine! We are nowhere near finished discussing my involvement with my daughter!'

'Yes, we are! There won't be any if I can help it,' she exclaimed.

'Come on, be reasonable! We are supposed to be logical and professional. Hamid bellowed, beside himself. 'You have no right to deprive me of my child. No Court will agree with you!' Each word was coated in despair.

'Take it to Court then!'

Hamid rose to his feet. For a few seconds, they stared at each other with pure hatred, before Jasmine heard herself say:

'I think you better go now, don't you?. I want you out of my life, out of Esme's life! And that's the end of it.'

Without another word, Hamid turned round, went out to the hall, grabbed his jacket and rushed out of the door.

Jasmine slammed the door behind him, stormed up the stairs and threw herself on her bed.

෧෬

After the swings, Karin, Tilly and Esme went to the river to feed the ducks. The sun lay on the pond making the water droplets sparkle and giving the trees a golden glow.

'We have been away for two hours. I think we have given them enough time.' Karin was anxious to find out the result of this frustrating afternoon.

'I think Esme is getting tired, too,' agreed Tilly. So they went home, Karin's strides getting longer as they approached the house.

When they entered, they sensed immediately that things had not gone well.

Chapter Twenty-Three

CৠৎO

When Ali returned to the hospital there was chaos. A great number of ambulances raced up the drive, sirens blaring, blue lights flashing. Had there been a pile up on one of Dhaka's congested roads?

As he entered, doctors and nurses were rushing along corridors disappearing behind doors labelled 'operation theatre'. Ali pushed his way through the throng, being jostled and bumped into, pressing himself several times against walls to get out of the way. He finally reached the intensive care station but when he entered, he could neither see Martha nor Vijay. He looked around in case the patients had swapped beds – a silly idea, he dismissed instantly – but the other young patients were still the same; only Vijay's bed was empty. Oh my God, he thought panic-stricken just when the nurse came in.

'Where are they, nurse, Vijay and my wife?'

'Don't worry. Vijay has been transferred to a regular ward. We have an emergency and need beds,' she explained and gave Ali instructions how to get to where they were now. Off he trotted again, down the crowded corridors. By the time he found the ward, Martha knew already something about the emergency: A clothes factory had collapsed burying hundreds if not thousands of workers, most of them girls and young women. Hundreds were already confirmed dead; hundreds more were injured and about a thousand were still missing.

Vijay seemed unaffected by the rumours and was happy to be in a general ward, free of needles and wires linking him up with machines. It was so much nicer to be in this huge, white-washed room which was divided up into sections of six beds each, three facing another three on the next stud-wall, a little bit like big pigeon holes. As so many children and teenagers occupied it the atmosphere was one of lively chatter and laughter. However ill, children were astonishingly resilient. Ali suspected that some of the young patients thoroughly enjoyed their spell in hospital, being cared for by the staff in clean, light and airy surroundings, so different from their own homes.

After Vijay had eaten his first meal, he leafed through the comics Ali had bought on his way back from the Minister. Soon he began to chat to a shy boy in the bed next to him who, he heard, had had his appendix taken out the day before.

'I think we can chance it to leave Vijay for a while. Shall we have a look at Dhaka tomorrow?' Ali asked Martha.

'We could visit your relatives,' Martha suggested in the knowledge that he had felt guilty for quite neglecting his late father's family. They had just been so busy

'Would you mind?'

'Of course not! I am curious what they are like and I imagine they will pamper us like only Bengalis can.'

'In that case, I shall take you out tonight for a slap-up meal, just the two of us, to celebrate this young man's recovery.' Vijay grimaced: 'You go ahead. I don't need you anymore!' He was getting better; banter ruled.

Martha was so happy to have the Ali back she had fallen in love with. Somehow and inexplicably they had re-aligned their wave-lengths.

'You know what I really fancy,' she said with a cheeky grin, 'is a pizza. Is there such a thing in Dhaka?'

'If there is, we'll find it!' Ali was relieved that the tensions of the past days had dissipated.

The boy in the next bed knew where to get one: 'Pizza Hut,' he beamed. 'All over Dhaka!'

They didn't care where it was; a baby taxi would get them anywhere.

Martha quickly changed into some fresh clothes she had found at the bottom of Ali's bag, a night-blue sarong-type skirt and an ice-blue blouse with a small, round collar, short puff-sleeves and little buttons all down her back. The female attendant in the

143

toilet had to help her to do them up. Ali just changed into another white shirt to go with his jeans.

'Let's go!' They were excited like teenagers on a first date, pushing aside all thoughts of the disaster which had befallen so many families in another part of the city. As they made their way through the hectic of a hospital in emergency mode, it crossed Martha's mind fleetingly how quickly one became immune to news of disasters in a country where they were a frequent occurrence and woven into the fabric of life.

However, this was their evening, the first since they had arrived; they were both desperate to retrieve closeness, their love and the dreams which had brought them here.

ॐ

Ali asked the hospital receptionist to call a proper taxi; it turned out to be a good idea because it could use the Dhaka Highway as a short cut, avoiding the congested, dusty inner city roads. Night was falling within minutes like a dark, heavy curtain at the end of a play; thousands of electricity wires hanging over the roads sprang into action and produced millions of flickering lights at their ends. It was like driving under a canopy of crackling spider webs.

It had taken just twenty minutes before the driver stopped, demanded his fare and pointed to a huge illuminated advertisement, saying PIZZA HUT.

The heat of the day still hung in the air like a cloud of midges, stiflingly oppressive, making tops and shirts stick to people's backs and showing up patches of sweat as dark shadows.

Martha and Ali held each other round the waist and stumbled across the unmade forecourt towards the restaurant door. It was so strange to be in the middle of Dhaka, Bangladesh, and 'to go for a pizza' as they might have done in America.

The waiters were still reassuringly Bengali in their typically solicitous way ushering them to a table, pulling chairs from under it for them, handing them enormous menu books bound in fine leather and the word Menu embossed in gold, and spreading large white starched napkins over their laps. A tea light hidden in a gold-coloured little pot flickered on the table and a *shapla*, a water lily, the national flower of Bangladesh, floated in a glass dish.

Martha knew what she wanted without looking at the menu: A four-season pizza with lashings of grated parmesan. Ali was considering for a moment whether to choose a pasta dish but then joined Martha in ordering a pizza with pepperoni, roasted peppers and lots of tomatoes and cheese.

'Do we want any of the healthy stuff?' Martha asked, 'like salad?' Ali hesitated and then agreed to share a portion for one. To their surprise Pizza Hut, Bangladesh, also served wine and they boldly ordered a bottle of the house red.

'This is a feast!' Martha laughed, conscious of the contradiction – at home in the USA it would have been a quick take-away meal after a busy day and no time and energy to cook.

They didn't have to wait long to be served although the restaurant was full: full of young Bangladeshis, a couple of families with young children and a few foreigners. Most youngsters were wearing jeans and T-shirts; including some of the girls; the one at the table next to them spoke English with an American accent.

At last, I blend in, Martha thought wistfully. It was a surprisingly good feeling.

The pizzas were delicious; they had only a thin base, heaped high with fillings. Ali and Martha ate languidly, savouring every mouthful.

While waiting for their ice creams, Martha looked, happily and flushed with the effects of a couple of glasses of the house red, at her husband and said:

'This is lovely. Please, Ali, let's stay like this forever. Please, stay on my side!'

Ali looked taken aback and replied cautiously:

'I am always on your side, Darling.'

'It doesn't always feel like that.' She didn't notice that Ali began to shift uncomfortably in his seat.

'I know,' he tried to be conciliatory, 'but there is not much I can do about the customs and attitudes of the people here. I shall always protect you and defend you but I can't promise that I shall win against their traditional ways of doing things. After all, we are the guests and incomers and can't expect the country to adjust to us.'

145

Throwing caution to the wind, she pressed on: 'But you can stand up for me. I don't want to be the pushy and screaming American who wants to change things and impose American ideas, but I do need a purpose in my life, even here; especially here! That's what I have come for, to use my experience and knowledge to help. I can't just be a lady of leisure or a house wife. It's not in my nature. I see so much that needs to be done, and I want to do it, not be blocked from doing anything useful because I am a woman. Ali, we were always mates, you always understood what I am about! And I hope you still do!'

As the words burbled out of her, she looked pleadingly at him. Ali began again to shift uncomfortably in his seat. Of course, he still knew what she was about; of course, he remembered the plans they had made how to apply their combined professional experiences and turn them into helpful and useful practice to the benefit of the orphans.

However, once they had arrived, the realisation had set in that this was not a western country. Men were not used to career-minded women. Women were given what they needed, often even what they wanted as long as it referred to objects, jewellery, clothes, not things like careers, independence and self-fulfilment. Most women knew nothing else and were happy with their lot. In return they were expected to always consider the reputation of the husband and his family; they would not dream of doing something which would bring shame and tarnish its name.

And as he and Martha lived here now they had to integrate which neant to respect the rules, consider their hosts' feelings and adjust to local sensitivities. He would hate to disappoint the expectations of his Headmaster and colleagues by failing to adjust.

He wished Martha would understand his predicament.

On the other hand, how could he ever expect to squash an American woman's spirit into a mould like this? It went against everything she had grown up with; everything she had acquired, learnt and fought for: independence, self-confidence, self-reliance; she was somebody who needed a purpose in life, even a mission; she had an unshakable belief that she was good, strong and intelligent enough to tackle almost everything, the hardest of tasks; and the lovely thing was, that whatever she did, she never did it for money, personal gain or aggrandisement; she did it out of compassion and idealism and with a warmth of heart that almost always won people over.

However, he had his misgivings that she would succeed in this society, far from everything she had ever known.

How could he ever tell her that? Tell her that it might have been a mistake to bring her to Bangladesh?

He finally said to his wife who was looking expectantly at him with her big shiny eyes, twirling dark curls with her fingers and finally tucking them behind her ear as she usually did when she was nervous:

'Martha, I cannot change an entire society but I will try to fight your corner. I have to be diplomatic. So let me first get settled into my position so that I have more influence. The bull in the china shop tactic just doesn't work here. You have to be patient, darling. Please, don't think I don't understand...'

He took her hand which had lain on the table and cupped it in his palms.

'Come on, let's forget it and let's enjoy tonight!'

They remained silent while licking their ice creams from the spoons. The magic had gone.

Ali paid and ordered two pizzas to take away, a surprise for the boys in hospital.

Ali put his arm round Martha's shoulders in the taxi on the way back; he well knew that this was frowned upon in public. Luckily, the driver seemed to turn a blind eye.

Martha sat there stiffly and unresponsive.

It isn't good enough, she thought; it's not as if I demand the earth. I want to work. I want responsibility. I'll die of boredom and frustration if I can't.

༄༅

The next morning, the Minister of Environment and Waterways was all over the papers, his unusually dishevelled portrait staring from the pages. People, who were not digging with their bare hands to try and rescue their loved ones from under tons of rubble of the collapsed factory, began to launch accusations at the factory owners, developers, construction companies and the Government.

It transpired that this particular Minister, the main owner of the garment factor, had advised his staff to skip regular health and safety inspections, and had ordered the entrance and exit gates to be locked during working hours, so that none of his workers could sneak out without permission; hence nobody could escape when the five storeys had begun to collapse. There were rumours of shoddy building work and constant pressure on the workers to produce ever more garments during their twelve to eighteen hour shifts, for – the newspapers reported – £1.50 a day, a salary Western workers would laugh at.

Soon not only the national, but also the international press picked up on survivors' accounts describing working conditions as diabolical: Stifling heat, locked doors and windows, inhumanly long shifts with hardly any breaks, the latter spent at work benches, and supervisors modelled on slave drivers. The Minister appeared several times at the place of the disaster, protesting his innocence into microphones stuck under his nose by journalists in scoop frenzy. He hoped that his sad face and compassionate words might absolve him from any blame.

The irony of the outcry from the international public was that most garments produced under such regimes were sold to European shops which in turn would charge an amount for each item, the seamstresses in Bangladesh could only dream of.

The Minister attempted at first to defend himself, trying to shift the blame to elsewhere, with his usual arrogance. This was followed by insincere condolences for the bereaved families, in the hope to appease everyone with grovelling apologies, excuses and complicated explanations to the world's press. In the end, the Minister capitulated and thought it wise to resign. The police asked him to make himself available for further interrogation.

Ali checked that he hadn't lost Satija's card. He might have to use it after all now that somebody else would be in charge of the allocation of grants.

೫ಜ

The boys had been very happy with the pizzas and encouraged Ali and Martha to go out again the following morning.

'You might bring some more pizza?' they hinted hopefully.

'We are going to visit relatives,' Ali said which was met with expressions of regret.

'Did you have good time last night?' Vijay winked.

He is definitely on the mend, Ali thought and nodded. Martha was playing the dutiful wife but frost was still covering their bond.

सोचर

Priti lived in Gulshan, a leafy residential area for the well-off. They had been able to move there when her husband had been made Lieutenant General of the Army. The roads were wide and framed by the luscious front gardens where dark red roses, the spidery white blooms of the bakul, strikingly coloured bougainvillas, the tall, lanky branches of the somalu holding delicate pale yellow flowers into the air, where the bold yellow kolkephul and white, heavily scented jasmine jostled for space, softening any impression that one was in a city of 15 million people.

Only residential traffic occasionally disturbed the peace.

Priti hadn't changed much. She still loved to dress in stunning colours. This time it was a lemon yellow, from the hair clasp to her sari down to her sandals. She almost squeezed her cousin and his wife to death with the joy of seeing them.

'So sorry, we haven't visited before, but it was so hectic these last few months,' Ali explained.

'We thought as much. So what has brought you to Dhaka? The orphanage is not exactly nearby.' To Martha's astonishment, Priti's English was faultless and only the rolling 'R's hinted at an accent.

They explained briefly what had happened and that they hoped to take Vijay soon back to the Children's Village.

'So you won't be able to see any of the other relatives this time? I couldn't get hold of anybody at such short notice.'

Ali knew that visiting a Bengali family was always a big affair. Nobody wanted to be left out.

'That suits us perfectly,' he said. 'Martha is still getting used to the crowds in this country. We'll save it for another day.'

'I shall be nailing you down with a date before you leave today!' Priti threatened laughingly but she seemed pleased, that they had chosen to visit her before anybody else.

'The children will pop in soon and Ansar will try to finish work a little earlier. So I shall have you all to myself for a while.' She undoubtedly relished the prospect.

'Tell all!'

She was particularly interested in their work with the children and kept looking at Martha who had gone quiet.

'You worked in New York with disadvantaged teenagers, didn't you?'

Martha nodded: 'From that point of view this is a doddle.'

'And how is my beloved auntie doing in England?'

They told her, that Karin was living with Jasmine who was aiming to become a barrister, and that they thought that Jasmine was taking advantage of her mother whom she had installed as a permanent child-minder.

'I am sure Karin loves being a grandmother,' commented Priti.

'Well, it's none of our business but I hope Mum will say if she begins to feel exploited.' Ali said what he honestly thought.

Martha quickly tried to soften the harshness of his statement: 'She has got this friend now. They go on outings together, and the latest we heard was that they were thinking of joining a club'.

'I must write to her sometime. She was always so good to me.' Priti's fondness shimmered through her words.

At that moment, two of Priti's children and noisy grandchildren descended and the conversation was interrupted.

Since Ali had seen them last, at the time of his father's funeral, the daughter Miriam had added a third child to her family, now a boy of six months whom she clasped to her bosom all the while. Pran and his wife Amira had brought their pride and joy, a two year old girl with a big pink bow in her black hair and the biggest brown eyes Martha had ever seen. Little Jenny had also inherited her grandmother's and father's dimples which appeared every time she laughed, and she laughed a lot.

150

'Will you stay for dinner?' Priti asked her brood, but they all shook their heads and professed that they had a busy evening ahead of them; particularly the two older grand-children who groaned at the thought of homework.

'I have a singing lesson in an hour,' said a pretty ten-year old girl in jeans and a rainbow-coloured Benetton T-shirt, hugging her grandmother.

'And I have to go to cricket practice tonight,' confirmed a tall teenage boy proudly whose spindly arms and legs defied any athleticism.

'Alright, alright! We believe you,' Priti laughed, enjoying their exuberance. ' Go on then, and ask Abdul to give you something to drink and a snack. He is in the kitchen.'

They came back, munching samosas in one hand and carrying a glass of freshly squeezed lemonade in the other.

There was time for chats.

Pran was most interested in hearing about life in the USA as he was seriously considering taking his skills as a computer expert there.

Miriam's husband, who had not been particularly well educated when they had met, had soon after their wedding joined the army and enjoyed the protection of his father-in-law.

'And how is Hameed doing?' Hameed was Priti's second son.

She threw up her arms in mock despair and declared: 'He is hopeless! He is doing very well in business but he is still not married! And he is such a good-looking boy!'

They all consoled her that sooner or later, he would find a wife. Once he would fall in love that would be it.

'He is so fussy and doesn't seem to be interested at all!' Priti sighed. 'It would be such a weight of my mind if all my children were married!

Miriam and Pran departed with their families and soon afterwards, Ansar, the Lieutenant General, Priti's husband, arrived. After the first polite exchanges, he dragged Ali into his study.

'Call us when dinner is ready,'

Martha was surprised, but Priti seemed pleased to get rid of the men.

'Now you tell me how life is for you in Bangladesh!' she demanded.

Martha's face reddened. She was torn between loyalty to Ali and the urge to confide in someone, someone who understood, another woman. Would a Bengali woman understand? Or would she think that Western women made a fuss about nothing?

'You have been very quiet all afternoon,' Priti encouraged her. 'I shall be discretion personified.'

Martha's eyes brimmed with sudden tears.

'Oh dear,' said Priti seating herself next to her bhabi on the diwan, giving her a daintily embroidered handkerchief and a hug.

'I am not allowed to do very much, Priti. All the responsibilities I had in New York don't count for anything because – and I can't believe I am saying this – because I am not a man!'

'I thought you might run into difficulties,' Priti sighed in solidarity.

'How on earth do you women cope here?' Martha burst out, 'You are intelligent. I am sure you want to do something other with your life than cooking and having babies.'

'We do and… we chip away.' Priti said quietly. 'Some women are happy the way things are. Not many though nowadays; certainly not the well-educated ones. Too many of us have travelled and seen, how women in other parts of the world live. News travels and seeps into all layers of society. But of course, we have to be diplomatic.'

'Do you go to work, Priti?'

'No, but I have done charity work for UNICEF for many years, and, now I am studying child psychology.'

'Does Ansar object?'

'He did at first. He was probably afraid that I would neglect the children or his dinners, but I proved him wrong. Of course, he was also worried what his family, our friends and his colleagues would have to say about it.'

'Yes, the honour of the husband,' Martha muttered bitterly.

'Yes, that's still deeply ingrained in our society: Don't bring shame on the family. Luckily, you have an English husband.

She looked at Martha what effect the statement would have on her but there was no perceptible reaction, so she continued: 'Slowly, I worked my way up in the Shishu Hospital, where your student is, and now Ansar is used to it, and I think he is even quite proud of me.'

'It's not that Ali doesn't want me to do things. He never minded me working all the hours God sent in America; but here, he doesn't stand up for me, fight for a decent job for me; he won't even let me speak to the Headmaster about it.'

'Martha, I understand you so well; but I feel for Ali, too, what you are both up against. My eyes were opened when I saw how hard your mother-in-law worked in Germany when I first met her. And when she came to Bangladesh, she wasn't even allowed to do charity work. It was crazy. She would still be here, a credit to us all and a blessing for our country, if she had had a more enlightened husband.'

'What do I do, Priti? I can't stay here doing nothing. I am so frustrated. It feels as if someone has put me in a straight-jacket. On the other hand, I can't ask Ali to give up his job for me, and I would hate to leave without him.'

'Hold on, Martha! You mustn't think like this! Do give it some time. It doesn't pay to be impetuous! You have to learn to be more like us: patient, diplomatic, wily; occasionally even devious; remember: Always chipping away.'

'And how do I do that?'

'Look, I first went to the UNICEF Hospital as a visitor; then I began to occupy the children there with games and crafts; then I got into some counselling. You can do the same: Offer to do some voluntary work, something nobody else wants to do or has thought of, introduce some after school classes, art or music, some sports for the girls, a film club or choir, anything. Make yourself indispensable but always in context with the girls and women. Make a concerted effort to impress the Headmaster. Be reverent. If he becomes your ally, Ali will have a much easier task to change things in your favour.' Priti smiled at her with confidence hoping a few specks of it would rub off.

'And if all else fails, come and cry on my shoulder. We need women like you to help us grow more independent. Don't run away. Help us by staying and supporting our cause. These girls in the orphanage need you to set an example. You were lucky enough to have grown up in freedom, knowing that you can do anything. We need your example; teach us and show us the way!'

Martha was overwhelmed by this heartfelt plea. She couldn't make any promises the way she felt at the moment, but she would certainly give it some thought.

So she said simply: 'Thank you, Priti. You are an angel!'

The men came out of the library.

'Is dinner ready?' Ansar asked impatiently, raising his eyebrows in military disapproval.

'There we go,' whispered Priti with a naughty grin.

Ali and Martha had to leave straight after dinner.

'We shall be busy for the next two Sundays, but the one after, we could drum everybody together for a family party?' Priti suggested, beaming at the prospect.

'That's a date!' replied Ali for both of them. He had noticed that Priti and Martha had got on well; more contact with family might sooth Martha's dissatisfaction.

When they sat in the taxi, Ali put his arm around Martha's shoulders, pleased that the afternoon had been a success. He also noticed that Martha didn't shrug him off this time but rather leaned into him,

'What nice people,' she said, clutching a parcel of delicacies for the boys in hospital. She would give Priti's advice a go, to be positive and to simply chip away.

Chapter Twenty-Four

⋐3⋐⋄

Karin's and Tilly's first Gilbert and Sullivan rehearsals were a hoot.

The group had chosen one of the less well known of the comic G & S operas, Iolanthe, and in the pre-rehearsal discussion where everyone sat in a circle they were briefly introduced to the world of the librettist and the composer: Iolanthe, so they learnt, had been performed for the first time in the early 1880s at the Savoy Theatre in London which had been the first to be entirely electrified. This allowed the use of special effects which had been unheard of before. The Savoy had also boasted a recent invention, the telephone, which had given the composer Gilbert the chance to listen in to rehearsals through his own newly installed telephone at home. It was said that at Gilbert's 41st birthday party even the Prince of Wales, Edward VII, had been listening in to what could be considered the very first public broadcast ever.

Tilly had pointed at the picture on the front of their music sheets which represented Alice Barnett, the star actress of that time.

'She looks more like a grumpy baby elephant than the Fairy Queen,' Tilly whispered which set the two friends off giggling.

There were plenty of ladies in the group to choose from for the chorus of the fairies, most of them near Karin and Tilly's age. They would be required, they were told, to wave sparkling magic wands which brought on another bout of uncontrollable laughter.

'All these ladies of a certain age waving silly wands,' Tilly covered her mouth with her hand, just before being told that they were both to join the chorus. Tilly converted her spasm of helpless laughter into a cough, whilst Karin quickly rummaged around her bag to hide her mirth.

'*Iolanthe* is the story of 'mortal love' wreaking havoc in the tranquil world of women, portrayed by the fairies; it is the story of the veritable battle of the sexes,' explained the choir master, 'so please, we need to perform this with passion!'

Looking again at the picture of the Fairy Queen on the cover, Tilly blurted out: 'Look at her! I am not surprised she won!' Karin struggled to keep a straight face while nudging Tilly with her elbow.

'Let's concentrate on the singing,' she said finally having regained her composure, 'otherwise they will throw us out on our first evening.'

After about two hours, rehearsals stopped and they all piled into the nearest pub. Rob, the choir master, paid for their 'welcome' gin and tonics and they had the opportunity to ask him about Gilbert and Sullivan.

'Don't set him off!' said the group's Fairy Queen, a large woman called Penelope. 'You will still be here at midnight.'

However, they found it quite interesting to learn that the librettist W.S. Gilbert and the composer Arthur Sullivan had worked together from 1871 to 1896.

'Actually, after *Iolanthe*'s success, Sullivan was knighted by Queen Victoria, not for the work he had done in collaboration with Gilbert, but for his serious compositions. He then wanted to concentrate on those and leave the partnership, but he had signed a contract which obliged him to produce more operas within the following five years. No wonder, the next one, Princess Ida, was a flop. His heart wasn't really in it.'

'So they worked together until the end of their lives?'

'Not quite. Sullivan died four years after their collaboration ended and Gilbert lived until 1911.'

Karin and Tilly enjoyed a few more chats with other members of the cast, before saying their good-byes. Marching happily home, they had their arms linked, glowing with the effects of the joyous evening and the rare treat of a G&T.

'I could get used to this,' stuttered Tilly.

'We might have to,' replied Karin quite ready to give in.

'We better be quiet not to wake the girls!' remarked Karin before putting the key in the lock. This did not have the desired effect; Tilly started to giggle again, and the front door shut behind them with an almighty bang.

'Oh dear! It's like sneaking in when we were teenagers,' whispered Tilly with a wide grin, not much perturbed by possible consequences.

The precautions had been unnecessary. To their astonishment, Jasmine was still up, sitting on the sofa, a glass of red wine in hand, deep in conversation with Serena.

'Hello, you two.' Karin beamed.

'Hello. Had a good time?' Jasmine asked back, her ironic smile giving away that she knew that they had.

'Shall we demonstrate that we weren't just in the pub?' whispered Tilly, and Karin could just stop her bursting into song.

'The people were so nice, and we belong already to the chorus of the Fairies!'

Now it was Serena's and Jasmine's turn to snort with laughter.

'Glass of wine?' Jasmine offered, and when the two hesitated, looking sheepishly at each other, she encouraged them: 'Come on, be a devil!'

They gave in graciously and flopped into the two arm chairs. Tilly almost fell through the modernist one before announcing:

'I think I have to sleep in this. I shall never get out of it!'

To the hilarity of the other two women, Karin pulled her friend up with both hands from the modern contraption and installed her in the chintzy arm chair; then she squeezed herself between the sofa arm rest and Serena.

With the two finally settled, Jasmine surprised everyone with a toast: 'To women's friendships!' and they all replied in unison: 'To women's friendships!'

'Now,' Jasmine continued, 'while you were out singing, we sorted out the world's problems.' She sounded bullish and more cheerful than she had done in weeks.

'And mine,' Serena added in a low voice as if embarrassed.

'Why, what's happened?' asked Karin, not sure what to make

of this comment. She hoped fervently that it didn't have anything to do with her marriage to the lovely Mohsin or the well-being of young Omar.

'The College has thrown another huge assignment at us at short notice, and it looks as if I shall have to work all weekend on it. Mohsin will be on call at the hospital which means, I can't rely on him. So I came to ask whether Omar could stay with you for a couple of hours tomorrow.'

'Of course…' but Karin was interrupted by her daughter:

'It's all sorted out, Mum. Omar is already sleeping in Esme's room, and I shall take the entire weekend off and have fun with the children.'

This was an entirely new side of Jasmine which Karin had rarely glimpsed. A couple of hours with Serena seemed to have done her daughter the world of good. As she sipped the wine, she heard Jasmine say:

'There is a fun fair nearby; I haven't been to one of those for years, and on Sunday, well, I am sure I can think of something exciting.'

'Excellent!' said Karin. She liked the new Jasmine — however short-lived she might be — and was relieved that she would not be involved in any weekend duties.

'So you wouldn't mind me going back to Manchester with Tilly until Sunday evening?'

'No, not at all!' Jasmine seemed to relish the thought of being in sole charge. It would be the very first time without her mother on standby.

'Beddy-byes, I think.' Karin drained her glass and put it on the coffee table.

'Yes, I must go as well,' Serena was suddenly in a hurry and got up. 'I better make a start with that blasted essay. Thank you so much, Jasmine! Give me a ring if you are getting fed up.'

'Don't worry, I shan't.' Jasmine smiled. 'Shall I drop Omar off on Sunday night?'

'I can't ask you to do that as well!'

'It will be nice to go on a little drive. We can actually bring a take-away which would save us all cooking.'

'Tell you what, I shall prepare a quick curry and we have that together when you come.'

'If you are sure…?' Jasmine loved curry, particularly home-cooked ones.

'That's the least I can do!' said Serena

'Good night all,' said Karin finally. 'Good luck with the essay!'

Serena shrugged her shoulders faking exasperation. 'I shall need it!'

Jasmine accompanied her to the front door, and Karin could hear her say:

'Good night, Serena. And thank you for listening!'

I wonder what that is all about, thought Karin.

As the two ladies walked up the stairs, Tilly muttered:

'Oh dear, oh dear.'

'What is it, Tilly? Are you out of puff?'

'No, no, I am only worried that you might not like staying in my flat.'

They reached the top of the stairs and stood outside the guest bedroom door:

'Nonesense! Look at me, Tilly. I say this only once more: I come to be with you, for your company, not to judge yourr flat. Is that clear?'

'You can sleep in my bed but it's only a one-bedroom flat, and the bathroom is tiny.'

'If you can live in it, so can I? I have slept on mats on the floor in my time.'

'You were probably a lot younger then.'

'And my flat in London was rather small and threadbare, too; nothing to crow about. Such things are not important. Our friendship is!'

'That's very nice of you to say.'

'I won't hear of you giving up your bed. Have you got a settee?' and when Tilly nodded she insisted: 'So that's where I shall sleep. We shall have a great time!'

Tilly still looked worried.

'We could try and get last minute tickets for the theatre tomorrow night,' she suggested tentatively.

'There you are! That's the spirit! That will be great!'

They hugged and disappeared behind their respective doors.

ഇറ

When Karin returned from her weekend in Manchester on Sunday evening, she could already hear the excited little voice of her grand-daughter before she had even opened the door.

'You are in good spirits,' she laughed.

'Oh we had a wonderful time. We have just come home ourselves,' said Jasmine cheerfully, helping Esme to take off her little shoes.

'I was carousel and…and… bicycle.'

'Have you then? How exciting!'

The little girl, now in socks, jumped up and down, clapping her podgy little hands and shrieking with delight.

'Yes, we went to the fun fair on Saturday, and today, we hired bikes, and cycled first around the park to practise and then along the river. Esme was riding in a trailer attached to my bike, and now we have just come back from dropping off Omar and having a wonderful curry dinner. We had a great time, hadn't we, Esme?!'

And when the little one confirmed this with vigorous nodding and a few more shrieks, her mother promised: 'We shall do it again!'

Karin was amazed at her daughter's sudden enthusiasm for motherhood and the joyful spirit with which she had tackled the considerable task of looking after two children all weekend. Once she puts her mind to something…, Karin thought with some admiration.

'Had a good weekend yourself?' Jasmine turned to her.

'Yes, we went to see a Noel Coward comedy in the theatre last night and went for a two hour walk in the park today. Tilly wants to get fitter, so we have put gentle exercise on our agenda.'

And then Karin couldn't hide her curiosity any longer:

'What was it, you talked to Serena about? She managed to cheer you up no end.'

'Well, all sorts of things. She is so sensible!' She grabbed the squealing Esme under her arm and said: 'Let me take this young lady to bed, and when I come down, I shall tell you all about it.'

Chapter Twenty-Five

 ⊂ЗᏏᎧ

It took only another day until Vijay was declared fit enough to be discharged. Beds were at a premium after the factory disaster. Vijay looked still painfully thin but at least all the symptoms like headaches, nausea, vomiting and lethargy had disappeared; even the lesions were healing well. Martha and Ali were slightly dubious about the haste but the hospital doctors pointed out to them that the boy would be discharged into the capable hands of Dr Chowdhury at the orphanage.

Vijay exchanged addresses and telephone numbers with Ravi, the shy boy in the bed next to him, who promised to visit the Children's Village sometime soon. It was a cheerful journey home in the car, Dr Abdullah, the Headmaster, had sent. It was driven by a very excited Harun, the caretaker who had only been to Dhaka once or twice before. The passengers grinned at each other as the poor man lost his way several times and finally got totally stuck in a traffic jam; a bullock cart had overturned its cargo of hundreds of cans of food which were now rolling around in the middle of a crossroads so that traffic was halted in four directions. A great mass of gesticulating and shouting passers-bye kicked the battered and dented tins to the edge of the road where they were picked up and spirited away by the poor and canny of the City.

As they were waiting, Harun looked more harassed than excited and the strain began to show in Vijay's face as well. They all breathed a sigh of relief when, after a considerable time, traffic began to move again and they reach the country road leading out of the city.

The staff and children at the Children's Village had organised a little reception committee for their friend. They wanted to express how happy they were to have him back safe and sound, and pat him on the back, but Vijay couldn't raise more than a weak smile and was quickly whisked away by Dr Chowdhury.

'He is out of the woods, children, but he is still recovering. So we all need to help him to build up his strength and spirits. I shall see to the first, and you can take care of the second by visiting him. But for now, he needs rest.'

The two of them walked off – very slowly – towards the clinic, the doctor supporting his young patient by putting an arm around his waist and Vijay resting his arm on the doctor's shoulder. The three nurses were already waiting by the door to take over.

The children suddenly realised how ill their friend had been; they could have lost him: it also dawned on them how easily it could have been them ending up in hospital, had not the staff reacted so promptly by diagnosing the problem and taking action.

The welcoming committee dispersed and went back to their class rooms in shocked silence.

℘℃℞

The following morning, Martha lost no time putting her good intentions and Priti's advice into practice. She would voluntarily introduce some after-school activities. She wouldn't tell Ali until she had concrete plans and a good idea how to organise them. She didn't want anybody to stop her or put obstacles in her way before she had even started.

First she would lobby the girls. She heard many of them singing to themselves during the day, sometimes even in groups in the workshops or kitchen. She hoped she could persuade them to join regular singing sessions. Surely, nobody could object to a choir!

Next she considered sport. There were two criteria: It had to be inexpensive in terms of equipment and the girls could do it dressed modestly which excluded sports like tennis, swimming, gymnastics and athletics; football, rugby or boxing were too physical and would certainly not be encouraged.

Martha settled on cricket and rounderss. They had the boys' bats already and many of the girls enjoyed watching the games. She had never played them herself, so Ali would have to help with the rules.

Martha was quietly pleased to have found such easy solutions. However, it occurred to her that it might be wise to run them past someone; someone well-established and courageous enough to help her implement the plans, someone loyal and spirited. She needed an ally who would support her. There was only one person she could think of: Sara, the receptionist and general factotum. She was always friendly, helpful and willing to have a go at anything, and she had a way which never seemed to annoy the men.

Martha went across the square and looked at the Banyan tree with its low hanging branches and aerial roots, bending graciously to the ground as if courtesy-ing. Every time she saw the branches swaying in the wind she was tempted to hold on to one and to swing with it like a little girl. Pity, but that wouldn't do for an adult woman, and moreover, the wife of a senior teacher. She looked up to spy the little bird which sang its heart out high up in the crown. I wonder whether this is a doel, she wondered, the national bird of Bangladesh. She hadn't seen one yet since they had arrived.

She craned her neck but still couldn't see it; it was hidden by the maze of roots and branches

Aha, she just had another good idea: Bird watching! Another inoffensive choice! Ideas just tumbled into her head. She felt invigorated by her renewed zeal and the pleasant late afternoon sunshine on her face. Soon the incessant monsoon rains would begin, she had been forewarned.

Martha met two of the nurses from the clinic, Shazia and Sufi. 'You look cheerful.'

'Isn't it wonderful to have Vijay back?' Sufi exclaimed. 'We are just stretching our legs and filling our lungs with fresh air,' Sufi laughed happily.

'Ladies, I have a project: I am thinking of starting a choir. Would you join?'

'How wonderful,' Shazia beamed. 'Will it be for children as well?'

'I thought of children and staff. Whoever wants to participate, really.'

'Count us in. When is the first rehearsal?'

'Not quite sure yet, but I shall let you know.'

That went well, Martha thought; she hoped Sara would be equally enthusiastic. On her way to the office, Martha bumped into two of the girls she and Ali had given career advice.

'Good morning, Mrs Khan,' they shouted from afar. Their respectful, formal address always took Martha by surprise.

She had been used to her charges in New York calling her by her first name at best; more often than not, her first contact of the day with them had been a rebuke for calling her something nasty. They hadn't known any better, and their behaviour had been reinforced daily by their uncouth families or gang friends. Martha had coped well with such pressures but relished dealing now with respectful, grateful and polite youngsters.

'Good morning, girls,' she replied. 'How do you feel about joining a choir?'

They looked at each other and giggled. Sultana was the first to speak: 'You haven't heard us sing yet!'

'No, but I am grateful for any support.'

They giggled again looking at Salma. 'She sings like a man.'

'Well, that's not a bad thing. We need altos as much as sopranos.' They looked baffled, so Martha explained briefly that a choir needed high, middle and deep voices for harmonies.

'Where are we meeting?'

'I haven't thought about that yet; we shall probably start in my bungalow. I'll let everyone know soon.'

The girls went their way, discussing this hot new topic.

'Hi, Beautiful!' It was Ali.

'Just on my way to Shamsur. What are you doing?'

She took the plunge. Sooner or later he would have to know anyway:

'I am recruiting for our new choir.' There was no point of keeping it from him. Soon the entire Village would be abuzz with the news.

Ali whistled. 'Can I join?'

'I thought to start with a girls' choir,' she said, 'I am trying to keep out of trouble, so no boys to start with.'

Ali laughed. 'Any details yet?'

'Rehearsals will be twice a week after school in our bungalow.' He might as well be prepared. She raised her eyebrows looking for an objection in his face but he seemed delighted.

'Okay,' Ali banned all thoughts that he might have to curtail his wife's enthusiasm further down the line.

'What are you going to sing?'

'I am working on that. I have to do a lot more research but how about a mixture of classical, folk and modern music or popular film songs; something the kids like.'

The latter didn't sound a great idea but Ali kept his counsel.

'Have you told the Headmaster?'

'Do I need to?'

'Of course, it's his school!'

When he saw Martha's smile vanish and her face darken, as if the wind had been taken out of sails and clouds had covered the sky, he said quickly: 'Tell you what: I think it's a great idea and if it's alright with you, I shall submit it to Shamsur during the meeting.'

'I would give you a very passionate kiss right now, if I was allowed to,' she joked, nodding in the direction of the erect figure of the headmaster, crossing the square at a distance. It made Ali's heart sing when he saw the sparkle back in her beautiful grey eyes.

৪১৯৫৪

'Priti, it's Martha.'

'Oh hello!' Priti sounded anxious: 'You are not going to cancel, are you?'

In her zeal to set up the choir, Martha had totally forgotten about the family reunion.

'Now, now!' said Priti sternly with the tone of one of those fearsome elderly women in white saris who considered themselves the arbiters of morals and good behaviour - the only role left to them after being widowed.

'Of course not,' Martha reassured her, pressing to get to the point of her call.

'Good, I have already thirty-two acceptances. Everybody is

dying to meet you; well, not literally but they are madly curious who their new American cousin or auntie is.'

'Thirty-two? Are they all relatives?'

'Yes, and there are still a few outstanding. We are a big family.

We mustn't leave anybody out otherwise we shall never hear the end of it. The grapevine is working extremely well in our society!'

I shall never remember all their names, thought Martha.

Priti seemed to have read her thoughts: 'I shall stay at your side and introduce you to them, and I told them already that nobody is allowed to ask you for help with a Green Card to work in America.'

Martha laughed. Yes, there had been quite an influx of Bangladeshis to the United States in the past decade. Young, educated Bengalis did not have the patience to wait until their own country had progressed to anywhere near the standard of living of the Western World. They wanted a good life now and were prepared to study and work hard for it. Of course, there were now mobile phones, computers, coffee bars and pizza restaurants available for the better off but they were the superficial signs of improvement. Real career opportunities were few and far between a fact which took the young people mainly abroad.

'Don't worry, Priti. We are coming. It's in the diary…'

'Excellent! That's settled then…. Was there anything else, Martha?'

'Yes, I have taken your advice and have started a project.'

'Bravo, Bhabi.' Martha felt honoured to be called 'sister'; it felt like another small step towards acceptance.

'I am starting a choir with the girls, but I don't know much about Bengali music and I don't think American pop music would go down well. Any ideas?'

'Not many, but I can find out. In the meantime I shall send you some of my CDs; I am afraid most of them are schmaltzy love songs from popular movies.'

'I thought of starting with a mixture of classical, folk and modern. We have to tread a fine line: The children have to like it, and it has to be acceptable to the Headmaster.'

'I shall make enquiries. My granddaughters will be a good source of information.'

'You are a star, Priti! Thank you. I shall keep you in the loop.'

'In the what?'

'Informed, I mean.'

'Please do. Speak to you soon. Bye, Bhabi.'

The following lunchtime – Martha was just walking back from her class room to the bungalow – she heard a car drive up the long drive. She watched it approaching, circling round the Banyan tree once and stopping outside the reception. The man who climbed out was Ayub, Priti's driver. He had been dispatched early in the morning to deliver the promised CDs.

She walked over to him as he climbed out of the car.

'How kind of you to come all this way, Ayub!'

He smiled with pride and modesty, obviously pleased that he had discharged himself of the task well. In spite of the long journey and early start, he still looked professional in his white, starched shirt, neatly ironed fawn trousers and a smart navy blazer. However, his tidy uniform was in stark contrast to his face flustered with heat and thirst. He handed over the music discs.

'Would you like me to show you round?' Martha offered.

He shook his head: 'Memsahib need car afternoon to visit sister,' he said politely, lowering his eyes.

'Well, can I at least offer you something to eat or drink before you turn back?'

He nodded gratefully but stood there with bowed shoulders and eyes to the ground, until Martha waved him to follow her to the kitchen.

The smells of the food, the women were preparing for the children's lunch, were tempting but Ayub was aware of his duty and only accepted a cup of milky tea with cardamom pods and a couple of salty butter biscuits. In the meantime, Martha rushed to deposit the music CDs to the bungalow and to write a quick 'thank you' note to Priti..

Ayub was already sitting in his car, ready to drive all the way back to Gulshan, when Martha ran up to his wound-down window: 'Thank you so much, Ayub, it was very kind of you. The discs will be very helpful.' She handed him the envelope: 'Please, give this to your Memsahib.'

He looked slightly bewildered about this American lady praising him for no reason at all.

'And please, tell her that I am very grateful, and that you must all come out to our first concert.'

He replied with a shy smile as if embarrassed by her gushing politeness; after all, he had only done his duty. He finally said:

'I shall give message to Memsahib, and thank you for tea.'

With his words still hanging in the warm air, he drove off, back to the choked roads of Dhaka.

ৎৣৎ

Martha had no more lessons to give that afternoon and spent the time sifting through Priti's CDs. One name kept appearing more than any other: Hemanta Mukherjee. He seemed to sing everything from classical raghs to poetic Rabindra *sangeets* – poems of the famous national poet set to music – some folklore and popular film songs. One of the melodies soon kept going round in her head, and she began to hum it. It was tuneful and the rhythm recognisable to a Western ear.

When Ali returned at the end of afternoon lessons, he found his wife looking up Bengali music scores on her laptop whilst humming: *Oliro kotha shune bokul haashe.*

'That sounds lovely,' he said pleased to see her so cheerful.

She closed the lid of her laptop, gathered the music sheets she had already printed out and packed it all neatly away in one of the low plywood cupboards. She turned the key but left it in the lock.

'Just to be on the safe side, run it past the Head.' Ali didn't see Martha's defiant grimace as she walked into the kitchen.

ৎৣৎ

'Right, girls,' she began their first rehearsal on the following Wednesday afternoon. There were twenty girls of all ages; the younger ones were in their usual uniform of blue dresses and black trousers. The older girls looked gracious in their light blue kaftans, white trousers gathered tightly around their ankles, and white scarves draped across their shoulders. They stood silently in the narrow hall, looking at their teacher full of expectation.

'Come on in! You will tread on each other's toes out here.'

Slowly they filed into the large, airy sitting room and sat as told on the floor cushions, and three of them squashed themselves together on the old red settee. The rotating fan on the ceiling made constant whirring noises.

'Welcome!' Martha began. 'We are here to form a choir. Our first task is to choose some music. I have made my own enquiries, but as you are the ones who will have to sing, I wondered what songs you like and would like to learn.'

Martha was pleased: The three nurses had turned up and Sara, the receptionist, had managed to recruit twenty girls of mixed ages. Some began to giggle; others held their hands in front of their mouths in shocked amazement that they were asked for their opinion; usually they were simply told what to do. The rest had lowered their eyes, waiting.

Suddenly a hand went up.

'Yes, Rihan?'

'What sort of music are we allowed to sing, Miss?'

'Anything we please as long as it is melodious and has nice words.'

Again, a respectful silence filled the space which seemed to last far too long for Martha's taste.

'I thought of something classical, something poetic and something modern.'

'Like *Wahid* and *Salma*?' a thin voice piped up somewhere from the depth of the squashy settee.

More giggles and a couple of deep intakes of breath at the speaker's audacity.

'Are they your favourite pop stars?'

Many nodded.

'Alright, we shall include one of their songs. But you have to make the choice as I don't know them at all.'

Their eyes widened. Were they really allowed to have a say? Martha smiled reassuringly and presented her suggestion, the song she had hummed since she had listened to it for the first time: 'There is one song I really like. Have you heard of Hemanta Mukherjee?'

Martha noticed a few grins.

'I think he is dead,' said one of the girls.

'No he isn't! I have heard an interview with him on the radio.'

Martha could hear supressed giggles. The girls seemed to come out of their shells of polite reticence.

'Well, that's neither here nor there. The song I want you to sing, my choice, is Oliro Kotha Shune Bokul Haashe. It's a tender love song and has an easy tune; though, you'll have to tell me what it means, just to be on the safe side.'

More giggles.

Martha handed out the music sheets she had copied and then played the CD.

Soon everybody hummed along or beat the rhythm with their fingers, on their forearms, in their laps and the girls sitting low, tapped on the floor.

It seemed a good choice. They learnt it quickly, line by line, soon able to sing the entire song. It was a satisfying and liberating start.

'So next time,' Martha said at the end of the session, 'I want you to submit y o u r favourite song. Maybe discuss it amongst yourselves and have a vote on it?'

Martha was curious what they would come up with but trusted them to choose something quite acceptable to Dr Abdullah.

'Mrs Khan?' A hand went up just as Martha was about to dismiss them.

'Yes, Rihan?'

'You said firstly we need to choose a song. What was the second thing?'

'Oh,' Martha laughed, 'I am glad you reminded me. The second thing is, of course, our choir needs a name.'

They were already putting their heads together, chattering like a flock of birds, as they walked away from their choir master's bungalow.

ℬↃℭℛ

At the next rehearsal, they suggested a Beatles' song, 'Those Were The Days, My Friend' and the National Anthem; nothing spectacular, nothing rebellious. There would be plenty of opportunities later to perform something classical, when they had actually found and refined their voices.

My American pupils might probably have insisted on some dreadful rap glorifying crime and drugs, Martha thought. The flicker of nostalgia was quickly replaced by gratitude for these gentle and considerate children. They only needed a bit more encouragement to be self-confident. That was something she would be good at.

They were, the girls said at their second rehearsal, still debating various names for their choir and hadn't come to a unanimous decision yet. Democracy in motion! Martha was impressed.

Chapter Twenty-Six

Karin didn't find out what the two young women had discussed until the following weekend.

With one thing or another, mother and daughter simply couldn't find the time. Jasmine had come home late most evenings during the week and had often brought work home with her. Striving to become a barrister seemed to leave no room for family matters. Karin was glad she could help.

On the Friday Jasmine was as good as gold, surprising everyone by bringing home ready-made cannelloni and already washed mixed salads for dinner. Tilly had arrived, too.

'You ladies need stamina for your rehearsals,' Jasmine joked and opened a bottle of wine.

They agreed that this was a lovely start to the weekend and left straight after dinner when their offer of help to clear away was refused.

'You go off. I have all evening and after all, I have a great helper.' She smiled at her daughter and put her arm around the little shoulders.

Karin and Tilly had enormous fun again at the Gilbert & Sullivan society and made great strides in being fairies in the choir. They were praised that they fitted in well. They were certainly enthusiastic.

Afterwards, the women popped into the pub with the choir members, had a quick half pint of Guinness before Karin accompanied her friend through the balmy evening air to the station. Tilly had to return to Manchester as she was expecting someone on Saturday morning to repair her washing machine.

'What a nuisance,' she moaned, 'but I guess I have to be grateful that somebody is coming at all. Strange day though, Saturday! They had all week to arrange it, but I am convinced that had I said no, I would have gone back to the tail-end on the waiting list again.'

☙◌ଓ

When Karin arrived back home, Jasmine was sitting at the dining table, writing a letter.

'No Tilly?'

'No, she had to go home.'

Jasmine only nodded and carried on writing.

'I shall go to bed then and have an early night,' said Karin and was about to leave the room, when Jasmine stopped her: 'I am writing to Hamid.'

Karin was lost for words and just looked into Jasmine's green eyes. They didn't sparkle with anger; they didn't sparkle at all. Her forehead was wrinkling as if questioning the wisdom of what she was about to do. Karin imagined that her daughter would approach the task with calm confidence and logic, like solving a puzzle. She just hoped that Jasmine would find some heart to sprinkle amongst the words.

'I would like to read the letter to you before I send it off.'

'Okay, I'll stay.'

'There is some wine left,' Jasmine pointed in the direction of the coffee table. Karin went over, poured herself half a glass and settled in her favourite arm chair; occasionally, she took a sip while waiting for Jasmine to finish writing. There were some holiday brochures lying on the settee; Karin hadn't seen them before. They were all about cycling and hiking in various parts of Europe. Karin liked particularly the image of walking through the Provençal lavender fields and another route leading across Tuscan hills, promising scrumptious picnic lunches and local delicatessen for dinners.

'Are you planning a holiday?' Karin asked.

Jasmine didn't look up, still engrossed in her letter, mumbling: 'Not for the moment, but I want to do something special to celebrate when my pupillage is over, hopefully next year.'

173

I should be proud of her, really, thought Karin, conveniently forgetting any heartache her daughter had caused her.

Karin, still reading, heard the dull thud of the pen being put firmly onto the table top followed by the rustling of paper.

Jasmine got up, walked across, pushed another arm chair close and sat next to her mother.

'Do you want to read it yourself or shall I read it to you?'

'You read,' said Karin too lazy to go out into the hall to get her reading glasses she kept by the telephone. She took another sip from the excellent wine.

'Dear Hamid,' Jasmine began.

'This is not a solicitor's letter; I am writing to you privately.

'I realise, that I was selfish to plan not to involve you in our daughter's life, and that I hurt you by not even telling you that I was expecting your child. To be frank, I was as much taken aback by my pregnancy as you would have been, had you known.

'I am sorry and I shall try to make amends for the sake of our daughter.

'My First Six is coming to an end and I expect to be given the Provisional Practising Certificate from the Bar shortly; of course, it still depends on my supervisor's report. The Second Six will be even more challenging, I presume. Leisure time will be at a premium.

'As you know, my mother is looking after Esme during the week but if you would like to spend some time with your daughter, you would be welcome to do so. Sundays would be particularly suitable.'

Karin's heart sank. Her daughter, ever the pragmatist! I wonder whether Hamid will fall for this, she thought before listening to the end of the letter.

'Let me know what you think,

'Kind regards,

'Jasmine'

Jasmine looked expectantly at her mother.

'You obviously had a change of heart! Is that the result of your chat with Serena?' Karin enquired cautiously.

'Yes. She actually caught me at a bad moment, but now I am glad. She is very easy to talk to. She understands.'

'How did she put it?'

It never ceased to amaze Karin that parents could submit perfectly sensible ideas to their off-spring only to have them rejected; however, if their peers suggested the same thing, suddenly it was acceptable and wise.

Jasmine spoke again: 'She pointed out that it would be detrimental to Esme's development if she grew up without a father; we don't even have a grandfather for her. Serena is doing some research on this topic for her degree. She is shocked about her findings; the statistics for single parent children going off the rails are horrendous! Particularly children, who haven't got a father figure in their lives, miss out tremendously. Of course, sometimes, it can't be helped – but I can help it."

Karin nodded in agreement. It wasn't news to her.

'Secondly, Serena mentioned, as you did the other day, that it helps with practicalities if there is another grown-up around, especially one who takes an active interest. You know, it was quite touching: Serena likes to be married. They have their ups and downs but, she said, that doesn't detract from the fact that being a team and living together is better than each struggling on their own.'

Never mind loving each other, Karin thought.

There was no need to say anything further. Jasmine knew her mother's position: she whole-heartedly agreed with what Serena had said.

Jasmine fell silent, and Karin took the opportunity to say good-night. For a moment, she wanted to stroke her daughter's hair but Jasmine's posture radiated prickliness. So she simply reassured her: 'You are doing the right thing, Darling. Have a good night!'

As Karin walked up the stairs she thought gratefully: Well done, Serena! Thank you!

Chapter Twenty-Seven

C3※O

'This is my nephew, Kirash Abdullah. He is an accountant, and will take over the funds and grants for the building of the new wells.'

Such was the headmaster's introduction of the young man of about twenty-four, looking haughtily around the circle of assembled staff, as if to establish his superiority over them all. He was much shorter than his uncle, slim, dressed in a well-cut but slightly shabby black suit complimented by a silver and black-striped tie. Both looked like hand-me-downs. His black hair was neatly trimmed, meticulously parted on the right side of his head and glistened with Macassar oil in the sunshine; not one strand was out of place.

Martha looked amused. She stretched out her hand to the newcomer, as Ali had done to welcome him with a warm handshake. It was ignored.

Please yourself then, she thought and turned away.

'I shall show my nephew round the Children's Village,' Dr Abdullah announced importantly as if he were in charge of an honoured dignitary, and they disappeared towards the Mosque. It would take them a while; there was a lot to show: The bungalow-type classrooms, dormitories, kitchens; tailors', carpenters' and blacksmiths' workshops; and the paper production for charity cards to be sold in England; there would be the grounds comprising of sports' fields, paddy fields, vegetable plots and the lakes for fishing and last but not least, the various offices, Dr Chowdhury's clinic, the library, the pride and joy of Mr Abdullah stuffed full of old and newer copies of

Bengali and English literature, and finally the new treasurer's office.

'I wonder how well that will go,' mumbled Martha. 'He looks hardly out of university.'

'He probably just qualified and was looking for a job,' Ali agreed.

'Isn't it a bit unwise to hand over our funds to such an inexperienced young man?' Martha wasn't convinced.

'Let's hope Dr Abdullah knows what he is doing!' Ali was non-committal and willing to trust his boss's judgement.

'Does Mrs Belamy in England know about this?' Martha kept on; to her this appointment felt ominous.

'I doubt he needs to ask her for permission to employ a new treasurer.' Ali shrugged his shoulders as if to say: Nothing to do with us; let's keep out of it. 'We'll just have to wait and see and hope for the best.'

Martha wrinkled her nose as if smelling something unpleasant.

'Don't let anybody see you do that!' Ali laughed but she realised that it was a veiled warning not to let the side down.

'Will you have the choir in tonight?' he changed the subject.

'Yep, choir practice tonight,' Martha confirmed more cheerfully. 'You know, I was thinking of adding some boys to give the sound a bit of gravitas. At the moment we sound like a choir of angels or castratos.'

'What's wrong with that?' Ali feared that Martha was on another path to controversy.

'Well, men's voices give a choir a fuller sound and more scope for harmonies.' she said as if it was a silly question and the answer obvious.

Ali didn't reply but said instead: 'Okay, I shall get on with some paper work in the office.' He was quite happy to escape. He might even give him the chance to have a diplomatic word with Shamsur about the new appointment.

෴

During the following days, teams of engineers and labourers moved into the compound to begin building works on the new wells. There was the matter of finding the right locations which would guarantee enough water of good quality. Those new locations also had to be nowhere near the poisoned aquifer and the village's sewage system. The school staff could often hear raised voices, loud arguments and shouted orders.

And of course, there was the matter of the approaching Monsoon rains to consider. So far the air had been hot and humid but the threatening monsoon clouds had not yet made an appearance. Everybody would know when they did: Blustery winds would change direction and the heavens would open, releasing big, hard drops of rain in quantities resembling waterfalls, battering the landscape beneath, drenching everything and everybody that lived there. The rivers would swell, breaching their banks, fields would be submerged and houses flooded.

From August they could even expect destructive cyclones! Ali looked up at the still blue sky which gave no indicated of things to come. One learnt to be grateful for small mercies in this country and to live from day to day.

After a few days of testing and scouting for the most suitable place, the chief engineer seemed to have made up his mind where the new wells should be. The inhabitants of the Village could see a few of his colleagues shaking their heads but he seemed to have won the argument with his authority and the help of the orphanage's new recruit, Kirash. He seemed to be on friendly, almost familiar terms with the chief engineer.

'Do you think, they knew each other before?' asked Martha, suspicion written all over her face, her lips curled to a sarcastic grin..

Ali shrugged his shoulders. He did not want to encourage her to pursue another trail of dodgy goings on. However, he had to admit that the same thought had crossed his mind. He hated corruption and would hate even more having to look on, powerlessly, as it was going on under his nose. He had accepted this job with the purest of charitable intentions but refused to be drawn into a world of ducking and diving, having to grease palms to achieve his goal, a world of cover-ups and whitewashes.

On the other hand he realised that he was a guest in this country and doubted that it was his place to take a stand.

It seemed to be second nature to Martha: She would always

make a stand for the sake of the powerless, vulnerable and poor. She was a good person to have on your side because she would fight for you, fiercely, determinedly, without any regard for her own position and safety.

She really is quite something, Ali thought realising that his diplomacy might in truth be more of a wishy-washy, duplicitous, even cowardly way of sitting on the fence. It might prove good manners but was it leading to a result he could be proud of? Or did he just capitulate under the pretext that this was the way things were done in this country; that it was customary and had to be respected?

'I bet they were at college together…' he heard her mutter.

Martha looked at Ali whose fingers fidgeted with each other in indecision and unease, and he was grateful that she did not speak. It would have undoubtedly ended in an argument. When she realised that he wasn't going to say anything more, she turned round and stomped back to their bungalow.

A shadow of sorrow settled on Ali's heart. He hoped that he would be able to bridge the gap between Martha's wishful thinking and reality; he hated that she felt rejected and disillusioned, even disappointed in him, after having moved here, ready to give one hundred percent of her energy and dedication to the orphanage. He feared that by now she might feel like a runner shackled to the starting blocks. He couldn't imagine how he would react if the roles were reversed and he had to feel the full force of discrimination.

I must tackle the headmaster once more. It's only fair, he thought. It was something positive he could do.

With this in mind, newly inspired by his decision, Ali made his way past the Banyan tree, along the dormitory buildings and the workshops.

He could see neither the chief engineer nor any of his crew. Where had they got to? It was only just gone eleven in the morning, too early to stop for lunch. Ali walked around the back of the buildings and ended up at the mosque. Would the workers be praying now? He wouldn't have thought so. As he carefully pushed aside the spiky branches of a bush which had barred his path, he heard male voices and laughter, and not many steps later he discovered a group of men sitting on the ground playing cards, throwing coins onto a handkerchief lying in the middle of their circle. Ali stared furiously at them.

'What on earth is going on?'

They scrambled up quickly, brushing dust and sand from their trousers; one of them gathered up the coins from the handkerchief with a speed Ali hadn't thought possible. Within seconds all proof of what had been going on had disappeared.

'Where is your boss?' Ali asked, his eye brows almost knitting together with disapproval. He knew he wasn't tall but he felt he grew threateningly in stature as he spoke.

'Where is your boss?' he almost bellowed.

Some shook their heads. Someone murmured: 'Not know.' Most of them looked away sheepishly Ali had expected them to scuttle off but they didn't seem to know where to. He would have to go back and ask the headmaster whether he knew what was meant to happen; maybe he would even find the chief engineer with him.

At that moment, he heard approaching steps and someone clearing his throat.

A pompous young man in a fine suit and trilby hat, a cigarette hanging out of the corner of his mouth appeared and with him the new treasurer, Shamsur's nephew, Kirash.

'What are you doing here?' Kirash screeched with an effeminate high voice. 'This building site is dangerous!'

'Hardly,' said Ali sarcastically, pointing to a forgotten playing card on the ground. 'There was no one supervising the workers. There was no work going on. As you will know, we cannot afford for people to waste precious time.'

'I shall take over now,' Kirash waved Ali away with the dismissive hand gesture usually reserved for servants.

Ali refused to budge as his suspicions of this young man's integrity and credentials grew.

'So what is today's object?' Ali persisted to the visible annoyance of the chief engineer and Kirash who both had turned their backs to him.

'We are looking for a better location for the new wells. It is not easy!'

'I thought that's what you had been doing so far, obviously without success! Well, I can make it easy for you.' Ali was livid

180

by now, his whole body tense like a coiled spring: 'The Minister himself had plans drawn up weeks ago, where to locate the new wells, how deep to drill, all the details. If you look at the government plans you will find that the chosen location is not anywhere near the mosque!'

Obviously, the new wunderkind had not yet bothered to look at the paperwork.

'Well, nobody told us...' Kirash sounded prickly with embarrassment and frustration not to be able to get rid of Ali. The chief engineer kept quiet to save his own skin.

'I expect you in my office in ten minutes to inspect the Government's plans which we have to adhere to, as you well know. And I shall expect digging to begin this afternoon! You can tell that to your working party who have so far done nothing but play cards!'

They muttered something he couldn't understand but he didn't care. He would have to keep a constant eye on the daily progress to avoid that the funds, he and Martha had fought so hard for, would not be squandered. Now, he would inform the headmaster!

ॐ

'Shamsur, have you seen the construction plans for the wells? They were on my desk.'

'No, I haven't been to your office.'

'Do you think the working party borrowed them?'

'Surely, they would have asked?'

'Exactly my thoughts! I wanted to show them to the chief engineer because he doesn't seem to be aware of them.'

'But he has seen all the papers from the Ministry on the first day he arrived.' The headmaster began to sound worried.

'Has he now!' Ali wasn't surprised.

Dr Abdullah raised his eyebrows.

'To be honest, Shamsur, they just told me that they didn't know about any plans.'

'Who are "they"?'

'The chief engineer and Kirash.'

'What's Kirash got to do with it?' The headmaster was baffled.

181

'He obviously thinks that overseeing the accounts means also to oversee the entire project. I just met them together, while the members of their working party were playing cards.'

'Oh dear, oh dear!' wailed the headmaster. 'I am getting too old for all of this. I am sure there is a simple explanation. Kirash is a good boy and was a superb student; he had the best graduation results of his year in the whole of the country.'

Ali felt sorry for the older man who had gone almost purple in his face with the strain.

'You are right, Shamsur, there might be a totally innocent explanation,' he relented, 'maybe they work so closely together to find clever ways of stretching the money.'

'Yes, that's probably it.' The headmaster clutched eagerly at the straw extended. 'Will you keep an eye on them, Ali? It's all too upsetting, especially after poor Vijay nearly died.'

'Of course, I will, Shamsur.' Ali tried to sound reassuring. 'And as we said, it is probably nothing. I shall keep you informed.'

'Thank you.'

Before leaving the room, Ali turned round and saw the Headmaster sitting at his desk, scribbling something in his diary, looking haunted and hunching his shoulders in dejection.

§℧℞

Ali went back to the bungalow and told Martha about what he thought he had discovered.

'I wouldn't be surprised if…' she began to speculate.

'Don't,' Ali stopped her. 'Let's hope not – for Shamsur's sake and the sake of the Children's Village!'

§℧℞

Ali kept his promise and used the ten minute slots between lessons plus lunch and afternoon free time to supervise the digging of the wells.

He often heard sniggers or sarcastic comments about him turning up again, but he couldn't have cared less. If these people couldn't be trusted to work reliably without someone breathing down their necks, he would be the one to keep at them. Nobody in the village knew how hard he and Martha had fought for every penny, what they had to endure to whittle it out of the Minister. They had never told anyone about the Minister's insolent proposition and arrogant condescension. Furthermore, there was always the chance that the new man in charge at the Ministry – and it was bound to be another man rather than a woman – might withdraw the grant and any future financial support which would leave them with poisoned drinking water and only half-built new wells.

He hadn't told anybody that there was a little light on the far-away horizon.

Ali had begged his mother in England to contact Mrs Bellamy, the founder of the charity, to ask how much they could afford to contribute. Their skeleton staff had sprung into action immediately, sending out leaflets to their members and regular donors. People had turned out to be kind and generous as usual; the considerable sum they had collected would help tiding the project over to the next stage but it would not be enough to finish it.

However, he was not about to disclose to Kirash that more funds would be coming their way.

It was the Thursday afternoon of week two. On the following day, the Friday, the men were expected to go to their mosques to pray; work would come to a halt for the day.

'Good afternoon, Sir,' he called out to the chief engineer, who only gave him a furtive glance, muttering something under his breath. He sat on a folding camping chair, obviously his campaign headquarters, and stared sullenly at the plans which had mysteriously reappeared.

'Is everything going well?' Ali asked in a conciliatory tone.

The chief engineer only grunted and continued to ignore Ali.

'I wondered whether you could explain to me what the stages of building the wells are. I don't know much about it; certainly not as much as you do.' It was surely worth trying to get the man on his side.

The chief engineer looked suspiciously at Ali, fearing a trap or criticism. Ali smiled to reassure him and eventually, the man got up from his unsteady chair, made an attempt at smoothing down his crumpled and sweat-drenched shirt, put on his beige jacket and fastened his tie. He did not want to be caught at a disadvantage, looking dishevelled while talking to his masters.

'I am Ali Khan, Dr Abdullah's deputy.' Ali introduced himself, clarifying his position to counteract whatever Kirash might have said about him. He stretched out a hand and wished he hadn't when it was clutched by the strong fingers of a hardworking man. A man drowning couldn't have gripped any harder.

'What's your name?'

'Mamun Hossain.'

He was a short and slight man, not unlike Kirash, but looking almost undernourished; he had darting, furtive eyes like black currants and, in spite of his relative youth, wrinkles all over his face as if life had treated him badly.

'When did you qualify?' Ali asked, not meaning to check his credentials but rather to kick-start their conversation. The suspicious look crept back into Mr Hossain's face.

'I qualified two years ago from Dhaka University!' he said sulkily.

'Did Kirash study at the same time?'

'He graduated a year ago but couldn't find a job so far.'

That explains a lot, thought Ali. Obviously, the headmaster had been fibbing.

'You must be very proud of your achievement,' Ali said meaning to put him at ease. He didn't get an answer, only a silent, haughty pursing of the lips and a provocative look directly into his eyes.

'Now, can you please explain to me the various stages of constructing a well? I am really interested.'

It was obviously not Mr Hussain's favourite occupation to explain what he was doing but he realised that he couldn't possibly decline this request. Reluctantly, he picked up the plans from his wobbly chair and waved Ali to come closer.

'As you know, we have to drill quite deep down to avoid the poisoned aquifer. We found one considerably deeper and flowing from a different direction; once we have drilled down we shall take samples and have them analysed.

'But,' interrupted Ali, 'I thought that that was done weeks ago by the people the Ministry sent.'

'That's right, but before we let you all drink from the water, we have to be absolutely sure that it is safe.'

'And if it turns out not to be?'

The chief engineer shrugged his shoulders unhappily as if he were the one who would be blamed in the event.

'So what has been done so far?' Ali took up the thread of their conversation again.

'So far, the men have dug with their spades and shovels which is very tedious and time-consuming, but next week we hope for the drilling machine to arrive. It will be a first class one, a rotary drill which can go down to three thousand feet.' Mr Hussain seemed to lose his inhibition and became unexpectedly animated, almost excited about the wonders of modern technology.

'We hope to drill down up to nine hundred metres' he explained further with passion and sparkling eyes. 'What we are looking for quality and volume of water.' The chief engineer, pleased with the attention, Ali paid him, chatted away.

'Thank goodness, finally he has relaxed, Ali thought supressing a smile.

'And once the holes are dug, what happens then?' Ali moved on quickly before his mirth could be misconstrued.

'The holes will have to be sleeved. We have applied for steel but might have only enough money for PVC. The pipes will have to be around six metres long and up to twelve inches in diameter...' The chief engineer was now in full flow.

'Yes and then?' Ali interrupted. He didn't want him to get bogged down by details however fascinating to the expert.

The chief engineer snapped his mouth shut, realising that Ali did not share his enthusiasm for the finer points

'Then it is a matter of choosing the appropriate pumps,' he continued talking in short, precise sentences, obviously piqued, 'and filters, and of course, the wells need to be capped against animals falling in and misuse,' he concluded his summary having decided that his listener wasn't worthy of more elaborate explanations. The last word, misuse, was spoken with distaste, a disclaimer for any problems after he had finished with the project.

'So how long do you think it will all take?'

The chief engineer had a way to shrug his shoulders whenever he didn't want to answer a question.

'Inshallah, about four weeks!' he said finally with a deference which he hoped would absolve him from all responsibility.

185

It seemed an enormous length of time to Ali, but maybe Mamun was right.

'Thank you,' Ali smiled apologetically like a particularly dim pupil. 'That was very informative, Mr Hossain. I better get back to my classroom now. I shall have to give a lesson in a quarter of an hour.'

The chief engineer remained stony-faced. He watched Ali walking away, and shrugged his shoulders in the conviction that the last half an hour had clearly been a waste of time.

Chapter Twenty-Eight

Hamid's reaction to her letter was not what Jasmine had expected. She had thought he might jump at the chance to have regular input in his daughter's life. As it was, she didn't hear from him for a month.

Good for him, Karin thought with glee. She doesn't need another person around her to dance to her tunes. It will concentrate her mind if somebody plays hard to get.

It didn't help that little Esme who, with the intuition of a child, had sensed that Hamid had to play a more important role in their lives than others and kept asking her mother when 'Uncle Hamid' would visit again. Jasmine almost choked on the term 'Uncle Hamid' but of course, she had only herself to blame as she had introduced any man, who had come into contact with them, as 'Uncle'. She realised now that, at some stage, she would have to tell Esme that Hamid was actually her Daddy.

What a strange thought! While waiting for Hamid's answer, Jasmine had plenty of time to sooth the turmoil in her heart and mind, and to get used to the realisation that she would not go through life entirely on her own, even after all her valiant efforts at evasion. She wasn't entirely sure whether she felt relieved or horrified. Well, she could still preserve her privacy and keep an emotional distance. It was about Esme, not herself.

Hamid's silence and absence annoyed her; it had ruined her plans to involve him as soon as possible in the care of Esme. She would have transferred responsibilities to him immediately in order to fill the gaps her mother had created by her bid for more independence! Why did she have to take up with a new friend and join the Gilbert & Sullivan Society just when she, her daughter, had to work extra hours to achieve her professional goal and needed her support more than ever?

'How is Jasmine?' asked Tilly innocently when Karin picked her up from Poynton Station.

It was pouring with rain, and Karin held a big, black umbrella over the two of them. The summer seemed to tease everyone, pretending to be autumn. Karin shivered and pulled her trench coat tighter around herself.

''Moody,' was all, Karin could bring herself to say without spoiling the day.

It had become a tradition that Tilly would arrive on Friday at lunchtime; this would leave them a couple of hours to chat without disturbance before Esme needed picking up from the local nursery. The little girl had started going there two afternoons a week, Thursdays and Fridays, which freed up some of Karin's time. Then they would cook together in time to have dinner as soon as Jasmine would be home; usually a little earlier on a Friday.

This week was different: Tilly had to arrive a day earlier and stay until Monday morning because the rehearsals for Iolanthe had entered a serious stage. The dress rehearsals would be on Thursday afternoon and Friday morning. There had been mutterings amongst the cast that this was rather inconvenient for those who had to work for a living, but the artistic director had fixed the dates and rented the Hall before turning to the hard task of reassuring his actors and singers that they were ready to perform. Tickets had been printed, and demand for them had surged as soon as the posters had been hung up in public places, announcing and promising a rip-roaring, fun-filled treat. To everybody's surprise, tickets for the two evening and one matinee performances were sold out within days.

So, on Thursday afternoon, the two ladies left with accelerated heart beats for the dress rehearsal. The other 'fairies' were also more a-flutter than usual. One was desperately searching for her sparkling wand until the costume designer relented and gave her a spare one.

The scenery had not been quite finished and the artists were working furiously to complete their job, but also trying to keep out of the way of the people rehearsing. More than once there was panic as they just managed to move a pot of paint or a scenery panel out of the path of a fairy scurrying towards the back of the stage.

'It would have enhanced her complexion. She looks awfully pale,' commented Tilly when Penny, the Queen of the Fairies had almost collided with a panel still glistening from being painted in bright red.'

There was no titter, not even from Karin; everybody was very serious.

Oh dear, thought Tilly. What a pity, no time for banter anymore; and there were so many things she found hilarious. Funny how people change when they were under pressure...

Quite a number of their peers complained about their outfits. Someone seemed to have ordered the wrong sizes. Fairies and soloists kept pulling at tight, scratchy sleeves, tight skirts or had to hold on to their far too wide trouser waist-bands.

Coordination seemed to be suddenly elusive: several times the accompanying pianist, usually a marvel of precision and a master of improvisation, shot ahead of the choir in tempo, and once he played on regardless although everybody had fallen silent. The conductor tried with a desperate wave of the hand to catch his eye, until he finally felt compelled to hit the music stand several times with his baton to stop him.

'Will you listen to the choir or at least look at me, Geoffrey!' he shouted in exasperation. 'You were all better three weeks ago than you are today!'

Only the Lord Chancellor seemed to remain calm and confident, and lost in a little world of his own preparations.

They all looked at each other and decided that they would pull themselves together, nerves or no nerves and give it their best shot.

The predicted three hours turned into four until someone had the courage to yawn, and, when reprimanded, to say that she was getting tired and needed a break. The cast were grateful to this brave soul, and Karin and Tilly breathed a sigh of relief, too. Reluctantly the choir master let them go, reminding them to be punctual on the following morning.

When they arrived back home, they found that Jasmine had picked up Esme and prepared a light dinner of coronation chicken on a bed of mixed salad accompanied by toast.

Karin and Tilly exchanged glances saying: What turned her into a domestic Godess? Answered by: No idea!

In spite of their lavish praise, Jasmine frowned constantly, looking unhappy.

'Anything the matter?' Karin asked, hardly daring to look at her.

Jasmine shook her head.

'Heard anything?'

'No,' was the brusque answer. She obviously did not want to discuss her problems in front of Tilly.

'Let us tell you a little about the shambolic rehearsals. That will cheer you up!'

'Story?' asked Esme excitedly.

'Well, we don't want to tell you too much as you are going to see it on Sunday afternoon, but I think we can tell you a little bit. Tilly, will you do the honours; you are more into the whole thing.'

Tilly sat up in her chair, pulling her cardigan straight and began with a mock-serious dramatic voice: 'Story time! There was a fairy called Iolanthe, who many years ago, had made the mistake to marry a human and to have a little boy called Strephon. The fairy was banned from fairyland and lived for twenty-five years in a frog pond. However, the other fairies missed her and badgered their Queen to allow Iolanthe to come back. She did. Iolanthe brought her boy with her. Now, the fairies are said never to grow old.'

'And now it gets a bit complicated,' Tilly said with importance, 'Stephron was in love with Phyllis, the ward-of-court of the Lord Chancellor who himself would have liked to marry Phyllis. When Strephon asked for her hand, the Lord Chancellor refused; after all, a shepherd was not good enough in his opinion. Instead he suggested two noblemen from the House of Lords. Those two spied on Strephon and saw him embracing his mother who like all fairies looked really young. They told Phyllis that her

190

boyfriend was cheating on her with another woman. Phyllis was so cross that she decided to marry one of the noblemen, but wasn't interested in which one. Then the noblemen offended the fairies by thinking they were a class of school girls. The Queen of the Fairies was furious and gave Strephon special powers: He turned into a nobleman himself in the House of Lords and could introduce any law he wishes. The fairies went along to cheer him on, but soon he missed Phillis and wanted her back. So his mother, Iolanthe spoke to the Lord Chancellor, who turned out to be her husband, Strephon's dad.'

'What happened to the two men who wanted to marry her?' interrupted Jasmine, curiously spellbound.

'Well, they decided that they were such good friends that they preferred their friendship to Phyllis. Now, by speaking to the Lord Chancellor, Iolanthe had broken the fairy code again and had to be punished, but then it turned out that all the other fairies had fallen in love with the peers in the Parliament, and even the Fairy Queen quite liked Private Willis, the guard of the gates of the Houses of Parliament. So they simply changed the law. And when you have seen the performance, you can tell me how they changed it.'

Esme smiled a little bewildered.

'I shall check on Sunday evening,' Tilly smiled back and turned to Jasmine: 'This was as much for your benefit as for that of this young lady here.' She added, gently tweaking Esme's cheek.

'At the rehearsals,' continued Karin,' one had lost her fairy wand and another trod on her frock and ripped it from her waist. The men looked quite aghast!'

Everybody tittered.

'Right, young lady,' Jasmine broke up their gathering, turning to her daughter. 'Bath and bed!'

'And a story,' the little girl reminded her.

'Yes, and another story,' Jasmine sighed.

'Will you come down again?' asked Karin.

'No, I think I shall have an early night, too. And by the way,' she sounded as exasperated as the choir master, 'I shall work from home tomorrow so you don't have to worry about Esme.'

Karin and Tilly looked at each other:

'That's very thoughtful of you,' Karin said eventually, and Tilly added: 'We had planned to take it in turns to look after her during rehearsals,' added Tilly, 'and then take her to the nursery.'

'No need. Good night.'

'You and Esme will come to the performance on Sunday, won't you? We have bought tickets for you.'

Esme looked with big, pleading eyes at her mother.

'Of course, we shall be there.' It sounded more like a duty than pleasure but at least it was a 'yes'.

'Lovely! Good night then, you two, and sweet dreams!'

'O-oh ddd-dear!' was all that Tilly could bring herself to stutter, while Karin only shook her head, picked up the crockery and carried it to the kitchen.

Of course, the Friday and Saturday evening's performances were a great success. Nerves had turned into excitement and jollity. The fairy's costume had been mended, the men's uniforms adjusted. The scenery was finished, installed and looked splendid. Even the lost fairy wand had been retrieved having been found on the high window sill in the ladies' loo. The pianist had calmed down and played as magnificently as everyone knew he could, and the audience laughed, cheered and applauded wildly. Occasionally, the cast could even hear someone in the audience hum along to a familiar tune.

When Esme and Jasmine joined them in the hall on the Sunday, the play was well established, the actors, experienced and in full flow, and seeing the end of the feat in sight, were almost recklessly joyous in their performance. When the curtains had come down for the last time after a standing ovation from a delighted audience, the members of the cast hugged each other as if they had been rescued from a great disaster.

Jasmine and Esme came to the dressing rooms to pick up Karin and Tilly.

'Congratulations; you were great!' said Jasmine and Esme added: 'Grandma and Tilly.'

'Now did you pay attention, Esme and Mummy?' asked Tilly. 'Which law did they change?'

'All the fairies had to marry a human,' Jasmine mouthed slowly, word by word which Esme repeated. The little girl almost fell over with delight, hopping and clapping her little hands, because she knew it was the right answer.

'You clever girl!' Tilly picked her up and swung her round.

When the cast had changed back into their ordinary clothes everybody piled into the Boar's Head again for celebratory drinks. Even little Esme was allowed to come along for a while and have a fruit juice, until her mother took her home.

'I need to get ready for work tomorrow,' Jasmine announced predictably.

'You go ahead.' Karin and Tilly were not prepared to have their euphoria dampened.

When they got back to the house a couple of hours later, Tilly went straight up to her room. Karin went into the kitchen for a glass of water and found an opened letter on the breakfast table, a little yellow notelet stuck to the envelope in Jasmine's handwriting. It said: 'So much for his desire to do his bit for our daughter!'

Karin folded the sheet and left it there. She would read it in the morning

Chapter Twenty-Nine

❦

Ali tried to keep to a non-invasive but thorough inspection routine: He greeted the working party in the mornings when it arrived, made sure they had tea and biscuits around ten o'clock, provided by the ladies in the kitchens. Around twelve thirty, the labourers went to the dining hall for lunch while the Chief engineer, accompanied by Ali, inspected the morning's work. Unfortunately, it wasn't really the right time of year to undertake such work. Daily monsoon rains raged and drenched everything and everybody to the bone.

Ali had agreed to a siesta-type break after lunch when the workers could take a shower and rest in the shadows of the trees. Sometimes he saw them listening to a small transistor radio for the latest cricket results or the music hit parade or reading a newspaper the school library provided; one or two of them just had a smoke and a rest. Several workers had taken up permanent occupation of the ground around the Banyan tree like old travelling traders had done in other parts of Asia centuries ago.

However, for a lot of the time, blustery monsoon winds drove water-laden black clouds across the sky, on their daily journey from the Bay of Bengal to the Himalayas. They were the harbingers of more downpours sending the men scuttling to hastily cover up the newly drilled bore holes with plastic sheeting before retreating themselves to the dining hall. Minutes later, the clouds would shed their copious amounts of rain onto the already sodden land below.

In a way, most people in Bangladesh welcomed the monsoon

season as a blessing: It relieved the unbearable heat of the summer months; it helped with keeping the paddy fields submerged; but it also brought untold misery to the villages near rivers which invariably flooded, destroying houses ruining crops other than rice. The monsoon rains caused another, much more long-term problem, the erosion of the river banks, which not only threatened the villagers' homesteads but also the land they cultivated to be self-sufficient.

The Children's Village, however, was well prepared for these enormous amounts of water pelting down. Dr Adullah had insisted from the outset that lakes should be dug to collect rain water and a drainage system should be established which would cope with the needs of the inhabitants, however many in numbers.

Now, the drilling sites needed protection, and work on the new wells came to a standstill when the heavens opened.

Mamun Hossain's attitude had subtly changed. He didn't seem to mind Ali's company and even took to informing him when they were ready to recommenced work, and when they decided to call it a day. Work progressed reasonably well under the circumstances, particularly after the much admired drilling machine had arrived and put into place; large holes appeared quickly at the far corner of the vegetable patches near the fishing ponds; PVC pipes were strewn around nearby to be installed later. The vegetable plots were a sorry sight, showing heavy boot prints between plants. The builders had tried to tread carefully but hadn't always succeeded, sliding around in the mud. It just couldn't be helped. For a few more weeks, the dinner ladies would have to go to the local market and buy huge quantities of provisions there. The local farmers were delighted with the unexpected increase in sales and loaded up their primitive stall tables with whatever they could offer. The orphanage's gardeners could start their own production again once the wells were finished and the workmen had left. The older children had already mentioned that it would be a blessing having the new water supplies so close to the vegetable plots which would save them carrying heavy watering cans long distances as before.

Ali insisted that the engineers put up barriers and signs in case some of the children strayed, overcome by curiosity to view the building site. After the turmoil with Vijay's illness, a child falling into a freshly dug well, would be unbearable.

Ali kept the Headmaster informed, and the new treasurer seemed to keep a low profile, until he crossed Ali's path again and berated him for interfering in his domain. Ali pointed out that his uncle had instructed him with supervising the on-going work but Kirash stormed off threatening to demand clarification from his uncle and the re-instatement of his position as the man in overall charge.

Do what you like, was Ali's first reaction but then remembered the crest-fallen expression in the headmaster's face when Ali had hinted at mismanagement. He didn't want to upset the old chap again: 'Why are you so upset, Kirash?' he tried to pacify him. 'You are Head of Finances, that's plenty of responsibility.'

Ali suspected that what Kirash really resented was Ali's newly close and friendly relationship with the chief engineer. He was sure that there was something those two shared and didn't want him to know.

'He is up to something,' was Martha's opinion when Ali told her. She was in a hurry to prepare the next choir practice. The girls would come to the bungalow in an hour.

Sara was the first to arrive. She had taken to coming early in case Martha needed some help with the music sheets, either printing or collating them. It also gave them a chance for a chat.

'What do you make of the new treasurer?' Sara asked not looking up from the pile of music sheets she was straightening up.

'Why do you ask?' Martha did not believe in gossip but knew that neither did Sara. She must be worrying about something.

'Well, Dr Abdullah seems to be impressed by him.'

'I know.' Sara nibbled at her lower lip and looked away.

Martha tried to catch her eye:

'Is anything the matter, Sara?'

'I don't know. I don't want to bad-mouth him but he is slippery; he doesn't look properly at you; and if he does he sneers. He certainly doesn't think much of women – me, in particular!'

'He probably thinks he is God's Gift to the financial world, and we are all dunces. It doesn't make him a bad man; only an unpleasant one.'

Sara sunk into thoughts of her own.

'Just keep your eyes and ears open and let me know,' Martha whispered before welcoming the first of the choir girls.

∞∞

They were belting out Those were the Days, my Friend when Ali arrived back at the Bungalow.

He had had an interesting chat with Dr Abdullah who seemed to worry that he might have made a mistake employing his nephew but couldn't quite get himself to say so. After all, to preserve family honour was one of the priorities in Bangladeshi life. Ali wondered why that should be so. Had he stumbled on a family secret?

Ali had also discussed with him whether there wasn't a possibility to transfer more responsibility to Martha, or at least let her have a full timetable, but, after lots of mumbling and clearing of the throat, it sounded as if the Headmaster's hands were bound by financial constraints.

'I am sure she won't mind taking lower pay for the good of the children,' Ali said but Dr Abdullah wouldn't hear of it. The rest of the conversation consisted of ramblings about the trials of old age – as far as Ali knew, Shamsur was in his mid-fifties, so in Western terms, no age at all. The arrival of his nephew seemed to have aged him rather than made his life easier.

'What are your plans for the future?'

Ali did not know how to take this. Was this an overture to dismissing them both?

'Well, we haven't thought about it. As far as I am concerned, we shall stay here and work with you.'

'We haven't put you off yet?' Shamsur chuckled through gritted teeth.

'No, Shamsur, not at all. Martha feels a little underused and undervalued, which I am sure you can understand, but with time it will change. She is a highly qualified, intelligent and efficient woman and isn't used to playing second fiddle.'

197

'Wouldn't this be an ideal time to start a family?' Dr Abdullah almost bit his tongue for being so outspoken.

'We were only married last year. I think she first wanted to do something worthwhile for the children of the village, establish herself here and achieve some goals before having babies of her own.'

The headmaster nodded in recognition of the logic but looked as if he thought it a pity that Martha should miss this opportunity of time on her hands.

'You haven't been on a holiday since you arrived, have you?'

'We have been to Dhaka for a family reunion and of course, with Vijay.'

'Well, the hospital and your negotiations with the Minister were hardly a holiday,' Dr Abdullah reminded him.

'You are right,' Ali agreed.

'Why don't you take Martha on a long weekend to Sunderban? We can cover you two for a couple of days. It will do you good, and you need a bit of privacy now and again.'

Ali smiled because privacy was not a concept Bangladeshis understood easily: 'That's very generous of you, Shamsur. I shall submit your proposal to Martha. I think it's a great idea. I haven't been to Sunderban either, at least not to the deep heart of it. We shall make enquiries and let you know the outcome.'

'Good!' The headmaster seemed relieved that at last he had found something positive to help that delightful young couple he had employed. He felt for them because he knew how hard adjustment could be. He only had to think back to his days as a University student in London. There had been many things he hadn't understood, some he had learnt to love and others he had never got used to. It had been an adventure but he had been glad to return home to his familiar surroundings and the moral safety of his society.

'Good!' he said again and closed his diary with a thump, a sign that Ali's audience was at an end.

৶৩৻৶

'Shamsur wants me to show you Sunderban,' Ali said when the rehearsal was over and they were alone.

'Why is that? It sounds to me as if he wants to get rid of us. Or maybe just me?!'

'Oh Martha! Don't be suspicious all the time. I think he feels a bit sorry for us and wants us to have some time together, away from the Children's Village and all its problems.'

'Okay, when?'

'One of the next weekends, and he will cover our lessons if we tag on a day or two.'

'Are you sure he doesn't want us out of the way for some reason?'

'Oh please! Stop being paranoid! Let's just enjoy it. Get on the internet and find out about excursions. It will be a nice break and a bit of fun.'

'Alright, I'll shut up. Come to think of it, it's quite exciting travelling around Bangladesh!'

'That's the spirit!' Ali sighed with relief.

ఠఇఞ

They chose Eid-ul-Adha, the 'Feast of the Sacrifice', remembering Abraham's willingness to sacrifice his first born and only son to God. It was a little way off but it would also fall towards the end of the monsoon and cyclone season.

Ali and Martha usually loved festivities, their preparations, decorations, rehearsals and finally the performances, the excitement of the children and the specially cooked Eid food. There was always an atmosphere of expectation beforehand and pure joy and fun on the day with the after-glow of happiness and pride of everyone's achievements still lingering for weeks.

They would miss it this time but they were getting excited about their own plans which they had quickly finalised: They would spend one night with Priti in Dhaka, take a flight south to Jessore and then join a group of tourists and approved guides.

They had no idea what Sunderban would be like. To be on the safe side, they had hired experts. These people would also provide them with permits to visit this World Heritage Site.

Martha laughed uproariously when she read the description of the river boat which would take them into the mangrove forests: It boasted capacity for thirty-two passengers, various cabins with two to four beds, two English commodes and two French toilets, whatever that meant.

'If necessary, we can hang our bottoms over-board,'

'And be bitten by a crocodile?' Ali was not so keen.

Martha giggled but they hoped it wouldn't come to that; certainly not if there were thirty-two other passengers.

'I wonder what the 'moving place' is going to be like,' Ali wondered.

'Oh, it's probably the deck,' suggested Martha, 'where we shall be sitting in deck chairs or lie in hammocks with a gin and tonic, looking out onto the mangroves and the wild animals.'

'Don't be too hopeful,' Ali warned, 'there is a review which complains that they didn't see any animals and I doubt there will be gin and tonic – it's still a Muslim country.'

'You spoil-sport! Let's wait and see. We are always lucky! They need our custom!' she countered with spirit and a twinkle in her eyes.

ℰᏅℛ

They set off on the evening two days before Eid-ul-Adha. The roads into Dhaka were busy as always but not as bad as they would have been during the national holidays.

Priti was delighted to see them again: 'I am so pleased to have you all to myself this time. Everybody is at school or at work. The reunion party was nice but I didn't get to talk to you at all. Everybody hogged you to themselves,' she chattered happily, grabbing Martha's arm and dragging her into the garden.

'We shall have dinner outside today,' she announced.

'I know you like that sort of thing. The monsoons are letting up; this is such a lovely time of the year when everything is green and lush, it's not quite so hot, and there is not so much rain, and all the flowers are out.' Priti stretched her arms towards the sky in delight.

They walked into a green paradise which was interspersed with pink, red, yellow and white blooms. The scent seemed to get stronger as they got closer. Priti's gardener proceeded with the evening's watering; from time to time, he filled up two watering cans from a tap on the side of the house.

'Have you ever heard of Reena's grandson again?'

'Dipu? Goodness! How do you come to know about him?'

'Karin told me, a long time ago and I don't know why, I suddenly thought of him. What is he was doing now.'

'Karin probably told you about his foul language and screaming and shouting last time she was here? Well, he hasn't changed: He still lives with his grandmother; he is still a hothead. He has the right name: Dipu, the Flame! Only now he is involved with Jamaat.'

'Who are they?'

'I'll tell you later,' Priti whispered, pointing to Ali who had already sat down at the table where they would have dinner.

He put down the newspaper he had been reading: 'Isn't it glorious,' he said. He had no intention to intrude into the girls' conversation. He was just so pleased that Martha felt comfortable enough to chat away.

Sitting there, in the cooling air, bright sunlight, dappled by the trees, they raked over family gossip and tried to untangle the memories of the family reunion, who was who and whether Priti had heard from them since. Most of them had at least rung if not written or popped in again, and given their mainly favourite oponopn of their new relatives.

'Only my mother-in-law thought you were a bit outspoken,' Priti looked at Martha and thought it was a hoot: 'Don't worry, she was the one in the burkha. My girls are always outraged when she turns up in it. What century do we live in, they say, but of course, our family is lucky because we are more modern than the majority of the population and that is due to our enlightened husbands.'

She said that last sentence, just as her husband Ansar stepped out into the garden where they were sitting sipping lassi, a refreshing yoghurt drink.

'I am gratified that you think so,' Ansar smiled, walked over to her place, put his hand on her shoulder and planted a kiss on her hair. Priti beamed like a child delighted with an unexpected present.

'I'll quickly go to the kitchen and tell cook that you have arrived. Dinner in half an hour?'

'Yes, I shall have a quick shower and I'll be ready.'

They spent a very pleasant evening, chatting, laughing, talking about history and politics, the family and the most recent fashions.

Priti never forgot to ask about Karin and her life in Manchester. She couldn't quite understand what Jasmine's problem was and thought that the girl should be pleased that somebody, especially the little girl's father, wanted to marry her.

'He sounds a nice chap,' she said.

'…and quite enlightened, as you would put it,' Ansar finished her sentence.

'It might be remnants of the trauma she suffered when they left Bangladesh and her father?' Martha suggested.

'That was years ago! Selfish genes more like it!' Priti said with conviction. 'She is her father's daughter after all.'

'Now, now, prio tomo, don't be catty,' Ansar cut off the topic. 'What about your trip? What are your plans?' He looked at Ali and Martha.

We shall fly to Jessore tomorrow. From there a mini-bus will pick us up…'

'We hope,' Ali held his fingers crossed.

'That will take us to the cruise boat and the rest is up to the guides, I reckon.'

'That sounds quite safe,' said Ansar. 'They will get the permits for you and pay the taxes. We are often asked by the embassies to accompany foreign visitors. They are well organised down there, but if at any stage you are not happy, give me a ring, and I shall send one of my boys down. It could well be that they take you to places where you won't see a lot of animals. You might have to travel further down to the Gulf of Bengal to see the wildlife enclosures.'

'We didn't know about that.' Ali and Martha looked at each other. Martha admitted that they might not have enough time to go further.

'I think we shall be taken as far as Katka.'

'That's beautiful, stunning!' Priti chipped in. 'So romantic!'

'Thank you for the offer, Ansar,' said Ali. 'It's reassuring to know that we can count on your help should things go wrong.'

Martha hit him gently on the arm: 'See who is pessimistic now!' she laughed.

Ansar wrote down his work telephone number and something else in Bengali scripture and handed the note to Ali.

'That should impress whoever you show it to,' he laughed.

ॐ

The following morning, Ayub, their driver, took the young couple to the airport.

'Oh look,' exclaimed Martha, 'there is the Radisson Hotel Karin stayed in last time. It looks splendid!'

Ali was checking the departure board. They would be well in time.

Chapter Thirty

⚜

"Dear Jasmine," Hamid had written, "I am sorry that I didn't reply to your letter earlier. I was in America, partly on business and partly on holiday. In fact, I had gone there for a job interview.

"I have read your letter with great interest. The tone seemed to be different but as I read it again I felt that you only want me more in your and Esme's life as a convenient child-minder, rather than as a permanent fixture, as her father. You still want to call all the shots and push me around as it suits you. I shudder to think what will happen to such an arrangement and my relationship with Esme, when you will have achieved your professional goal. By the sound of it, I might be discarded.

"Jasmine, I have always been fond and proud of you but I am no pushover, not for anyone! I really think it is time you made up your mind whether we should be a proper family – mum, dad and child – or whether you want to return to the status quo, as it was before I found out that I was a father; anything in between will only be confusing for our little girl. I don't want her ending up as a pawn in selfish negotiations. It goes without saying that leaving you both behind would be heart-breaking but if that is what you want, so be it!

"It is crunch time, Jasmine!

"If you decide that you favour a future with me as your husband and father to Esme, we can begin to work on our relationship, on being a team as a couple and a strong family unit for our daughter. If your answer is 'no' I shall accept the job in New York. You have two weeks to let me know.

"With best wishes
"Hamid"

Karin had come down to the kitchen before everyone else would wake up, so that she could fully concentrate on reading Hamid's letter. It had bothered her all night, jagged jolts interrupting her sleep.

No wonder Jasmine had been upset! Hamid had rejected her idea of a loose arrangement where he would have access to his daughter, mainly when it suited her. He was right, that this could only be detrimental to the emotional well-being of the child: Esme wouldn't know from one day to the next who would be in charge of her, her mother or her father, two people with wildly differing ideas about her upbringing. Hamid saw himself as a husband and father while Jasmine was still clinging on to the idea that she could remain an independent single mother, quite happy to be so, not really needing a man as a permanent fixture in her life. He would be tolerated when needed, but the emotional distance would remain.

He obviously knows her better than she does herself, Karin thought. He had looked through her and her - probably instinctive rather than devious – scheming. However, he wasn't going to accept the crumbs she had offered. He insisted to know where he stood, so that he could build a future with or without her. He had made it clear, that the least he demanded was respect from her, if she couldn't summon up love.

Karin felt admiration for the man who might have been her son-in-law.

She did not expect Jasmine to discuss the matter with her, certainly not while Tilly was there; but Tilly would be gone by the afternoon and maybe, just maybe Jasmine might open up and for once listen to her mother. She was afraid for her. It couldn't be easy, going through life constantly trying to avoid emotional involvement, being suspicious of any attachment.

There surely must be times in her daughter's life when even she needed a shoulder to cry on or simply to snuggle up to someone who was on her side. And how would all this to-ing and fro-ing affect Esme's childhood and development? Would s h e ever be able to trust anyone? If Jasmine made the wrong decision now, it could leave them both scarred for life. Was there anything she could do without being accused of interfering?

Karin sat down at the kitchen table to sip her second cup

of tea. For memories sake, she dropped a cardamom seed into it to give it the flavour she had loved when she had lived in Bangladesh.

It was such a long time ago, but she did often think back: It had been a romantic and, in parts, dramatic courtship, Raj having been trapped in his country and she having to battle against her parent's disapproval and society's prejudices, until fate finally had reunited them.

She had entered her marriage to Raj with great idealism and full of plans to do good works in his country, one of the poorest in the world. As it had turned out, he had belonged not to the starving masses, but to one of the noblest families who ran the country as they saw fit: With some sympathy for the poor, but mainly for their own benefit. Of course, they hadn't been all bad, corrupt and greedy, but the few who weren't, didn't really get anywhere with their efforts. They were shrugged off as do-gooders. She had wanted to be one of the latter, but then, in a Muslim country, women rarely won the arguments. To her disappointment, she had found out that there was nothing she could do without her husband's permission, which had been very rarely granted. At first, she had thought that, ringing shame on the family, would apply only to blatantly bad behaviour, but soon she had found out, that the tiniest and most well-intentioned deviation from the traditional role, a woman was expected to play, was sufficient to disgrace her and the family. There were broad guidelines, a strict code of conduct, which had been outlined to her, but they had seemed to hamper everything she had in mind to do.

She had clung to her exotic dream for a long time and had concentrated on bringing up her children, Ali and Jasmine, but ultimately, she had felt isolated and unhappy. When she had found out about her dashing husband's infidelity, and when her three year old son had told her, 'that Mummy doesn't sing anymore', she had known that, for her sake and theirs, she had to put an end to it.

Karin, still sitting at the kitchen table, shuddered thinking back to the day, when she had fled, with only Priti's knowledge and help, clasping the children to her body. She had gone through hardship and emotional turmoil; her parents' accusing looks, saying 'we told you so'; a deepening feeling of guilt at not having said good-bye to her husband's family; and most of all, guilt towards her children, who were totally confused. They soon had given up asking when they would return to Abbu.

In the end, the silent recriminations and her struggle to come to turns with being a single mother had made her accept a job in London. She had needed a fresh start, and however hard it would be, she would get through it, and she would make sure the children were happy and had the best education she could afford. She had aimed to be self-sufficient, unimpeded and un-influenced by anybody but herself. She had succeeded, but it had also been a lonely time.

Suddenly, this sort of containment, single-mindedness and insistence on struggling on in solitude and isolation sounded horribly familiar. Was that what Jasmine was striving for, to be a control freak? One thing was for sure: Karin knew that it would not make Jasmine happy. Moreover, it would turn Esme into a shy, socially awkward and prickly adolescent or, if Jasmine was unlucky, a tear-away, denouncing her mother.

I must speak to her, Karin thought hoping fervently that she would find the right words.

Chapter Thirty-One

Cৎৎৎৎৎ

It was a short, rattling flight; the plane was almost empty. They wondered whether it wouldn't have been safer to travel from Dhaka on the Rocket Steamer which would have taken them down stream on the Buriganga river until it met with the Meghna. However, when they had checked the tourist reviews on the internet, there was mention of problems with finding the correct boat in the crush of Sadarghat harbour, particularly if one only spoke English. There were also warnings that the trips were often cancelled because the three ancient steamers – only one of them, the Ostrich, had first class accommodation – needed repairs. The least appealing aspect of going by one of those three boats would have been a journey of at least six hours which would have ended even before Khulna, the gate town to the Sunderbans; the review mentioned that this was due to lack of water in the tidal channels.

'Is that the official language that the river has silted up, and the people couldn't be bothered to do anything about it?' said Martha waspishly underlining the sarcasm with a double *acha*-tilt of the head. She was really letting fly.

'Darling, Martha!' Ali put his arm around her agitated shoulders leaning over from his seat. 'We are not going on a crusade. We are not going to change the ills of the world, not this weekend, please! We are going to have a holiday, see one of the last and biggest mangrove forests in the world and hopefully, at least some of its wild animals. Let's just relax and enjoy it!'

He knew when she was agitated because she would always twirl a lock round a finger as she did now. She stayed silent though.

Once they had arrived at the ramshackle airport in Jessore, they were picked up by the promised mini-bus, its driver and an official guide who introduced himself as Tahir. He was a dark-tanned, tall chap with floppy black hair falling into his forehead and a ready wide smile to welcome his charges.

They were only joined by a young Australian couple who, judging by their luggage, seemed better equipped than the usual backpackers. Honeymooners, Martha speculated.

There was also an elderly Bengali man who had his nose constantly in a book which looked like a travel guide.

After driving for quite a while on a dusty country road past bony, grazing cows, village people looking up briefly to stare at the bus, and wooden houses which would be classified in America as shacks – but were obviously the villagers' homes. They stopped at Bagerhat, a City famed for its Mosques, particularly the Unesco World Heritage Site of the Sixty-Domed Mosque. They entered through the expansive and lush gardens.

'How extraordinary!' exclaimed Martha 'and,' she whispered into Ali's ear, 'mole hills on the roof.'

'Shh!' he put his finger on his lips. 'Don't get us into trouble.' She put quickly a hand in front of her mouth, though he sparkling eyes above it gave away her amusement.

They walked around the gardens a little longer under a cloudless blue sky and a bearable sun. As non-believers they were not invited to go inside the Mosque. In the end, they were glad to climb back on the bus and to check into their hotel in Mongla a few miles along the road.

The hotel was not exactly the Hilton or the Radisson, which Karin had described to them: with fluffy towels, chocolates and shaplas (water lilies) on her pillows, but with its clean beds, an mosquito net which was intact, a simple wardrobe with a rail and two drawers and most of all, a working shower and toilet next door, it was adequate. They slept fitfully, arms slung around each other, making unexpectedly love the moment they woke up, The place was beginning to weave its magic and even the trickling shower and missing toilet seat couldn't dampen their spirits. They laughed hysterically, when it turned out to be a toad which had attacked Martha's bottom while she was sitting on the porcelain.

They ate heartily at breakfast trying everything on offer: stuffed cheese potato cutlets, *aloo tarkari* served with *puri*, *channa bhaji*, a chickpea dish; prawn cutlets, mutton *nihari*, a curry, pickled *parathas*; and various sweet dishes like *dudh sevalan* which was vermicelli in milk, semolina *halwa*, *bhapa pitha* made with rice, coconut and molasses; and an intriguing jam called raw mango *murabba*. All this was accompanied by bowls full of plain rice and its more glamorous version of *polao* cooked in clarified butter and spices, adorned with sliced almonds and peas.

'I don't think I can walk up the stairs,' laughed Martha before they went to their room. They had eaten far more than they did usually for breakfast: a boring slice of toast with honey or chocolate spread and plenty of coffee.

They grabbed their two small rucksacks, which lay ready packed on the bed, and boarded the mini-bus which had come to deliver them to their next stage, the river boat harbour.

It was a lovely boat; not the most recent model but it looked seaworthy enough and romantic. As the young Australians and the older man were the only other passengers, Martha and Ali had the feeling that they had the boat almost to themselves. They had booked a two bed cabin so that they didn't have to share with somebody else. As soon as they entered, they heard the river water gently lapping under the small bulls-eye window.

They were lucky that the 'French' toilets of perfectly normal size were only a few doors away, and found that the 'English commodes', a little further along the corridor, were not as bad as they had sounded, just wooden seats with a hole in the middle and a can full of water to flush.

The perception of foreign national habits was interesting, though.

'Perfect,' they agreed; not too much luxury, just a few comforts.

'I bet the food will be divine,' Martha smacked her lips.

'I could have prawn cutlets morning, noon and night!'

'My mother used to like them,' Ali said, and for a moment they both thought of the woman whose past had brought them to this country.

The boat's engine roared into life and they settled on a bench

210

on deck which they had all to themselves, sipping iced water which a steward in livery had offered together with cha and slices of fresh mango.

'Lunch will be served in an hour,' boomed the captain's voice over an old-fashioned, over-sized loud speaker.

'In the meantime, enjoy the view of the river, the mangrove forest and the wild animals.'

Ali had remembered to bring binoculars, but in spite of them they could detect nothing but various birds singing, twittering and calling. Ali leafed through a small bird book he had bought at the hotel and tried to identify them but it was difficult to match names with birds he had never seen or heard.

'Heaven!' said Martha sleepily. The sun was shining brightly but again not unbearably so. Soon she was dozing. Ali watched her chest peacefully rising and falling in regular intervals; her curls framed her face; her legs hidden in white jeans; and brown feet peeping out, one sandal having already fallen off. I am a lucky guy, he thought looking at his sleeping wife.

She awoke when lunch was announced over the crackling tannoy.

'How can I fall asleep with all this beauty around us!' she scolded herself.

'You obviously needed it,' Ali smiled at her.

'I thought, I could never ever eat again after our huge breakfast but I think I am surprisingly peckish,' she laughed and dragged her husband by the hand to the dining room below deck.

'It will be much nicer eating upstairs,' Martha decided but as soon as she emerged from the door, flying insects of all sorts descended on her plate.

She quickly fled downstairs to a laughing Ali, bemused looks from the other three passengers and grins from the staff.

'It's as bad as at home,' the Australian woman remarked. 'Unless we have a barbie fire burning we don't eat outside.'

'Are you here on holiday?' Martha felt a little foolish and tried to change the subject.

'We are here on honeymoon,' said the young woman proudly flashing her wedding band at them.

Martha looked at Ali triumphantly as if to say: 'I told you so!'

'And you?' the young man entered the conversation.

'We are working in another part of Bangladesh – at an orphanage,' replied Ali and felt a tiny bit proud.

'My Goodness!' exclaimed the honeymooners in unison. 'And what is it like?'

'Fine but challenging,' said Martha diplomatically, adding quickly: 'By the way, I am Martha.'

'Kerry,' said the Australian and shook the extended hand. 'And that's my husband Tom.' She was obviously very proud of Tom.

'I am Ali,' the men exchanged handshakes as well.

'Are you coming as far as Port Canning?' Tom asked. 'That's near Calcutta.'

'Kolkata,' Kate corrected him, 'it's now pronounced Kolkata!.' She looked apologetically at Tom which Martha thought rather endearing.

'I don't think we do travel as far as Port Canning,' Ali replied. 'We have only four days leave; then it's back to Dhaka and the children.'

Martha really wasn't in the mood to think about their return journey and munched through various plates of curried lamb, chicken, vegetables and finished with lychees from the fruit bowl.

Tahir mingled with his guests and finally asked for their attention: 'We shall be at Daingman Forest Station in half an hour where I shall get your permits to enter Sunderban. While I deal with officials, you can climb watchtower and see wild animals. We shall also be joined by armed guard.'

In the event, it took them a full hour to reach the Forest Station and another to procure the permits. The two guards who would from now on be in charge of the visitors' security, looked grim and important with rifles slung over their shoulders; they were short, wiry men who undoubtedly intended to take their task seriously.

While waiting, Ali managed to see some birds in the woods across the river. He thought he had identified a *doel*, a *myna* and something that had looked decidedly like a kingfisher.'

Tahir the guide, nodded vigorously when asked: 'Yes, *machranga* – kingfisher!' He couldn't have been prouder.

After permits had been secured to everybody's relief, the group and the guards boarded the boat. As it jugged along the river, Tahir pointed out a small herd of spotted deer which were grazing on the long, tough grass near the river bank.

Suddenly he screamed with excitement: 'Red-whiskered bulbul! Red-whiskered bulbul,' he shouted, and everybody stared in the direction of both his extended arms towards the tree tops. They heard the bird before they saw it which sounded a little like 'pettigrew, pettigrew'.

'Is saying "welcome to Sunderban",' Tahir beamed.

Through the binoculars, which were handed round, they could just about make out a medium-sized bird with a white belly and dark-brown feathers covering its back as if it was wearing the long-tailed jacket of a morning suit. What was extraordinary about the bird were two bright red dots on each cheek over the vents and whiskers and a tall black, pointed crest on its head like a fashionable fascinator.

The visitors felt they had done very well so far and were happy to decamp at the next Forest Station to have another sumptuous meal before falling into beds protected by almost weightless mosquito nets.

'Why are we having such early starts?' mumbled Martha, bleary-eyed, the following morning just after sunrise.

'Because the air is still fresh and the animals are more likely to be out?' Ali guessed. He could see in her crumpled face that she would have fancied a lie-in for once.

Back on board, with the small group of tourist around him, Tahir, their guide, launched his first lecture of the day with a question: 'What do you think 'Sunderban' means?'

Everybody looked at him eagerly for the answer but the older gentleman, a camera on a strap round his neck, had found it already in his guide book.

'Something to do with the trees here?' he suggested.

'Excellent, excellent, Sir' exclaimed the guide excitedly as if he was addressing an outstanding pupil. 'The mangrove forest is full of Sundari trees which used to provide fuel for the local population. Now of course, this is a World Heritage site and National Park of Bangladesh, so people have moved away.'

I wonder how willingly, a little rebellious thought popped into Martha's head, but she kept quiet.

And then Tahir launched into the statistics: 'Sunderban

stretches over two countries: Bangladesh and India. It is one of the largest, if not the largest, mangrove forest in the world, covering an area of around 38,500 square kilometres. It forms a bay of 256 kilometres or 160 miles along the Gulf of Bengal and is the delta of the rivers Ganges, Brahmaputra and Meghna. These tidal river estuaries have carved up the area into thousands of channels and fifty four islands which are covered by Sundari forests. There is a bird sanctuary at Sajnekhali and a crocodile hatchery and sanctuary at Bhagbatput which is totally uninhabitable, and that is also, where the tigers live, safe from poachers; there are about four hundred of them left.'

Tahir took a deep breath before launching into the rest of his speech: 'You can also access the Sunderbans from Canning Harbour in India' He didn't seem keen to give that information and hurried on. Martha could hear Kerry whisper: 'That's where we are going,' before she was shushed so that Tahir could carry on:

'The wildlife sanctuaries were founded in 1966 and have been very successful. We think,' at which point Tahir raised himself visibly to include himself in this illustrious group of savers of the forest, 'there are now 30,000 spotted deer, 400 Bengal tigers, 120 species of fish, 260 species of birds, eight species of amphibians and five types of salt-water crocodiles, crocodiles paresis, the only ones in the world. There are, of course, also monkeys, butterflies, parakeets and wild boar. Today we might see any of them, if we are lucky,' and here Tahir looked dreamily into the distance, 'crocodiles basking in the sun or swimming across a river, monkeys swinging from tree top to tree top – if we are lucky,' he added again.'

Everybody looked appreciatively at him.

'And tomorrow,' this seemed to be the piece de resistance, 'we shall take boat to Katka, very special Heritage Site. We shall climb wooden watch tower, forty feet high and have wonderful view over Sunderban and later walk to beach where you might see white-bellied sea-eagle.' Tahir looked as if to say: I rest my case!

Ali and Martha slung arms round each other when they heard the word 'beach'. They would definitely make use of a beach if there was one!

'Thank you so much,' said Kerry loudly, to atone for her interruption earlier. 'You are very knowledgeable, Tahir!'

The little group burst into applause.

Tahir bowed, obviously gratified: 'I have degree of Science from University of Dhaka,' he said proudly and then turned away as if embarrassed about boasting.

'Do I smell food again?' whispered Martha into Ali's ear. 'I shall put on a ton at this rate!' She didn't really mind; the food was simply wonderful.

'Looks as if I shall have a feast day taking photographs,' said the Bengali man to no one in particular.

'Is that your hobby?' Martha asked politely. She had the feeling that he might be a little lonely or did he not want anybody to intrude into his personal space? It was hard to know…

'Yes, it is!' he replied. 'I belong to a club since I retired, and we want to enter our best pictures into a national competition this year. So I hope for something spectacular.'

Martha couldn't tame her curiosity any longer: 'I hope you don't mind me asking,' she began, 'your English is flawless and even almost without an accent.'

'Oh yes,' he chuckled a little shy, 'we spent most of our life in England, in Oldham until my wife got sick three years ago. She wanted to come home to see everybody one more time and be buried here; so I retired – I was a GP – and came back to care for her. She died eighteen months ago.'

'That must be so hard,' Martha commiserated. He only nodded.

'Have you been back to England?'

'No, and I don't think I will ever again. I don't know anybody there anymore. Once you have left, people forget you and move on with their lives.'

'That's true! You don't have any children?'

'Yes, a son who lives in America, in California; so it is a long way for him to come and for me to get there.'

Martha filled the ensuing silence looking at him full of sympathy but he just kept staring at the floor, avoiding her eyes, as if it had suddenly dawned on him, how far it really was and how lonely he had become.

'You know,' she broke the silence, 'if you ever feel you want to visit England again, my husband's mother and sister live in Manchester. I am sure they would put you up in their guest room.'

'That is so kind of you!' he smiled faintly, 'I don't think so but just in case, I shall let you have my address before the end of the trip. When are you flying back to Manchester?'

'We are not. My husband Ali and I work here in Bangladesh for a children's charity north of Dhaka, and we are going to stay there for the foreseeable future.'

'But then you must come and see me!' he exclaimed with great pleasure.'I live in Gulshan.'

'So do Ali's relatives! We shall definitely call on you next time we visit them… And you must also come to us. It's in the countryside, so plenty of opportunities to take lovely photographs!'

'That would be delightful!'

Martha felt as if she had made the man's day.

Soon afterwards, the boat stopped, they were told to disembark in order to climb up the viewing tower at Kotchikhali where they were all straining their eyes to look out for wildlife. It was elusive apart from the noises and flutterings. This stop was followed by another view point an hour later whose name they couldn't quite catch; the last one of the day was at Mandarbaria.

The drill was always the same: the captain of the boat would announce the stop over the loudspeaker, the guide, Tahir, would get into position at the railings and mention for the umpteenth time the animals they were looking out for, they would leave the boat accompanied by the armed guards, be ushered to the watch tower but left to their own devices on the platform. By now they were sharing the binoculars with the others and the older gentleman, whose name, they found out was Ali as well, managed to take reel after reel of photographs in the hope to catch one of these elusive creatures. They did see quite of few groups of deer and a couple of monkeys. Sometimes the birdsong was deafening. Of course, they were all straining to discover a crocodile or a tiger, but even passing by Tin Kona Island, where some of them were known to live, they had no luck.

'Maybe on the way back,' they consoled each other. As it was, they were very tired by the evening from eating far too much, getting on and off the boat and gazing into the beautiful forest to maybe, just maybe, see a rare animal.

The last two nights would be spent in their cabins in the bunk beds on board and everybody professed that they looked forward to waking up to the dawn chorus and noises of the jungle.

It was less of a dawn chorus than a cacophony of screaming, screeching, shrieking, rasping, knocking, wings-fluttering, not to mention the rhythmical bumping of the boat.

'I hope that's not a crocodile looking for its breakfast,' Martha hung off her top bunk and blew a kiss down to Ali who was rubbing his eyes,

'And a lovely good morning to you! You will make a tasty snack!'

Martha threw her thin pillow at his face before retorting with glee that he would be a more substantial portion for any animal than she could ever be.

They heard noises outside their door and decided that they did not want to miss their own breakfast. Ten minutes later, they sat down to more prawn cutlets, chutneys, *parathas* and *dhal* and the only concession to the foreign visitors: toast and jam.

No sooner had they left their narrow bench and breakfast table, they could hear and feel the boat chugging gently along the river. They took up their by now established positions on deck and listened to the noises of the jungle. They saw shadowy, gangly bodies swinging from tree to tree and everything from tiny songbirds to birds of prey with huge wing spans, inspecting with beady eyes the water furrow, the boat made, for scraps.

The deep forest on either side of the river changed into grassy planes where large groups of white spotted deer grazed, At first the animals took no notice but raised their heads as the boat approached; a stag, a little distance from his does, stood motionless, carrying his branchless antlers – two beams only like a tuning fork – on his elegant head.

A beautiful butterfly, brown with vivid white markings, erred onto the boat and sat on Martha's shoulder, just long enough for Ali senior to take a snapshot.

They passed fishermen, in white, sleeveless vests and *lunghis* hiked up to their knees. They were standing in water spreading a net next to their own flat boats near the river's edge. The tourists could hear the men's excited chatter before the tourists were discovered and greeted with waving hands.

A little further downstream, they saw something large floating on the surface, bobbing up and down with the waves the boat made. At first they thought it was a huge lump of soil but as they got nearer it turned out to be an uprooted, crownless tree. It then occurred to them that this part of Bangladesh would always be hit first by the unavoidable autumnal cyclones.

'Tahir, when is the cyclone season? Not now, surely?'

'We do not have excursion when cyclone is announced, but we had, I think, eight last year. October and May are bad, and sometimes November, but now is okay.'

'That's a relief!' Kerry chipped in. 'What is it like?'

'Very windy!' they all laughed when Tahir stated the obvious. He looked a little bemused by this hilarity and blamed himself for not having described it properly. So he tried again:

'Very high tides, all of Sunderban flooded, trees falling over, animals drowning,' he took a deep breath, 'devastation!' They stopped giggling and made a big effort to look concerned.

However, this bit of reality was soon forgotten; after all, they were on holiday.

'Is this still part of the Ganges?' asked Tom pointing at the water.

'No, the big rivers like Ganges, Padma, Jamuna, Meghna, have spread into many little rivers and channels. This is called river Balu.' Tahir seemed to know everything about the area. He was a great guide!

'On the map, you see these big rivers approaching the Sunderbans and suddenly they divide into many thin ones. Have a look.' He offered his map and they bent over it.

'Yes, you are right,' Martha remarked, 'the delta looks like a multi-fingered glove.'

'You are turning into a poet,' Ali grinned to which she stuck out her tongue, feeling quite embarrassed about it a second later.

'I think we are reaching our destination soon,' she said quickly, pointing to the two armed guards who were getting ready, slinging their rifles over their shoulders.

Sure enough, ten minutes later, the boat docked and they were asked to leave it and to follow Tahir, flanked by the armed men.

'We are first going to watch tower!' he announced. This one was a de-luxe version with three storeys to climb, about forty feet high. Tahir led his little group up to the first platform while the armed men took up positions at the foot of the tower.

Martha and Ali climbed up to the top where they had the highest platform all to themselves. The view was breath-taking: In front of them by a wide, sandy beach and the glittering waters of the Gulf of Bengal; to the left they saw the beach stretch into the distance framed by forest. As they looked, left they could see the narrow water lane they had come from, their boat moored at the bank, and the mouth of the river Balu emptying its waters into the sea. On the other side of the river spread out the green finger of another island which was the home to Hiron Point, said to be a more touristy attraction. The brochures had said that it was home to the greatest population of Bengal tigers; Ali and Martha had decided that that was in some way contradictory. They were happy with the type of journey they had chosen with the right mixture of natural beauty, lazy days and just a few basic comforts.

As they turned away from the sea and the river, they looked over the lush green canopy of the mangrove forest, still like a green roof, only disturbed in the distance by monkeys clambering around like little fleas. Through the binoculars, they discovered birds they hadn't ever seen before.

'I wonder what that is…'

'Let me see…' it was Tahir who had appeared, breathless from the climb. Ali pointed out to sea.

'That is sea eagle,' Tahir announced proudly. 'And over there, pelican; and there a pair of buzzards, and on the beach oyster catcher.' The binoculars whizzed from one side to another: '… and down there, red jungle fowl and purple moorhens and up there parakeets. You lucky!' Tahir, forgetting English grammar in the excitement, was pleased with the performance his beloved Sunderbans gave.

'What's that down there in the sand,' Martha almost fell over the balustrade pointing at something far below in the sand.

'Could be tiger foot print,' said Tahir mysteriously, observing her reaction. First horror, then excitement glinted in her eyes and then she realised that he was teasing her.

'Do they really come here?'

'Sometimes, at night. They keep to the truly wild islands, away from people. But sometimes, you can see foot print in the sand.' He smiled and made his way back down to the others.

They had been wondering, looking down from the viewing platforms, what their crew were doing down there in the sand; they had looked like busy ants. Now the visitors found to their surprise that they had prepared a picnic for them. It didn't take long until everybody was seated on blankets tucking in heartily. Martha couldn't believe how juicy the mangoes were and ate two.

After lunch, everybody dispersed into a private corner to have a snooze, to read or to chat. Ali and Martha decided to walk along the water's edge, listening to the waves, the gentle humming and buzzing; the loud noises had abated in the midday sun. The imprints in the sand they had discovered from above did indeed look like paw prints of a very large cat but they just took a photograph of it and kept it to themselves. What a treat thinking that they were walking in the footsteps of such a noble creature. What a privilege! It didn't matter that they were not likely to see the real thing; it was safer that way, for all concerned!

Finally, they sat down in the sand, Martha cross-legged and Ali supporting himself with his hands behind his back. They saw the young Australian couple playing with something that looked like a Frisbee.

Ali seemed to be fishing for something in his trouser pocket until he revealed a tiny parcel wrapped in white tissue paper and bound together by a straw ribbon.

'Sunnah,' he said simply, 'Happy Eid!'

'I didn't realise that you exchange presents on Eid Adha as well.'

'I am not sure myself but I saw this…'

'…and thought of you!' Martha finished his sentence and they both burst out laughing.

Martha un-wrapped it and out came a little Bengal tiger, made of clay and painted in rather striking colours.

'Just in case, we don't see the real thing,' Ali grinned. The real thing would probably look nothing like it.

'Thank you,' said Martha, looking furtively around and once

sure that nobody was watching she leaned over to him and kissed him passionately on the mouth. 'You are very sweet!'

They fell into a lazy silence, the little Bengal tiger sitting between them on the sand.

'This is heaven.' Martha said. 'Let's always be so happy!' Her eyes sparkled and she looked full of determination and hope.

'Yes,' said Ali simply. He didn't want to break the spell.

They sat there till late, the big, yellow sun throwing a golden mantle onto the water's surface before turning into a fireball and painting the Bay of Bengal crimson.

Within minutes it sank below the horizon like a stone and left only darkness and the black outlines of the forest behind. The air was still and the animals had fallen silent as if a door had been shut.

Tahir and the crew took out their torches and led their mesmerised guests in single file back to the boat.

Chapter Thirty-Two

Karin tried twice to have a word with Jasmine about Hamid's letter but for some reason or another, her daughter managed to cut short all her attempts; they were politely interrupted, postponed and finally ignored.

Jasmine strode around with her official courteous face grimly set into fake-smiles.

How does she do it? Karin thought, am I the only one who is distraught at the possible consequences? Who can't get the thoughts of what might happen out of my mind; the only one with a heavy heart? How can it be that I feel closer to Hamid than to my own daughter?

And there she is, going about her business, efficient as ever, without a sign of being in turmoil or torn between the choices that could change her life forever.

Until one morning, Jasmine mentioned casually at breakfast – when Karin had made another attempt at finding out whether her daughter had come to a decision – that yes, she had replied and had wished him all the best for his career in America. After dropping this bombshell into the early morning, Jasmine got up swiftly, grabbed her coat and bag, planted a kiss on Esme's forehead and left hurriedly for work.

Karin was so stunned and deflated that her usual good-bye got stuck in her throat as she heard the front door shut with a bang.

What was the point of giving your children any advice if they went off and did exactly the opposite?

She cleared up the breakfast table with little Esme as a keen helper, carrying the not so precious bread basket out into the kitchen. They then set off to do a bit of shopping at the village grocer's and the bakery, went to the swings for a little while, but the wind and rain set in and drove them home.

'We are going to pick up Omar from school today; his Mummy has to stay in school for a parents' evening,' Karin said to her grand-daughter who was delighted; the two children liked each other.

When they got home, they unpacked the shopping and settled down to some colouring-in followed by a puzzle and finally preparing lunch. Esme had hardly settled for an afternoon nap when the telephone rang.

Karin put the newspaper, she had just opened, on the coffee table and went out into the hall.

'Hello?'

The line was crackling. Bangladesh, she thought immediately, before she heard Martha's excited American drawl:

'Hi Karin! It's us. We are back from the Sunderbans, and it was awesome!'

'I am so pleased! You sound as if they have done you a world of good!'

'They have and to Ali as well.' It was so romantic, and wild and peaceful.'

'Did you see any animals?'

'We saw loads, birds we have never seen before, butterflies, monkeys and hundreds of white-spotted deer.'

'So, no Bengal tigers?'

'No, and no crocodiles either, but it didn't matter. The landscape was stunning. It wasn't too hot or humid – well, the usual sort of thing for Bangladesh in autumn – and of course, the food was divine!'

'Marvellous, so back to the salt mines now?'

'What do you mean?' What was the saying again? America and England, two nations divided by a common language!

'Back to work.' Karin explained.

'Yes. Ali has already disappeared to see whether there is any progress with the wells; lessons will start tomorrow again. There were Eid celebrations going on while we were away, so the children have not missed out at all. And how are you, Karin? Everything going well?'

A big sigh travelled all the distance to Bangladesh.

'I shouldn't have asked, should I?' Martha laughed. 'Let me have a guess: Jasmine?'

'Yeah,' Karin didn't feel like laughing.

'What has she done now?' Martha had immediately picked up on her mother-in-law's sombre mood.

'She told Hamid in a letter that she wished him the best of luck in his new job in America.' Karin almost burst into tears, as she said the words out loud.

'She didn't!' Martha was as horrified as Karin.

It was nice that at least one young person shared her opinion. She sometimes felt so out of step with her daughter's thinking that she had begun to wonder whether she was in the wrong, just simply growing old and staid.

'Poor Hamid! I am sure, that that is not what he wanted,' Martha guessed correctly.

'I wish I could change her mind, but she won't listen to me, literally. She simply walks away, when I broach the subject,' Karin said miserably.'

'Well, 'making your bed and lie in it' springs to mind. You said he was quite nice, didn't you?'

'He is − well-mannered, intelligent, with a good job, obviously with some sense of responsibility otherwise he would not have made so much effort as soon as he knew he had a child. I understand that he wants a firm commitment rather than a loose arrangement, from which Jasmine could pull out any time.'

'Very unsatisfactory! Esme would never know where she stood.'

'Exactly! Jasmine seems to put her principals as an independent woman before her daughter's welfare. What did I do wrong bringing her up?'

'You know, Karin, I don't think it's the upbringing parents provide. It's more the influences, after we leave them that we choose from. We seem to cling on to our first independent decisions, we are so proud of, but they are not always the best for us. Jasmine has obviously trouble getting past that stage. Only when people can combine the two, upbringing and own experiences, are they truly mature. So don't blame yourself! You have done an excellent job, certainly with my husband. So if Jasmine is different and prefers to complicate her life, it's not your fault.'

'Thank you, Martha. You are a great comfort!' Karin sighed, feeling slightly less guilty.

'Anytime,' Karin heard her daughter in-law's happy laughter. 'I have to rush off now. We have choir practice tonight, and I haven't prepared anything yet. Stay calm, Karin. Love you!'

Karin replaced the receiver gently, wondering why her daughter couldn't be kind like that. Martha was right she shouldn't worry so much about something she couldn't change.

She heard Esme stir upstairs. Another five minutes and she would have to respond.

She dialled.

'Hello Tilly. It's Karin. Can I spend the weekend with you?'

'Of course, you can! There are no more rehearsals for this year, are there?'

'No. And in this weather I don't even like country walks.'

'Well, you know what I am like with walking...' Tilly cackled, sounding like a chattering dolphin. 'You come to me, luvvie; Come as early as you can! I am sure we shall find something to amuse ourselves.'

'Just what I need!'

Tilly didn't reply to this dark remark and only said, after a little pause: 'See you Saturday. Let me know which train; I'll pick you up.'

Chapter Thirty-Three

༕

'Can I come in? I'm a bit early,' Sara called through the half-open door of the bungalow.

'Of course,' Martha appeared in the wide open door, wet curls dripping on the floor. 'You can help me with the music sheets. I am miles behind. I am still in holiday mood!'

She stopped short and looked again at Sara who stood still in the door frame grinning as if overcome with shyness or embarrassment.

'Come on in! What's the matter?'

Sara made a few steps inside and shut the door behind her.

'I have some news…'.

Martha raised her eyebrows, put an arm around her friend's shoulders and led her gently into the sitting room. She pressed her onto the settee and demanded:

'Spit it out!'

'Aresh, Dr Chowdhury, and I are engaged to be married.' She smiled as if she had done something naughty.

Martha was so surprised and delighted that she threw herself next to Sara onto the settee, gave her a big, warm hug and exclaimed: 'That's wonderful, Sara! I am so happy for you both!'

It was heartfelt! Sara had proven to be a good friend over the last months whenever Martha had felt isolated, frustrated and bewildered. She had even confided in her that she had her doubts whether Ali was still on her side, which had made her feel disloyal.

'Of course, he is!' Sara had listened patiently and then reassured her, 'you have the most wonderful husband in the world! Trust him!' Sara had been the best support she could have wished for, and now she had found love herself.

'You are the first to know.'

'Thank you, my dearest friend!' The young women embraced and Martha stroked Sara's hair tenderly. Then she held her face in both her hands and look at her with love and seriousness: 'And I shall always be there for you to listen, too! And I shall keep your secrets!' she added cheekily.

The news spread immediately round the choir whose members found it hard to concentrate on anything else that evening.

'How did it happen?' one of the girls wanted to know. 'You dark horse!' said another. 'Obviously, it happened while we were in Sunderban,' added Martha; and then, of course, they had found another topic to embark on at great length. No one had ever been there, so Martha had to tell them all about it. In the end, they had not practised one song and decided to leave it at that. They would start again at the next rehearsal.

'You won't leave us, will you, Sara?' Martha asked anxiously. 'I mean when you are married? You don't plan to move away, do you?'

'I don't think so,' Sara answered. 'Maybe, we might build a home outside the Children's Village but we shall still work here. To be honest, we haven't discussed future plans. We still try to get our head round the fact that ...' She couldn't finish the sentence bursting with happiness and simply smiled the biggest smile Martha had ever seen. It brought tears to her eyes to see so much hope for the future in her friend's face.

By the next morning assembly, everybody knew, so Dr Abdullah thought it wise to make an official announcement to stop the gossip. There were 'oohs' and 'ahs' among the few who hadn't heard the news yet, and then all of a sudden applause broke out over the entire assembly. Sara and Dr Chowdhury were very popular.

They had to endure another day of shaking congratulatory hands before everybody went back to their routine.

'Any idea when the big day will be?' Martha asked tentatively.

'We have to get married quite quickly because it is not really acceptable that bride and groom live in the same place before the wedding.'

'You have done so for months,' Martha was tempted to remark but thought better of it. She was slowly learning not to point out the logic of things – it didn't apply here.

'So, next weekend Aresh will go and see my parents to ask for my hand in marriage.' It sounded terribly quaint and formal. 'Then the week after, I shall go and stay with my parents until Aresh picks me up at the weekend. We won't have the full works because he hasn't got any family, but we shall celebrate with mine for about two days and then we come back here to work.'

'As Mr and Mrs,' Martha completed and gave Sara another hug.

There isn't much time for preparations, thought Martha. It was correct that Dr Chowdhury had no blood family anybody knew of; the Children's Village had become his home over the years and the people in it his family. Surely, the children would love to honour the event and greet the young couple in style. She would have to put on her thinking cap, sharpish.

ဆာၛ

'Shamsur is furious,' Ali reported to his wife on the following evening.

'Why?' Martha was preoccupied with a list of suggestions for the happy couple's after-wedding reception.

'Well, this thing with Sara and Aresh getting married seems to have set off a couple of our teenagers. They were caught embarking on shenanigans behind the mosque.'

Martha giggled: 'To be honest, I often thought that we were lucky that nothing of that sort has ever happened; somebody must have fallen in love here before in spite of all the rules and customs. They just managed to keep it quiet. Well, I am pleased to hear that young Bengalis are not immune to feelings.'

'Just as well Shamsur can't hear you,' Ali couldn't help grinning. 'He is mortified and thinks it's totally immoral, but what can he do? He can't throw the boys out before puberty; and the girls certainly need our protection until they either marry or start working in a secure job.'

'I wonder whether farming out the boys to families nearby would help?'

'What do you mean?'

'You know, a type of foster families, not too far, so that we can supervise them. It would do the boys good to be part of a proper family, and they still could come back to play for their cricket or football teams and to meet their friends.'

'Another one of your good ideas?' Ali teased her but was secretly impressed; his wife had a sharp and quick mind; but, of course, there was always the hurdle of overcoming the headmaster's opposition to most things new.

'Would we find anybody willing to house the boys?' Ali wondered.

'Against payment? They would jump at the chance of additional income, and it would give us a lever to insist that the boys would carry on studying rather than be treated as servants.'

'I think you should present this yourself. It's a brilliant idea!' Secretly Ali hoped that by letting Martha submit her solution to the problem, she might redeem herself with the headmaster.

'By the way,' she caught him before he could slope off to the bedroom, 'we must organise a celebration in honour of Sara's and Aresh's wedding. They won't have a big do at her home because he is an orphan and they don't want a fuss anyway, but we should all put our heads together and organise a party and a present. In a way, we are the only family he has got, and Sara is like a sister to all of us.'

'Any plans yet?' Ali asked hopefully. He longed for his bed.

'No, but we really have to make a move to organise something because they are getting married in a fortnight.'

Never a dull moment, Ali thought, chuckling while finally getting ready for bed.

ॐ

Shamsur seemed difficult to get hold of. In the end, Martha confided in Sara who suggested making a formal appointment with him.

'It's a bit silly, isn't it?' Martha raised her eyebrows. 'His office is only on the other side of the Banyan tree.'

'I'll pin him down for you,' Sara was amused. 'Anything urgent?'

'Fairly, but I also have a new idea.' They both burst out laughing.

'Not another one,' quipped Sara when they had recovered.

'Don't you start! Ali is bad enough!'

Martha submitted her idea of foster parents and Sara fully approved.

'If he throws me out you know why.' Martha shrugged her shoulders in mock despair. 'By the way, where is he?'

'No idea. He seems to have lots of meetings with his nephew and the chief engineer, and today he travelled to Dhaka.'

'That's odd! Isn't that Ali's domain? I thought he wanted to get rid of the burden and that's why he put Ali in charge of supervision?'

'I don't know either,' Sara shook her head in mild disapproval. 'He is looking peaky these days.'

Martha looked at her. 'Peaky' was not a word Sara would have known a few months ago. Dr Chowdhury's English seemed to be rubbing off already.

'Ah well, let me know when he has a moment, she said 'I shouldn't keep him too long.

The next morning, Sara summoned her to the headmaster's office.

'Good luck,' she whispered as she opened the study door and shut it quietly behind her friend.

'Good morning, Martha? How are you?' the headmaster asked politely rather than with warmth.

'I am fine, Shamsur, and I hope you are, too.' He nodded distractedly.

'I don't want to impose on your time, so I shall come straight to the point. Two points, in fact.'

Shamsur sat down in his leather chair without offering her the seat opposite.

Martha took a deep breath and began:

'Point one is Sara's wedding. They will get married in her village, but we are the only family Dr Chowdhury has, so I would like to suggest that we organise a little celebration in their honour, preferably on the day of their return.'

The headmaster sighed: 'What did you have in mind?' he asked brusquely.

'A nice lunch or afternoon tea and cake, a performance of the choir, a traditional dance by the girls and a cricket tournament for the boys – Dr Chowdhury could be the referee; the children can make their own presents; generally a nice pleasant day with lots of cheering.'

'Will you organise it?' was the distracted reply. He did not want to get involved, that much was clear.

'If you agree, I shall.'

'Good. That's settled.' He got up from his chair as if it were the end of the meeting but Martha stood her ground:

'My second point is something quite different, a suggestion, a possible solution to our recent problem.'

Shamsur breathed out audibly and sat down again resigned to listen to some more drivel.

'Go on,' he snapped.

'We could find foster families in the nearby villages for the boys before they get interested in the opposite sex.'

She looked at his face which expressed surprise, dismay and embarrassment. It was not a topic to be discussed between a man and a woman. He was annoyed that Ali had told her at all.

'Are you mad?' he barked.

'Hear me out, Shamsur, please!' she ploughed on regardless. 'We could pay the families which would give them an income; the boys could still come back for their sports and to see their friends; and maybe one of us could inspect the arrangement regularly to make sure the boys are happy, treated well and go to school as they would here. And I am sure they would benefit...'

Martha was interrupted in mid-flow: 'No thank you,' the headmaster roared. 'I am sick and tired of you and your new ideas. We leave things as they are, and that's that! Now, anything else?'

She desperately wanted to finish her sentence, expressing her belief that the boys would surely benefit from the experience of family life. Few of them had ever had it, and those who had, not for long. All their children had to suffer loss, pain, abandonment and had to grow up quickly.

'They are fine where they arem' Dr Abdullah croaked.

Martha stopped and stared at her boss. He didn't look well: He had stood up and was now holding onto the top of his desk, swaying a little, head bowed and his face a colour which made her fear that he might collapse or burst into tears at any moment.

'Are you alright? Can I get you a glass of water?' she offered.

'Just go,' he mumbled hoarsely and with rasping breaths.

'If you are sure…' She went backwards until she had reached the door, her eyes still fixed on him. He didn't look up once and remained silent. Martha opened the door quietly ad slid out.

She met Sara as she walked along the corridor.

'Sara, he isn't well. It can't be just me and my silly ideas.'

'Oh dear, it didn't go well then?'

Martha only shook her head: 'Better have a look whether he needs anything.'

Sara nodded and walked towards the headmaster's office.

'He hates me,' she said to Ali in the evening. She had thought over her conversation with Dr Abdullah, at first upset and outraged at his closed mind and inflexibility, but even more about what he had said: 'I am sick and tired of you and your new ideas.' She was calmer now but the statement still hurt.

'Don't be silly,' Ali consoled her, 'you probably caught him in a foul mood.'

No, she was convinced that his dislike of her ran deeper; he obviously thought that she was somebody who was rocking the boat; who wasn't easy to fob off; and who would discover any flaw in the fabric. She was convinced he hated her presence.

How could she continue to work here? None of her efforts would ever be good enough; there would never be any appreciation, only rebuke, resentment and attempts to stop her.

I might as well not be here,' it suddenly dawned on her. It made her very sad, not only for herself, but also for Ali.

How was she going to tell him? She would organise Sara's wedding party and then think again.

Chapter Thirty-Four

Karin was just about to ring Tilly to make arrangements for the weekend when the shrill tone of the phone in her hand startled her.

'Hello?' She wondered whether Tilly was telepathic, but then she shook her head as if to scold herself: You don't believe in things like that, do you... Do you? There had been a time when she had been wrapped in such theories in an exotic world in which feelings and emotions ruled more than logic. It was a lovely, woolly, silky world which had wrapped itself round her like the saris she had dressed in every day.

Tilly probably didn't believe in telepathy either; there just wasn't enough space and time for it in the noisy, modern world.

Karin pushed all thought of it aside, cleared her voice and said again more firmly: 'Karin Khan speaking.'

'Karin, it's me, Martha.' Her daughter-in-law's voice was faint and brittle.

'Martha, how lovely! Where are you? In Bangladesh? You sound awfully far away.'

Martha spoke up a little, but it didn't make much difference:

'Yes, I am still here – though I am not sure why!'

'Well, aren't you there because of Ali and the children?' she reminded her, but suddenly her instincts told her that Martha wasn't in the mood for jokes.

'Yes, that's true, but they are the only things which keep me here.'

'Why? What's happened?'

Martha launched into her list of sorrows and Karin could hear the bitterness and disappointment: First came the story of the arsenic poisoned wells, her vigil at Vijay's hospital bed, her fight to fend off the press and the ghastly Minister, whom Ali had eventually managed to shame into providing the funds for the new wells; and then, when they had returned to the Children's Village, her struggles had continued, this time with the Headmaster, who had rejected every one of her proposals: Her simple request for boys to join the choir to give its sound more depth, her latest idea to find foster families nearby before the older boys' interest in girls could manifest itself, and worst of all, Ali's suspicion that Mr Abdullah's nephew, the new treasurer, was not entirely to be trusted with the grant money. It was tight enough; any misappropriation of funds would result in abandoned, half-built wells and financial disaster for the orphanage. She described how Ali tried to keep hold of the reins but that the young upstart nephew seemed to have pulled the wool over his uncle's eyes.

However, what had hurt her most of all – and she almost burst into tears relating this to Karin – her boss thought her a nuisance and was sick and tired of the sight and sound of her.

'That can't be true, Martha. He employed you. He wanted you.' commiserated Karin. 'It seems quite foolish not to make use of all your expertise and enthusiasm. Are you sure, it's you he is cross with?'

'He might be secretly worried about the finances, but whenever Ali mentions, that he would like to check the accounts, he gets short shrift. The nephew is the new 'Golden Boy'.'

'What is he like?'

'Cocky, poor eye contact, shifty, smarmy – you get the picture?'

'Yes, I see. You don't like him very much,' Karin dared to chuckle.

'To be honest, I have met Mr Abdullah only once,' said Karin, 'and he seemed to be honourable and reasonable. I wonder what's eating him. He was really keen for you to come and work with him.'

'I think he wanted Ali, and I was just thrown in for good measure. But I must say, he didn't look well when I saw him last. I obviously upset him.'

234

'In Bangladesh, few people live as long as we do here, but he is only in his fifties, isn't he?'

'I would have thought so.'

'There is something nice to report,' Martha tore herself away from her misery, 'Sara, Mr Abdullah's PA, is getting married to our doctor, and we are preparing a wedding reception. At least, the Headmaster didn't object to that!'

'There you are; something positive to look forward to.'

'Yes. I shall stop moaning now.'

'Don't be silly! I wish Jasmine was wearing her heart on her sleeve like you do! I never know what she is thinking. I wrote to you about her reply to Hamid, didn't I?'

'Yes. It's such a pity. I had the feeling that she could have been happy with him.'

'I sometimes think she doesn't want to be happy. She has thrown herself into a totally mad work schedule. She'll know in a few weeks whether she has succeeded.'

'That will be a great achievement!'

'Yes, and by then, Hamid will have gone to America.'

'I feel really sad for the three of them, but mainly for him and Esme.'

'So do I! Now, listen to us two: from one drama to the next. How about coming over sometime soon? You sound as if you could do with English pampering.'

'We just had the holiday in Sunderban, but now it feels as if it never happened.'

'I mean a break from Bangladesh. You have been there almost a year. Sometimes a short spell of change can make a big difference. You might even see things from a different perspective…'

'That's very tempting and very sweet, Karin, but as I said I am preparing Sara and Aresh's wedding reception, and I would hate to abandon Ali right now.'

'Maybe some time soon, at Christmas? With Ali? Keep it in mind!'

'I shall! I better go now. Thank you for talking good sense.'

'You are a wonderful person, Martha, and don't let anybody tell you otherwise!'

'I'll try. Thank you for listening! Byeee!'

Karin put the receiver down wishing there was something she

could do for her dear, impulsive and warm-hearted daughter-in-law.

Actually, there was something she could do, and it had just occurred to her: 'Tilly,' she said over the phone, 'are you any good at fundraising?'

'I don't know. What for? And where are our Headquarters?'

'You clever thing! I hadn't even begun to think of practicalities. We shall have them here, and if you don't mind, you could move in here for the duration. And it's for the children's charity in Bangladesh where Ali and Martha work. They need money to finish those new wells, so that the children have clean and safe drinking water.'

'Good! When do we start?'

'As soon as possible! Tomorrow?'

'Done! I shall put my thinking cap on in the meantime.'

'You are a treasure, Tilly! See you tomorrow.

The next person Karin planned to contact was Mrs Bellamy, the founder of the Children's Village. As far as Karin knew, she was still running the charity from England. Maybe her members could be persuaded to donate for the new wells?

No time like the present! Karin spurred herself on, looked up the charity's telephone number and dialled.

₮ℂ℟

Fundraising wasn't as easy as they had imagined. First they made a list of events they could organise: A coffee morning; a jumble sale; a street collection; a charity stall at the local market; door to door collections, standing at the local supermarket with a tin; a raffle.

They looked at each other with dismay; there wasn't enough time to do all of this, so they had to choose. They went over the list again.

A coffee morning for neighbours, friends and family on a Saturday morning seemed feasible; they could even include a raffle or ask for people to bring and buy;

A jumble sale looked like enormously hard work for days without a guaranteed profit.

'I once helped at a church jumble sale, and the things people donated!' Tilly's disgusted facial expression made Karin laugh.

'So we cross out jumble sale.'

Street and door-to-door collections were possible but they had to ask Mrs Bellamy first whether there would be any formalities to be cleared with the Town Hall. Her charity would have to direct and support them with advertising material. Karin put a question mark behind 'collections'.

The same actually might apply to collections at the local supermarket; they could imagine that they needed at least the store manager' consent. They would have to make enquiries.

And the charity stall at the weekly market sounded as if it required a lot of form filling and applications as well.

'Until we have found out more about collecting in public, we are left with the coffee morning and a raffle or bring and buy.'

'I can't see why we couldn't do that fairly soon?' suggested Karin. 'All we need to do is put leaflets or posters in letter boxes and advertise in local shops.'

'Great, let's get started!' Tilly was rearing to go.

‽‽

They decided to host the coffee morning on the following Saturday.

For the next few days, they designed a poster, leaflets, invitations, and bought a book of raffle tickets. Mrs Bellamy had sent copies of the charity's newsletters describing life and work in the orphanage and a short letter explaining why they were so desperate for money now,

'Aren't those children adorable?!' Karin showed the most recent photographs of toddlers and their carers.

'I couldn't go there,' Tilly remarked, 'I would want to adopt each and every one of them. Look at their big, dark eyes and huge smiles!'

Karin understood very well, how easily it was to fall for them.

'They really do seem happy there, which is certainly more than they had ever before in their young lives.'

'One wonders why the Bangladesh Government didn't start a centre like that. Why do foreigners have to set up places and be the driving force?'

Tilly was right. Why?

'And the foreigners are not always welcome,' Karin said, thinking of her charitable and caring daughter-in-law.

Tilly looked at her, raising her eyebrows in anticipation of an explanation, but Karin didn't elaborate.

'Right, back to work. This afternoon, we have to distribute all this material and on Monday, we hang the posters in the shop windows.'

'How many guests do we expect?'

'That's a point. We couldn't take hundreds, unless we stagger them. I better put RSVP, so that we shall get a vague idea about numbers.'

Monday and Tuesday were hectic, launching the advertising assault on the community. The response was immediate and encouraging.

They even had a call from the choir master of the Gilbert & Sullivan Society offering another performance or two of *Iolanthe* and donating the proceeds to the Children's Village.

'I have spoken to most of the cast, explained what it is for, and they all wants to help. Almost everybody is free at the weekend in two weeks' time, so if it is alright with you, we shall advertise for two repeat performances, one on the Saturday and a matinee on the Sunday again. And we shall have the buckets out for extra donations!'

'You are a treasure, Rob! That would be wonderful!' Karin was almost overwhelmed by the generosity of the people around her – considering that she didn't know them all that long. She felt keenly that, when all this was over, she should pay back some of the kindness and join the Volunteers; maybe she could persuade Tilly to do the same.

However, first things first. They had to concentrate on their coffee morning. The local baker's had already promised a chocolate and a cheesecake with some doughnuts thrown in for good measure.

'I shall do fruit flans', said Karin, neither an enthusiastic nor a successful baker. 'Well, I shall buy the bases and put custard, bananas, grapes, mandarins and pineapple pieces on it. I can't really go wrong with it.'

'And I shall make tons of scones, so you only have to buy the jam and whip the cream.'

They asked other neighbours: An elderly woman promised a walnut loaf, a young mother was happy to contribute a pavlova, which was the favourite of her own family; someone else promised a lemony sponge cake; someone ambitious offered a tart tartin, and several people were honest enough to own up in advance that they would go out and buy something from the supermarket.

Karin and Tilly made a list of positive replies to the invitation. They were astonished how many people wanted to come.

'Tilly, I think we should decorate the room.'

'With balloons and tinsel?'

'No, I mean, in a Bangladeshi style.'

Tilly looked lost. 'I haven't got anything.'

'Of course, you haven't!' Karin laughed. 'You are doing enough as it is. I thought of draping my old saris, offer some Bengali Cha and Bombay Mix; I can bring some souvenirs down from my room, a bit of Bengali music – I have a few CDs.'

'That sounds lovely – different.'

'Yes, I hope it puts everybody in the mood for giving. We'll lay out the charity newsletters which people can take away with them; they might even become members and support the Children's Village regularly.

'You think of everything, don't you,' Tilly patted her friend's shoulder in admiration. 'I think we are set! Roll on, Saturday!

They had another big surprise – they hadn't realised that there was a Bengali family living in Poynton. Karin had never met nor even seen them.

On Tuesday morning the doorbell rang, and when Karin opened the door, apron clad and covered in flour because they had started baking Tilly's scones, a Bengali lady, a coat over her *sari*, and her black hair wound into a *beni*, stood outside, greeting her with a shy smile.

'You organise coffee morning?' she began in heavily accented English.

'Yes, we do; for an orphanage in Bangladesh. Are you Bengali?'

'Yes, and I want to help. Can I bring home-made sweets… or savouries… on Saturday?'

'That would be perfect. Thank you so much for offering. Come on in. My friend Tilly and I are just baking scones for Saturday. What's your name?'

'Ruma. We live other end of village.'

'Tilly, this is Ruma, and she will bring Indian nibbles on Saturday.' The three of them grinned at each other. They had found another team member, a kindred spirit.

৲৩ন্ঞ

The rest of the week went in a hectic blur. Jasmine and Esme had helped to pick up contributions from the shops, but then Jasmine had taken her daughter away, anticipating a crowd of adults and not much fun for a little girl. Karin, Tilly and Ruma continued to set up the buffet with food and drinks – coffee, tea and soft drinks – and when all was done, they waited for those guests. who had promised to add to it or tothe bring-and-buy table. Tilly suggested that she should stand by the door with the raffle tickets trying to corner people as they entered. However, Karin objected.

'We don't want to harass our guests the moment they arrive.' Karin wrinkled her forehead while weighing up what would be best. 'I think you should take one of the trestle tables and sit prominently in a corner, but let people come to you.'

'Okay,' Tilly relented, and Ruma added diplomatically: '…but you must have sign 'Raffles' and I am sure, they not mind you call them or walk around to offer tickets.' This was the longest sentence in English they had heard Ruma say, since she had joined them. She herself seemed to be taken aback by her audacity, but when she saw the two women grin, she smiled with modesty and a little pride.

'Great idea!' Karin agreed. She felt nervous and was glad to have these two excellent women at her side.

'How many are coming?' she asked for the umpteenth time, and Tilly only laughed:

'Roughly a hundred at the last count.'

'Goodness!' Karin clapped her hand over her mouth. She certainly hadn't expected such a good response.

'My Bombay Mix looks meagre next to the Indian snacks. What is in them?' Karin felt tempted by their smell to try one

240

of each but they would have to fulfil a function: To please their guests enough to donate handsomely.

'I make lamb and vegetable samosas,' she accompanied her words with sideways nods of the head, 'onion *bhajis* and spicy vegetable *pakoras*; two hundred – enough?' Ruma looked at her new friend anxiously.

'You must have taken all week to make them! Thank you so much, Ruma!'

'It is pleasure,' she said modestly, 'it is little I can do for children at home.'

Tilly quickly wrote a big sign saying RAFFLES, and a couple of minutes later, the first visitors arrived. After an hour, most of Poynton's residents huddled in Karin's sitting room, some little groups having spilt into the corridor and even the kitchen. Ruma was in charge of the drinks, Tilly proved to be extremely cunning with selling her raffle tickets without upsetting the guests; most of them left her table laughing. The raffle prize table had filled up with alcoholic bottles, hand-knitted dolls, embroidered doylies and a cushion cover, even some home-crafted necklaces and greeting cards. Someone had brought an expensive looking vase, whispering while handing it over, that the owner had always hated the brash colours. There were pots of home-made marmalade, jam and chutneys and a couple of tins of soup and chickpeas.

Poynton had done itself proud and Karin felt a sudden surge of great happiness at the thought that she had moved here.

At times, the crush in the sitting room was a little dangerous with everyone holding a cup and saucer or a glass, until people put them down on window sills and every other available space to take a plate and serviette and storm the buffet like locusts.

To Karin's joy, Jasmine and Esme returned earlier than planned: 'She wanted to be part of it,' said Jasmine with mock exasperation.

'Of course, she would!' said Karin, relieved that her daughter had at last shown some sensibility.

'My daughter, Jasmine, and my grand-daughter Esme,' Karin introduced them to the assembled crowd.

Guests, who had been preparing to leave, were captured by this vivacious child and put yet another donation into the basket proffered by the little hands.

When people finally began to drift away after much longer than Karin, Tilly and Ruma had anticipated, the hosts were showered with compliments about the food, the décor of draped saris, the Indian music piped discreetly into the room, the charity work they were supporting, the hilarious raffle ticket prize giving – someone had recognised an item which seemed to have made the rounds of several earlier village events – and the jolly atmosphere.

'We all live in the same village, but we never see each other from one week to the next,' said one woman, 'unless somebody organises something like this. Thank you! And I hope you will do it again!'

Karin wasn't sure about that, but she smiled obligingly and thanked the lady for her generosity. Glancing furtively at the various baskets labelled 'donations' and placed discreetly round the room, she judged that it had been well worth doing.

'And don't forget the *Iolanthe* performance next Saturday evening and Sunday afternoon,' they reminded everybody before they left. In fact, quite a few members of the cast had turned up, too, and rolled their eyes jokingly: 'How can we, we are in it!'

'Keep us informed about those wells,' said a gentleman whom they knew as the local plumber, 'the least these children deserve is decent water. I have taken a few leaflets and shall give them to my colleagues and customers.'

Another young chap, who said he was a businessman and in computers, promised similar help, and the local doctor, who had popped in for a short while, took the rest of the leaflets and a poster to display in his surgery's waiting room.

'Always a good idea to show people that others are worse off than they are!' he said tapping the side of his nose.

When everybody had left, Karin, Esme and Ruma threw themselves onto the settee, while Tilly announced that she would make a strong cup of tea for everybody.

'Shall we open the bubbly?' asked Karin, but they shook their heads.

'Keep that for when we are not quite so exhausted.'

They couldn't believe how generous people had been; they counted the money from the baskets and the proceeds from the raffle tickets: nine hundred and twenty-five pounds and thirty-two pence. They grinned at the tuppence but somebody might have simply rid their purse of small change.

'I shall make that up to a thousand pounds,' announced Jasmine perched on the settee's armrest; it earned her a warm hug from her mother.

When they related the good news over the telephone to Mrs Bellamy at the Charity's headquarters, they were told that her own fundraising efforts had been equally successful: 'We are lucky,' the founder said, 'that we have a couple of wealthy members in London and the southern counties. So I have the pleasure of announcing that so far, we have raised fifteen thousand Pounds.'

'That's wonderful,' Karin exclaimed and added: 'And of course, we still have the proceeds from the Gilbert & Sullivan show to come. Will that be enough for the wells?'

'It will take us certainly a good deal forward. And best of all, one of our kind members has underwritten to pay for the rest; whatever is needed to finish it all.'

Karin just stopped herself from saying 'wonderful' again – but wasn't it just!

'So now, I shall call Dr Abdullah in Bangladesh and tell him the good news. I shall probably fly out in a couple of weeks to see what's happening and to take the money with me. In any case, they can get on with it now. For the moment, they have the Government grant to pay the labourers and engineers.'

An hour later, they had an excited call from Ali and Martha thanking them for their efforts.

'It is such a relief!' Ali said. 'I don't know what's happening here. Everything has come to a standstill, and the Headmaster looks continuously worried. Tell your friends that you are all angels, and that we are very grateful!'

'I think, I will get out the bubbly,' Karin announced. It had been a good day!

Chapter Thirty-Five

༃

Ali crossed the yard from his class room, walked underneath the swinging roots and branches of the Banyan tree for a quick visit to his study next to the Headmaster's office.

He was happy with this afternoon's teaching. He had managed to introduce a group of older girls to Elizabeth Barrett-Browning's love poem: How do I love Thee? Let me count the ways, a small extract from her Sonnets of the Portuguese. As he had expected, the girls found – once the lines had been translated with Sara's help – romantic, and at the end of the lesson, they walked out slowly with dreamy eyes and entranced smiles. Success! Ali had asked each of them to learn a couple of lines by heart, which ever ones they liked best.

The newly introduced debating class for the older boys, which had been the last lesson of the afternoon, had also gone better than expected. Bengali children were hardly ever asked for their opinions but rather expected to do as they were told by their elders. Ali hoped to change that in small steps so that the young men in his care would learn to stand up for themselves later in life and could hold their own with confidence. Drawing on his recent experience of Sunderban, Ali had chosen a debate on environmental protection with particular reference to landscapes, animals and birds. As usual, his students had surprised him with their thoughtfulness, quick grasp of the subject and logical arguments. They brought up the topic of dredging rivers, without prompting, to stop flooding; then drilling proper wells for safe drinking water which, after what had happened to their friends, was no surprise; then the topics just tumbled out of them:

Stopping the extinction of rare animals by a hunting ban; for over-fishing the rivers and seas which included the shrimp farms in the south of the country destroying natural habitats and the livelihoods of local farmers; and, deviating a little from the topic, arguments for improvements in the population's general hygiene for the sake of everybody's health, in particular that of children; someone also mentioned birth control but the question was followed by an embarrassed silence which Ali quickly dispersed by suggesting that that could be a topic all on its own for a future debate. However, he was astonished and heartened when a final vote among his students resulted in the unanimous support of the protection of nature in their country. There you are, Ali thought. They put us adults to shame; the politicians better listen to the new generation! Everybody had shown courage to express their ideas and opinions and had put them forward eloquently and well thought out, sticking to the maxim Ali had introduced of 'first think than speak.' It had been a good afternoon indeed!

Ali hastened his steps. He would only have a quick glance at today's mail and deal with it tomorrow morning during his free period after assembly. Tonight, he wanted to cook a nice meal for Martha who was busier than ever organising the after-wedding reception in secret. Only he knew how much she needed cheering up.

Elizabeth Barrett-Browning's poem would be most suitable, it suddenly occurred to him. It could be either declaimed by one or each line by a different student. I shall suggest it to Martha, he thought.

He opened the unlocked door to his office. Keeping doors unlocked was a principle of the Headmaster. It meant to instil trust and respect for each other.

The mail lay on Ali's desk; Sara usually brought it in as soon as it was delivered. Nobody had touched it; it was still in a neat bundle held together by an elastic band. He took it off and glanced at the names of the senders. There was nothing urgent by the looks of it. Only one envelope intrigued him. He opened the unusual envelope sliding his finger underneath the flap and ripping it open. It was a bill from the company who had provided the pipes for the new wells. Ali hadn't expected the total amount to be so high. He stared at it until it suddenly dawned on him that the bill had been issued for the purchase of steel pipes, not the plastic ones that had arrived. It was baffling. There surely must be a mistake! Ali looked at the top of the letter which, he only noticed now, was addressed to Kirash, the new treasurer. There would be hell to pay, if Kirash found out that one of his letters had been opened. Ali looked again at the envelope: No, it was addressed to The Children's Village. The only sentence added in spidery handwriting at the bottom of the bill referred to negotiations between the company and Mr Kirash Abdullah and the special arrangements they had agreed on. What did that mean? Was the Children's Village supposed to pay this huge amount to the manufacturers which had delivered much cheaper products?

Ali took the receiver and rang the number on the letterhead. This needed clarification. All of a sudden, Kirash stormed into the office, snatched the invoice out of Ali's hand and said in an almost hysterical, high-pitched tone, rolling his 'R's furiously: 'This is for me! I told you to keep away from my responsibilities!' Then he stormed out, purple faced and with a flapping jacket.

Ali's suspicions were heightened and he decided to make this phone call after all. A flustered secretary put him through to the Managing Director of the pipe manufacturing company. At first, he took Ali to be Kirash and chatted on that, once the invoice had been paid, he would transfer the amount they had agreed on, to his private account.

'What amount are you referring to? Can you give me the exact amount again?'

'You know, as discussed, the difference between this invoice we sent and the original invoice for the plastic pipes. We had agreed to split the difference, hadn't we?' The Managing Director obviously was worried that Kirash might have changed his mind and would demand a bigger share of the loot.

'Interesting,' was all Ali said.

Only then did the Managing Director become suspicious that the silent at the other end of the line might not be the same as the one with whom he had made the corrupt arrangements. He began to stutter and then fell silent himself.

'You misunderstand,' he suddenly spoke in broken English.

'He bully me; he force me. I not guilty.'

'Thank you,' Ali interrupted him curtly and hung up. He would make sure that this particular bill would not be paid, at least not in full.

Luckily, he had taped the conversation on his mobile for future reference.

ஐௐ

The Children's Village was abuzz with preparations to send off their beloved Dr Chowdhury who was about to visit his future wife's parents for the first time. He intended to ask for her hand in marriage. Vijay quipped that he had no chance; they would not give their lovely daughter to him. Dr Chowdhury waved his cupped hands in the air, as if to strangle the boy.

'You_wouldn't do that! You just saved my life,' the boy laughed and ran away.

Lessons were disjointed and the children inattentive because nobody wanted to miss the moment when they would send off the prospective groom. This was one of the highlights of every Bengali's life; of course, they had to be there!

Ali finally had enough of the exasperatingly distracted students and sent a note round to Dr Abdullah for permission to dismiss classes for the rest of the day. It was granted, and an hour later, the entire school stood at the gates, waving off a suddenly coy and nervous looking man, carrying a battered suitcase full of presents for the people he hoped would become his in-laws.

Sara stood at the back biting her lip and twiddling a lock of her black hair. She waved wildly after the disappearing figure but was sure that he couldn't make her out in the crowd.

Falling in love had been a surprise; being asked to marry the object of her secret affection was overwhelming. Now that it was really happening and her family would soon know, her knees buckled, her head was spinning and her heart thumped like blows of a woodpecker's beak.

It was almost too good to be true.

No doubts, no obstacles too high, she and Aresh had agreed, Only love, loyalty and cooperation.

They would have a wonderful life!

Two days later, she received the news that her parents had

accepted Aresh's proposal and that they had begun arrangements for the wedding. Could she please, travel to her home village as soon as possible?

'Of course, you must go immediately,' Mr Abdullah insisted, but Sara had suddenly become tongue-tied and almost panicky.

'Go now,' Martha laughed and gave her a reassuring hug. 'All brides are nervous and in panic. It is a big decision and the most important time in your life.' And looking at her totally flustered friend, she took her by the shoulders:

'Come on, I'll help you pack. I reckon the first thing you will do when you arrive, will be buying your wedding sari. Your family will drag you from shop to shop to buy it.'

'There aren't many shops where we live,' Sara whispered pathetically, 'and frankly, I am past caring.'

'You will love the celebrations and you will love to be married, Sara. And we shall all wait for your return to give us a blow by blow account; and you must bring your wedding sari back; we want to admire you in it! And just imagine, you will come back as Mrs Chowdhury and live happily ever after.'

Martha realised that she was going over the top but she hoped she could make her friend snap out of her anxiety to enjoy the wonderful prospect of what was to come.

'And you won't be alone for long. Aresh and your family will pick you up from the other side of the river and I bet they will insist on heaping flower garlands around your neck; everybody will be so happy to see you!'

'I think they had given up hoping that I would ever get married,' Sara joked with a meek voice.

'There you are then,' Martha padded her on the back.

Finally, Sara was ready, and the children and staff managed to give her an equally boisterous send-off before Harun, the caretaker, drove her in the school's battered Morris Oxford to the nearest ferry port. As they rattled out of the gates, Martha saw her friend turning in the seat and waving frantically through the rear view window. Be happy! Martha blew her fervent wish towards the disappearing car and was rewarded by Sara's huge and happy smile.

℘ℭ

Ali's conscience was heavy with the discovery of what the Headmaster's nephew was up to.

On the one hand, he felt like storming into Shamsur's office to tell him about the invoice and to play the recording to him. He knew he would cause distress in one way or another: distress over the protégé's fraudulent dealings and distress of the discovery of it. Ali couldn't imagine that Mr Abdullah would condone corruption, but he was also old enough to realise that one could never be entirely sure about people's motivations and what really lay behind their actions.

Ali half expected that his boss might feel compelled to defend Kirash and the family honour. On the other hand, he might resent that his own reputation was put at stake and resort to protecting it. All these years of dutiful service to the charity, it would surely be unbearable to lose the confidence and trust of his staff and employers. Ali knew that much though, that whichever path the Headmaster would choose, it would cause the old man great pain.

Martha had been predictably on the side of honesty and, if necessary, confrontation.

'You can't let that young rogue get away with it. If he isn't punished now he will just carry on to be dishonest all through his life and be one of the thousands who squirrel away the country's money in their private bank accounts. What Bangladesh needs is a whole generation of people who actually want to help their country, protect it, use every penny they earn or are given in aid to improve its infrastructure and genuinely make the lives of their own people better,' she argued hotly and added with indignation: 'Not somebody like him – selfish, self-serving and not giving a damn about his fellow citizen!'

'Here endeth the next lesson,' Ali quipped. Martha was absolutely right but there was still the small matter of how to tell the Headmaster.

Ali waited for a quiet moment when the children would be tucked up in bed and most of the adults had settled in their own quarters to read, check their e-mails or potter. Ali caught sight of the Headmaster as he walked towards the bungalow next to the offices which served as his residence.

'Good evening, Shamsur. Can I have a quick word?'

'Joining me for a nightcap, Ali?'

Only the most trusted members of staff knew that the Headmaster was partial to a glass of port in the evenings. The supplies were usually smuggled in when Mrs Bellamy, the Charity's English founder, and her husband came for inspection visits. It was seen as a kind gesture, nothing extraordinary in England but a fact to be kept quiet in a Muslim environment. Ali and Martha thought this little weakness quite endearing.

'I will, Shamsur,' Ali agreed.

The Headmaster's sitting room looked out directly onto the yard with the Banyan tree in its middle. It was furnished with old rattan armchairs, made more comfortable by green and white patterned seat cushions. Shamsur uncorked a bottle and took two plain wine glasses from a mirrored cabinet. He put them on the low coffee table between them and filled them half with the thick, almost black liquid of vintage port.

'Ah,' Shamsur visibly relaxed at the glugging sound of port being received and cradled by the glasses. He sat down opposite Ali and savoured the first careful sip. 'Ah,' he said again, leant back in his chair and closed his eyes in rapture. As if emerging from a dream, he smiled at Ali and said:

'Fire away.' Ali was tempted to say that it was nothing; that it could wait. It would be a pity to destroy the man's peace of mind and the tranquillity of the evening. There was no way to soften the blow, to embellish the truth; the news would have the same effect in the morning or at any other time.

Ali felt Shamsur's eyes on him, waiting, observing. Looking up from his hand holding the stem of the glass, he took courage, looked him in the face and told him what he had discovered.

To his surprise, Shamsur did not get upset. He sat there calmly considering his glass of port as if he had fallen into deep thought.

'I wanted to tell you before anybody else noticed.'

'You did the right thing.' Shamsur said, his words detached from his feelings and the stark truth as if still in a trance.

Ali drained his glass. 'Will you be alright?' he asked.

Shamsur nodded: 'Oh yes!' It sounded determined and deeply disappointed at the same time.

'If you want, we can talk it over. I don't mind being your sounding board.'

'No, no, Ali. You go home to your wife. I shall deal with this.' and like an afterthought he added: 'I would be grateful if you didn't tell anybody else.'

'Of course, not!' He wanted to reassure his boss that he could always count on his support and discretion, but Shamsur had got up and had escorted him swiftly back to the entrance.

As Ali stood in the open door, he turned round:

'I'm so sorry, Shamsur.'

'That's quite alright. You did your duty.' The Headmaster looked suddenly old and tired beyond his years; his body seemed to be shrinking, together with his will to carry on. His eyes had dulled as if they had developed a grey film to keep reality outside. Ali failed to find words to console him.

'Good night then.'

'Good night, Ali.'

৪৩০০৪

That night, ominous news trickled through the villages along the river banks until it flew through the gates of the Children's Village: An over-crowded ferry had capsized in the afternoon. No one knew how many passengers had survived.

Chapter Thirty-Six

❦

'Martha … Martha… please, slow-down.' Karin could hardly understand the garbled half-sentences which were tumbling across the vast distance, accompanied and blurred by hysterical sobs. All she had figured out so far was that there had been an accident and that someone from the Children's Village had been involved.

'Is Ali there? Can you give the telephone to him, Martha?' What if it was Ali who had been hurt? Fear struck Karin's heart.

'It's Sara, my best friend,' was followed by uncontrollable sobs. 'She drowned.' Martha screamed into the mouth piece, 'The ferry sank and Sara drowned.'

'What's the matter?' asked Jasmine who had just come down the stairs and had overhead her mother's efforts to come someone down, whoever it was at the other end of the line.

'It's Martha,' Karin mouthed; 'something about a ferry disaster and her friend Sara drowning.'

What?' Jasmine, who had just sat down on the settee, was stung into jumping up and staring at her mother with horror.

'But Sara is the young woman who is getting married to the doctor next weekend.' She whispered, unexpected tears welling up in her eyes.

'Can I speak to her?' Her mother handed over the receiver, numb with shock.

'Martha, it's Jasmine here.' The hysterical sobs had turned into whimpering like that of an animal in agony. 'Martha, we are so sorry! Is there anything we can do? Is Ali with you?'

'No, all the men have gone to the ferry port.' The sentence was almost too long to sustain. The pain shredded the voice.

'Martha, is there anything we can do? Do you want us to inform Mrs Bellamy?'

'Yes, I suppose so.' The silence was only interrupted by groans.

'Do you want us to come over?'

In the midst of this agonising turmoil, Karin listened up to process what she had just heard: Jasmine offering to abandon work and flying out to help?

'Everything is going wrong,' she heard Martha wringing for breath.

'Everything is going wrong; nothing is going right. I wish we had never come!'

'Let me speak to her again,' Karin reached for the receiver.

'Darling Martha, would you like to come over for a break; to gather your strength and to have some thinking time?' Silence… 'Maybe not immediately; but do think about it. I hope Ali returns soon to be at your side…' They knew that every word of consolation was futile; nothing they said would make a difference. No words were adequate to describe the tragedy.

'The Headmaster is here to keep things going.' Martha said out of context.

'Stay close to him until Ali gets back. You all need each other now. He must be terribly upset himself.'

'And poor Aresh!' Martha burst into bitter tears again and moaned with pain. 'They were supposed to get married at the weekend…'.Martha's heart was beaten to the ground. The world was dark and cruel and closing in on her.

They heard a male voice in the background: 'I have to go now; I am calling from the Head's office,' Martha whispered hastily, and her words were trailing away.

'Let me speak to him briefly,' Karin coaxed her gently. The sobs retreated into the background: 'Abdullah speaking. Is that Mrs Khan?'

'Yes, it is. We are so shocked and sorry about your loss.'

'Thank you. You are very kind.' The Headmaster sounded heartbroken.

'Your son Ali has gone to the river bank to fetch Sara's body and to bring Dr Chowdhury home.'

'Will you keep an eye on Martha for us? She loved Sara and she is totally distraught. We wish we could be there with you and share your pain and to help... but could you please look after Martha until Ali gets back?'

'Of course, I will. Thank you for your concern. This is not an easy time for any of us.'

'I know, and we share in your grief. We shall inform Mrs Bellamy if that is okay with you.'

'Oh, would you? That is one less thing for me to think about.'

'That's the least we can do. And we shall stay in touch. May we ring again?'

'Of course! Your emotional support is very important.' There was nothing more to be said, and they both hung up.

'Isn't life fragile; everything can change in a moment...' was all Karin could bring herself to say. It was the first time that she saw tears streaming down her daughter's face.

𖠿𖠿𖠿

Karin and Jasmine took it in turns to ring every two hours. Sometimes they got through; at other times the line was crackling or faint; once they spoke to one of the older girls who seemed to stand in at the reception desk. Finally they got hold of Mr Abdullah again, but the news was still the same: Ali and his colleagues were still away to identify and bring back Sara.

According to the Headmaster, Ali had rung in only once in the middle of noisy chaos just to let them know that he had located Dr Chowdhury and Sara's family, who were understandably distraught and frantically searching for her.

'We might still be here for a couple of days,' Ali had said. 'It is mayhem!'

'I did tell him to take his time,' Dr Abdullah sounded defensive through the phone, as if someone had accused him of some indefinable negligence: 'I did tell him to look after himself.'

'That's good,' Karin tried to sooth the poor man's anxiety of having failed in some way: 'Thank you, Mr Abdullah. That is very kind.'

'I would have gone with them, but somebody has to keep the Children's Village safe.'

'Of course, you do! It must be so difficult to keep the ship steady when there is so much turmoil!'

'Thank you for your understanding.' Mr Abdullah had obviously been fighting an inner battle about his decision not to join the other men. He had himself had needed somebody to confirm, that he had done the right thing.

If they could have seen him through the telephone, they would have been shocked: His face was ashen with dark circles underneath his eyes, framed by bags like dunes around a black beach. With one hand, he had to hold on to the edge of his desk to steady himself while holding the receiver with the other.

'How are the children coping?' Karin asked.

'Some of them are beside themselves; others are very subdued; most of them are crying…' There was a pause, as if the Headmaster himself had to wipe tears away. 'Martha is a great help,' he finally continued haltingly, 'we have carried on with some sort of teaching, the female staff covering for their male colleague. But it's hopeless…' He didn't have the strength to say more.

Judging by the silence in the background, Karin imagined that the children were walking from class room to classroom in a hush, their cheerful chatter and raucous laughter having died.

'We are all heart-broken…' The Headmaster sounded as if he was going to collapse.

'We are praying for you, and if you don't mind, we shall ring again.'

'Thank you,' was all Karin could understand before she heard the click ending the call.

໓໑໕

Even thousands of miles away, the gloomy shadow of loss descended and a painful daze gripped the house in Poynton.

Jasmine waited till the evening meal to impart her news:

'I know this is not a time for celebrating; I just wanted you to know that I have passed my exams.'

'Does that mean …?'

'Yes, I am a barrister.' Jasmine said simply.

Something has happened to my daughter, Karin thought.

She has turned some sort of corner. She has become more thoughtful, considerate, aware of other people's feelings. She got up from the table and gave her a hug:

'Congratulations, darling!'

Jasmine smiled almost apologetically.

'You have a very clever Mum, Esme. Do give her a hug, too!'

They were standing together, united in a small circle of warm light, like sheltering under a parasol against the harshness of the world; they felt safe and strong.

They thought of Sara, her poor fiancé, her family, the staff and children at the orphanage, but most of all, they thought of the two people who belonged into this circle, however far away they were. They had to be strong for them.

ഇറങ

In the evening, they sat on the stylish furniture, pretending to read a book or magazine; nobody felt like a glass of wine or nibbles; even little Esme had gone to bed without a word of protest. Tilly, whom they had called for moral support, was the first to turn in, yawning behind her hand.

'You don't mind, do you?'

'Of course, not! I just think I won't be able to sleep,' replied Karin.

'We can't even console ourselves, that tomorrow will be a better day; tthe pain will still be there,' Tilly murmured sadly. 'Good night then.'

Karin and Jasmine continued to read for a few minutes until Jasmine put her newspaper down onto the low table and looked at her mother:

'Are you willing to talk?'

'Yes.' Karin knew that any 'You know that I am always willing,' or 'of course, you should know that,' would have been counterproductive; not a good way to encourage her daughter to open up.

'I don't know any more whether I am doing the right thing about Hamid.'

'Go on.' No remonstrations or taking of sides,' Karin reminded herself; she had learnt to hold her tongue. Jasmine paused as if waiting for an 'I told you so'. When it never came, she carried on: 'Esme does like him to be around, and I have begun to wonder whetherI am depriving her of the right to know, that he is her father. I might also do an injustice to Hamid. I do like him, I always did. He is a steadfast man; he was always good company, and he is obviously loyal and prepared to take over his share of responsibility. The only thing is, I just don't know whether I'll be any good at a relationship, living with somebody.'

'You live with me.' Karin pointed out, 'and Esme and sometimes Tilly. You are doing pretty well with.'

This took some time to sink in. Obviously Jasmine had not considered that she was already sharing her house and life with people.

'That's true,' Jasmine finally conceded. Karin saw a little pleasantly surprised smile playing around Jasmine's mouth. 'I just don't know whether I can love him!'

'Do you mean "again"?'

Karin wouldn't have put it past her daughter to have entered the relationship with Hamid with a cold heart. Maybe it hadn't been a relationship at all; maybe Esme had been conceived in a one-night-stand? But then, would Hamid be so adamant that he wanted to be part of his child's life and even offer Jasmine a permanent liaison? Karin realised that she knew absolutely nothing about her daughter's fling with Hamid. If he hadn't turned up, she would have remained forever in the dark.

'How long were you with Hamid?'

Jasmine swallowed hard: Confessions and revelations had always been difficult for her, but she realised that this time she couldn't shrug the question off with a simple wave of the hand, followed by clamming up.

'It happened before you moved here. I was looking for a BPTC (Bar Professional Training Course) provider; so was Hamid and we met trying to get into a very heavy door. Hamid let me go first and held it open for me. Afterwards we went for a drink together.'

Karin held her breath: So it was a one-night-stand?

'We kept in touch, went to restaurants, until one evening he cooked for me, and it led to other things.' She searched in her mother's face whether there was any sign of shock.

'For goodness sake, Jasmine, you are a young woman. Why shouldn't you have a love life?' Jasmine looked amused at her mother's outburst.

'Well, that's what we had for a few months, until he started to talk about moving in with him and meetings his parents. I just panicked, but he didn't understand why. So one day, I decided, I wouldn't answer his calls anymore. Of course, he came to my office – I had never given him my address – and I told him, that it was over; that I wanted out. Luckily, he didn't discover that I was already pregnant.'

'And that's when you rang me in London?'

'Yes, Mum. I just couldn't cope with career, baby and a husband. I had it all mapped out: The first would be fine with your help, but a man constantly interfering, telling me what to do, having a say in my decisions. And then I thought of you and Abbu; that you gave up your career to be with him; that you were supposed to be happy with just making him happy, pampering him, having no say in major decisions…' she paused before continuing: 'After all, Hamid had had the same sort of upbringing. I wouldn't have lasted in your marriage five minutes! How you stuck it out for years I shall never know!'

Jasmine was exhausted. She had hardly ever produced such a flow of thoughts, tinged with genuine anguish.

'Is Hamid really like Abbu?' Karin asked. 'For a start, he belongs to a new generation. He grew up in England, he is an intelligent, professional man, and probably much more enlightened than your father's generation was able to be. Did you ever feel that Hamid tried to bully you into things?'

'If I am honest: no! It was me who panicked at the first whiff of commitment.'

'You didn't give it a chance, did you?' Karin tried to sooth away any feelings of guilt, blame and stress. 'It might have turned out fine, maybe even brilliant. You have a good head on your shoulders, darling. Start again! Make the right decision this time! And then you must talk to Hamid and tell him about all your fears, your insecurities and their background, so that he can understand. He will probably have some reservations after what you have put him through, but if you work together, respect and cherish what binds you together, why shouldn't it work?'

Jasmine got up, walked over to her mother who sat in her favourite, chintzy armchair and planted a kiss on her forehead.'

'I should have talked to you a long time ago, shouldn't I?'

'Better la…'

'Yes, I know. Thank you.'

When Jasmine had gone upstairs, Karin allowed herself a tiny triumphant victory gesture and a whispered: 'Yes!'

Things might turn out well for her daughter and granddaughter after all.

ॐ

They heard from Bangladesh daily. Everybody there sounded distraught, disheartened and exhausted. In spite of the tragedy, the school and workshops still had to be run; the wells were not completed and half the workforce had disappeared. Nobody seemed to know why. tThe oh so brilliant and slippery new treasurer kept a low profile, and the Headmaster had taken to locking himself into his study.

It was Martha who kept the family in Manchester informed, as the week went on, with more and more distress in her voice.

'It's all falling apart. We have cancelled everything, the cricket tournament, disbanded the choir – nobody feels like singing; Sara played such a big part in everything.'

'And how is Ali?'

'Busy and … distant.' Karin had never heard Martha so dispirited. 'He hardly talks to me.'

'Do you think you could take a few weeks off and come here? We would love to have you, and it would give you an opportunity to recharge your batteries.'

'That would be nice. I'll think about it. I am not sure if I can, but thanks for the offer.'

ॐ

Karin found the phone call unsettling. Martha sounded, different, unhappy, deflated, dispirited. Yes, there had been the tragedy of Sara's death and worries about money matters to get the wells finished, but her unhappiness seemed to go deeper. Did she really mean that Ali was distancing himself from her? Was that because he preferred to bottle up his pain, to cope with his own feelings? The last thing Martha would expect was that he would shut her out. She would want them to stand together as a couple, unite in grief and adversity and decide on how to go forward together. Instead she felt stranded in isolation.

How sad for them both, and how frightening for Martha,' Karin thought, stroking absent-mindedly an invisible wisp of hair out of her face.

It never seemed to stop, this worrying about your children!

Chapter Thirty-Seven

ᙄᘓ

Martha waded through the dark days like an automaton. She had taken it upon herself to keep some resemblance of school activities going. Stretches of extreme busyness let her forget for a while her pain of losing her best friend Sara and the void of Ali's absence.

The headmaster seemed invisible; so was his nephew who had actually taken himself off in his swish car and had not been seen for two days. The children were tip-toeing around like little shadows and made every effort to be particularly well behaved which was a great help. Martha thanked them in assembly for being so considerate and making her task of keeping the teaching programme running, much easier.

Life was in suspense; everybody waited for Ali, Dr Chowdhury and their colleagues to return. The latest report had said that Sara would be buried in her home village, and that the men would all attend. Martha knew that Muslim burials took place rather quickly after someone's death and that women were discouraged from attending. To her great sorrow, she would not be able to say good-bye to her friend. It broke her heart! It was the men who would accompany Sara's body. They would have to stay until the ceremonies were over. It could still be days until they returned.

When they did, they looked grey, defeated, dragging themselves over the ground as if all energy had been sucked out of them. Dr Chowdhury had red-rimmed, almost inflamed eyes. He didn't say a word.

'We are here for you, Aresh,' she whispered. He only managed a nod, and after Martha had given him a silent hug, he retired immediately to his bungalow.

Then she turned to her husband who stood there with a blank stare and an almost a hunched back.

'Come on, honey. You must rest.'

Only then did she notice a young woman holding a baby, standing at a distance, sobbing silently into her achol. She must have come with the returning men who by now had deserted her and rushed to their quarters.

Martha walked over to the tall, painfully thin figure, who clutched her baby as if afraid that somebody might snatch it out of her arms. Martha bent her head in respect and said:

'*Salaam alaikum.*'

'*Walaikum salaam,*' the young woman whispered, barely audibly.

Martha saw Vijay rushing towards her:

'How is Mr Khan?' he asked, the question accompanied by short, fast breaths. His recovery had been slower than expected.

'He is fine but exhausted. Listen, could you ask this lady who she is and what she is doing here?'

As Vijay translated without hesitation, she thought that he might make a brilliant interpreter one day: charming, personable, great linguistic skill' definitely bright feathers in his cap – a chink of hope in an otherwise dark day.

'She says she was on the ferry. She lost her husband; her family doesn't want her back.'

'Why?' Martha was outraged.

'Two more mouths to feed.'

'And what about her husband's family?'

Vijay translated and Martha could see in the young woman's furtive glance that she was scared.

'She is afraid of her in-laws.' Vijay confirmed. 'She will end up being their servant.'

'How disgusting!' Martha was outraged. Vijay grinned apologetically.

'She will just have to stay here. Ask her if she would like that?' Martha did not hesitate a minute to take the decision upon herself. Well, nobody else was available or in a fit state to discuss it with her.

'She said, Ali invited her already,' said Vijay without addressing the young woman again.

'Did he now…' The words were like a warm shower to her heart; this impulsive compassion was one of the things she had always loved about her husband. It had still been lurking under all his diplomacy. He was not so different from her after all!

'Vijay, could you please ask one of the girls, Shazia, Safda or Sufi, to take her over to the accommodation and help her to settle in? They can explain to her what we are about. And tell her that if she likes it, she can stay.'

'I shall.'

Martha smiled at Vijay who was growing into such a nice, reliable young man.

'I have to see to Ali now.'

'Of course, you do. Leave it to me!'.

As she walked away, she observed him bending down, saying a few soothing words to the young mother, stroking the dark shock of hair of the baby boy, sleeping, his head on his mother's shoulder. Then he led them over to the Village's little hospital to find the nurses. He had matured indeed!

I don't even know her name; I forgot to ask, Martha scolded herself as she strode back to the bungalow.

As she opened the door, she could hear her husband's noisy and regular breathing. He lay sprawled on top of the bedspread, fully clothed and fast asleep. She planted a gentle kiss on his soft lips. Then she lay next to him, a protective arm over his chest.

I better tell Shamsur that a new mother and her child have moved in,

Martha thought with a start. She got up silently, disentangling herself in slow motion, not to wake Ali. He seemed oblivious to the world.

She rushed across the yard and knocked on the Headmaster's door.

'Come in,' she heard the tiredness in his voice.

He was sitting in his leather chair, hands folded on a pile of papers on his desk and looking at her through his reading glasses.

'Shamsur, I just wanted to tell you that Ali has brought back one of the ferry survivors with her baby.'

'Why hasn't anybody informed me?'

'Sorry, we were all busy. I sent her to the nurses to check her over and to help her settle in.'

'She can't stay here. We haven't got enough space, and we are running out of money.'

Martha thought she had misheard and carried on:

'Shamsur, we can't send her away!'

He looked at her menacingly.

Martha was aghast; he wasn't serious, was he? He surely could not be so cruel? Was he losing his mind?

'She has just survived a ferry disaster,' Martha pleaded even more fervently, 'her husband drowned, she has a baby, her parents don't want her and she is frightened of her in-laws; and you want to send her away?'

'We can't help everybody.' He shouted not even looking at her.

'Shamsur, if that is your last word, if you think there isn't a spare bed for her, she will live in our bungalow. I am not sending a vulnerable young woman with a baby out into the world before she is ready. She is traumatised and she needs our help. A bed is the least we can give her!'

'Are you defying me, Mrs Khan?' It sounded odd and more like a threat than a question, mirrored by his steady, hostile stare.

'Oh, I have been relegated to being Mrs Kham now, have I?' she shouted back.

'I am still the Headmaster here; I make the rules, not you!' He waved her away, but she was not about to let it go.

'Shamsur, when I came here, I thought you were wonderful: compassionate, kind, enthusiastic, you had great presence and authority without being overpowering. Most of all, I admired your wisdom: Nothing was too much for the children and the young mothers. Now you are mean, ungenerous, unkind and obstructive. What has happened to you?'

The two looked at each other like prize fighters in the ring.

Martha took a deep breath and realised that she had overstepped the mark.

'If that is what you think of me you better not work here! This is my Children's Village, and I have been here a lot longer than you have. I suggest you leave as soon as possible.'

264

'And where does that leave Ali?' Martha was frantically afraid that she might have ruined both their careers.

'That's up to him.'

'Shamsur, I am sorry if... I just think we can't...' Martha felt sick at what she had done.

'Go!'

She looked at him pleadingly: 'Can't we at least discuss...?'

'No! Why don't you go and have a baby – like a normal woman.' It hit her like the hiss of a whip.

'I don't believe you said that, Shamsur!' she whispered.

Outside she allowed herself to let her tears flow. She didn't want Ali to wake with the news. He deserved a peaceful rest. She sat on the step of her bungalow and cried.

೮೧೮೩

Ali found her there an hour later, still sobbing. She told him in a few words what had happened. He didn't seem quite as perturbed as she was.

'We are all upset about Sara. I am sure he didn't mean it.'

The way the Headmaster had looked at her, full of hatred and disgust she didn't hold out much hope.

'You better see whether Monjuri needs anything.'

'Is that her name? And the baby?'

'I think she called him Robin... Don't worry. I'll speak to Shamsur.'

೮೧೮೩

Ali waited for an opportune moment when he thought the headmaster might have mellowed with his glass of port. In the event, his audience didn't last more than five minutes. Shamsur was abrupt and unfriendly; in fact, he was downright discourteous. Ali had never seen him like this. 'You better send that wife of yours back to America,' were his last words before he turned his back on Ali.

This was not like the man who had employed him. He understood that everybody was under great strain with Sara's death, Vijay almost dying from arsenic poisoning, the water wells still not being finished and the funds allegedly dwindling.

However, Ali suspected that there might be some other pressures at work,. For as long as Dr Abdullah kept them hidden, there was nothing Ali could do to help.

Now he had the unenviable task of suggesting to Martha that it might indeed be better if she left for − at least a while − until everything was back to normal and the emotional upheaval had subsided. He knew, Martha would hate to leave him to cope on his own but the way things were, she couldn't be of much help anyway.

✆✆

'I can't believe he spoke to you like that,' was Martha's horrified comment when Ali told her about his brief meeting with the Headmaster.

'He is upset but I think there is something else brewing; I can't quite put my finger on it. He is hiding something...' Ali mumbled to himself, not even looking at Martha.

'Did you ask him what else was bothering him?' she asked more sharply than she had intended. 'After all, you are his deputy and confidant − at least, you should be!'

'No. It's no use; he won't tell me anything. It's as if he is terrified to lose control and, even more so, to lose face.'

'As if 'saving face' is important when you try to help him solve a big problem! What happened to Say what you mean and mean what you say, our very own motto? Did you not have the courage?' Martha's voice almost flipped over with anger.

'It wasn't the right moment.' Ali looked at her with despondence, bewildered by an attack from a quarter whose support he had taken for granted.

'And did you talk about me?' Martha began to wonder what Ali really a had discussed during his brief attempt to sort things out.

'Yes, you were right: he does want you to leave. You both being at loggerheads, it might be the best solution; not for long, obviously; maybe just for a holiday until everybody has calmed down.' Ali brushed a strain of hair out of his eyes with a worn-out, slow-motion gesture. 'And please, don't shout at me.' She didn't hear his plea.

'You didn't think of defending me, did you?' Martha's thunderbolt accusation crushed him as if being hit by an avalanche. He stared at her in disbelief. Was that what their aims and dreams had come to?

'There was no point,' he said finally in a whisper, 'I did my best but he even shoved me out of his bungalow.'

'You could have tried a bit harder, Ali. I would have defended you to the death. I would have screamed and shouted, begged and negotiated hard. I would not have allowed him to throw all your good work and intentions back into your face. I would not have allowed him to send you away…!' Her voice flipped over with screams of frustration, bitterness and disappointment until they ended in more heart-breaking sobs. He took her in his arms, stroked her hair and shoulders and told her that he loved her.

By the end of the evening, he had soothed his wife, and they had agreed on a solution. Maybe they did need a break from each other.

'It's only for a short while,' he consoled her. 'If not, I'll come and join you.' Would he really? They had stopped looking at each other and to speak more than was necessary.

Like in a daze, they rang his mother and booked Martha's flights. Ali would take her to the airport at the weekend. They decided on a joyless truce for the last few days before her departure.

'I want to take part in Sara's memorial,' Martha said simply.

She felt more than ever, that Sara had meant an awful lot to her. She had been the one person she had turned to when she hadn't understood the customs of the land, the thinking of the men, the embellishments of facts, which drove her crazy because often they bordered on lies, complicating the simplest of truths. Sara had only shrugged her shoulders in resignation and sighed, pulling a funny face: 'They will learn sooner or later. Englishmen have learnt, so there is hope.'

Would Sara have found the right words to console her, now that she had lost Ali's support?

Sara had always managed to make her feel better. Nothing was too much. She was fun on top of being a moral support, very much like a beloved sister. She would miss her dreadfully!

For all she knew, she might even have lost the only other important person in her life, the only person she trusted with her life, the only person she allowed herself to lean on. She felt so alone…

The memorial service took place in the mosque, for the men only. When Martha had heard about that particular plan, she was outraged and planned her own celebration of Sara's life. It took the shape of a school assembly outside in the fresh morning air, the birds singing and the children performing.

Ali's students declaimed the love poem they had learnt originally for the wedding reception.

'How do I love thee…' a girl said, 'Let me count the ways… continued another…and so they took it in turns with sombre voices until they heard a deep sob and somebody running to bring a chair, so that the distraught Dr Chowdhury, as good as a widower, would not collapse onto the ground. Martha's heart went out to him but nobody in this world could take the pain away from him.

The younger girls performed a sombre dance they had practised for the young couple, and finally the choir sang Sara's favourite song: *Oliro kotha shune bokhul ashe* with Sufi, one of the nurses, singing the solo.

Finally, the Headmaster said a few closing words mentioning how everybody had loved and respected Sara, that she had been an efficient receptionist, and that she would have made a good wife to 'our beloved doctor.'

Surely, that can't be it, Martha thought. She looked around her. Pupils started already to shuffle their feet.

'I would like to say a few words.' Martha looked at Ali who nodded encouragingly, while the Headmaster kept his eyes fixed to the ground and his jaws clenched.

She didn't care anymore, stepped forward and spoke.

'Sara was my friend. She was everybody's friend. She would do anything for anybody. She was kind, generous, intelligent, patient and funny.'

Appreciative murmuring came from the children's ranks.

'Each of you will have a very special memory of her, like kind deeds, she distributed so liberally, a nice moment with her, something funny she said. To me she was the person who made

268

it easy for me to understand my new country, your country. She made me understand the differences and helped me to settle in, and she consoled me when both were hard to achieve. I owe her a great deal! We all have our own memories of our wonderful Sara and I would like to challenge you all: To commemorate her forever, to make her a firm part of the Children's Village's history. I want you all to write down or draw your memories of Sara, and I shall make them into a book for everyone to read. And I also challenge the boys to think of something to make in her honour, something lasting, something which reminds us every day of her. My husband Ali will collect your ideas and discuss them with you and your teachers. I shall be very curious what you come up with. But always remember, it is to commemorate a very special person.'

Martha stepped aside to a great, solemn silence, and then suddenly the children clapped their hands wildly and began to chant in unison: 'Sa-ra, Sa-ra…Sa-ra!' until Martha put her finger to her lips. 'Quietly,' she said with a smile, and they went away in orderly rows. Martha quickly checked whether she had offended the Headmaster again, but he had already disappeared.

On the last evening before her departure, Martha opened the door of her bungalow to a small delegation of teenage boys who shuffled shyly into her sitting room. Ali looked up rather baffled.

'Sir, Mrs Martha, we have discussed with teacher our project for Miss Sara.' They told her what they had decided on and that it should be kept secret until it was finished.

At first, Martha was speechless, shaking her head in disbelief at the ingenuity of these children.

'That is absolutely wonderful!' she finally exclaimed, forcing herself to be cheerful. In happier times, she would have given a hearty hug to each of them. Instead she said: 'Sara would have loved it! Good luck with the carpentry!' They shuffled away again. As they walked away back to their dormitories, she saw them congratulating themselves for their brilliant idea, slapping each other on the shoulder and holding their heads up high with importance.

'You are good with youngster, Martha,' Ali stood up and kissed her tenderly. 'They will miss you and will want you back. And so do I!'

'We'll see,' she couldn't be more specific than that.

269

Chapter Thirty-Eight

Jasmine and Karin rushed to the airport with a heavy heart. Ali had warned over the telephone that the Martha they would pick up, would be terribly upset, firstly, because she had to leave him behind and secondly because it could mean the end of their Bangladeshi dream.

'She didn't deserve the treatment she got,' he hinted. 'Nobody bothered to understand her. It was always about them, their customs, their feelings. And now she has lost the only person who had made an effort…'

So nothing much has changed, Karin thought, remembering her struggles to do something useful in a country which needed every help it could get. She hadn't stood a chance, forty-odd years ago because she didn't even have the support of her allegedly westernised husband. She had found out that the broad-mindedness, he had been so proud of, had only been skin-deep and had floated away at the slightest whiff of social scrutiny.

Karin closed her eyes for most of the drive to the airport while Jasmine made the most of her brand new BMW's powerful engine along the motorway. Both women were subdued because it was the last thing they had expected: That their golden couple would separate. Ali hadn't specified for how long Martha would stay; he had mentioned that, if possible at all, he would come as well, if only for a very short holiday.

At least little Esme was excited at the prospect of seeing her auntie Martha again: 'Will she get married again?' she asked hopefully; they knew she had been telling everyone about the wedding for weeks afterwards.

'No, darling, people are supposed to get married only once!'

The disappointed pout disappeared as soon as she saw Serena and Omar who were going to look after her, while Mummy and Granny would pick up auntie from the plane.

When the two women had arrived at the airport and parked the car, they jostled their way through the waiting crowd in the terminal and were shocked when they finally spied Martha, who looked thin, gaunt, her curly hair pulled severely out of her face and tamed with a grip at the back of her head. She had one suitcase which she dragged carelessly behind her on its wheels.

'Hi there' she said sadly and gave them a silent hug, gulping with emotion, unable to say more.

They raced back along the motorway and were glad when they arrived home, picking up Esme on the way. The little girl provided some much needed relief, giving auntie Martha a guided tour of the house, introducing her to her dolls and finally asking her to read her a story; she had already selected which ones and had the books ready, *Peter Rabbit* and *Jemima Puddle-Duck*.

'I like them, Auntie Martha,' she announced standing in front of her reader with arms folded across her chest.

'I haven't heard of them, honey, but if you like them I will like them, too.'

'*Peter Rabit*? And *Jemima Puddleduck*?' Esme's eyes widened in disbelief. Everybody knew the rabbit and the duck!

'No, Honey, remember, I grew up in America. I remember reading *My Friend Flicka* which was about a horse. But I am really curious now, so let's read them!' Esme settled next to her on the bed.

Jasmine and Karin left them both there. It was a welcome distraction. They would have days to talk about Martha's problems. In any case, they had agreed, they would not press her for information; they would wait for her to indicate that she was ready to tell them, what had happened. They were supposed to look after her and let her heal.

The new week began with mundane but good news: Serena's endless stream of essays had been accepted and been given reasonable marks. This left her free to look for a job, and before she could look at advertisements, the school she had spent the last few weeks at, had made her an offer. She would be starting as a junior teacher, working three days a week with the prospect of a full-time appointment once Omar would be in full-time education.

'That's fabulous. Serena! Congratulations!' They couldn't help feeling happy for her, in spite of their own worries.

'Why don't you come round one evening, so that we can have a proper talk, not just on the doorstep?'

That would be lovely. Friday okay?

'Friday will be absolutely fine. Jasmine will be here, too, and probably Tilly, so it will be solely a girls' evening.'

'Perfect. I could do with one! Shall I bring some snacks?

'Bengali?'

'Of course!'

'Yes, pleeease!' Karin drooled at the thought; Jasmine rolled her eyes which made everybody laugh even more.

୫୨୭୫

Martha spent most of Monday sleeping, reading and speaking to Ali on the phone as if to reassure herself, that he was still there, that she still had a husband somewhere in the world. Karin could feel, overhearing snippets, how dreadfully she missed him. This had never been part of their plan.

It was Tuesday, as Karin and Martha were washing up and drying late breakfast dishes, that Martha's dam of pent-up emotions burst. Luckily, Esme was already playing devotedly with her dolls in her room.

'I wonder sometimes whether this charity lark does any good,' Martha began.

Karin kept quiet.

'Most of the time I feel they don't want us there.'

'Go on…'

'It's not the work that is hard; it's battling against their old-fashioned and frankly sexist views; their antipathy of being told anything by Westerners, particularly Americans and – shock horror! – a woman!' she added sadly.

She told Karin about the poisoned drinking water and her outrage that hardly anybody with any official clout had taken much notice: 'Vijay almost died. How can they ignore such a fundamental catastrophe? If we hadn't taken action, many more children would have died and nobody would have cared.'

'I am sure, Mr Abdullah always cares.'

'I don't know what's wrong with him. He introduced this buffoon of a treasurer, a boy just out of college, to take over the entire budget of the orphanage, including the Government grants. And the Headmaster claims that he is running out of money. Where are the funds, we fought so hard for?'

'I am surprised you secured a grant.'

'Well, that's another story.' She told her mother-in-law in a few words what had gone on. Karin was horrified.

'I can't believe that there are still men in high places, who are so behind times. They call themselves westernised but when it comes to giving up some of their privileges in order to give women a chance, the veneer falls off. It's scandlalous!'

'Ali and I try as gently as we can to set a different example to the boys and girls in the orphanage. We teach them respect for one another and self-confidence in what either of them can achieve – but some of the girls are so brain-washed that they will never stand up for themselves.'

'Look, Martha, you can only do your best, and if you turn around only a few lives, you will have done your bit.'

'Karin, I could do so much more! I see things, I could do so much better than they are done, but they won't let me. I don't even dare to offer help anymore.'

'I know… It's almost impossible to curb one's energy drive and tread carefully instead. It's difficult for the first year or so, but it will get better. They will get used to you.'

'You know, what really gets to me, is how so many people at the top are still corrupt. Corruption in Bangladesh has been in the world news for years, and they still dare to syphon off money which isn't theirs. Why does the West bother with their Foreign Aid budgets? They never reach the people who really need them!'

'…because whatever does trickle through helps at least somebody, I suppose,' Karin said.

'If I were a President or a Prime Minister, I would only send aid money with people I trusted; no transfers into private accounts of officials overseas! I would make the bearer personally responsible to deliver and to administer the money and to lead the projects the money was for in the first place. He or she would have to account for every penny and I would send an expert to check that everything has been done as planned and that the materials used were the ones that had been quoted for. If people knew how much money disappears in private pockets or pays for office staff of charities, nobody would give anything.' Martha's voice somersaulted with exasperation and emotion.

'Let's have another cup of coffee, and then I shall tell you about my experience,' said Karin and filled the kettle. When they sat in front of their steaming mugs, she picked up the threat of her story:

'Before I moved to Bangladesh with Raj, a terrible cyclone had hit Bangladesh. It was estimated that one million people had died and millions more had lost everything, including their homes, their clothes, their belongings, everything. While I was still in Germany, a radio station started to collect, not money, but clothes, blankets, anything that could be useful for the survivors. The mission was called 'A Ship for Bangladesh'.

In the event, the listeners of that radio station filled not only one but three ships. They were duly dispatched. Soon afterwards, I moved to Bangladesh with Raj. One of his relatives was the Head of Customs at Chittagong Harbour. Out of curiosity, I asked him to check whether the ships had arrived in good time and the cargo distributed to the needy. I didn't hear for a while, and when, weeks later, I met the Head of Customs again, he was sheepish and tried to avoid me. I managed to corner him, and he had to tell me the sorry tale: The ships had docked in Calcutta first; there the relatives of the local officials thought they had first choice. Why? I asked. The only explanation, he could come up with, was that India had helped Bangladesh to win the Independence War. What the rich and wealthy Indian families had to do with it, I never understood. And what happened to the stuff they didn't want? I asked. It was burnt, he said. I have rarely seen somebody so embarrassed.'

'That's appalling!' exclaimed Martha. 'What did you say?'

'From then on, I said to everyone who would listen: Poverty is neither God's will nor the people's fault, because of something they have done in a previous life. It is the fault of the educated, successful and rich section of the population. The West has given billions of dollars, euros or pounds but nothing will ever change unless the so-called elite, the five percent of immensely privileged citizens of the country, alter their attitude towards their own people.'

'That's damning.'

'It is the truth. One member of my family felt so ashamed that he went with a cheque for a few thousand takas to the then Prime Minister, who had been a childhood friend, to open a fund for the underprivileged. A fat lot of good that did! Of course, it disappeared into a black hole. On another occasion, one of Raj's cousins, who was a civil engineer in the Government, a decent enough chap, came and told us excitedly that the American Government, had freed a huge sum of money from the United Nations to dredge the main rivers, which flooded every year and brought misery to the people living nearby, fishermen, farmers, poor people who couldn't move away. The money duly arrived, and when years later I met the civil engineer again and asked what had happened to his plans, he just shook his head. Nobody knew where the money had gone; it certainly had not been used for what it had been destined.'

Martha had gone very quiet.

'I don't want to put you off, Martha, but if you want to carry on, you must insist that either you or Ali is in charge. Only if you deliver charity yourself to the needy, can you be sure, it will arrive.

'Food for thought,' Martha said wistfully and began to cry again.

They heard Esme coming down the stairs asking whether they were going for a walk soon. Fresh air would do them all good, so they wrapped up against the autumn wind and made for the playground.

෫෩ඇ

Friday night came round quickly. Tilly had decided not to join them to give the family privacy.

Serena was as good as her word and spoiled everybody with her famous Bengali snacks of *samosas, bhajis,* mini egg rolls and diamond shaped *nimkis.*

'Can I tuck in?' asked Karin shortly after everything was laid out on the table. She simply couldn't help herself.

'Please, do,' Serena laughed, 'I don't want to take anything home!'

Jasmine was in charge of drinks, everything from wine and beer to fruit juices and mineral water. Serena opted for a cup of cha while Martha longed for a glass of good Rioja after months of having to abstain.

'I don't mind, not drinking alcohol, when I am in another country. It feels offensive, and it doesn't seem important, but this is nice!' She raised her glass and snuggled into the colourful Indian cushions which, over the months, had found their way onto the designer settee to liven up the grey fabric. Serena took a selection of her snacks to Martha and sat down beside her. Karin settled in her comfy armchair, and Jasmine sat in her permanently reclined modernist chair. She seemed to be the only person who ever sat in it and actually managed to get out of it.

'Now who is first?' asked Karin. 'You each have something to discuss.'

How about you, Serena? You don't have a problem, you only have good news.'

Serena was inexplicably overcome by giggles: 'I am so relieved,' she said, 'I have almost finished my training, and the results so far indicate that I have passed. And…!' she made a dramatic pause, 'I have been offered and have accepted my first job; part-time with the prospect of a full timetable when I am ready.'

'A toast is in order,' suggested Jasmine, 'to education and the teachers who provide it!'

'To education and the teachers,' they chorused and clinked glasses and porcelain.

Mohsin must be so proud of you!' Karin remarked.

'Yes, he is. He is also pleased, that soon life won't be quite so hectic.

I couldn't have done it without his support, and of course, not without your help either, Karin – child-minding whenever I needed someone for Omar. Thank you.'

'It was a privilege and I hope we won't see any less of you in the future. You have become part of the family!'

276

'I know, and it's lovely!' After a little pause, she added: 'So that's me done. Who is next?'

'I'll go next,' said Jasmine to everybody's surprise. She was usually not one for confiding in others, but she began immediately.

'You all know about my dilemma concerning Esme's father. I have thought long and hard about my future and of course, that of Esme. I also had a few talks with Serena, a few run-ins and finally a proper talk with Mum. And this is what I have decided and done: I have written a letter to Hamid to accept his offer to have a go at proper family life, so that Esme can grow up with a mum and dad.' The reaction was stunned silence and open mouths.

'I can't believe it!' said Karin at last, and added quickly, 'and I am so pleased! Come here, and let me give you a hug!'

'You are not going to change your mind?' Serena's facial expression was a mixture of hope and doubt. 'I don't want to be the one who talked you into it!'

That would be a first, thought Karin and listened with baited breath to her daughter's answer: 'As you know, talking me into anything is a feat. No, I have weighed up the pros and cons carefully, and I think I can risk it. Whether I shall be any good at it, remains to be seen, but I shall give it my best effort!'

She took a deep breath, waved at them to be silent and continued: 'Well, that's not all,' said Jasmine, amused at the effect her first announcement. 'Yesterday morning, I had a phone call from Hamid to say that he has declined his new job in America, and that he will try to come tomorrow around lunch time to have the in-depth discussion, we should have had months ago.'

'In that case, congratulations are in order! Martha's spirits soared and she raised her glass: 'To Jasmine and Hamid!'

'...and Esme,' added Karin, a huge load falling from her heart.

They raised their glasses and tea cup again to toast Jasmine's decision.

'You won't regret it,' Serena said. 'Look at us. We don't always live in harmony, but if one of us is down, the other will be there to talk to, to lean on. It's a great feeling!'

Jasmine raised her shoulders in mock-resignation: 'We'll see how it goes. Hamid will have to be very patient!'

'I think he will,' Karin said with conviction and hoped that she was right.

'Uh, I can hear wedding bells ringing,' Martha chuckled for the first time in days. Suddenly a burden had lifted; the stresses and strains of the last months had disappeared. She felt accepted, understood, at home, amongst friends and family.

And now it was her turn. They looked at her and waited:

'I had a horrid first year in the Children's Village,' Martha began, 'not because of the children – I love them dearly, they are gorgeous, and I think they like me, too – no, the adults made my life a misery, in particular the men.'

To put Jasmine and Serena in the picture, she went again over the arsenic poisoned wells; her time at Vijay's bedside in Dhaka; the nasty collisions first with the journalist and then, even worse, with the creepy, revolting Minister; Ali's bribery to extract funds from that man for the building of new wells; the obstacles thrown in her way, whenever she wanted to make changes and her subsequent row with the Headmaster; and finally, the shock and tragedy of Sara's death, just when everybody was so looking forward to the happiest event of the year, the wedding of two beloved members of their community.

'Why did the ferry capsize?' asked Jasmine, nibbling at a nimki.

'Like all ferry disasters in Bangladesh,' said Serena , 'from overcrowding.'

'Aren't there any rules?'

'Of course there are, but which ferryman refuses passengers who want to get on and pay? It's every year the same thing. Life is cheap and people are so poor, that in order to earn money they take risks.'

'It's the same with the factory workers,' Martha continued. 'They will work under the most appalling condition because they need every penny. The supervisors lock them in. There are no decent emergency procedures never mind drills. Every year fires sweep through factory floors, killing hundreds of people; or as happened this year, a whole factory fell in and buried a thousand women and young girls underneath the rubble.'

'Girls? You mean child labour?'

'Of course there is child labour. The poor families can't afford

278

to send their children to school, so they send them out to work. Every taka counts and most of the factory owners don't give a damn. It's not in their interest to check. They are happy as long as the profits keep rolling in.'

'What happened to the owners of the factory which fell in? It was big news here, too.'

'One of them was that ghastly Minister. He has been arrested and freed on bail. They probably hope that the bereaved families will shut up, when they have received their paltry compensation. They only offered compensation because the world's press had gathered and well-known western clothes shops had been involved. Suddenly everybody was horrified and fiercely against child-labour, but nobody had bothered to enquire and check beforehand.' Martha sighed: '…and you know what? I think, once the furore has died down, these owners will all get off scot-free.'

'That is dreadful!' exclaimed Jasmine and turned to her mother, 'did you know about that?'

Karin only nodded and turned to her daughter-in-law: 'And how has Ali shaped up as a husband?'

Martha took a deep breath and spoke: 'Ali is still hanging on to that dream, that you had, Karin. He wants to do his bit to save the world, in particular the children of this world. He always says, that they are the most vulnerable people, dependent on us; they don't deserve what life has put on their slim shoulders.'

'Do you still agree with him?' Karin's voice trembled.

'Of course, I do!' Martha surprised herself with this emphatic statement.

Up to then, she hadn't known that that was how she still felt about their mission. She suddenly knew that she would return to her husband's side and help him as much as she could. Her hurt feelings and frustrated efforts were not really important in the great scheme of things.

She could tell him when he came for his short visit.

'Good girl!' said Karin, relief in her voice. 'I am even playing with the idea of visiting you there for a while. How does that sound?'

'That sounds wonderful!'

The women looked at each other, pleased with the evening's problem solving. Life had a way of sorting itself out.

Jasmine went out to the kitchen to make coffee for everybody, when the phone rang. It was Ali to say that he wouldn't be coming after all.

Chapter Thirty-Nine

❦

'Come on in, Mamun.' Two weeks after Martha had left Bangladesh – the children thought she was visiting a sick relative – the chief engineer stood in the frame of Ali's study door, shuffling his feet and looking embarrassed.

Ali smiled at him encouragingly. Slowly, Mamun shuffled over the threshold.

'Can I help you, Mamun?' he addressed him again.

'Sir …'

'Ali,' he corrected him.

'Ali, I wondered whether you could find out when my labourers will get paid.'

'Don't they get paid every week?'

'No, they haven't been paid for three weeks, and they are getting angry.'

'Of course, they do. I had no idea but I shall find out for you. In the meantime, give them my apologies! I shall come and speak to them as soon as I know more.'

'That's good; thank you, Ali.'

How odd, Ali thought. As far as he knew, Kiresh was in charge of paying wages. Not that he had seen much of the financial Wunderkind.

He went to the Headmaster's study and knocked.

'Come in,' was followed by a clearing of a voice.

'Sorry to disturb you, Shamsur. The chief engineer just came to ask when his workers would be paid. Is Kiresh in charge of that or are you?'

'Kiresh,' was the clipped answer.

281

'Okay. I shall go and find him.' He took a double-take of the bowed figure. 'Are you well, Shamsur? You look a bit off colour.' In fact he thought that his boss looked ashen.

'Fine,' was all the headmaster could get himself to say.

Ali walked over to Kiresh's office. Nobody answered his knocks; after a while, he tried the door. It was unlocked. Ali entered an almost empty room. Only the desk, telephone and bookshelves, now empty of files, were left.

Ali closed the door quietly and stepped outside, walking past the Banyan tree across to where the two cars were usually parked, one belonging to the orphanage and the other Kiresh's bright red sports model. The old, trusty Morris Oxford was still there but the new, shiny sports car was gone.

Ali walked back to the headmaster.

'Shamsur, do you know where Kiresh has gone? His office is empty and his car is gone, too.'

'He might have gone to Dhaka about another grant.'

'Shamsur, I mean his office is bare, stripped of everything. Are you sure he is still with us?'

The Headmaster became agitated, got up at once, almost overturning his desk, rushed past Ali and out of the door.

Ali followed him at a distance back to Kiresh's office. For a few minutes the headmaster stood forlornly in the empty room. He came out slowly leaving the door ajar, not saying a word. Before he disappeared in his study again, he turned round to face Ali and said with bitterness: 'I shall make a few phone calls, Ali. I shall keep you informed.'

An hour later, Ali was summoned back:

'Have a seat, Ali. This is all rather difficult. I should never have involved my family. The truth is, Kiresh has disappeared; nobody in the family knows where to. And worst of all, he has cleared out our grant account, so there is no money to pay the workers. I shall have to pay them from my personal savings account.'

Ali sat there, stunned and disbelieving; it was worse than he had imagined!

'How dare he!' he shouted. He felt upset not only for his and Martha's efforts to secure the project, but also for the headmaster whose trust and kindness had been betrayed.

'You are right, Ali: How dare he! And I owe you and Martha

an apology. Kirash hated you being here; especially Martha. He called her a brazen American. I should have listened to you and your concerns. I should have kept my belief in you rather than in my nephew. I have no idea, what I was thinking of; family loyalty is no excuse. My first responsibility is to the children and staff here. Will you accept my sincere apologies?' The headmaster was swaying, his eyes looked overcast and his breathing was fast and laboured.

'There is no need to apologise, Shamsur. We all make mistakes.'

'I shouldn't at my age and with my experience.'

'You did it for the best of reasons, to help your nephew. You were not to know that he was easily tempted.'

'I should have seen that he was arrogant, ruthless and totally unsuitable to work for a charity!'

Ali felt great sympathy for his tormented boss and didn't know how to console him. Suddenly he remembered:

'I have some good news, Shamsur. My mother and Mrs Bellamy have been fundraising in England, enough to finish the project of the wells. Mrs Bellamy intends to bring the money over in the next couple of weeks.'

'People are so kind,' the headmaster sounded tearful and defeated 'that's why it is all the more humiliating to have to admit to them that the grant money has been stolen by a member of my family!'

'They will understand, Shamsur. It was not your fault.'

'I am so ashamed…' He suddenly grabbed his left arm, wrinkling his nose and eyebrows as if wondering what was happening to him. He was obviously in pain. All of a sudden his hand flew up to his throat, his eyes were bulging and his breaths came in loud staccatos.

'I am getting Dr Chowdhury. You are not well, Shamsur. Hold on for a moment!'

Ali ran to their little clinic and shouted before he had arrived: 'Aresh, Aresh come quickly!'

One of the three nurses appeared first.

'It's the headmaster. He has some sort of attack.'

She grabbed a bag and ran ahead to give first aid. Ali found the doctor patching up one of the cooks who had cut herself in the forefinger.

'Shazia, you take over here.' The doctor issued short, precise orders like a general before a battle. 'Sufi, you come with me.' and then they all ran to save the headmaster.

When they entered the study, the old man was still seated in his leather armchair but his upper body had flopped over onto papers on his desk. They couldn't see his face at first, but the doctor up-righted him, checked his pulse and any drooping of the face, eyelids and limbs.

'Call the ambulance, Sufi,' he ordered, 'Safda, get some blankets and lay them out on the floor. Ali, you have to help me to get him out of the chair and onto the blankets,' and with a deep sigh he added sadly: 'I think we are too late.'

ₛ₧

Late that evening, Ali rang London to tell the founder of the orphanage that Dr Shamsur Abdullah had died from a heart attack. Mrs Bellamy asked Ali to take over as acting head for the time being; she would make every effort to fly out within a couple of days.

His next call was to Poynton. It was Jasmine on the phone.

'We'll come out with Mrs Bellamy and we shall bring Martha.'

For the first time in his life, his sister sounded warm and compassionate, exactly what he needed now.

Chapter Forty

⁓

Ali had hired a people carrier from Priti who was delighted to help and to hear what he needed it for: Martha, Karin, Jasmine, little Esme and Hamid plus Mrs Bellamy, the founder of the orphanage, were expected to arrive this afternoon at Dhaka airport.

'You know what our family is like,' she said when he came to take up her offer, 'we never go just in twos or threes; it's always a crowd, so there are quite are few mini-busses and huge cars in the family and you are welcome to use them any time.'

'You are a treasure, Priti,' he laughed exuberantly and made an attempt at twirling his cousin around.

'You'll do yourself a mischief,' she laughed, happy to see Ali cheerful again. 'Off you go then! You don't want to keep your wife waiting!'

While driving out on the long and ever widening road to the airport, he had plenty of time to reflect on the turn of events. A couple of weeks ago, his wife had left. She had kept assuring him that it had been hard to leave him but that she needed a different perspective to assess their situation at the Children's Village; only then could she make a decision on their future. He had clung to the word 'their'.

Martha had left open all possibilities: staying in Bangladesh, staying in the job with her unsatisfactory share of it; maybe she could find work somewhere else, but why should she? This had never been the plan.

On the other hand, she might decide to stay in England or return to the United States. Where would that leave Ali, if indeed he would remain a part of her life? 'The latter certainly isn't in doubt, I hope,' he had said sharply into the telephone's mouth piece. She had kept quiet and a ghastly feeling of doom had spread in his stomach.

She loved him dearly and she understood that he had to be diplomatic to hold on to his job, but she had expected him to defend her more vigorously than he had done. Though, he had made attempts, she had to concede; and he had never ceased to be a loving husband.

As so often happens in life, fate had intervened. The Headmaster had died, the man who had employed them both.

Ali had speculated many times, why Shamsur had done so. He must have known that a couple of foreigners would bring in new influences, new ideas, different dynamics to what he was used to. Mr Abdullah had been an intelligent, well-educated and kind man; and Ali could not explain why, when they had arrived, he had suddenly changed his mind wanting them to conform, to be like Bengali teachers as if he had lost confidence in his own courage and open-mindedness. Ali had foreseen some difficulties of adjustment but nothing like it had turned out to be, no concessions, no compromises, making Martha thoroughly miserable and objecting to her every move.

Now that the orphanage was rudderless, and he had unexpectedly found himself in charge for the time being, he needed Martha more than ever.

The day after he had cancelled his visit to England, Martha had rung to say that she had spent the afternoon walking in Lyme Park, on her own, where they had got married.

She had said that she had needed to get away from all influences to think her very own thoughts and to come to her very own decision. She had followed the paths the carriage had taken them on their wedding day. She had rested at the lake, where they had been served their wedding lunch, and she had marvelled again at the Hall. All the while, she had weighed up the pros and cons of their relationship and what the work in Bangladesh had done to it. And then it had dawned on her that, of course, she wanted to remain married to Ali; of course, she still wanted to do charity work; they were a team and nothing could and should destroy their bond.

On reflection, the only fly in the ointment had been that she had been virtually ignored and side-lined – mainly because she was a woman which was a fact she had found hard to swallow. Foolishly, she had battled against existing rules and perceptions like Don Quixote tilting against the windmill; she had wanted to alter things, to change the opinions and attitudes of the Headmaster and Bengali men in general. She had wanted to teach them respect for women.

How naïve! She had behaved like a brash American after all.

'I must make changes within myself,' she had said during the call to Ali, 'be more diplomatic; more patient. Oh God! Priti told me all this weeks ago.'

'Martha, you mustn't beat yourself up over this! You are a great asset to the Children's Village. The youngsters and staff would be devastated if you left for good. Doesn't that mean that you have already made a great impact on their lives? And aren't they really the people who matter, not some narrow-minded bigots?'

'That's true, Ali, and… that's the conclusion I have come to myself: You and the orphans are the main source of my happiness and must remain my main focus. I have been selfish and impetuous and paranoid and unkind to you. I am so sorry, darling! It was all about me and my ambitions… and it shouldn't have been.'

Ali burst out laughing with relief; she sounded funny when she was contrite: 'I see, Lyme Park has done its magic again – wonderful! And when are you coming back?'

'I shall try to attach myself to Mrs Bellamy who is definitely flying out soon.'

Now three days later, his entire family would arrive from England. He couldn't wait and began to sing loudly and out of tune with happiness. Only at the end did he realise that he was humming Martha's and Sara's favourite tune about the bokul flower, the bees and the birds and an unrequited love.

Their love could have so easily gone that way but luckily it hadn't!

ഇൻങ

When he finally saw his family waving and smiling broadly, his heart swelled: There was his beloved Martha falling round his neck and making her curls yoyo around her face; there was his mother who had obviously taken to enjoying life to the full and looking radiant as never before; his glance fell on his sister, demure but strikingly stylish in her Armani tailored summer suit; little Esme who was the cutest little girl in a similar butterfly dress to the one she had worn for his wedding; he was introduced to a chap called Hamid, Esme's father, and took to him immediately like to a brother.

'We are engaged to be married,' came forth the astonishing pronouncement from his sister, who duly blushed and was overcome by uncharacteristic shyness. That won't last Ali thought winking at her, something he had done frequently when they had been children and had to cover up each other's mischief. Her green eyes glittered as if to warn: 'Don't you dare say it!' Could she still read his thoughts like she had often done when she had been a little girl?

He was delighted to see Serena, Mohsin and Omar again and pleased to hear the good news about her graduation and her job. They were waiting for a connecting flight to Sylhet but had come out to the hall to say hello.

'You wouldn't want to work for us, would you, Serena, now that you are a qualified teacher?'

'Tempting!' she joked back.

All this time, Mrs Bellamy had waited patiently in the background, amused and touched by the closeness of the family and their friends. What a wonderful bunch of people! She couldn't have wished for better to look after her charity.

Ali became aware of his dereliction of duty, baffled for a moment how to greet their VIP: 'I am so sorry to keep you waiting, Mrs Bellamy. Welcome!' He extended both his hands and shook hers heartily.

'I had fun watching you all,' she said smiling broadly. 'It is a privilege to meet you finally in person, Ali.' Ali knew immediately that they would get on.

'Let's go to the Village. The children are already excitedly waiting for you. We could hardly get them into the class rooms this morning.'

'See you back in Manchester,' said Serena, 'unless you all decide to stay here.' The Khans waved after their friends' disappearing backs and then made their way to Ali's car.

'Have you gone up in the world?' Martha teased him pointing admiringly at the huge car.

'Yep!' he answered proudly. 'It was Priti's. At first she said I could keep it for the duration of your visit, but last night she rang to say that she had talked it over with her husband and that they would like to donate it to help with the running of the orphanage.'

'Goodness,' said Mrs Bellamy, 'that is so kind! Are they members?'

'No, they are family. Our Bengali family,' said Martha proudly.

'We shall make them honorary members of the Children's Village!' Mrs Bellamy declared. 'My first decision on Bangladeshi soil and it's a good one!' She looked around and only read approval in everyone's faces. 'Let's go and tackle the rest!'

They clambered in and drove off.

Chapter Forty-One

The three nurses had made it their business to prepare the guests' bungalows. They cleaned and scrubbed so that everything sparkled with cleanliness whilst also making sure that the incense pots in the corners were attracting any foolish mosquito, daring to be indoors, and burning it. They checked any loose wall tiles in the bathrooms for cockroaches. Finally, they unfolded the mosquito nets and, when they had ascertained that there were no flaws in them, they draped them around the beds.

The bungalows were situated at the far end of the ponds in a little clearing sheltered by palm trees.

'You want to be woken by birdsong, not screaming kids,' said the resolute Safda.

'That wasn't necessary,' Mrs Bellamy assured her, 'but it's very thoughtful. Thank you!'

Martha, of course, moved back in with Ali; they were both overwhelmingly happy that they were reunited. The family breathed a sigh of relief.

'Acting headmaster,' Martha remarked mischievously, rolling the words over her tongue, twirling her locks, 'the title suits you!'

'Don't get your hopes up. Mrs Bellamy has come over to appoint someone permanently. I have no idea whether I shall be in the running.'

Martha shrugged her shoulders as if she knew better.

Time to change the topic: 'Has anything been prepared for the memorial service?'

'Not as far as I know.'

'Okay, acting headmaster, can I call rehearsals?'

'No objection whatsoever!' Ali was glad that Martha was herself again, enthusiastic and indefatigable.

At first, she called the choir, then the dancers, then the group who was going to recite poems. She spoke to the cooks to come up with suggestions for a particularly festive menu and, the rest of the six hundred children and staff, she had asked to produce decorations and another book of memories, this time for Dr Abdullah. Everybody was encouraged to contribute in a few words or drawings how they would remember him, maybe through an anecdote, a kindness experienced or a quality they had learnt from him. She also reminded them to make sure that they had handed in their contribution for Sara's commemorative album if they hadn't done so yet.

By the evening, everything was in place and everybody knew what to do.

Ali could only marvel, and when he told the guests, why they hadn't seen much of his wife that day, they were mightily impressed.

'It was rather foolish not to harness her energy and give her full reins beforehand,' remarked Jasmine with her inimitable logic and bluntness.

With children, sadness rarely lasts long, Martha thought, looking at the hive of industry, activities erupting all over the Village: The needlecraft sheds were busy sowing bunting and making decorations like paper garlands and snakes; there was constant banging coming from the carpentry workshop which had the important task of producing the biggest memorial item. Only Ali and Martha knew what it was. The carpenters had willingly agreed that it should remain a secret; however they found it hard to keep people from wandering into their workshops as usual in spite of the big sign they had hung at the door shouting: KEEP OUT. Sometimes the heat in there became unbearable and they counted their blessings that it was not summer time anymore.

As Martha walked to the back of the buildings to the assembly lawn, she saw girls practising their traditional dances. The choir, whose numbers seemed to have swelled enormously, could be heard practically whenever the children had a break from lessons. The normal timetable had been suspended and lessons consisted of writing and polishing stories or poems in memory of the two people they had lost.

Mrs Bellamy went on an inspection tour guided by Ali. She was appalled by the unfinished wells which were not even particularly well secured. With six hundred children, however well behaved, living nearby, it was a hazard and a scandal.

'It's still mainly bottled water you are drinking, is it?' she asked.

'Afraid so,' Ali replied. 'I would love to ring up the chief engineer and ask him and his crew to come back but the grant account has been cleared out. We have to think of some fundraising...'

'That won't be necessary, Ali.' Mrs Bellamy beamed with the good news, 'Our English members have already done so, and your mother and her friend Tilly were instrumental in getting everybody going, including the local Gilbert & Sullivan Society. And to top it all, one of our main sponsors has promised to pay for anything above the amount we have raised, should it not be enough. His only stipulation is that we use good quality materials and install the best system available so that it can be used for years to come.'

'That's absolutely wonderful, Mrs Bellamy!' With one fell swoop, all the money problems were solved. I only wish Shamsur could have held on to hear this, he thought.

'Oh Ali, don't call me Mrs Bellamy. Call me Victoria. We are a team now and I hope we shall work together for a long time.'

'Martha and I hope so, too,' he said simply looking her straight into the eyes.

'I like the sound of that. So, I might as well ask you right now: Would you accept the position of headmaster at the Children's Village if I offered it to you?

It took Ali a minute, to take in her proposal but second by second, as it dawned on him what that meant, a smile first lit up his eyes and then spread all over his face. There was only one concern: 'Would you object if I chose Martha as my deputy?' Ali hoped it didn't sound opportunistic. When else would he be able to submit this proposal if not now? 'It's not about the money,' he added quickly, 'it's about harnessing her energy, experience and professionalism. She has so much to give!'

'You don't need to explain. Of course, she must be your deputy, Ali. I only need to look around to see how she gets this place organised; it's buzzing, and we only arrived yesterday.' and to herself she thought: This young woman will be like a breath of fresh air, entirely devoted to the children and totally incorruptible.

Ali laughed: 'She has a constant flow of innovative ideas.'

'Good for her! I shall discuss them with her while I am here so that I can give her targeted support, but first, I need to look into every nook and cranny so that I know exactly the state of affairs. After all, even I have to report back – in great detail I might add – to our sponsors in England.'

Victoria Bellamy scrutinised a list of things to do which she had written in the back of her diary:

'Now, tomorrow morning,' she continued,' I would like to visit the head office of our bank in Dhaka. Could anybody make an appointment and take me there, do you think?'

'Harun, our caretaker, could take you,' Ali suggested.

'Do you think the Village could spare you for the morning? I would prefer you to come along so that I can introduce you to the bank manager as our new man in charge. And when we get back, we shall make it public.'

෨෬

'I will have to give a lift to Victoria tomorrow morning,' Ali said with a grin to Martha just as she was preparing a plate of stir-fry vegetables.

'It's Victoria already?' she teased him.

'Now, now, young lady, the new headmaster deserves some respect!'

A little silence ensued before it dawned on Martha what he had said.

'Oh, you clever boy!' she laughed, put her arms round his neck, jumped up and slung her legs round his waste.

'And you haven't done too badly either,' he continued when he had freed himself: 'You will be my deputy.'

It looked like a crazy war dance they both performed from the kitchen to their sitting room.

'Oh, the vegetables are burning!' She stormed back into the kitchen still laughing with happiness.

'But keep it to yourself. It's still hush-hush!' he admonished her, putting his finger over his lips.

'Hush-hush,' she whispered gleefully, putting a digit over her mouth, making shushing noises.

Ali could only shake his head.

'I'll be a good girl,' she carried on whispering more like a cheeky one.

࿇

The next couple of days were filled with formalities like drawing upwork contracts, coordinating the resumption of work on the wells. Martha had several private meetings with Victoria to explain the innovations she had in mind, in particular the idea of farming out the older boys to foster families in the nearby villages.

'We have to consider that the young women might feel inhibited about living so closely with young men, who are not their relatives. Obviously, I would rather not, but it's about how they feel having been brought up in with traditional values.'

'It's laudable that you consider their feelings,' said Victoria appreciatively. 'We have to respect the local traditions and religious beliefs. We do not under any circumstance want to get a reputation that we try to impose western ideas and to be accused of encouraging loose morals.

'I would never do that,' said Martha looking straight at Victoria.

'I know, and I trust you; and the idea of foster families seems to me a good one, at least worth trying out. We can always revert if it goes wrong... By the way, how would you organise safeguards?'

'One thing is essential, and that's making sure the boys are happy and will continue to go to school. We don't want them to end up as personal slaves to the families.'

'That's a good point. And how would you do that?'

'Pay the foster families well to look after the boys, so that they will be encouraged to provide a happy family life. The boys will stay in contact with our community for events, sports and to see their friends. We could even plant a supervisor in each village where people have volunteered to host our boys, so somebody will constantly keep an eye on things, somebody the boys can turn to.'

'You really have thought it through, Martha. Let's give it a go!'

Martha was delighted. For the first time since she had arrived, somebody had listen to her ideas and allowed her to explain them. That had been all she had ever wanted: to be appreciated and taken seriously.

'We could also,' Martha pressed on, 'open a residence or hostel in Dhaka for our older girls and boys who want to study at University, a sort of safe haven.'

'Steady on, Martha,' Victoria frowned. 'Let's do one thing at a time and let's do it well.'

'Blast!' Martha bit her lower lip. She had promised herself not to overwhelm people, to listen more, to be measured and diplomatic. If even the ever so supportive Mrs Bellamy had to stop her in full flow, she had a lot to learn.

'Sorry, Victoria! You are right,' Martha conceded, twirling a lock. Victoria looked at her benignly and not a little amused: She thought she could still hear Martha's little grey cells buzzing away.

'One more thing, though. Would you mind if I turned the narrow patches of concrete strips running along the fronts of the bungalows into tiny courtyard gardens?'

'Go on,' Victoria leaned back in her chair in anticipation.

'I thought of decorating them with flower pots or window boxes. It would teach the children and young mothers gardening skills and would make the houses look pretty.'

'No objections,' chuckled Victoria, 'go ahead.' She couldn't help shaking her head in admiration and astonishment at this bundle of dynamism, all in the service of the children. They were very lucky to have her!

෨෬

There was also the matter of finding a new receptionist cum PA to the Headmaster and his Deputy. Sara was a great loss, and they knew that it would take a while to train somebody else.

'Cora might be good,' Ali suggested. 'She is almost ready

to leave the Children's Village. We could give her a job here instead.'

'Excellent idea!' Martha agreed. 'She is bright and reliable and has already stood in for Sara several times. Let's ask her.'

To their surprise, Cora had other plans. She had decided on a University course in business studies, aiming to run a business of her own. They were taken aback by her confidence and determination. Ali and Martha looked at each other: 'Are you thinking what I am thinking?'

Martha nodded: 'It's working – democracy!' she said with glee.

'Though,' Cora interrupted, 'I could train somebody while I prepare for my Higher Secondary Certificate. I was friends with Sara, so I know her job pretty well.'

They were amazed at the young girl's practical thinking and clear vision.

'Have you got anybody in mind?' Ali was only teasing her.

'Oh yes,' she said as if that had been the easiest of problems to solve. 'I think that this new young woman, Monjuri, would make a good PA. She is friendly and willing to learn and grateful for any opportunity to better herself. She needs stability.'

'We shall have a word with her, Cora. That might turn out to be a most inspired choice. Well done you!'

'Is that all?' Cora asked briskly, her shiny eyes giving away her pride at the praise.

'Yes, thank you, Cora,' Martha said.

No sooner had the girl disappeared, they burst out laughing:

'I bet she will have her own business,' said Ali, 'and she will be a brilliant employer! Congratulations, Martha – your first Bengali feminist!'

Martha looked ever so slightly smug. Finally, things were going her way. She would be cleverer this time round. Eventually she would reach her goal to instil in these young women that they were as good as the men; that they could do anything if they put their mind to it; that their success did not depend on anybody else but themselves; and that being clever, educated and having a career did not preclude them from get married, having children and finding happiness. They just would have to find enlightened husbands who were confident enough within themselves, not to see their successful wives as competition and a threat to their reputation…. And then, of course, there were the boys who needed to be re-educated… Martha sighed. This could turn out to be her life's work. However, nobody needed to know just yet.

'Cora is a good girl!' she said simply, stood up on the tips of her toes and gave him a quick kiss.

ഇറൽ

The day of the memorial celebrations dawned to the song of birds in the trees, chattering noisily, sometimes screeching with outrage. The sky was already a glittering canopy of blue velvet and the sun shone benignly radiating warmth rather than heat. The year was coming to an end; it was the season everybody had looked forward to.

Slowly, the birdsong was joined and, soon afterwards, drowned out by the sounds of the Children's Village waking. Children shouting, giggling or singing; adults calling out to each other; pots clanging from the kitchen where the women were in the process of preparing breakfast; loud banging of doors being hastily opened and shut; even the chief engineer had turned up unexpectedly early with a couple of labourers who were now making familiar thudding noises with their tools. It had been arranged to everyone's relief that work on the new wells would recommence the day after the memorial. The outstanding wages had been paid and everybody was happy to come back to work with newly ordered, good quality materials, replacing the plastic pipes with steel ones and a pump which included safety mechanisms.

The ceremony would begin at 10 o'clock, enough time for another quick rehearsal of the various performances. Muffled voices could be heard coming from buildings. The excitement was palpable, filling the air. It had been many months that the Village had been celebrating anything. Today of course, was a sad occasion but it was also time to celebrate the lives of two people who had given so much to this place and its inhabitants; it was time to celebrate their friendships and kindnesses. It would be a joyful occasion; the adults had reassured the children.

'We don't want the guests to be sad,' said one of the younger children, and he was right.

At a quarter-to-ten, Ali walked out of his office, shaking rhythmically a big hand bell which he had found among Shamsur's belongings and which he intended to use for the start and finish of each school day; he would have it fixed somewhere permanently, and he would appoint a team of older children to the privileged position of bell ringers.

There was a huge bulge around the Banyan tree wrapped in jute sacks for protection from prying eyes and bird droppings. Ali could guess easily what it was but didn't know yet what it looked like. Even he had been kept outside the workshop. The carpentry students and their teacher must have furtively and noiselessly installed their gift last night when everybody else had gone to bed.

On the dot of 10 o'clock., everybody was assembled. Ali looked at the neat rows of children and staff – teachers, doctor and nurses, maintenance men, even the ladies from the kitchen had left their cooking – each standing to attention in front of a chair. The children's freshly washed faces gleamed and their still wet hair glistened in the sunshine. Everybody had made an effort to be well groomed and dressed in freshly laundered clothes.

The front row of chairs had already been occupied by the guests, the founder Mrs Bellamy, Karin, Jasmine, Hamid and little Esme.

Even the chief engineer and his team had changed and turned up in their Sunday best, standing in the back row, shuffling their feet nervously.

Ali was facing the assembly, waiting for Martha who had for some reason been delayed.

'Not a good start,' he thought but retracted it the moment he saw his wife. Everybody gasped as nobody had ever seen Martha in a sari. The green sari, a gift from her mother-in-law, was beautifully draped around her, pleated silk springing out like a fan with every step. As she approached, she saw Karin in the front row wiping away a couple of tears of emotion.

'You look gorgeous,' Ali whispered.

'Cora helped me' she whispered back and stood next to him surveying the surprised crowd with amusement. It felt like a home-coming.

Ali cleared his throat and spoke: 'I welcome you all from the bottom of my heart. We are here to remember and celebrate the lives of two very important people, Sara, our dearly beloved receptionist, and the headmaster, our headmaster.'

He paused. For a moment the task ahead and his new responsibilities, crowding his head, almost overwhelmed him. He straightened himself up to stem the rising panic and to remind him of his duty: 'As was said before and as we all know, Sara was more than a receptionist: She was the Headmaster's Personal Assistant but also an assistant to all of us; to some of us, she was our bhabi, our sister, our best friend. Nothing was too much for her; whenever someone needed help she volunteered; she was kind, generous and forever cheerful. We miss her dreadfully and shall continue to do so; and we have every right to be upset that instead of celebrating her marriage to Dr Chowdhury we are here to commemorate her.'

Ali could see the doctor lift his glasses and wipe away tears with a handkerchief. He felt immensely sorry for him.

'The headmaster's equally untimely death,' Ali went on, 'is a great shock to us all. He was a dedicated headmaster, loving you all very much, looking out for you, always providing the best education, the best of everything for you. You were his family, his own sons and daughters. He gave this Children's Village the best part of twenty years of his life and, as he always said, he enjoyed every minute of it. He set an example with his kindness and integrity and instilled in all of you that you can achieve anything you want if you work hard. He also kept reminding you how important it was, to be honest, truthful and reliable. But above all, he wanted you to grow into happy, kind and successful adults. The headmaster was a wonderful man, and I personally am going to miss his wisdom and gentle humour. So let us now for two minutes be silent and remember him and Sara, these two remarkable people to whom we owe so much and who gave so much of themselves to make us happy.'

It was a melancholic silence; not a sound from the children and grown-ups; only the birds in the surrounding trees would not be silenced.

It was Mrs Bellamy who broke the silence after the two minutes were up: 'Thank you all so much for your excellent behaviour, children, and thank you also for your kind welcome to us, your guests. I heard that in honour of Sara and the headmaster you have worked hard and rehearsed often, but before we carry on, I want to tell you some good news: We have raised enough funds in England to finish the building of the new wells within the next few weeks, and I think, we should thank Mr Mamun Hossain and his men for making sure that in the future, you will have best possible quality of drinking water and superb wells to take it from… Please, show your gratitude with a big round of applause.'

The children were a little taken aback that they were allowed to clap at such a solemn occasion but did so heartily.

Ali looked over to Vijay who was clapping with more fervour than everybody else.

'I also,' Mrs Bellamy waved her hand for them to be quiet again, 'would like to thank Mrs Khan from Manchester, her daughter Jasmine and her friends, some of whom can't be with us today, for making such a magnificent effort to add a considerable sum to our funds by organising coffee mornings and theatre performances in their home town in England. We are very much indebted to them, so let's show our appreciation with another round of applause.'

This time the children were more audacious and clapped enthusiastically.

'And lastly, I have an announcement to make: I have appointed Mr Ali Khan,' and she smile fondly at the man standing just behind her, 'as the successor of Dr Abdullah, and I am pleased to say that he has accepted to be your new headmaster. You all know his wife, Mrs Martha Khan. I am delighted to say that she has agreed to be your deputy headmistress.'

This time, the children needed no encouragement to applaud wildly and someone even dared to whistle. It went on for a couple of minutes until Ali stepped forward and announced the start of the performances.

The members of the choir assembled in front of the audience and sang several songs they had practised under Sara, ending with her favourite, the love song *Oliro kotha shune bokhul hashe*. They sang with gusto fired up by Sara's spirit.

This was followed by a dance: A group of five young women stepped forward, the three nurses, Shazia, Safda and Sufi, plus

Sultana and Salma, the girls who were destined to go to university. They looked beautiful and elegant in their white saris with orange and gold embroidery borders and white lotus flowers fastened to their black hair. They danced to the music of a classical song called *Dry Leaf* written by the famous Bengali poet Kazi Nazrul Islam. They swayed their arms in unison, passing each other, forming a circle one moment and a line the next, tapping their feet to make the little bells of their ankle bracelets tinkle to the rhythm of the music. It was a gracious dance which ended with the girls joining hands at a point in their midst and spinning like a wheel.

The next item on the program was Elizabeth Barett-Browning's poem once again. This had meant to be a group effort but ultimately the children had decided to let one of the older girls, Rani, recite it. She had a beautifully sonorous voice and perfect diction. She poured her heart and soul into the words:

'How do I love thee? Let me count the ways.
I love thee to the depth and breadth and heights
My soul can reach...'

As she continued, a deep sob rose from the direction of Dr Chowdhury, mourning his bride's death and the future they had lost.

The applause was suitably mute.

There followed another dance. The girls had changed into bright blue saris and white blouses and were joined by Vijay, Ismail, Sajaad and Iqbal, the boys also heading for university at the end of the school year. The boys wore cassocks of the same blue over black trousers pretending to be fishermen casting nets. The girls floated around them to the sound of a folk song, admiring the boys' non-existing catch.

Giggling could be heard from the junior section of the audience, turning into happy cheering at the end of the dance.

Tariq, the tall, skinny boy, appeared holding a sitar, smiling shyly as if he had strolled onto the lawn stage by mistake. He waited until everybody had quietened down; only then did he sit on a hastily provided chair, positioned his instrument and began to pluck the strings. It was a magnificent rendition of a classical song by the nation's favourite poet, Rabindranath Tagore. Many had heard Tariq strumming and tinkling in his dormitory over the last few months but nobody had realised how dedicated he was and how competent he had become.

At the end of his playing, he sat on his chair for a moment, his head still bowed over the strings and his fingers still on them. The mesmerized silence erupted into thunderous applause. Tariq just stood there, amazed by the effect his playing had had on his listeners.

That boy has real talent, thought Ali, and made a note in his mind to give Tariq more support in the future, maybe lessons by a professional and definitely a new sitar to replace this rickety old thing.

Someone took the still transfixed Tariq by the arm and gently led him away to clear the stage for the last performance.

It was another dance, but of a different kind – a group of under-tens walked on, holding hands, dressed in bright yellow costumes with tails sown onto their bottoms and wearing orange beaks over their mouths. When a grey duckling turned up it was soon apparent that they were performing the story of the ugly duckling, quacking and paddling and generally bumping into each other. The children in the audience laughed helplessly, released from the pressures of sadness. When the yellow ducklings crowded around their ugly brother, Cora, the instigator and choreographer, stepped in to help them, pulling out white feathers from his costume to turn him into a beautiful swan.

Happy cheering, hysterical laughter and exuberant clapping erupted, and some of the children got up from their chairs and jumped up and down with delight. The adults let them have their moment of relief from the pressures, worries and terrible events of the last year.

As soon as the mayhem had subsided, Ali got up to speak: 'I think I can safely say that Mr Abdullah and Sara would have been very proud of you all. Let's give our singers, dancers, speaker and sitar player one more round of applause.'

There was no need to say it twice. After a few minutes, he cleared his voice and indicated that he had more to say.

'May I also remind you that we want everybody to write their memories and thoughts about Sara and Mr Abdullah down which we shall collate, bind each into a book and put on permanent display in the library! So make your entries good because they will be on show for all to see.' Ali took a deep breath, pleased with the way his first official function as the new Headmaster had gone.

'Now it's time for lunch,' he said in a brisk routine manner, 'May I ask the older students to return the chairs to the hall so that we can have our meal on the lawn. Our guests will sit at the tables in the dining hall.'

However, Mrs Bellamy wouldn't hear of it and insisted that she and the other guests would love to join everybody for the picnic.

The cooks had done themselves proud and earned another round of enthusiastic applause while serving plates full of delicious food.

They were just finishing when Ali saw Habib, the woodwork teacher, from the corner of his eye; he lingered in respectful distance from where Ali sat with his family.

'Oh, I almost forgot,' exclaimed Ali and got up to call again for the children's attention.

'There is one more ceremony to perform in memory of Sara and Dr Abdullah. Our carpenters have a surprise for us. Please, form orderly queues, walk slowly to the front of the office and stand around the banyan tree.

The adults followed the children and Mrs Bellamy was invited to unveil the surprise. She peeled away some of the bulging jute sacks from the snakelike thing around the tree and gladly accepted the help of the proud carpenter apprentices to remove the rest.

They all looked in awe at the beautiful wooden bench which circled the banyan tree. One brass plaque had Mr Abdullah's name and the duration of service to the school engraved and pointed towards the Headmaster's office. There was a second plaque facing towards the reception remembering Sara. A red ribbon went all around the circular bench, and Mrs Bellamy was invited to cut it: 'This is a magnificent piece of craftsmanship, she said, 'a true master piece! The bench will be here for years to come and will remain a fitting and beautiful tribute to our dear departed friends.' She turned to the little group of carpenters shuffling their feet with embarrassment and sneaky feelings of pride. 'Thank you so much!' Mrs Bellamy added and declared the bench open.

Everybody was keen to shake the hands of these artists in their midst and to express their gratitude. Some of the younger children already sat on the bench trying it out and declaring it marvellous.

Guests, children and staff dispersed to have a little rest in their various accommodations to escape the still hot winter sun. They would meet again in the coolness of the evening.

ಬಿಲ

At last the day was done.

As Karin's family approached the new bench around the Banyan tree, they could see from afar that the Village's children had already taken possession of it. In an instant, it had become a gathering place, a chattering place, a restful but joyful place.

'Off you go now,' said Ali to them, 'you should be in bed by now.' He said it with authority, kindness and a twinkle in his eye. This was the way he wanted to rule, to give the children a home, to prepare them for the adult world, so that they may spread the qualities, instilled in them by the school, during their life time.

The children retreated with big smiles and a little wave to Martha which she returned.

'They are so cute, aren't they!' she said as if she was a little in love with them. 'They are incredibly resilient, always cheerful in spite of their backgrounds.

Ali went to his office and brought back a picnic basket with a bottle of champagne and flutes, a present from his mother.

'We have to drink it quietly before anybody sees us, but we deserve a glass to celebrate.

Aresh joined them wanting to be rather with his friends than on his own on this momentous day.

'So, what next?' he asked with the first smile in days that hardly dared to emerge.

'Well,' mused Ali, 'I reckon nothing much will change. We shall just carry on looking after the children.' Martha intervened, clearing her throat demonstratively several times and said with emphasis: 'There will be a few innovations.' She was stopped by gales of laughter from everybody else.

'Who would have thought it,' snorted Jasmine hitting her

304

thighs in helpless mirth, '...but only after consultation and discussions with everybody,' continued Martha regardless. 'I want the improvements to be for the best of the Village, not change for change's sake. I shall need everybody to help us to think through our proposals. We shall not dictate but consult! After all, we come from the lands of democracy.'

Everybody had recovered their composure and managed to grin silently at her emphatic speech. It made even Martha blush and she twirled her locks vigorously.

Ali quickly gave his wife a reassuring hug, chuckling away: 'You just stay the way you are!' he said overwhelmed by his love for her.

He was particularly gratified to catch a glimpse of Mrs Bellamy nodding in agreement.

The evening breeze was refreshing, even a little cool. Jasmine pulled a thin cardigan around her, looked at Hamid, took her daughter's small hand and declared: 'Hamid and I have decided that doing things by halves is cowardly and no use at all; so we shall return to Manchester, move in together and get married, and yes, little Esme, you will be the bridesmaid and you shall have another new dress with butterflies.' She ended by squeezing her daughter who squealed with delight.

Karin didn't dare to breathe in case she had misheard and a retraction was to follow. It didn't. When Jasmine relaxed her grip, a delighted Esme clapped her podgy hands, and the adults followed her example. For the first time, Karin saw her otherwise cold and calculating daughter kiss a man with warmth and affection, her green eyes sparkling with pleasure. What a man her son-in-law was; exactly what her daughter needed! The kiss was interrupted by the couple's little girl, clambering on Hamid's lap repeating her new favourite word: 'Daddy, Daddy, Daddy!'

'I guess, I shall just carry on fundraising,' said Victoria Bellamy taking up Aresh's question again. 'I hope to visit you regularly and to support you every step of the way. I am just so grateful that you young people have taken over the job that I have created but can't really do myself. It's wonderful to know that I can trust you implicitly to carry out my initial ideas and that the orphanage will be in safe hands for many years to come.'

'Thank you for your trust, Victoria,' said Ali from the other side of the tree. 'Martha and I feel honoured and humbled, and promise to give it our all. We won't disappoint you!'

Dr Chowdhury had remained quiet, head dropped to his chest, just listening to everybody's good news. Ali put his arm consolingly round the doctor's shoulders and said with feeling: 'I hope with all my heart, Aresh that you will stay with us. We couldn't bear to be without you; we need you; the children need you. It's no consolation now and you have heard it a million times, but time will heal and sometime in the future, you will be happy again. In the meantime, we shall remain your family.'

'Thank you for your friendship,' Aresh murmured to no one in particular, and then swallowed hard to supress tears.

'And you Mum? What will you do with Jasmine and Esme gone?'

Everybody round the tree leant forward and looked at Karin with curiosity.

'Oh, don't worry about me! I shall return to England and keep on the house; maybe I can persuade Tilly to move in with me – that should be fun! We shall work together with Victoria to do some more fundraising... that sort of thing...'

She stopped and everybody waited with baited breath for her to continue: 'But first of all, if you will have me, I think, I shall stay on a little while, to help, to visit Priti, to be a tourist for a bit, but mainly to make myself useful here during the transition. You probably can do with another pair of hands.' She looked around her, uncertain how her proposal would be received, until she heard everyone giggle and Jasmine blurting out: 'You always wanted to do charity work in Bangladesh – there is your chance!'

The evening breeze swept the roots and branches of the Banyan tree gently through the air as if agreeing.

Ali got up from the new bench and gave his mother a hug:
'Welcome to the Children's Village, Mom.'

THE END

306

GLOSSARY
Bengali-English

abba, abbu	father, daddy
acha	okay, often accompanied by a head side shrug
achol	often embroidered end of sari draped over one shoulder or over the head
alo tarkari	potato omelette
amma	mother, mum
bakshish	tip, donation
babui	chill
bakul	flower (minusops elengi)
bhaba pitha	sweet, made of rice, coconut and molasses
bhabi	sister
bhai	brother
bulul	chil bird
cha	spiced tea
chana bhajo	chickpea dish
dhal	lentils
doel	magpie robin (national bird of Bangladesh)
dudh shemai	sweet dish, vermicelli in milk
halva	sweet semolina dish
inshallah	God willing
lassi	yoghurt drink
lunghi	loin cloth for men, reaching over the knees
machanga	kingfisher
memsahib	mistress of the house
murabba	raw mango jam
mutton rehari	mutton curry
mynah	weaver bird
nimki	biscuit
pakora	savoury snack

paratha	flat bread, similar to nan bread but more buttery
polao	festive rice, cooked in clarified butter with spices, almonds and peas
puri or *poori*	deep fried, fluffy bread balls
rabhindra sangeet	Tagore poem set to song
ragh	classical song
salaam alaikum	welcome greeting
sari	five meters of silk or cotton draped around a woman as a dress
shalwar kameeze	trouser suit for women
snalu	flower (cassia fistula)
shapla	water lily (national flower of Bangladesh)
suma	gift
tuntun	tailor bird
tiya	green parrot
walaikum salaam	good-bye